CHILD *of* IMAGO

ALSO BY LYNN HARROD

The Queen's Angel

Keepers of the Night Garden

Lucky Five

Of Gods and Devils and All In Between
Book One

CHILD
of
IMAGO

a novel

LYNN HARROD

For information contact
www.deerwoodpress.com

Cover Design by Lynn Harrod/Deerwood Press
Art and Photos: Forest by Hans/Pixabay, Robot by Adobe Stock, Dog by Pohjakroon/Pixabay, Overalls by Jan Wennington/Unsplash, Wolfman by FBartonDavis/Pixabay, Soldiers by GMB Visuals/Pexels, Snowfall by Nicole Young/Nicolesy, Girl by A.M. Alvarez

Edited by William McCoy

ISBN: 978-1-7367234-2-5 (ePub edition)
ISBN: 978-1-7367234-9-4 (Paperback edition)

First Edition: January 2024

To Annabelle, how she brought everyone together.

———————————————

1

Wake Up

"Go away... come closer."

The desperate whisper floated across The Void, a barren expanse of enveloping darkness pierced by two stars shining in the distance. Nothing else could be seen or heard, as if all other light and sound were not merely absent but denied. In the silence, the emptiness, the endless space, the twin stars felt like the returning stare of the proverbial abyss. Standing on no ground, looking up at no sky, surely nothing could exist here.

Except her.

"Run far from us... return to us."

The Girl turned, tried to pinpoint the source, peering into the darkness for the person whose whisper shook her.

"Go away, far away... come back."

She felt her search was futile in such a confounding, surreal place, but upon hearing the whisper again, she knew the soft voice, young and female and familiar, came from the twin stars. She realized the voice contradicted itself not out of madness but from opposing pleas, for there were actually two whispers in The Void, speaking one after another.

"Get out, save yourself while you can... join us and we'll save each other."

The Girl looked at the two stars, separate but aligned along the invisible horizon, and struggled to remember their two souls who became one. She didn't know whether to fear or follow the whispers.

"You're alone from this moment... you'll always have us."

She walked forward through The Void but made no progress, called out to the twin stars but made no sound, and as despair crept in, an icy sting struck her forehead and ran down her face.

A rain drop.

* * *

The Girl woke from her dream, still in total darkness, but now curled on hardpan dirt, her hands around her bent knees. A sliver of sunlight beamed in from above, shining into her hazel eyes. A few more drops of cold water fell onto her as if riding the light, and the sound of a slowly building rain could be heard pattering leaves and plopping onto soft ground.

She outstretched her arms and felt walls of warm wood around her, the space barely big enough for her small folded body. She slid her hands on the walls until she reached a spot that felt like stone. Resting on her back, she pushed the stone with her hands and feet, encouraged by its slight movement. She kicked several times, grunting with the painful effort, until the stone fell away, revealing the exit.

She emerged, worn and weak and disoriented, from what she had believed was a small cave or alcove. Instead, she discovered she'd been lying in the hollow of a large oak tree. Someone had placed a boulder beside it to act as a heavy door. She couldn't remember if the crude set-up was meant to imprison or protect her. Perhaps both.

The Girl stood under a drizzling overcast sky on a steep hillside dense with ancient oak, walnut, and ferns. Their unchecked growth covered whatever tracks were made leading to her cramped shelter. She spied a large puddle and knelt beside it for a bitter drink and a cold splash to further awaken her. As the puddle settled again, she caught her reflection in the muddy water, interrupted by the droplets of rain, and saw her face for what seemed like the first time.

The Girl looked to be fifteen years old, with long curly brown hair framing her soft features and a puzzled stare from those hazel eyes. She rummaged her foggy mind for any memory of how she arrived at that oak tree high up the slope of the hillside woods but recalled nothing, not even her name. Rising to her feet and looking about the trees with not another soul around, she briefly felt a stirring within for the twin stars of The Void in her dream.

The stars had voices.

The stars knew her.

She took off her blue canvas jacket – two sizes too big – and recognized its camouflage pattern as military wear. A soldier had placed it on her, likely the same soldier who tucked her into the tree. The steadily increasing rain and the chilly air forced her to put it back on, for her thin blue cotton dress alone wouldn't do. She removed her knee-high combat boots – also slightly too large

– and dumped out damp dirt. As she placed them back on her feet, she noticed a mark atop her right hand, peeking out from the jacket's sleeve. She pulled up the sleeve and saw a tattoo, three bold, black letters... DOT.

The Girl surmised that "Dot" was her name, or must be for now until she learned more about herself and the unknown soldier who brought her here. Her curiosity broke as a savage hunger clawed at her, forcing her to choose a way forward. Dot could either make her way up the hillside or wander down through the ferns until she found something, anything.

A distant, lingering howl from above gripped her in fear, prompting her to choose an immediate descent.

* * *

Through the light rain, Dot made her way down the steep slope past oak, walnut, birch, and mossy boulders until she spotted a road below. She doubled her efforts through the thick foliage and felt a strange relief upon setting foot on pavement, a relief short-lived for only when she stood on level ground did she notice the other people, none of whom were in any condition to help her.

A short distance from her exit from the woods lay the bloody aftermath of a skirmish, a firefight between opposing troops.

She saw men and women dressed in blue camouflage fatigues, like her jacket, dead on one side of the cracked wet pavement. Some were out in the open, while others lay near large transport trucks and small utility vehicles, as if they died while ducked behind cover.

Across the broken road were men dressed in green, their bodies riddled with bullet holes, their vehicles still smoking from a battle that took place not long before. Among them were a set of

Lynn Harrod

triplets, perfectly identical soldiers, all clean-shaven with short, dark hair, and all dead.

Between the two factions, the weathered road was strewn with rifles, knives, and large, ominous weapons she didn't recognize. The air smelled of sulfur and gunpowder, and the engines radiated heat. She stood beside the hood of a large transport for a moment of warmth as the soft rain continued around her. None of these gruesome images summoned any memory, yet she'd clearly been part of it. She deduced that a lone soldier led her away from the battle, up the hillside, to the protection of the hollowed tree she awoke from. A panic set in as she quickly regretted her choice of trekking downhill, returning to the danger she'd been spirited away from.

Dot climbed into the transport truck to search for something to eat, unnerved by the three bodies she had to pass to reach the lockers within. She found many more weapons, but no food.

She searched the dozen vehicles, resorting to rifling through the dead soldiers' uniforms, but pulled out their pockets empty-handed. A cargo van at the head of the convoy was all that remained, but it turned out to be worth the wait. A canvas bag held three sealed ready-to-eat meals. It felt like discovering treasure.

Grabbing a nearby combat knife, Dot slashed one open and devoured its contents with barely a glance at what she shoved into her hungry maw. After five desperate swallows, she slowed down and started chewing. She tasted macaroni and cheese, corned beef, biscuits, and sweet corn, the latter being her old favorite. Her memory wasn't a complete wasteland after all.

As she sat on the rear bumper of the van, shoveling corn into her mouth with a plastic spoon, she spotted an overturned motorcycle a short distance away. It had a boxy metal sidecar attached to it, resembling a reinforced cage. As she pondered the idea of searching it next, she froze in fright when she saw it move.

Her fear heightened when she heard a whimper from the cage.

2

Gypsy

After ravaging two of the ready-meals, Dot tucked a third under her arm and looked to the hillside for a quick escape from the unseen lone survivor trapped in the motorcycle's sidecar, but paused when his whimper became a moan of misery. Perhaps it was another prisoner, like herself, if that was even the case. Perhaps it was a soldier in need of help. The dead driver of the motorcycle laid across its handlebars, dressed in blue like her unknown savior. Whoever laid trapped in the overturned sidecar cage might have been an ally.

Fighting the instinct to flee, Dot approached the sidecar, startled by the louder moans that soon resembled howls. She realized the poor soul in the cage wasn't a man at all, and upon peeking through its flat bars, discovered a dog, a German

Shepherd wearing a blue vest, his leg pinned to the road by the frame of the cage. The dog's black eyes stared at a river that ran alongside the road, crossing underneath a bridge ahead. Dot grabbed a shovel from a nearby truck and used it as a lever to lift the cage slightly, allowing the dog to scurry out from beneath.

Even as she provided aide, she imagined the war dog tearing her to shreds the moment it was free, but was surprised to find it docile and attentive, standing beside her as she lowered the cage back to the ground. She wanted to believe it meant no harm, but saw it was as weak as she had been moments before, likely stuck there as the soldiers killed each other around it. Blast marks scarred the cracked pavement only a few feet from where it laid.

"Are you alright, boy?" Dot said, curiously hearing her own tender voice for the first time. "You've been through a lot. Me, too. What's your name, boy?" She knelt down and carefully petted the dog, a highly trained canine asset of the blue troop. He allowed her to grasp him, to pet his back, the top of his head, and under his collar, and it was there she saw the dog's name embossed in leather: "Gypsy."

For that fleeting moment of peace and silence between them, Dot neglected the looming, unknown danger and cut open the last of her ready-meals. She poured out Salisbury steak and potatoes into a nearby helmet and slid it toward Gypsy like a dog dish. He ate its contents within a minute. A sealed oatmeal cookie accompanied the dinner. She pocketed the treat for herself, happy to somehow know that dogs shouldn't have sweets, another memory intact.

Dot looked ahead to the bridge, now aware of the sound of the rushing river below, for some kind of sign of where she should go next. Judging from the layout of the bodies, she gathered that the convoy of blue soldiers was heading toward the bridge when it fell victim to an ambush by the green soldiers. She concluded they

Lynn Harrod

staged the attack to prevent the blue troop from crossing. A small roadside sign revealed what lay ahead: "Kellan 6 KM."

She felt two opposing voices within, similar to the whispers in The Void. One voice told her to continue on to Kellan as the blue soldiers had clearly wanted. The other voice urged her to avoid that path, for surely another attack awaited her on the other side, or perhaps at Kellan, whatever place that was.

"What do you think, Gypsy? Do we cross the bridge?"

The dog stared up at her and seemed to let out a long groan, but she turned and saw the agony came from a man on the road not far behind them. She stared at the still man, his legs barely moving, and felt the need to tend to him as she had the dog. He likely faced death, but he might have had answers.

Dot clutched her combat knife, still streaked with cheese sauce from her ready-meal, and cautiously approached the man. Unlike the others, he wore black overalls and wasn't so easily identified with one of the two troops. She felt no choice but to reveal herself to him.

"Are you okay, mister?" she asked as she came closer. Passing other dead soldiers, her eyes widened as she realized that most of the men in green appeared identical, far more that the triplets she first spotted. They were small in stature, a little over five feet tall, with short, thin black hair, brown eyes, and similar facial features, as if one petite man was duplicated to create an entire troop. The identical soldiers' only distinguishing features were the tattoos atop their right hands – like her own "DOT" – only theirs were three-digit numbers.

She saw 048, 099, 107, 391, 224.

The man in black, struggling with his life, was Soldier 113.

"Mister, are you gonna be okay?" Dot asked as she reached him, kneeling beside him. She noticed Gypsy, who had stayed close to her, now kept his distance.

Soldier 113 strained to look up at the girl staring down at him. He smiled and offered his hand. She took it and helped him turn over, revealing the extent of his wound. His stomach brutally lacerated, his innards spilled out, having been held in place only by his torso being pressed to the road. Thick gray blood seeped out, something Dot knew to be unnatural.

"You're alive," he groaned, "and you're here."

"Yes, but what about you? Your blood's turned gray! Is there a first aid kit somewhere?"

"My truck..."

Soldier 113 pointed to a utility transport behind him. Dot ran to it and rummaged through its cab only to find the first aid kit was destroyed from the firefight. She called out to the soldier in black.

"This one's no good. I'll keep looking..."

Dot stopped herself when she spotted the soldier's green jacket draped across the front seat. It gave her a bad feeling. She turned back to the man in time to see him pull a handheld radio from his vest.

"She's here!" Soldier 113 said into the radio, wheezing with urgency. "I've got her! She's alive, at the west bridge over the Miracle River! All converge on my location! All converge..." The alarming command was the last thing the soldier said as he succumbed to his wounds.

Dot looked around, expecting a swarm of soldiers in green to come barreling down the old road at any moment. Ignoring the bridge ahead and the mysterious destination of Kellan beyond, she left the road immediately. She snapped her fingers at Gypsy, and the two of them ran up the hillside, back into the trees whence she came. She'd wanted to search the wreckage for better-fitting clothes and more food, but suddenly felt out of time.

Hidden once again in the dense woods, climbing high above the road, the girl knew she'd made the right decision when she heard a dirge of trucks and motorcycles approach from the distance.

3

Wellspring

"Go west and never look back... go east and save us all."

Dot stood in The Void again, surrounded by darkness and silence, with only the two whispering voices speaking in turn. She recognized them as feminine voices before, but could now clearly hear their timbre of adolescent youth. They sounded similar, like girls her age.

"If you go east, you'll die... if you go west, we die."

They sounded like Dot.

Knowing now she stood in a dream, she turned within The Void and faced the twin stars again, only this time they seemed closer. She peered into the distance and saw shapes within the glowing lights, the auras of two girls wearing what appeared to be pointed hats and flowing dresses.

"Who are you?" Dot asked, surprised that her own voice traveled across the expanse where it hadn't before. "Do I know you?"

"You don't know us, and you never shall... we're all that you have ever known."

Dot felt something rub against her leg. She looked down and felt puzzled to see Gypsy standing next to her.

"Are you really here, boy?" She knelt beside the dog and stroked the fur atop his head. Though she knew she was in a dream, she felt that he was indeed there somehow.

"Return down the river... travel upstream, against the river."

"How can I do what you both ask?" Dot said to the silhouetted girls. "You want opposite things!"

"Avoid the towns... stay away from the towns."

Dot stood puzzled.

For once, the whispers agreed.

* * *

Dot awoke from her dream surrounded by juniper bushes enclosed within the shared canopy of a circle of trees, a seemingly safe shelter she found the night before after four hours of trudging uphill away from the skirmish near the bridge. She'd kept going until the sounds of the military vehicles had faded away, collapsing to the hillside once she felt satisfied that no one was trailing her.

She felt ashamed of her relief after the last soldier died. She was unable to help Soldier 113, but he was unable to tell his comrades which way she fled.

Gypsy laid at her side, curled atop her legs like a bundled blanket. He stood up in a thicket of leaves and made a hungry whine, both sounds drowned out by the cascade of the nearby waterfall. It occurred to her that resting in such a noisy spot was foolish for she and her dog wouldn't have heard intruders in the wee hours of the night, but she couldn't bring herself to think with logic and strategy as she drifted asleep within a minute of her head touching the mossy ground.

Dot stepped out from the junipers and gazed at the wide waterfall, its mist soaking her clothes and making her shiver. She and Gypsy needed to find a proper shelter, preferably with food and a decent place to sleep so she could clear her head, perhaps regain her memory. She felt certain that one of the many things she inexplicably forgot was the key to her dilemma.

Just east of the waterfall, Dot spied rooftops poking up over the trees. Houses. Surely, someone there would help her. She concluded she had to continue uphill toward the cluster of homes, though it was hardly a decision as a descent back to the broken road would likely deliver her to the soldiers in pursuit.

The Broken Road.

More than a description, that's what it was actually called, another recovered memory.

Blue, green, she didn't trust either troop. Soldier 113 may have been delighted to see that Dot survived the ambush, but there was no care or concern in his tone. To him, she was only a mission objective for reasons that still eluded her. She tried to put him out of her mind as she and the German Shepherd moved on.

After another twenty minutes of hiking uphill, the terrain leveled as it entered a small residential community. Dot had imagined a neighborhood of homes but stood surprised to find the remains of a small downtown. A worn sign revealed she was in a place called Wellspring, "Home of the Wellspring Warlords," a high school football team for a town that no longer held a population. A ghost town. She didn't know how long Wellspring had been abandoned, but she figured it to be many decades from seeing how nature had so thoroughly reclaimed it with tall weeds growing through cracked pavement, moss and mold covering walls, and climbing vines overtaking buildings.

Dot and Gypsy walked the desolate streets, the military dog leading the way as trained. His calm demeanor put Dot at ease within the eerie, liminal state of the town. If there was trouble to be found around the corner, she knew her alert companion would sniff it out before they ran into it.

"Keep your nose sharp for people," she told the dog, "and anything resembling food."

Though the citizens were long gone, their messages remained. Graffiti sprayed high and wide across every surface screamed "Hybrids die!" and "Only pure humans!" Posters plastered across storefronts and wrapped around lampposts depicted "The Purists of the Earth" as brave militant heroes to be celebrated, identical soldiers in green carrying menacing weapons. Most disturbing were hand-painted signs that warned "No Born Tomb or Born Boom Allowed!" whatever that meant.

After ducking into several shops only to find their shelves and cupboards bare, Dot and Gypsy came to a large, ornate structure in the center of town. A tall building with a steeple adorned with a large iron cross welcomed them with its open double doors. Defying her fragmented memory, she recognized it as a "church," a place where people would gather to worship "God," whoever or whatever that might have been.

A sign stood at the church entrance, announcing the times of Sunday worship, food distribution, and "Final Rest." Entering the old wooden church, she quickly surmised what that rest entailed as she finally found the town's citizens gathered together.

Sitting in the pews of the old church were hundreds of people – men, women, elderly, children hugging their fathers, babies held by their mothers – all slumped over dead, plastic cups in hand. Seeing their dry, decomposed bodies seated evenly across the rows, she wondered how long they'd been there and how they departed. Perhaps they died of disease. More likely, they died from their chosen drink. Final Rest, indeed.

Dot started to think that the antagonistic whisper in her dream that urged her to flee was the wiser of the two, the voice whose warnings she should have heeded, though both of the star girls told her to avoid towns.

"What happened to them?" Dot asked Gypsy. She shook from both the chilly wind that blew through the busted stained-glass windows and the macabre sight of so many content corpses. "They came for worship, for food and protection, but ended up staying forever. What would make them choose to die here? What would bring an entire town to this?"

Gypsy led Dot to a large market nearby – a "supermarket" she recalled – its sliding glass doors permanently jammed open by the invasive roots of nearby trees. The sight of cans and boxes on shelves beckoned her, and she entered the store ahead of her guardian despite his hesitation to continue. This excitement, this anticipation of a much-needed meal, led to her surprise meeting of the town's one living resident.

"New to Wellspring?" a male voice asked from another aisle.

Dot froze upon hearing the question, her arm outstretched to a can of beef stew. She turned her head and saw Gypsy at the doorway as if standing guard. She ignored the voice and picked up three cans, careful not to make a sound.

"You don't have to tiptoe around here," the young male said. "It's just us."

Dot placed the cans in her jacket pockets. She couldn't see the man, but knew he stood near.

"What do you mean it's just us?" she asked, daring to speak aloud.

"Everyone else is dead."

"Why? Why are they all dead?"

"Maybe ask yourself, why are we not dead?"

A seventeen-year-old boy revealed himself at the end of the aisle. Tall and lean, his stringy black hair dangled over his pleasant face. A long bow and quiver were slung on his back, his body wrapped with a gray trench coat with black boots. He raised his spread hands as a show of good faith.

"Who are you?" the girl asked.

"Who am I?" he said. "Who are you? You're the one sifting through my stash."

"Your stash? There's enough food here for more than just one person."

"Not if it's meant to last the rest of my life," the boy said, "and I intend to live a long time. You didn't even think to ask permission before taking those cans."

Dot felt the three cans of beef stew hanging heavy in her jacket. She wanted desperately to rip them open and pour their cold contents down her gullet, but conceded that this old market was the armed boy's claimed territory.

"Might I have a few cans?" she asked.

The boy approached, his hands still raised, and looked at the young girl up close. As he loomed over her, he saw her tired expression and her firm grip on the shape of the cans through her jacket. "You can have as many as you'd like," he said with a smile. "Thanks for asking."

Dot nodded and took three more large cans. Her jacket could carry no more.

"My name is... Dot."

"Dot? Dot what?"

"Just Dot."

"What clan are you from? What village?"

She thought for a moment, as if a direct question might dislodge the block in her memory. Nothing came to mind. She shrugged without an answer for him.

"Is it short for something?" he asked. "Dot."

"Just Dot."

"Nice to meet you, Just Dot."

His grin was unnerving, as if he knew more than he let on.

"I'm George Brook," he said proudly, as if he came from noble stock. He held out his compound bow, a long, curved, imposing weapon of wood and steel pulleys, engraved with ornate crescent moons and stars. "I'm a ranger from the South Lands."

"Hello, George Brook." Dot felt more comfortable with the boy.

"Welcome to George's Supermarket, the finest store in all of Wellspring." He smiled as he gestured for her to follow him. "Since you're a tourist, I guess I should give you a tour."

"This is your town?"

"Actually, I've only been here a week."

"I just got here," the girl said.

"I gathered that. Is he yours?"

Dot and George looked over at Gypsy, who remained at the door, now with a slight scowl. The German Shepherd suddenly burst into a sprint and ran toward the boy.

"No, Gypsy!" Dot said. "Down boy!"

The dog instantly heeled and sat upon the floor like a perfectly trained guardian.

"That's some dog," George said, slinging his bow behind him again. "I can tell he's trained to obey your every word, probably been with you a long time."

"No, we just met," Dot said, "but it feels like Gypsy's been with me all my life. I think he just loves people."

"Except me," George said with a laugh. "I mean, you did save me from him just now."

"I suppose I did."

He knelt down and offered his hand to the dog. Dot nodded to Gypsy. The dog leaned forward and took in George's scent.

"Good boy, Gypsy," Dot said.

"I like his name," George said, "and I like his vest. Kevlar-carbon weave over non-Newtonian fluid pockets."

"What's all that mean?"

"It means your dog can take a bullet. A lot of bullets. Hell, he can probably take a bomb blast and hardly feel it. He must be military."

"No," Dot lied, not wanting to reveal any secrets about her past she had yet to uncover herself. "I found the vest on the side of the road. I pulled it from a wrecked truck."

"You sure he ain't military?" George asked, petting the top of Gypsy's head. "It would explain how well trained he seems."

"Those kinds of animals kill on command. Gypsy wouldn't kill anyone."

"That's a relief. A moment ago, it looked like he was gonna rip my guts apart!"

"Like I said, I think he just loves people, once he gets to know them, I mean."

George reached into his trench coat and pulled out a small bag of jerky. He handed a piece to the dog. As Gypsy ate the small strip of dried beef, the girl saw he now had the boy's complete confidence.

"Well, military or not," George said, "you don't see too many dogs anymore."

"Why not?"

"Because they've mostly been eaten. German Shepherds in particular are a delicacy."

Aghast, Dot glared at him, not sure if he was joking or not. "People don't eat dogs," she said.

"What do you think is in those cans you're carrying? Cows?"

Dot searched her memory for a moment. "Isn't that what beef stew is made from?"

"Not anymore. 'Beef' is a very loose term nowadays. The Worm took out most livestock."

"The Worm?"

"You really don't know, do you?" George briefly considered explaining what he meant, but just as quickly shrugged away the notion. If she wasn't familiar with The Worm, she surely didn't know The Story of the World, and he was in no position to enlighten her. He envied her ignorance.

George led Dot and Gypsy through the supermarket to another aisle of cans. "These are vegetables, fruits, sweets. Those big ones are tomato sauce. Some of them have fish, might still be good." He picked up a basket from a nearby counter and filled it with cans. "These here, I can tell you for sure are okay to eat."

"And the others aren't?"

"Well, you're taking a chance on those. They might be too old. They'll taste fine, but you'll get a twisted gut later when you're trying to sleep."

"How do you know?"

"From experience, sadly." George clutched his stomach with a grimace. He reached into his coat and pulled out a four-inch knife, holding it out to Dot. She flinched, thinking he was about to assault her, but her instant of mistrust faded as she traced his warm smile.

"What's this for?" Dot asked. "Protection?"

"You're gonna want to open those cans, right?" The girl nodded and took the knife. "And you're gonna want to cook it?" Again, she nodded, still unsure about the boy.

"I don't imagine any of the town's kitchens still work," Dot said.

Lynn Harrod

"Nope. Not for a long while. Gas lines are dead, and no electricity, of course. Wellspring still has plenty of goods for the taking, considering relief shipments continued for a long while, but utilities ran down long before either of us were born. You can always tell by the rust and the dust. But hey, don't you worry. We'll make a fire, have ourselves a nice little supper. How's that sound?"

"Supper?"

"Dinner."

Dot nodded. She knew that word.

George walked out of the market with his basket of cans. Dot followed with heavy pockets, Gypsy close behind.

"Where are we going?" Dot asked.

"I got a place down the street. We need to get there and board up the door before sunset."

"What happens at sunset?"

George turned and stared, bewildered by the girl. She seemed bright and articulate, traits he rarely saw in his travels – especially in fellow youngsters – but truly knew nothing of The Worm. She couldn't even recall her clan, and she didn't know about the night raids.

"At best, the Gardeners come to scavenge around," he said. "At worst, the Purists roll in. Either way, we'll need to be out of sight before dark."

4

The Library

The light streaming through the wood slats nailed to the windows dimmed with the setting sun as Dot and George warmed themselves by a fire surrounded by tall bookshelves. They sat in the center of the remains of a grand two-story library. Thousands of books lined countless tall shelves all around them with hundreds more stacked in piles on the first floor, the mezzanine above, and on the steps of the wide central staircase that connected them.

George had built a fire pit with stones and gravel behind the old librarian's desk. He assured Dot that the fire was contained and that they'd be safe there, that no passing patrol would spot the flames or feel its heat.

"You said you've been here a week?" Dot said. She sipped hot vegetable soup directly from its can that had simmered over the fire moments before.

"Nine nights and eight days, actually."

"Where were you before that?"

"Everywhere," the boy said. "Most folks roam the wild in groups, but I prefer to go solo."

"Why is that?"

"I know I can trust myself." He passed her a can of warm apple pie filling. Though it was well past its shelf life, it remained edible and served as a fine dessert. "I can't say the same for anyone else."

"What about me?"

"I trust you, I suppose. You stopped your 'not-military' dog from feasting on my insides."

George looked at Gypsy by the door, admiring the way he stood watch like a steadfast guard. Though the door stood boarded tight like the windows, he could still see the town square through thin gaps in the wood.

"Where are you from?" Dot asked. "Surely, you haven't been roaming all your life."

"I already told you. I'm a ranger from the South Lands." He couldn't bring himself to mention the village name, and Dot didn't press him.

"Aren't you young to be a ranger?"

"In The South, we actually considered seventeen old for a ranger. When I was fourteen, I was made Senior Woodsman in charge of two dozen scouts. We ventured out at night, mapped the region, hunted game, and scavenged goods."

"You ate a lot of dogs?" Dot asked, dreading his likely response. "Delicacies like German Shepherd?"

"No, mostly fish, birds, sometimes hares. Like I said, you rarely see dogs anymore." He reached for his quiver resting beside him and pulled out an arrow. The way he expertly spun it in his hand as he spoke told Dot he'd been an archer his entire life. "The boys all listened to me. I was a pretty good shot. I still am."

"It wasn't just your marksmanship," she said, surprised by her vocabulary. "Being a 'pretty good shot' isn't enough. It sounds to me you were a pretty good leader."

"Senior Wainright was our leader. He taught us all about life, about survival. He trained us well."

"Why'd you leave?"

George winced as his words came forth like jagged rocks. "I escaped three years ago."

"Escaped?"

"It's not the kind of place you live happily ever after, though I guess no place is anymore."

George recalled his upbringing in The South Lands, in the small hunting village of Colt, and the night his world went up in flames. The heat from his fire cruelly brought the grim memory to life.

All around him in the dark corners of the old library, he saw the burning doorways of his neighbors, the fleeing children, their parents begging for mercy as identical soldiers in shadow blasted anyone and anything in their crosshairs. At the top of the library's staircase, he saw his 14-year-old self hiding in a barrel, clutching his bow, peering out and waiting for his chance to run. Senior Wainright, the leader of the village and his surrogate father, had warned him to forget about fighting the soldiers and flee if given the chance. All the young rangers and woodsmen had been given similar orders, though most of them followed their instincts to help their families, ultimately falling to unrelenting gunfire.

"Anyone else escape with you?" Dot asked, jolting him back to the present. "I guess what I want to know is how a boy ends up alone in an abandoned town."

"Like I said, I prefer to go solo," George murmured, the only response he could summon without breaking down into tears. "That was years ago. I've been on my own ever since."

"I'm sorry," Dot said, recognizing the pain on her new friend's face.

"It's not so bad. 'He travels fastest who travels alone.' That's what Senior Wainright used to say. What about you?"

"What about me?"

"Do you remember anything? How old are you?"

"I'm... not sure."

"Fourteen or fifteen is my guess."

"Fifteen," Dot said, frustrated that she couldn't recall any further details about herself.

"I guess what I want to know is how a girl ends up alone in an abandoned town."

"I'm not alone," Dot said almost defensively. She looked at her loyal dog at the door and at the friendly boy by the fire. "Not anymore."

"You know what I mean. Surely, you remember something before running into me at the market."

Dot thought of cover stories to hide the fact that she fled a battle over her capture, a violent struggle that resulted in the deaths of two troops in green and blue.

She had a family waiting for her.

She'd been sent out on a pilgrimage.

She sought missing friends.

She'd been searching for her village after wandering off and getting lost in the woods.

None of her fabricated stories landed within her mind. Perhaps she felt that lying to George after just having met him was a poor start to a new friendship. Perhaps she simply felt scared to attempt any deception with a kind boy who offered her food and shelter and protection from nightly raids. None of it mattered, for George saw through her indecision.

"You don't know, do you?" he asked.

"Know what?"

"You don't know where you're from."

"Of course, I do."

"You don't know about The Worm and you don't know about the night raids, so it stands to reason you don't know much of anything."

"That's harsh," Dot said. "You make me sound like a fool."

"I'm sorry, Dot. I didn't mean it like that. It's just that... I think those memories are gone. Not blurred or blocked, they're gone. Erased. I've seen it before." George chose his words carefully for he knew he risked making her clouded mind worse. "It's okay, I won't keep nagging you to remember. I don't think you could if you wanted to."

Dot felt uncomfortable with George's assessment, though she couldn't deny it. As he laid out, it truly felt like someone had reached into her mind and plucked out specific memories of her life prior to waking up in that ancient oak tree.

She reached to a stack of books piled beside her and opened one to the first page. The blocks of text overwhelmed her, but only for a moment.

George laughed, walked to another stack, and gathered several large books for her. "This is where the picture books are in case you're curious."

To his surprise, the young girl turned to a random page and started reading, enunciating each syllable at first, soon flowing through the passage with fluency.

"There now came a sharp whistling in the air from the south," Dot read, "and as they turned their eyes that way they saw ripples in the grass coming from that direction also. Suddenly Uncle Henry stood up. 'There's a cyclone coming, Em,' he called to his wife. 'I'll go look after the stock.' Then he ran toward the sheds where the cows and horses were kept. Aunt Em dropped her work and came to the door. One glance told her of the danger close at hand."

"Are you just making that up?" George asked.

Dot shut the book and read its ornate cover.

The Wonderful Wizard of Oz by L. Frank Baum

She picked up another book, opened to a page and read again.

"Nous étions à l'Étude, quand le Proviseur entra, suivi d'un nouveau habillé en bourgeois et d'un garçon de classe qui portait un grand pupitre. Ceux qui dormaient se réveillèrent, et chacun se leva comme surpris dans son travail."

George sat flummoxed upon hearing her read the strange language. "You really can read?"

"Yes," Dot said, also surprised.

"What's that all about then? Those strange words."

"A girl. She's in a library like this one, I think. The man in charge is dressed up fancy. A boy came in, someone in her 'class.' He carried a desk. The others were asleep."

"Sounds like a school," he said. "Sounds like the man is their teacher." George took the book from Dot and glanced at the cover, its title unfamiliar. "Mad... madam... bover..."

"Madame Bovary," Dot said. "So you can read, too."

"Senior Wainright taught me a little. But the words in this book sound like some kind of special code."

"It's French."

"What's 'French' mean?"

"I'm not sure," Dot said. "I just know it's French."

George abandoned the picture books and sifted through the stacks beside Dot, flipping pages until he saw another language he didn't recognize. He held the book open for Dot to read. "What about this one?"

"Era un viejo solitario que pescaba en una barca en la corriente del Golfo y llevaba ochenta y cuatro días sin atrapar un pez."

Neither of them could realize that Dot's pronunciation was perfect.

"What's that say?" he asked.

"An old man is fishing in a boat. He's lonely, and he's caught nothing for eighty-four days."

"Damn, I know the feeling," George said. "But that doesn't sound 'French' to me."

"It's not. It's Spanish."

George felt genuinely confused and ever more curious about this mysterious girl.

"They're from different villages, I think," Dot said.

George thought about the idea of villages using different languages and remembered encountering hunters who had invented their own manner of speech so they could talk amongst strangers without giving away the location of their home or their numbers. He wondered if Dot had spent time in such a camp, though knowing more than one 'village code' seemed impossible to him.

"What else can you do?" George said with a laugh, impressed with Dot's self-discovery.

"Well, I know how to use that." Dot pointed to a display cabinet across the room that she'd been eyeing since she arrived. It held strange, beautiful objects of brass and wood and black lacquer, all covered in valves, buttons, and a thick layer of dust after hanging undisturbed for decades. They rested on hooks next to flags with different colors and patterns.

"Can you teach me?" George said. "Could come in handy."

He opened the cabinet and pulled out a long, black funnel, a tool alien to him as evident by his scrutiny. The boy carefully handed it to her as if it might crack or split with any sudden movement. He rubbed his hands by the fire and watched her every motion, expecting her to guide him through its use as a weapon.

Dot laid her fingertips on its buttons and pressed her lips to the pointy end. She blew into it, pressed the buttons in sequence, and George stared at the girl, enthralled by the lovely sound she made with it.

"It makes music," he said, realizing in awe.

"It's a horn," Dot said, halting her tune. "A wind instrument. It's a 'clarinet,' I believe. What were you expecting?"

"I always thought those things were guns, like the soldiers use, but I could never figure them out."

Dot laughed at the idea of a clarinet being a firearm. George laughed with her, feeling silly as he saw the bizarre shapes of the instruments with fresh eyes.

"I guess it makes sense that they're not guns," he said. "If they were, someone would have taken them long ago." He walked to the display case and spotted a large wooden desk sitting in front of it. "What about this? It's empty now, but it looks like something used to be stored in here, hung on all these wires."

Dot stood and walked up to the desk. Without knowing how, she lifted a cover, exposing a long keyboard. She played its black-and-white keys and a crude song emerged from its cabinet.

"Beethoven," Dot said, unsure of whether that was the song title or its composer.

"So that's for music, too," George said, fascinated by what neither of them knew was an upright piano.

"They all are."

A sense of dread overcame George. He quickly grabbed Dot's hands and shut the keyboard cover.

"What are you doing?"

"We're making too much noise," George said, suddenly whispering. "If there are Purists out tonight, they'll hear us for sure!"

The two of them backed away from the display of musical instruments, seeing them now as liabilities that could give away their shelter. George joined Gypsy at the boarded door and listened carefully. To his relief, he heard no scavengers exploring the town.

"We need to get some sleep," he said. He turned to find Dot looking through the picture books he offered earlier. For once, she felt confused by them.

"I don't know this one," the girl said, holding open one of the larger books. She showed him a children's book full of pictures of animals dressed and walking around like people.

Once again, George was stymied. "You know how different villages speak, you can read many codes, you can play music, but you don't know about hybrids?"

Dot flipped through the book, saw wolf women, lizard children, gorilla men, but didn't recognize any of them as "hybrids."

"Whoever wiped your mind really went deep," George said.

"What's all that mean? Wiped my memory? And what are hybrids?"

"We need to get some sleep," George said again, taking the children's book from her. As gifted as she was, he didn't want to further splinter her fragmented mind. "We need to rest while we can."

5

Night Raid

Dot awoke to a loud clatter, like a loaded toolbox dropped to the ground. She opened her eyes and remained still, lying on the floor, staring up at the mezzanine high above. The sudden metallic crash may have shaken her from an uneasy slumber, but it was the many footsteps, crunching on dirt outside, that brought her panic.

"George," she said, keeping her voice to a whisper. She silenced herself as the footsteps became louder, and she felt grateful to be hidden from view, flat against the floor in the dark behind the librarian's desk.

The darkness, silence, and biting cold made Dot turn her head slightly to confirm that the fire had gone out. A trickle of water crept across the floor from the fire pit and onto her arm. The wide puddle across the hardwood and the empty, overturned pail beside it told her the flames hadn't died on their own while she slept. They were doused in a hurry.

Dot slowly sat up and peered around the desk at the door where her German Shepherd remained on guard. Gypsy stood perfectly quiet and still, his hind legs bent as if he were coiled to strike at anyone that might pull down the barricade and dare to enter. She wanted to call her dog, to have him back away from the entrance for fear he'd be shot by the intruders, but she couldn't risk being heard by them.

She looked around for George, hoping he knelt ducked behind a bookcase or crouched by a window, but didn't see him or his longbow. She realized he must have heard the night raiders before she woke, quickly poured water onto the fire to help hide their position, grabbed his bow and quiver, and ventured out of the room. He was likely upstairs to better view the intruders, to assess the threat.

A wave of fear overtook her when she noticed that he'd taken more than just his weapon. He took all of his belongings, including his share of the food, a heavy sack of dry beans and canned goods. All traces of him were gone. It meant that he probably fled the town, leaving her and Gypsy to fend for themselves.

Clever boy.

"Shoot her on sight," a male voice said from just outside. "Injury only. We take her alive if we can. She must be near."

The order was given with the same monotone voice, stern tone, and distinguishing cadence of Soldier 113, the dying man she encountered on the road whose last words were a similar command. With seconds left to live, his final thought was dedicated to her capture. Now there was another man – many other men – on the same mission.

"She likely crossed the river," the man said, contradicting himself. "The West Wall isn't far from here."

"No, footprints place her heading north from the falls," he said, but from farther away. Dot turned to the distance voice.

"She looked for food and rest before hitting the river," he said, now sounding much closer.

Confused for a moment, Dot realized the soldiers all sounded the same just as they looked the same. To the ear, one soldier hunted her, but she knew there were at least three in the street in front of the library. Only their footfalls hinted at their true numbers.

Dot rose to her feet and joined Gypsy at the door. She knelt down, pressed herself against the barricade, and peeked through the sliver in the wood that let in moonlight. She saw five soldiers kick down the entrance of the tall building across the street – "The Wellspring Hotel" – and enter with rifles drawn. Another three forced their way into a building called the "Post Office" next to the hotel.

Soon, they'd enter the library.

Dot grabbed Gypsy by the collar and led him to the central staircase. The first step made a loud creak that she assumed gave away their presence. After pausing a moment and not hearing anyone give chase, she slowly ascended the stairs, her dog following her pace. Upon reaching the mezzanine, she looked around for a hiding spot and spotted a small, round window high above the bookshelves. It stood out because it was the only window not boarded up. With no other options, Dot climbed up shelving and stacks of books, stood on her tip-toes, reached out, and grabbed the window frame. The slight nudge from her fingertips swung it open to the night air.

Pulling herself up into the open window, she realized why no one had bothered to seal it. The circular frame was hard to reach,

Lynn Harrod

barely big enough for her to fit through, and led to a two-story drop to an alley. Crouched within the frame, she nearly lost hope before noticing an arrow embedded in the exterior wall beneath her. Below that were several other arrows, easy to miss in the dead of night.

George had formed a makeshift ladder.

Clever boy.

Dot cautiously placed a foot onto the nearest arrow, the moon offering just enough light to guide her.

The arrows were stuck into the wood trim of the old building at odd angles from George shooting them either from above or below, but each felt solid as Dot made her way down. Even if George's escape path had been spotted, none of the night raiders could follow because, like the small round window mounted high on the wall, the delicate arrow ladder could only be used by a child. She imagined young George, tall but lean, barely able to manage it himself.

Upon reaching the alley, she realized the downside of such a carefully planned, difficult path. Gypsy remained in the window above, stranded, unable to traverse the odd ladder. He silently looked down at Dot, content that she had found a way out, doomed to be cornered by the intruders once they eventually entered the library.

Dot stared up at her loyal companion. She searched the narrow alley for something for him to land on but saw only the cracked pavement, the brick walls of the library and the building behind it, and a small panel van. She considered the van's roof, but dismissed the risk as too great. They'd surely hear the dog leaping onto it.

She offered the German Shepherd one last look of apology before turning to run.

"Stay boy," she said in a lowered voice, failing to hide the pain in her voice. "You stay and hide." Gypsy's expression remained friendly during her goodbye, his black eyes shining in the moonlight. She would always remember that moment.

Dot reached the ground and crept into shadow against the back wall of the library, ready to slink past the town full of men hunting her, but stopped and gasped upon stumbling onto the dead body of a soldier, his chest impaled with two arrows.

"George," she muttered sadly. "How I wish I was a survivor like you."

She stepped over the corpse, keeping close to the wall, but was again halted upon spotting a single soldier standing in front of the van, thirty feet away, fixated on her. He wore black-and-green fatigues like Soldier 113 the day before. Dot had been so focused on her descent that she failed to notice the man when her feet touched earth.

Their eyes locked, Dot backed away from the soldier but froze when he pointed his rifle at her. He raised his radio to his face.

"Command 70," he said into the radio. "312 reporting."

"Report 312," an identical voice replied.

"Located the girl, in the alley behind..." Soldier 312 stopped and looked about him, unsure of his exact location.

"Which alley?" Command 70 asked over the radio. "Behind what? Respond 312."

"Behind the post office," Dot lied, desperate to stall for time.

Soldier 312 read her face for a moment. He shook his head in disappointment. "Bringing her to the transport," he said over the radio. "312 out." He pulled a pair of handcuffs from his belt and tossed them to the girl's feet, keeping his rifle at ready. "I may not know this town, but I'm not a fool, Princess."

Princess?

Dot picked up the handcuffs.

"Put them on," the soldier said.

Dot found it odd that he kept his distance, that he didn't restrain her himself, as if he was being careful not to come near her. She glanced over her shoulder, saw nothing blocking her path out of the alley.

"Try to run and I'll cut down your legs," the soldier said, pointing his weapon at her ankles. "Perhaps I should regardless. No more running."

"George is gonna get you," Dot said, hoping it was true, hoping her friend was crouched in shadow nearby, his longbow drawn.

"You mean the South Land ranger?" Soldier 312 said, to Dot's dismay. "He killed six of us on his way out of town. The boy's trail leads west to the river. Command sent half the troop after him. By now, he's either dead or gone."

"You lie," Dot said, though she had a feeling the monotone soldier wasn't trying to trick her.

"The ranger is not your savior. He's a survivor, just as you said. No, Princess, your 'George' will not get me."

As Soldier 312 aimed his rifle at Dot's legs, he fell, violently slammed to the pavement as Gypsy landed atop him, pouncing from the round window two stories above. The soldier quickly unsheathed a knife, but the dog tore at his arm with impossible speed and frightening fury. Dot could only watch as her canine friend ripped the soldier apart, spattering gray blood across the alley. Soldier 312 tried to scream for his comrades' help, but Gypsy clamped his jaws down hard and deep into his neck, crushing his windpipe and severing his vocal cords. The fatal blow silenced him, ending his life.

The brutality lasted less than a minute, but in that moment Dot saw the dog as a demon out to destroy anyone who posed a threat to her, ready to put himself in harm's way to protect her. The

German Shepherd released the pulpy remains of the soldier and once again stood at her side.

"We have met before," she said in realization, awestruck by how calm he suddenly looked. "We must have." After a moment of hesitation, she petted his head. "George was right. A dog like you is rare."

* * *

Dot and Gypsy spent the next late hour crouched behind buildings, shrubs, tall weeds that pierced the cracked pavement, and abandoned vehicles that littered the town's streets. The passenger vehicles were all different, colorful rather than military green, black, and gray. She remembered they were once called "cars."

She expected to see an endless army of green soldiers, but only saw nine. Four patrolled the main thoroughfare while peeking into buildings. The other five lay dead, their torsos struck with arrows, George's work as he navigated his early exit. Soldier 312 claimed George led most of his comrades west toward the river. For that reason, Dot and her dog fled Wellspring heading east. The troop was hunting her, not the boy, and would soon give up chasing him and resume its mission.

As she ventured away from the town to return to the woods, she passed the last of the derelict cars left to rot in a field. Dot wondered about the people who used to drive them, the people who used to populate Wellspring. She hoped they weren't all dead like the folks who ended their lives in the church. Perhaps they founded another town. Perhaps war forced families everywhere to join in a mass exodus and build anew.

She imagined a towering city, a rainforest paradise, and a sprawling network of tunnels, unsure if they were burgeoning memories or forgotten dreams.

They sounded like they could be The Story of the World, or at least part of it. There was also The Worm. The green and blue soldiers. Gardeners. Purists. Hybrids. The mystery of her friendly yet highly trained killer dog.

After another hour of tramping across wild fields and through dense woods, Dot felt a stinging hunger and seemed to feel her dog's as well. During their hasty flight from Wellspring, she neglected to bring her supplies from the supermarket, and though she didn't know it, her forgetfulness granted her escape. Finding a cache of canned goods threw off the soldiers' hunt, convincing them she fled with George or was otherwise still in Wellspring.

The stars along the horizon faded as the sun rose, shining light onto something Dot found curious.

A short distance away stood thousands of tall stalks aligned in a perfect row, spaced evenly, perfectly, a feat impossible by nature. Someone had planted those stalks, which meant they likely grew food. On closer view, she recognized their abundant offerings as ears of corn, the source of her favorite treat, canned sweet corn. It now and would forever remind her of George. She hoped he was well and that she'd see him again.

The corner of the field grew corn the size of her forearm. She picked an ear but stopped herself from grabbing another when she spotted more further along, hanging three times the size of the one in hand. She picked a giant ear, peeled back its husk, and bit into it with relish, leaving the smaller one for Gypsy. After making quick work of it, she ate a smaller one, using both hands.

With the sounds of the night raiders invading the dawn, their trucks and footfalls and shouts in the near distance, Dot held her dog close and remained hidden deep in the safety of the cornfield. After feasting on corn and having barely a collective three hours of sleep throughout the tumultuous night, the girl fell asleep with her dog curled in her lap as the sun started a new day.

* * *

The sputtering of a motor vehicle caught Dot's ear, waking her with a jolt, its slow approach clutching her stomach. It sounded similar to the convoy of trucks that had arrived at the bloody skirmish by the bridge while she retreated into the hills, only smaller, with a more irregular cadence.

The sunrise looked strange. Its yellow-orange beams of light still peeked up from the horizon, spreading across the cloudy sky, but from the opposite direction. She sat in the vast cornfield not during morning but the following sunset, having slept soundly for nearly twelve hours.

The motor vehicle sounded closer, and Dot quickly scrambled further into the cornfield on her hands and knees. Though she remained well hidden where she'd slept, she wanted to distance herself from the noise of the motor. Her crawl turned into a sprint as she went deeper into the field. The tall stalks disoriented her, removing all sense of direction. Even the setting sun was now hard to spot.

She froze, unable to backtrack to her entry point and not daring to step out of the corn any place else. Instead, she sat on an ear of corn the size of a log, each kernel like a lemon, and waited for the sinister motor to pass, to continue into the distance. It did not.

After another minute, the loud mechanical noise stopped quite near, replaced by a sharp whistling. Dot assumed it was the wind through the stalks but soon heard a lively tune within the whistle, followed by a jovial voice singing its lyrics.

Oh, I wish I was in the land of cotton
Old times there are not forgotten
Run away, run away, run away, Veggie Man
In farmin' land where I was born in
Early on a frosty mornin'
Run away, run away, run away, Veggie Man

Oh, I live up in the North Woods
Hooray! Hooray!
The farm is where I'll take my stand
To live and die in North Woods
Away, away, away up in the North Woods
Away, away, away up in the North Woods

The man repeated his song, switching from lyrics to whistling to humming and back to lyrics. His voice rose and fell in pitch and cracked at times, almost like a busted bicycle horn. His verses were punctuated by heavy loads being dropped into what sounded like a large wooden bucket. He toiled just beyond the edge of the field, harvesting the corn. Dot saw his shape pass several times before she crawled toward his voice, careful not to reveal herself.

She sat motionless and terrified by what she saw as she parted the stalks.

6

Vincent

Dot collapsed to her knees as she stared at the bizarre creature, its long, slender body bent over a small three-wheeled motor vehicle. Gypsy stepped in front of her and let out a low growl, instantly alerting the towering thing now standing before them. With the eerie sound of twisting dry straw, it turned and looked around, under and behind the small vehicle. After a minute of Dot holding her breath, the creature's large, deep-set black eyes caught sight of the dog through the stalks. Gypsy met the locked stare with fangs bared and hind legs poised to pounce. His attack stance may have blown their cover, but it also kept Dot from retreating into the depths of the cornfield. She thought back to what her canine friend did to an armed soldier, something that horrified her before but now offered strange comfort.

Lynn Harrod

Silhouetted by the setting sun, the monstrous creature soon noticed the girl and stared back with equal curiosity. She had assumed it was a man, but was no longer sure. It certainly resembled a man, a most unusual one who stood eight feet tall with long slender arms and legs on an almost impossibly thin frame. Despite its spindly appearance, its limbs were covered in what looked like long, green muscles. It wore stained denim overalls, worn work boots, and a hood made of woven straw.

The vague similarities to any normal man ended there.

"What... happened to you?" Dot asked, her instincts telling her it was a gentle monster, at least for the moment. "Your arms and legs... your eyes..."

"My eyes?" the thing said with an amused smirk. His high-pitched voice cracked at the start of each sentence. "Have you seen yours? They're brown! Both of them! Brown like hazelnuts!"

"That's odd to you?"

"Odd? No, I'm not for sure about that. It's just that I've never seen hazelnutty peepers before."

The strange man's deep black eyes were double the size of an average person. They resembled ebony porcelain saucers with thin colorful streaks delicately painted across them. Their rainbows of veins made them look like delicate flowers. Upon each blink, the floral patterns changed, widening, darkening, their multi-colored veins shifting. They contrasted with his deep green skin, yellowish lips, and light brown face grooved deeply as if made of ancient wood. If not for his facial expressions, one would assume he wore a crude oaken mask.

Most striking were the creature's many dark green tentacles protruding from his sleeves and backside, like wild wisteria. Their many small jagged leaves, similar to those peeking out from his woven hood, revealed they were indeed living vines. They moved like long snakes poised in the air, twisting and curling about him.

Simply put, the curious creature looked like a giant walking, talking plant.

"Are you a pig?" it asked, its voice cracking again as he lowered it to a whisper. He pointed to Gypsy, still ready to attack. "I know he's a dog... I'm pretty sure he's a dog... but I'm not for sure about you. Pig, right?"

"I'm not a pig!" Dot said. "How rude! Why would you ask that?"

"An albino lizard?" he said. "No, not a lizard. No scales. Sorry, I don't mean to be rude."

"I'm a human."

"Well, of course you're a human! But a human what? Not a human-pig... sorry, didn't mean to be rude... and not a human-lizard. Maybe a human-chimpanzee? No, not hairy enough."

"I'm just a human, like my friend is just a dog."

"Oh, I see, you're a human-human, like Father," the creature said. "We thought he was the last one."

"Who's Father?" Dot asked. She stood and stepped out of the cornfield and onto the dirt trail that ran through it. "And who are you?"

"My name is Vincent!" The tall green man spoke his name with pride, extending a leafy hand toward her, his fingers like the branches of a mossy tree. "That's the name I like, but they also call me Vinny Greenblood, Veggie Vinny, Dim Vin, the Green Fool, Vincent Vines. I hate all those other names 'cause they used to poke and prod me while they teased me with those names... except for Father... but you can call me one of those names if you like. I won't mind."

"Vincent," Dot said, offering a slight smile. "I wouldn't want to use a name you hate. My name is..."

"Let me guess!" Vincent shouted, jumping uncomfortably close to her. "Arianna? Thea? Evangeline? Athena?"

"No…"

"Albertine? Petra? Jan? Zelda?"

"No, none of those!" Dot said with a laugh.

"No? Hmm, this may take a while…"

"My name is Dot," she said, amused by his childish manner.

"Dang, I should have known," he said, his wide smile exposing dense roots within his mouth. "It's so obvious."

"It is?" Dot hoped she'd met someone that could help fill in her memory.

"It says so right there on your hand. D-O-T. I can read, you know. Can I call you 'Dottie'? Father says I'm an excellent reader."

"Yes, you can call me Dottie. Tell me more about…"

"About Father?" Vincent said. "He always tells me what to do. He even made me a book."

With his spindly fingers, Vincent reached into the front pocket of his overalls and pulled out a small black book no bigger than a deck of cards. He flipped through its pages, muttering "new" and "stranger" and "visitor" until he found the page he needed. He attempted to read it, mouthing the words before turning it around and showing it to the girl. She read the header and its instructions aloud.

WHAT TO DO WHEN SOMEONE COMES TO THE FARM.

BRING THEM TO ME AT THE HOUSE.

"I got the first part," Vincent said slyly. "Thanks for getting the second part, Dottie. I always wondered what it said."

"Didn't you read that page before?"

"No, I got lazy halfway through."

"I mean, didn't you read it when others came here?" Dot asked.

"There were others?"

"Weren't there?" Dot's hope for familiarity faded.

"Nope! You're the first!"

"Vincent... how long have you been here?"

The green-and-brown man counted his fingers. He then picked up an oversized ear of corn and counted kernels, turned it over, counted again. "Umm, thirty."

"Thirty days?" Dot asked. "Thirty months?"

"No, what it is when you put days together? They make a week. Then you put weeks together to make a month, and you put months together..."

"Years?" the girl said, taken aback. "Thirty years?"

"That's it! You got it!"

"Thirty years and it's just been you and your father?"

"Yep! But he's not my father, Dottie. I mean, he's 'Father,' but not my father-father. Sorry if I don't make no sense. I do that sometimes." The plant-man suddenly smelled something. He leaned in close to Dot and sniffed her face, his black saucer eyes inches from hers. "You've been eating our corn!"

"Yes, we both have," Dot said, backing away a step. "I'm sorry, we didn't mean to steal from..."

"How was it?"

"It was... good."

"Nice and sweet?"

Dot nodded and smiled.

Vincent stood upright and raised his arms proudly. "I knew it was sweet! I wondered if it was maybe just me tasting it, but I had a good feeling it was sweet. We grew it special, you see. I had Father mix up some different seeds under his looking glass to make a brand new seed. Then I planted it, watered it, grew it, and I could tell it would be sweet corn. That's where I got the name from."

"What's it called?"

"Sweet Corn."

Dot laughed at how animated Vincent became when he boasted of his corn, twirling about, spinning on his boot heels in celebration.

"Should we meet... Father?" she asked.

"Yes! That's what the book says so that's what we'll do. He'll be sitting in the parlor now, ready to watch the sunset."

"How lovely."

"He also sits there to watch the sunrise, the afternoon sky, the stars, the rain, the fog, the hail, or just to listen to music on his big brass flower. I'd offer you something to eat, but you already had my special sweet corn."

Vincent set a second giant ear of corn onto the back of his small three-wheeled vehicle. He sat on its long seat and grabbed its handlebars. As he gestured for Dot and Gypsy to hop on behind him, his many vines grasped the corn while his hand flipped a switch. A quick down-kick of his leg started the throaty motor. It bellowed overwhelmingly loud as she had remembered, but it no longer sounded frightening like the soldiers' big trucks. This green monster of a man, with his large black eyes and meandering tentacles, seemed grotesque before. Now, after speaking with him for only a few minutes, he seemed like a gentle, innocent soul.

Dot placed her hand on Gypsy's head, signaling for him to heel. The sneer dropped from his face as he quickly calmed, always the obedient dog. They sat atop the oversized ear of corn which Vincent held to the long seat of what Dot recalled was a "motor trike." He shifted into gear and drove them further down the trail.

"What's his name?" Vincent shouted over the rumble of the motor. One of his vines slithered past Dot and rubbed the dog's ears.

"Gypsy."

"Like the flower!"

"There's a flower you call 'Gypsy'?"

"Cynoglossum officinale. The Gypsy Flower. Red and purple and yellow. Hairy leaves. Bristly fruit. Some folks call it Houndstongue. Hey, Houndstongue! Get it? Because your dog has a tongue! It's a real pretty flower, but it's a weed, so you gotta keep it in check 'cause it can get you sick."

"You sure know a lot about flowers."

"I grew some on my body once, on top of my head, under my hood. It was like a real pretty wig, but it's a weed so you gotta keep it in check 'cause it can get you sick. I know 'cause it got me real sick since it's a weed and you gotta... dang, I kinda said that already."

"Yes, you kinda did."

"I gotta remember to remember things, so I don't forget to remember them." Dot laughed at Vincent's looping logic, just as tangled as his vines. "Sorry if I don't make no sense. I do that sometimes."

Dot watched Vincent steer the motor trike while his vines held down the corn. She wanted to ask what kind of creature he was, but didn't want to cut into his polite, welcoming manner. His reference to growing plants on his body sounded like a chance to satisfy her curiosity.

"Vincent," Dot said. "Can I ask you a personal question?"

"Well, I am a person, and I'm pretty sure you're a person, so anything we say to each other is personal."

"What are you? I mean, you're not... human."

"Of course I am!" Vincent said.

"Not human-human like me."

"No, not human-human. I'm a human-plant."

"I figured that much," Dot said.

"Human-plantae-liana if you wanna get scientifical-like. Most folks just say 'Man-Plant' or other names which I hate, so I won't mention them unless you want me to, which I won't mind."

"I'll call you whatever you prefer."

"Thanks," Vincent said. "You really are like Father."

"How do you mean?"

Dot looked over his shoulder as they approached a farmhouse beside a barn. The house was surrounded by lush, oversized vegetables and immense trees offering with a variety of fruit, most the size of the girl's head.

"I mean, you're not like the other human-humans," Vincent said. "The ones in the old village... I forgot the name of where we used to live... you're nice to me, like Father."

"The other humans weren't nice to you?"

"Oh no, not nice," Vincent said, parking the utility vehicle in front of the farmhouse. "Not very nice at all. They tried to kill me for murdering their chief."

Vincent shut off the engine and hopped off the motor trike. Dot hesitated, remaining on her corn seat with Gypsy after hearing the plant-man's grim confession. Vincent saw the look on her face and realized he may have frightened the girl.

"Sorry if I don't make no sense," Vincent said. "I do that sometimes."

7

Father Young

"I was wondering who Vincent was talking to," the old man said from his corner chair in the parlor, having overheard him outside as he stepped onto the porch. A fireplace crackled and glowed beside him, offering a warm respite to contrast the chill outside. "Usually, he whistles or laughs at the jokes he claims to hear from the elm tree out front."

"Elmer doesn't tell jokes, Father," Vincent said with a sigh, as if for the hundredth time. "He tells funny stories."

"You're Father?" Dot asked, remaining at the open screen door.

"Francis," the old man said in his watery, tired voice. "Francis Young. Vincent calls me Father."

"He's not my father-father," Vincent said, forgetting he mentioned it earlier. "But he kinda is, but he's not..."

Lynn Harrod

"You wouldn't exist without me, boy, and that's as fatherly as a man can get."

Francis "Father" Young looked as old as the cracked, peeling walls around him. He spoke in wheezing exhales, stared at the ceiling, and sat nearly obscured by colorful flowers all about the room. Every color of the rainbow climbed the walls, swept across the floor, and stretched to the ceiling. Their blooms were the size of one's face, their leaves the likes of one's hands. The dense, lush flora breathed life into the otherwise ramshackle home. They starkly contrasted their decrepit master, confined to his chair, his arms and mouth attached by tubes to machines that kept him alive.

"You hungry, girl?" Father Young asked.

"She likes corn," Vincent said.

"Yes, sir, but I'd love anything else you have to offer," Dot said quickly.

"Boy, get her a bowl of stew and some... you like coffee?"

Dot somehow knew what was coffee was, but didn't know if she'd ever had it.

"Coffee with milk and sugar, maybe?" Father said.

"We're out of milk," Vincent said, "and we're low on sugar."

"Drop an egg in, then." The old man turned to Dot, not sure if she understood. "Ever had egg coffee? Dropping an egg in makes it go down nice and smooth."

"I can show you if you want," Vincent said.

"No coffee for me, thanks," Dot said. "Maybe some other time."

"Boy, how about you get her some tangerine punch?"

"And corn?" Vincent asked.

"I suspect she's had her fill of corn."

Vincent skipped out of the room, his many vines trailing behind him. Dot and Gypsy remained standing at the door.

"I apologize for stealing your corn," Dot said, realizing Father figured out her theft.

"Nonsense," Father Young said. "We have enough corn, squash, carrots, and string beans for a hundred girls and their hundred dogs. You take as much as you want."

"I'm very grateful."

"Now come in, girl. Unlike your furry friend here, I don't bite."

Dot shut the screen door and walked into the parlor toward the old man in his corner. She saw paintings on the walls, nearly hidden by the thick foliage. They depicted several plant creatures like Vincent working on a farm, playing with human children, climbing trees, and fishing along a lake.

"I painted all those," Father Young said, "while I still could. Vincent is in each of them."

"There are others like him?" Dot asked as she studied the paintings. "Plant people?"

"There were many others," Father Young said sadly, "but they didn't live long. Vincent was the best of them, for better or worse. He was the last one they made and ended up being the last of his kind. I guess I am, too."

Dot wanted to ask the old man about the soldiers, their hunt for her, and the fate of the Wellspring townsfolk, but she felt safe and welcomed in the ancient farmhouse. She didn't want to interrupt that hospitality. She felt at ease with her company and the home they shared. For the first time since she awoke in the hollow of the oak tree, she could relax and breathe. Still, Father Young sensed she had questions, as he surely had.

"What animal are you?" he asked. "I can't quite place the scent. Pig?"

"Vincent asked me the same thing," Dot said with a laugh.

"Chimpanzee? Orangutang? If so, the musk is mild."

"I'm human."

"Human-human?" the old man asked.

"Yes, sir, can't you tell?" Dot crossed the parlor and reached her host, realizing that the old man stared blankly into space with glossy white eyes. "Sir, are you... blind?"

"Blind as an earthworm, my dear," Father Young said. "Ironic, isn't it? Surrounded by beauty I can't see. Vincent's a sweet boy. He fills my little room with the most extravagantly colored perfumed flowers. He says they're good for me even if I can't fully enjoy them. His stew, I'm afraid, doesn't smell as good as it tastes."

Vincent returned with a large steaming bowl of vegetable stew and brought it to Dot. Indeed, the stew smelled like a barrage of pungent spice and burnt tree bark. He held a spoonful up to her lips, excited to see someone other than Father sample his cooking. Dot sipped the broth before eating the chunks of squash and carrot and turnip, pleasantly surprised by its unexpected flavor.

"It's delicious," Dot said.

"Smells atrocious, though, don't it?" Father Young said with a coughing laugh. "Just gotta pinch your nose when you eat it."

Vincent prepared a simple table setting for her, slid out a chair, and gestured for her to sit. He set the stew on a linen placemat along with a mug of tangerine punch.

"Such service," Dot said, sitting to her meal. She looked down and saw Gypsy already bent down over a bowl on the floor.

"That's always a good sign," Vincent said. "If a dog eats your cooking, it must be good!"

Gypsy devoured his stew within a minute. He backed away from the bowl and returned to Dot's side.

"What's your dog's name?" Father Young asked, glancing in the animal's direction.

"Gypsy."

"Glorious name. You come up with it?"

"No, sir."

"I see. So, it's sewn onto his vest and collar."

Dot stared at the blind old man, confused. "Yes, but... how did you know?"

"I can smell the gunpowder on it. Someone shot him."

Alarmed, Dot quickly knelt beside her dog and scanned the surface of his military vest. As Father Young surmised, a spent bullet was embedded in it, along the side of his belly. As George had told her, the vest easily stopped the bullet.

"Boy," Father Young said. "Take the dog outside for some fresh air and exercise before it gets too dark. I want to talk to our little friend."

"Come on, Gypsy," Vincent said, summoning him with his long, leafy hands. "Let's go visit Elmer!"

Father Young waited for his adopted son to leave with the dog before turning in the girl's direction as she dined on vegetable stew and tangerine punch. "You're the first human we've seen in a long time."

"Thirty years."

"So, he told you."

"He said you used to live in a village, but he couldn't remember the name..."

"We lived in Colt," Father Young said. "A human enclave, small hunting village in the South Lands. I was one of the elders."

"He was born there?"

"Vincent was never born, my dear. He's an early hybrid, created in a lab."

Hybrid.

Dot remembered the children's book from the library. She tried to hide her shock. "You made him?"

"In a way. I belonged to the team who made him. I took him and nine of his brothers and sisters with me when the Great Domain fell into chaos."

"What's the Great Domain?" Dot asked.

"A habitat for hybrids, largest ever built. We left the Domain heading west, ended up in Colt. It was a tough sell, convincing a bunch of hunter zealots to take in ten hybrids. But Chief Warren had a big heart, something rare in the South Lands. Remember that."

"Vincent said they tried to kill him."

"So, he told you that, too." Father cleared his throat, stifling an emotional response, and took a moment to breathe. "That boy sure loves to talk."

"Is it true?" Dot asked.

"A year after we took refuge in Colt, my special children had jobs, friends, even romantic relations with the villagers. They were hunters, teachers, artisans. Vincent tended the community garden, of course. His magic touch grew food for the people of Colt tenfold. I thought my boy and the rest of his siblings had been fully accepted by the villagers. I was wrong. You don't truly know where you stand with people, what they're capable of, until you see them in crisis. Remember that."

"What happened?" Dot hoped details of Father's story would tie into her own mysterious past, one that she still kept hidden from would-be allies and felt selfish for it.

"A troop of Purists descended on the village at night. They always come at night, girl. Remember that, too."

"Yes, sir." Dot thought of the night raiders at Wellspring.

"Vincent ran to Warren's house, wrapped him with his vines, tried to protect him."

"He said he murdered him."

"Yes," Father Young said, to Dot's surprise. "The Purists were there to hunt hybrids. It's what they do. Vincent stuck to the chief, refused to leave his side or release him no matter what anyone told him. Depending on who you asked, Warren died either from the suffocating grip of my boy's vines or from being gunned down in the crossfire. Either way, Vincent was inadvertently responsible for his death. Of course, the boy didn't know any better. That's why we left for the North Woods and settled on this old farm. I told him that his brothers and sisters remained behind."

"What really happened to them?"

"They... remained behind." Father Young didn't have the heart to offer details, but his dire tone revealed the truth.

"I'm so sorry," Dot said. She suddenly saw her simpleton friend in a new light. "I'm sorry for whatever became of your hybrids, and for the loss of your friend, Warren."

"So am I. Warren was my close friend. But I didn't weep when he died. He wasn't long for this world. He worked outside all day. The sun was inevitably going to get him."

"I don't understand."

"My dear, that's because you aren't asking me any of the questions swirling around in your little head." Father Young coughed a little laugh. "I appreciate your courtesy, girl, your interest in us, and your friendship with my boy, but I'm still waiting for you to ask me."

"Ask you what?" Dot didn't want to reveal her memory loss, still unsure who to trust.

"No need to hide your past from me." Father Young paused, curious at this mysterious girl. "Believe me, this blind old man you see sitting here, strapped to machines, living on an extended deathbed, is the least of your worries."

"I know, sir," Dot said, concluding that neither Father nor Vincent posed any threat. "I'm sorry if I seem guarded."

"I don't blame you. We're all on guard. We have to be, as I'm sure you know. Before I keep on blabbing, you never told me your name."

"Dot."

"Dot? D-O-T?"

"That's right."

"And you've been traveling alone?" Father asked.

"I've had Gypsy. And I met a boy in the nearby town, a brave ranger. But he's gone."

Father thought for a moment, fear and realization sweeping over him. "It's tattooed on your hand, isn't it?"

Dot looked at her name burned into the flesh atop her left hand in tall, thin letters.

"Tell me the truth, girl. Vincent and I shared our secrets. Now you spill yours. You are sitting in my house."

"Yes, sir," Dot said, reluctant, again confused. "On my left hand. How did you know?"

"Wrong question, my dear. The real question is, how do you not know?"

"You sound like George."

"George? Is he the brave boy gone away? He's been on your mind ever since, hasn't he?"

"Well..."

"They all eventually go away, my dear. Don't let it wound your heart. Everyone's just trying to survive."

"Father Young," Dot said, leaning forward, eager for answers. "You said I wasn't asking the real question. What don't I know?"

"The Story of The World," Father Young said, echoing George's cryptic words from the night before. "The truth is, you've been 'blessed,' my dear, and whoever blessed you went through a lot of trouble to keep you in the dark and likely gave their life for it."

Dot said nothing, ashamed at the many casualties in the hunt for her. "I want to remember. I owe it to them."

"The people who protected you."

"Yes."

"I'd feel the same way," Father Young said. "But if you truly want to honor your guardians, you'll remain safe in the dark."

"How can I honor their sacrifice if I can't remember what they were fighting for?"

Father Young sympathized with her. He had experience with The Blessing and knew well how cruel it could feel. "Tell me what you do know."

Though Dot now felt more comfortable with the old man, she hesitated to reveal her entire short, bloody history. It seemed that most of the world was out to get her, and she'd only met him moments before. If he didn't betray her, he might eventually die helping her, as George may have.

"You're scared," Father Young said. "I can hear it in your breathing. And I get it, my dear. Vincent was likely the first friendly face you've seen since 'waking up' from your Blessing. Everyone else is either gunning for you or gunning each other, trying to survive, trying to scratch out a life on the fringe with you stuck in the middle of it all."

"We were in Wellspring," Dot said, offering a bit of her brief past. "Me and Gypsy and the boy. But we were chased out by soldiers."

"They all looked alike?"

"That's right."

"Green uniforms?" Father asked knowingly. "Green and black?"

"Yes. They might have killed my friend. Who are they?"

"Those soldiers are with the 'Purists of Earth.' They might shoot you on sight or they might drag you back to their compound for testing. Either way, girl, you go with them, you'll end up dead."

"What about the soldiers in blue?"

"You've seen them, too?" Father Young said in a cough. "Blue, sometimes blue and gray, they call themselves the 'Loyalists to Man,' and they'll likely protect you at any cost."

"They paid that cost," Dot said. "They all did."

"Then it's their sacrifice that brought you here."

Dot thought back to the bodies lying on the road near the bridge to Kellan. That so many soldiers on both sides would die in the name of protecting or hunting her sent her mind spinning.

"You might be right," Father Young said. "Maybe you should know why. Maybe you should know everything that led up to you wandering onto our farm today. It's quite a thing to forget, and another thing entirely to remember."

"I can't forget them," Dot said, wiping away a tear. "They died keeping me safe. I must know why."

"Of course, my dear. And as much as I, too, want to keep you safe, you deserve to know why."

Father Young leaned over and opened a small window next to him to hear Vincent and Gypsy playing in the front yard.

"Vincent doesn't remember everything," he said. "He doesn't think to ask questions, and I'd like it to stay that way. But if he ever asked me why we left Colt burning in the middle of the night, why we left his brothers and sisters behind, or why we remained hidden here for so long, I'd owe it to him to lay out the truth."

"Do you owe it to me?"

"We just met." Father Young considered her words. "But I owe it to your creator."

"My... creator?"

"Like my boy, you were never born, either. I'm sorry if that comes as a shock."

Dot trembled upon hearing Father's alarming revelation. Of all her theories about her history, she never expected one similar to Vincent's. "You know him? My creator?"

"If you are who I think you are," Father Young said, facing the warm fire, "then yes, I confess I do. We worked together at The Great Domain long before I lost my sight, and like Chief Warren, I considered him a good friend."

"Why keep it from me?" Dot grew anxious, approaching frustration, as Father's secrets slowly unfolded.

"It was important that you shared with me first. I needed to know what you remember. Perhaps I shouldn't..."

"Who is he?" Dot blurted, the sound of Vincent and Gypsy playing outside a stark contrast to the tension in the room.

Father Young's expression turned sour, uneasy. "Whether or not he's still alive, still at the Domain, or whether or not he wants to reunite with you, I think you should know... you're a child of the great Domingo Imago."

Dot felt torn. She wanted to know every detail of her life, all the events that led to her wandering the land in the wake of intense violence. She also wanted to honor and protect the sacrifice of those in her service.

"Will you tell me about him?" she asked.

Father Young's life support machines beeped. Vincent burst into the room and adjusted the machines to keep his father alive.

"Father!" Vincent felt scared to continue. "I've never seen your numbers so high."

"Will you tell me?" Dot asked again, desperate for answers yet guilty for pushing the old blind man so hard.

"Tomorrow," Father Young moaned in agony. "I may tell you everything you want to know over breakfast... still not sure."

"But Father," Vincent said. "You need to take it easy, get your numbers down..."

"Breakfast," Father Young said again, insisting. "Now let me rest."

"Okay, sir," Dot said. "Over breakfast."

"Pain Perdu," Vincent said with a smile. He plunged a hypodermic needed into his own arm, pulled out an inch of his glowing green blood, and injected his father with it, calming him. "You ever had Pain Perdu, Dot?"

"What are you doing?" she asked, startled by the transferring blood.

"I'm giving him something to help him rest. I've done it lots of times. My blood is like medicine. Pain Perdu?"

"That's French toast," Dot said, remembering the dish. Someone used to make it for her every morning. "Un homme me le faisait tous les matins."

"What's that mean?" Vincent asked, his large black eyes blinking.

"It means she's had it many times," Father Young said, adjusting in his corner chair. His anguish subsided for now. "You speak French, girl?"

"Apparently, I speak several village codes."

"Good. The Blessing didn't erase them, the languages of the old nations. Whoever taught them to you and kept them intact wanted you to fit in wherever you might roam."

"And so you'll tell me?"

"Yes, yes, tomorrow," Father Young said, struggling to breathe. "Now, I need a long sleep. I'm no good to you until then."

Vincent pulled a lever on the side of Father's chair, reclining him to a horizontal position. He repositioned the old man's blankets, revealing his chair was actually a medical bed.

"I can't believe Imago did it," Father Young said as he drifted off. "After all this time. I've waited thirty years for you, kept breathing for you. I'm still not sure if I should rip open the seals in your tender mind, but I'm willing to stay alive one more day for it." He coughed and laughed. "No promises, though."

Gypsy trotted in, more comfortable with their new friends. The old man grabbed his son's leafy arm and wheezed into his breathing tube while pointing to the other room, gesturing for Vincent to take their guest away.

"Father wants me to take you to the room," Vincent said.

"What room?"

"Your room, the one we've been saving for guests. You're going to stay with us, right?"

"Yes," Dot said. "If that's okay."

"If it's okay with Father, it's okay with me!"

Vincent shut the window. He took Dot and Gypsy out of the farmhouse, leaving the old man and his machines to wheeze and cough and beep in the dark parlor.

* * *

Dot stood in The Void, once again staring across a vast darkness with two distant stars staring back. They seemed closer with each recurring dream, with the faint shape of people, though not close enough for Dot to be certain. That night, she had no doubt. The glowing beacons now had the shape of children – two young girls – with pointed hats, flowing gowns, and outstretched arms. She now felt certain that the two figures weren't emanating light but rather were silhouetted by it. Haloed by their glow, she could see one girl wore all white while the other wore all black.

"You're going to get killed... you're being protected..."

"What does that mean?" Dot asked.

Lynn Harrod

"There's safety in the West... your home is in the East..."

As before, the guidance of the two stars conflicted. One warned her to stay away, to run west, while the other summoned her east, where she supposedly belonged.

"You must save yourself and your friends... you must save us..."

The opposing orders may have been confusing, but they weren't alarming until the choice of whom to save was voiced by the whispering girls. Dot could save herself and those she befriended, or she could save the mysterious twins whom she now called the Dark Girl and the Light Girl. She couldn't quite tell where the whispers came from, but felt that the Dark Girl sought her own gain and wanted Dot to risk her life, while the Light Girl selflessly wanted only Dot's safety.

Or was it the other way around?

"Go away... come to us..."

"He needs you..."

The last whisper sounded different. Muted and echoed like the others, the unfamiliar voice mentioned someone new.

"He needs you..."

Dot looked around the darkness, expecting another star. Instead, she saw Gypsy at her heels.

"Gypsy, did you just... talk?" Dot asked the dog.

"He needs you... to wake up..."

8

They Don't Always Grow Back

Dot opened her eyes, ripped from her dream, and stared up at the tiled ceiling of her room. The bright sunlight startled her, making her feel vulnerable after days of hiding in the shadows of the night and scurrying in the tall grass and cornfields of the morning.

Before she could rediscover her surroundings, Vincent's wood-grained head and big black eyes head came into view as he leaned over her.

"He needs you," Vincent said. "Are you awake, Dottie? He needs you to wake up."

"Yes, Vincent," Dot said, yawning her first big breath of the day. "I'm up now."

"Good. For a moment, I thought you were stuck asleep like Father."

"How long has Father been... stuck asleep?" Dot asked gently, afraid of the answer.

She sat upright in the down feather bed Vincent had slid into a rear corner of the barn, part of a quaint "bedroom" he put together with old furniture scavenged from abandoned houses that sat along the road near the farm.

"Father usually wakes up with the birds, but today he's an hour late.... or maybe the birds are early?" Vincent stretched one of his vines out a window, letting the morning sun touch his palm. "No, he's late."

"Maybe he's just getting extra sleep," Dot said to comfort him, not wanting to hurt him with the likely devastating truth. "He's old and unwell."

"Yeah, maybe just sleepy."

"He did seem tired."

"Oh yeah, he's tired," Vincent said. "Or maybe he's dead."

Dot glared at him, shocked at how matter-of-fact Vincent seemed to be with the notion. He appeared to have no empathy, and she started to view the plant-man as deranged.

"You really think so?" she asked.

"I read that being dead looks like still being asleep... Father says I'm a good reader... at least it looks like that at first. Later, being dead is like when a pumpkin spoils. It smells bad, grows mold, gets all wrinkly, attracts flies and worms. Father smells bad, but it's his usual bad smell, and there are no flies, so I'm not sure if he's dead or just too stubborn to wake up."

Dot patted her leg, summoning Gypsy from the open barn door where he no doubt stood guard for most of the night.

"Can you tell me?" Vincent asked, looking at both the girl and her dog. "It's important, so I know how much Pain Perdu to cook for breakfast. Have you ever had Pain Perdu..."

"Let's go see him together."

* * *

Dot stood at the foot of Father Young's bed, draped in a thick blanket covered in purple flower petals.

"Lavender," Vincent said. "It wards off disease and evil spirits."

Though she had no experience with death by old age or illness, she'd seen plenty of people die in the few days she could remember, and she instantly knew Father Young would never wake up again. Though he offered answers to her many questions, it was his kindness and stories that she'd miss.

"Vincent," Dot said, unsure how to break the news. "Your father is dead."

"He's not my father-father, Dottie, but I call him Father..."

"Vincent!" Dot yelled, incredulous. "Whatever you call him, this man who took care of you is now dead! Don't you see that? Don't you care?"

"Of course I care!" Vincent said. "I know he's dead, so let's just leave him there."

Dot's heart broke for both of them. She backed away from the unfeeling mutant. "What happened to all the love he showed you? How he rescued you from the Great Domain, how he took you away from Colt when it was burning? Don't you remember any of that?"

"I remember each minute," Vincent said, looking up at the ceiling. "I relive them in my dreams. Every night, I see my old friends being taken away in chains, being branded, getting shot if they tried to run. Father thinks I didn't see those terrible things, told me not to look, but I did. I turned and looked back when he drove us away. I can see good in the dark, even when I'm crying."

"So, you can feel sadness," Dot said. "Is that how you feel now?"

"Confused is how I feel now. I need to know is how long Father's going to be dead! I have a bowl of eggs and cream waiting for bread in the kitchen, planned on frying two slices for each of us. If Father isn't going to eat right now, I could give it to Gypsy."

"I thought you read about death?" she asked. "What happened to Father saying you were a good reader?"

"I am a good reader," Vincent said, confused by the girl's agitation. "But Father took the book from me before I finished that chapter. He said it would upset me."

Dot felt ashamed for scolding Vincent as she realized why he seemed indifferent to his father's demise. Her simpleton friend didn't know the permanence of death and couldn't comprehend it, even as he imagined a pumpkin rotting in a field.

"What about the spoiled pumpkin?" Dot asked. "What happens to it?"

"The fruit may rot, but the plant keeps bearing fruit. Why are you upset?"

Dot took Vincent into the parlor and sat him by the dormant fireplace. Gypsy left the bedroom and took his station by the door, his slow movement suggesting that he, too, felt the absence of their friendly host.

"Father will never wake up," Dot said, holding her friend's leafy hands together. "Death is forever. He won't get better, he won't ever speak or sit by the fire again, waiting for you to finish your chores. He's gone."

Vincent looked at his father's open doorway, caught sight of his feet on the edge of his bed. "You mean like when a willow catches rust or a cedar has bark beetles, and you have to chop them down and burn the wood."

"Yes."

"And they don't grow back."

"That's right," Dot said. "Father isn't growing back."

Vincent felt an overwhelming sorrow as he imagined Father Young rotting from the inside like a diseased tree. He'd never fully understood the concept of death and now thought back to the many tribes of hybrids he saw fall to infighting at the Great Domain and the dozens of families he witnessed being gunned down at Colt. He assumed they all "grew back" after he left, but now knew they were gone forever like a once-towering sycamore grove succumbing to unchecked disease. In that cruel moment of realization, Father's death felt like the death of everyone he'd ever loved.

Tears streamed from his big black eyes, pattering onto his vines and leaves, and he saw his little friend in a new light.

"Does this happen to everyone?" Vincent asked.

"Yes, Vincent."

"Will you die?"

"Yes, one day," Dot said. "Everyone dies."

"I don't die." He sounded confused.

"We all do. Just not at the same time, and not in the same way. No one lives forever. It's okay. Death is part of life. I remember someone telling me that."

"Your father?"

Dot wasn't sure who told her that, her memory still eluding her, even during a time of grief.

Vincent stood and walked to the bedroom doorway, peering in to see his father's body in his usual corner as if for the last time. "What's going to happen to me?"

"You might not die for a long, long time, Vincent."

"I know that!" he said with a forced laugh as he wiped away a tear. "I mean, what do I do now? Father always told me what to do. That's why he made me the book." His eyes widened, remembering the little black book he followed each day, offering life lessons, reminding him of his chores, instructing him on what to do when there are visitors, storms, and night raiders. "I almost forgot! I have my book! He'll tell me what to do in the book!"

Dot felt for her friend as he rummaged desperately through his overalls for the little book, as if it would somehow ease his pain. She couldn't bear to look at him as he flipped through its pages for the next instruction.

"Vincent, it's okay to feel sad. It's good to hold on to his book, but it's not going to make things better."

"Right here!" Vincent said, reaching the page he needed. "The last five pages! I never made it to the last five pages. Father said if he ever had to leave me, I should look to the back of the book. I think this is what he meant!"

Vincent opened the book, attempted to read it, but turned it to Dot for help. An unexpected message awaited them, an ominous task in large letters...

WHAT TO DO WHEN I DIE

"Is that all it says?" Dot asked.

Vincent turned the page to the last entry, to a simple, three-word instruction...

PROTECT THE CHILD

Dot read the clairvoyant order aloud, which offered no clarity to the confused plant-man.

"The child?" Vincent said. "What child? Usually, his instructions are easy to understand. I don't know what he means."

"Did he write in this book last night?"

"Yes, he did! He asked me for the book and a pencil, and he wrote in it right before he went to sleep forever."

"It was his dying wish," Dot said, honored by the gesture. "He knew he wouldn't make it to morning, so he wrote one last instruction. I think I'm the child."

"I thought you were a girl?"

"A girl is a female child."

"Oh, I see, because you're not all grown yet." Vincent felt proud to figure it out.

"Vincent, I'm the one he wants you to protect."

"Then that's what I'll do!" He shut his book and slid it back into the front pocket of his overalls. "You and Gypsy can stay in the barn as long as you want. We have plenty of food. I even made extra Pain Perdu... or Frenchie Toast, as you call it."

"I'm not staying," Dot said. "Gypsy and I are heading east."

"I don't understand. Don't you like the farm, Dottie?" Vincent looked sad, torn by the idea of her leaving. "It's beautiful here, and usually quiet, and the trees are friendly, except on hot days. Elmer can get in a sour mood..."

"Of course, I love your farm, Vincent. To live here would be like remaining in paradise. But I have to go west or east, and I'm choosing east. It feels like I'm being pulled there. It's hard to explain..."

"Then... then I'm heading east, too!"

"I know what Father said, but you don't have to come with us." Dot didn't want to take Vincent away from his beloved farm, a secluded plot of land that offered familiarity and safety, a perfect home for a simpleton plant hybrid like him. She also didn't want him living alone, for he lacked the wits and wisdom needed to handle intruders who would take advantage of him. Despite her offer, she admitted to herself that they needed each other.

"It's okay, Dottie. We don't have to walk. We can take my trike."

"The three of us barely fit on it getting to the house. I don't think we could travel very far."

Vincent flipped open the book again and searched for a page, reaching another simple instruction...

IF YOU EVER LEAVE THE FARM

TAKE THE HORSE

"You have a horse?" Dot asked, startled by the fact that she knew what a horse was and by the idea that the farm had any livestock at all. According to George, nearly all animals died from The Worm – whatever that was – or were butchered for meat.

Without answering her, Vincent walked out of the farmhouse and headed back to the barn. Dot and Gypsy followed, barely able to keep up with the strides of his long legs. Upon entering the barn, she expected to see a horse that she perhaps hadn't noticed before, as unlikely as that might have been. They passed several empty stables before reaching one covered with a large tarp.

"Father's horse is in there?" Dot asked. Hearing no movement, she shut her eyes, not wanting to see the remains of a long dead animal.

Vincent reached up with his snaking vines and pulled down the tarp, revealing a large, old service truck, similar to the ones the soldiers drove.

"There it is!" Vincent said. "Father's horse! He said its motor has the strength of two-hundred horses!"

Though the vehicle was overgrown with decades of cobwebs, it appeared to be in exceptional condition. Its glossy paint and straight body suggested it might still be operational.

Vincent flipped through his book for more instructions. Satisfied, he reached into the cab, shifted the truck into neutral, and used his arms and many vines to pull the massive vehicle outside into the sunlight. It seemed easy for him, and Dot was astonished by his strength. Though his muscles weren't bulky, they were long and powerful, and it suddenly made sense why Father Young thought his adopted son could protect Dot on her journey.

"It needs to sit outside for a while before we can turn it on," Vincent said.

"The sun powers it," Dot said, spotting the thin solar panels on the roof and sides.

"It gives it energy. That means it makes it go."

"Of course."

"But first, we need to plant Father in the ground so his blood can feed the crops while we're gone."

"The book told you that?" Dot asked.

"No," Vincent said. "It just seems like the right thing to do. We come from the Earth, we return to the Earth. That's what Father always said. 'Remember that,' he told me."

While Father's "horse" recharged in the morning sun, Vincent and Dot wrapped the old man in his nightly blanket, adorned with lavender petals to keep evil spirits away. The plant-man wrapped his vines around his father, lifted him off his bed, and carried him into the crops. Together, they buried him in the field between the corn and the carrots, his two favorite foods.

"Goodbye, Father," Vincent said once the job was done. His voice cracked and wheezed, the farewell difficult for him. "I'll always miss you, even though you're dead. I know you weren't my father-father, but thank you for making me alive and raising me and teaching me stuff."

"You don't get more fatherly than that," Dot said, her head bowed. "I will miss you, too." She suddenly resented The Blessing and unknown The Story of The World, for they surely put pressure on him, a delicate old man in no state to handle the emotional task of undoing them. "When I finally learn the secrets of my life, I'll think of you in your corner chair by the fire."

A half-hour later, Vincent started the truck's silent electric motor and turned the steering wheel away from the barn with Dot and Gypsy sitting beside him in the front seat. The three companions drove away from the once-again abandoned farm, heading south down the Broken Road, bisected by its eternal yellow line. Despite his unflinching optimism, his vision of one day returning to the comforting routine and safety of his beloved crops, Vincent would never see his beloved farm again.

9

Emerald Pond

Father's Horse didn't make it far. Just over an hour south, the truck's dashboard beeped with blinking red lights. Dot scanned the gauges and saw that they were nearly out of power. Vincent had never charged the vehicle before, and Father hadn't driven it for years.

"I guess thirty minutes wasn't enough to recharge it," Vincent said. "We'll have to let it sit a little longer."

Vincent pulled over next to a large pond. An ancient, rusted sign by the road told them it was "The Famous Emerald Pond." The sign also boasted of "Food, Gifts, and Live Music," none of which were in sight. A single building on weed-strewn pavement stood nearby, looted and burned down long ago, no doubt a former tourist center. What was once a gathering place for fun and relaxation now stood as a charred ruin.

"While the horse soaks up energy," Vincent said, "we can go for a nice swim."

"You know how to swim?" Dot asked.

"Of course! Us plant hybrids love the water!"

"You go ahead. I want to look around. Maybe there's some food in that building."

"I brought plenty of food."

"No offense, but I'd like something other than raw root vegetables."

"I can cook them!"

Vincent's vines shot out in all directions, plucking twigs and branches from the tall weeds, gathering them into a pile along the edge of the pristine pond. He quickly dug a fire pit, stacked the wood into a conical shape, and lit it by rapidly rubbing his elbows together. A proper campfire was made in seconds.

"You really come in handy," Dot said.

"Father taught me everything I know."

Vincent grabbed a basket of potatoes, onions, and carrots from the truck and placed them by the fire. He expertly sliced them and tossed them in a pot of water. As they simmered on the fire, he decided it was a perfect time to take a dip in the pond.

"A nice swim before supper is always refreshing!" he said as he jumped high into the air and somersaulted into the water with a wide splash. Dot laughed at his little display. "It's just like the pond behind the barn, only bigger. You sure you won't come in?"

Dot walked to the pond's edge and shook her head no. As she watched her friend frolic in the water, she noticed something she had previously thought impossible.

"Are those... fish?" Dot asked.

"I see bluegills, minnows, sunfish. I think there are bass in here, too. Yep, there's one!"

"You know fish as well as you know plants. Pretty smart, Vincent."

"Nah, I'm not so fish-smart, Dottie. I only know them mostly by what plants are around them."

"Can you catch one?" Dot asked. "Do you have a fishing pole?" It was another thing she somehow knew, though she couldn't recollect from where.

Dot turned to the truck, ready to rummage through its cargo bed for fishing gear, but froze in place as a Largemouth Bass landed at her feet. Gypsy ran to the flopping fish and barked at it as if Dot were in danger.

"Easy boy," Dot said. "It's not a threat. It's lunch."

While Vincent enjoyed his afternoon swim, fully extending his many vines across the surface of the water, he looked at his little friend and her dog by the fire with curiosity. He saw the girl cut into the fish with his knife, pull out its guts, impale it on the blade, and hold it over the fire.

Dot had cleaned the fish and now cooked it as if she had done so many times before, another skill that remained despite its related memories having been erased.

"Did your father teach you that?" Vincent asked from the middle of the pond.

"I'm not sure," Dot said.

"Maybe your mother?"

"As little as I remember about him, I have no memories or feelings at all about her."

"Don't all human-humans have mothers?"

"Yes, but I guess we don't always remember," the girl said. "And Father Young said I was never born."

"Like me!" Vincent said. "We're the two never-born twins! We got a lot in common, Dottie, though you're missing your vines."

Whenever Dot tried to imagine her father's face, it felt like trying to recall a dream fleeting across an outstretched morning, but when she tried to picture her mother, nothing specific came to mind. No face or feelings. It was like trying to remember the details of a day yet to come or a night never seen.

"I don't think I have a mother," Dot said. "But I think I understand what happened to me. The moments and people in my memories are gone, but everything I learned from them is still somewhere inside. I discover new skills all the time."

"Now you're the one who comes in handy!" Vincent said as he splashed with his long toes in the cool pond.

Dot cooked the fish well and tore off a fillet for Gypsy. To her surprise, the dog didn't take the meat and instead cowered down into the grass. Dot ate the piece and continued to pull flakes of meat from the fish.

"Wait!" Vincent yelled as something dawned on him. "Dottie! Don't eat the..." His words were cut off by his panicked flailing in the water as he hurried to the shore. Dot assumed he wanted to dine with her, not expecting one of his long vines to reach out and grab the fish from her knife. He walked out of the pond and held the cooked bass to his face. "Yep, it's got it. That means you shouldn't eat it."

"But... I already ate it."

Vincent turned the large fish around to see that Dot had eaten half of it, a sizable portion for an adult, much less a child. He looked at her as if waiting for something to happen.

"Why shouldn't I eat it?" Dot asked, worried.

"It's got it."

"Got what?"

"The Worm." Vincent turned the fish around and pointed out small red and blue streaks about its head. "See those jagged lines? See the white eyes? The Worm made them, though I don't see any worms in it. How do you feel?"

"I feel fine. What's The Worm? Your father never told me." From her conversations with George and Father Young, Dot had a good idea about what The Worm was but was afraid of saying it aloud.

"I don't know much," Vincent said. "All I know is that animals with The Worm shouldn't be eaten. Father says you'll die on the spot! How are you still alive?"

Dot felt alarmed at the thought of eating poisoned fish, but felt no trace of illness. "Maybe Father was wrong."

"Father is never wrong."

Putting aside Vincent and Father Young for a moment, Dot tried to see the situation through George's eyes. The pond was filled with fish, to where Vincent easily grabbed one. If they were safe to eat, there would surely be survivors here now, catching them by the barrel instead of ransacking markets that had been picked apart many times over. Unlike the Young Farm, which sat hidden from view, Emerald Pond stretched along the road for all to see.

"Dot," Vincent said in a soft voice. "If you're not dead now, you might be soon. I want you to know I liked having you as my friend."

"Vincent, don't be silly."

"You're a kind person, especially for a human-human. It was good to know you."

"Stop it. I'm fine."

Vincent dropped the bass onto the ground next to Gypsy. The dog backed away as if instructed to avoid it.

"Even Gypsy knows better than to eat wormed fish," Vincent said.

"I think he was taught to not eat them," Dot said, remembering George pointing out Gypsy's exceptional training.

How she missed the boy.

"I think he can smell it," she said, rubbing Gypsy under his chin. "I think the blue soldiers trained him to detect The Worm."

"Gypsy was with them? The Blues?"

Dot had kept her brief history secret, but felt no need to hide anything from her plant friend now.

"I found him in the wreckage of a fight between two troops," Dot said.

"Greens and Blues, right?"

"Yes, their uniforms and their vehicles were colored either green or blue. Your father said they're called the Loyalists and the Purists."

Vincent looked at the dog's blue vest. "If Gypsy was with the Blues... the Loyalists... it means he was with the good guys."

"How do you know which side is the 'good guys?'"

"Father told me."

"Yes, but what makes them the good guys?"

Vincent had never questioned Father's wisdom before. He simply accepted the fact that soldiers roamed the land, that some were good and some were bad, and Father knew the difference.

Soldiers in blue were good and true.

Soldiers in green were bad and mean.

"Father says so," Vincent said. "That's what I know."

Dot remembered the Purists hunting her in Wellspring, kicking down doors with rifles in hand, though they didn't actually hurt her. Why were they looking for her?

In contrast, the Loyalists seemed to be protecting her, transporting her somewhere, but to what end? Father's story of the invasion of Colt sounded gruesome, but she couldn't be sure which troop was responsible.

"What else do you know about the soldiers?" Dot asked.

"They all look alike," Vincent said. "I figured they're all brothers."

"They sound the same, too."

"Yep. Brothers! I wish I had brothers. Two brothers that look alike are twins. Three are triplets. What's it called when there's a hundred?"

"What about the night you left Colt? You said you saw them. Did they wear green?"

"Oh, I saw them plenty, doing terrible things, but it was foggy and dark. They could have been wearing purple and yellow and I wouldn't know!"

"What about after that night?" Dot asked. "After you settled down here."

"Father and I ran into a bunch of them while we were out scavenging last year. I don't know what they looked like because Father told me to stay in the back of the truck, out of sight."

"He didn't want them to see you."

"Nope, and he didn't want them to follow us back to the farm, neither. After they left, we must have drove around for hours before heading back home, zig-zagging down every road and trail. Father was always careful that way."

Dot tried to piece together everything she and Vincent knew about the soldiers, tried to tie in what George had mentioned, but could only think of Father's advice.

Soldiers in blue were good and true
Soldiers in green were bad and mean.

It sounded too simple.

Until she got the answers she sought, Dot had no choice but to be wary of anyone in military uniform, regardless of color. There might very well be other factions looking to capture her for their own agendas.

BEEP BEEP!

Dot and Vincent turned to the sound. It came from their truck parked nearby.

"Father's Horse is charged up!" Vincent said, heading back to the large vehicle. "All the way this time. We'll be able to drive much farther."

The sun rested in the sky, just left of the middle. It had started its descent west toward the hills and would soon be behind them, throwing Dot and her friends into darkness.

"Let's keep going," Dot said, joining Vincent in the truck. She looked through the windshield at the Broken Road, continuing south. "We need to find a path that will take us east."

"It's up ahead," Vincent said. "Not close, but we'll get there soon."

Vincent started the truck's electric motor with a brief hum followed by silence. Dot waved to Gypsy, summoning the dog to jump into the cab between them.

"I see smooth sailing from here!" Vincent said as he pulled away from Emerald Pond. "That's what Father always said when I drove him around. He always knew the right words to put my mind at ease."

"Smooth sailing from here," Dot said, hopeful.

"You're still not dead. Maybe Father was wrong, or maybe I was wrong and that fish didn't have The Worm after all."

"Maybe," Dot said, thinking back to the prominent red and blue streaks through the fish's flesh.

She started to suspect why everyone hunted her.

10

The Loyalists

Dot grew tired after three more hours on the road. She kept an eye open for any path heading east, but saw only trees, rocky hills, and the ruins of houses and abandoned cars overgrown with tall weeds. With the sky approaching dusk, she worried that the turn to the east that Vincent said was "up ahead" might be a day's travel, or might not exist at all.

"We should set up camp soon," Dot said. "I don't think we should be on the road after dark."

"Certainly not," Vincent said, still as bright and chipper as the moment he woke up, something Dot found curious.

"Forgive me if this is a foolish question," she said, "but do you ever get tired? I know little about hybrids."

"Tired? Like Father?"

"Like me right now."

"No."

"Never?"

"Nope," Vincent said proudly. "I never get tired. I sleep so I can dream and recharge these muscles, but I actually don't need to sleep. Also, I never die. Sorry if I already said that."

"You really never get tired?" Dot asked.

"I haven't yet!"

"And you can never die?"

"I haven't yet!"

"That's amazing."

"Not dying certainly comes in handy," Vincent said, "as you might say."

"I'm sure it does."

Though Dot could accept the idea that her unique plant-mutant companion never felt fatigue, she knew no one was immortal and that he simply didn't yet understand his own delicate nature. A simpleton like Vincent only learns from experience, and a person's own death is a lesson only learned once.

Vincent pulled over and parked Father's Horse in a grove of trees near the road. As he shut off the motor, Dot peered ahead and saw what looked like a turnoff.

"Is that the road you spoke of?" she asked. "The road east?"

"That's it!" Vincent said, peering down the Broken Road. "Should we take it now?"

"No, let's get pitch camp. We don't know who or what is down that road at night."

"Very true. Father always avoided that road."

"He did?"

"Of course," Vincent said. "Father always said 'Never ever go past the pond.'"

"The pond?" Dot said. "You mean Emerald Pond? Where you went swimming and where I cooked the fish?"

"Yep. Father said it's dangerous to go past it."

"Vincent, that was hours ago! So, you've never been this far down the road?"

"Nope. Too dangerous, Dottie. We always kept to the North Woods."

"Where are we now?"

"The South Lands."

Dot again thought back to George, of his time in the South Lands and the violence he fled, his story similar from Father Young's. She quickly realized she had led Vincent down a path that had been forbidden to him all his life and felt regret for making him to break his father's strict rule. She also thought about the old man's last words as written in his son's little black book – "protect the child" – though he likely assumed they'd remain in the safety of their hidden farm. He had no way of knowing safeguarding her would mean traveling deep into unknown dangers.

Vincent unloaded their gear and pitched a quick camp within minutes, his many vines working independently to put up a tent and start a small fire, out of view of the road.

"Too bad we didn't catch more fish," he said as broke a stick off his body and tossed it for Gypsy to fetch. "Now that we know they don't really have The Worm, we could have cooked some more for supper."

"Maybe it's best we didn't. Maybe I just got lucky with that one."

"I'm a strict vegetarian, anyway."

"Me, too," Dot said. "Well, mostly vegetarian, I mean."

"We have plenty of potatoes and carrots," he said, grabbing two large sacks from the truck bed. "I can fry some with onions and..."

Vincent's dinner menu was cut off by the sound of gunfire.

Dot whipped around in time to see her tall friend mowed down by a hailstorm of bullets.

"Vincent!" Dot screamed.

"Run, Dot!" Vincent screamed back as he fell flat to the ground. Even as he laid motionless by the truck, another round of bullets peppered his body.

Vincent finally learned about death.

Gypsy barked madly and ran to the unseen threat coming from the road. A bullet struck him down, but not out, his vest halting the shot. Dot slapped her leg, summoning him back to her as she sprinted for the treeline to the west.

As they ran for cover, ducking behind every tree, she heard the frenzied footsteps of boots on the ground. She imagined an entire platoon of soldiers in pursuit, far more than she'd seen or heard in Wellspring. She'd evaded them before, in the town and near the bridge to Kellan, but couldn't foresee an escape this time. They sounded closer by the second, and it was only a matter of time before they reached her.

Her lungs ready to burst, Dot quickly gave up running and ducked into a bush, grabbing her dog and holding him close. Perhaps they could wait them out, stay out of sight until they gave up the hunt. She wanted to scream, "Why are you doing this?" She wanted to plead with them to spare their lives, to explain themselves, but knew it was ultimately pointless.

From her crouched position, she saw the silhouettes of two dozen soldiers spread out in the woods, backlit by floodlights from their trucks. She held her breath, hoping the bright light didn't reveal her hiding spot.

A single gunshot rang out, and one of the shadowed soldiers fell.

Another shot, another soldier down.

A moment later, the massive spotlight was shot out.

Before Dot could see what was happening, a clatter of gunfire filled the darkness of the trees, sending her hunters down to the dirt. Two grueling minutes later, her pursuers were all dead, like her innocent friend.

Dot clutched Gypsy tight and sobbed, no longer caring about who was behind or ahead of her. She only wanted the violence to stop before anyone else was killed. Her moment of torment was interrupted by the terrifying sight of a lone soldier standing over her, his glowing eyes staring into hers. To Dot's surprise, Gypsy didn't instantly pounce on him.

"Easy, boy," the familiar male voice said, the same voice she'd heard many times while fleeing Wellspring. The dog relaxed and sat on his hind legs, at ease.

Three more soldiers gathered around Dot's hiding spot. One of them shined a light on them.

"We found her!" he called out.

Though Dot still sat upright in fear and confusion, the tension faded as the soldiers turned on their flashlights and surveyed the area.

"Sweep the trees," another identical voice commanded. "Let's be sure we're alone out here."

"Are you hurt?" asked the soldier who discovered her. He flung his rifle behind his back and offered his hand.

Dot took the man's cold, clammy hand and stood from the bushes. With the area once again flooded with light, she could clearly see the identical soldiers around her.

They wore blue uniforms.

Lynn Harrod

* * *

With guns sheathed, the soldiers kindly escorted Dot and Gypsy to their camp only minutes away from where poor Vincent had parked Father's Horse, which had also been annihilated in the firefight. She considered herself lucky that her friend had unknowingly pulled over so close to them, but felt a pit in her stomach at the timing of their arrival.

An enormous bonfire in the center of their camp revealed their equipment, vehicles, tents, and their numbers. Four dozen soldiers in blue stood in awe as Dot and her dog entered their circle, as if the Queen of the Land had graced them with her majesty. They resembled the dead soldiers she saw upon waking up in the oak tree, and the night raiders that descended upon Wellspring, all of them five feet tall with smooth pale skin, brown eyes, and short black hair. As confused as she felt, their leader presented another mystery.

"I'm Sergeant Furst." At six feet, the man stood taller than the rest, with a thick brown beard and age spots across his face and neck. "Forgive me, Little Miss, if my men and I look astonished. After discovering the skirmish at the bridge, we were sure you were dead."

Wrinkles adorned the sergeant's cheeks, peeking out from the corners of his blue eyes. Dot stared up at him, the first soldier she'd seen who didn't look like the many others chasing her, and the first who didn't greet her with a rifle pointed at her head.

"You look... different," Dot said.

"That's because I'm human, like you," Sergeant Furst said. "Well, not exactly like you."

"Human-human?"

"Yes."

"And these men... they're not?"

"No, they're not."

"What going on?" Dot asked, exasperated. "My friend... he was shot..."

"We know, Little Miss," Sergeant Furst said sadly. "We found his body next to your transport."

"He was protecting me." Dot wiped away a tear as the sight of his grisly death replayed in her mind. "It was his father's last wish."

"Don't worry and don't wish," Sergeant Furst said. "You're with the Loyalists now."

11

The Story of The World

Three days before Dot met him, Sergeant Benjamin Furst – known by most simply as "Sarge" – intercepted a distress call. He took a squad of his most trusted soldiers, both born and artificial, to the bridge just east of Kellan, where he discovered the aftermath of a slaughter. Sarge found his fellow Loyalists had been ambushed, most instantly killed by explosives embedded in the deep ruts of the Broken Road. Their sensors likely didn't detect them until a moment before detonation.

The radio call for help came not from one of his men but from the enemy, a Purist heavy gunner. It doubled as a status report. "She's here!" Soldier 113 cried out with what would be his last words. "I've got her! She's alive, at the west bridge over the Miracle River! All converge on my location! All converge..."

If Sarge was to complete his mission and recover the girl, he needed to act fast before another Purist platoon arrived. Fortunately, his camp wasn't too far from the scene.

Sergeant Furst led The Mighty 13th Company of "The Loyalists to Man," a citizens' militia dedicated to continuing human life in the wake of The Worm at any cost. The Mighty 13th was one of the last active units in the western region as the lieutenants Sarge served under died at Beacon Hill earlier that year, all of which made him the de facto leader of not only his company but of the entire western region, despite his lower rank. In essence, he was the head of the Loyalists campaign and their 200+ humans and "Automen" in blue.

Opposing them were "The Purists of Earth," a vast military backed by the remnants of the old nation's governments known as "GARD" or "Global Allied Races Division." Their acronym – and the last word within it – proved fitting and ironic for it came to represent oppression rather than union.

The Purists were often called "The Greens" for the color of their uniforms and equipment. They were superior in numbers and firepower, supposedly devoted to the purity and sanctity of humanity. They regarded any genetic deviation, any hybrid, as an abomination and a threat to humanity.

Despite her appearance and innocence, Dot was viewed as such a deviation.

Sarge and his elite squad tracked Dot and Gypsy through the woods parallel to the West Wall, losing her trail in the abandoned town of Wellspring, where he saw the bodies of Purists littering the streets. He assumed another of his companies saved the girl from capture, but saw no blue marker and no identifying tire tracks to put him at ease.

Moments earlier, his men heard gunfire in the trees north of their base camp. Seeing the Purist soldiers converging in the

Lynn Harrod

woods, he surmised that a group of hybrids was in hiding. He felt shocked to discover the girl was their target, somehow evading an intense three-day hunt.

"You're one tough kid, Little Miss," Sarge told her as he led her through the woods to his camp, a third of his platoon trailing behind. "My guess is you made your way up to Brandywine Falls for the night."

"Yes, we slept by the falls," Dot said. "How did you know?"

"The sound and mist of the falls likely helped obscure you from their reconnaissance."

"Lucky us."

"And my guess is this old war dog also had something to do with your survival."

"Gypsy saved me in town," Dot said.

"Wellspring."

"Yes, that was the name."

"And the hybrid," Sarge said. "He must have been pretty brave, must have taken a liking to you."

"Vincent was my friend."

"Amazing. Veggies usually run from a firefight. I've never seen one face a platoon. I guess I still haven't."

"Veggie?"

"A plant-hybrid human. Where did you come across him? I thought they were wiped out."

"They are now," Dot said, bowing her head. "His father said he was the last of his kind. He told him to protect me."

"Veggies don't have fathers."

"His guardian, the man who kept him safe."

"Whoever he was, he knew your life was worth more than even the 'son' he cared for."

"Where are we going?" Dot asked.

"To my camp. We're almost there."

Dot looked around at the soldiers, all in blue, most identical to the green soldiers hunting her.

"The small ones... they all look the same," she said.

"My Automen?" Sarge said. "They may be fleshy like us but they're artificial, mass produced by the old nations. Mine switched sides."

Dot ducked under a tree branch, turned a corner near a rock wall, and saw the sprawling base camp of the company, a collection of tents, shacks, and trucks, surrounded by dozens more soldiers in blue.

"But not you," Dot said. "You're not one of them... are you?"

"No, Little Miss," Sergeant Furst said with a laugh. "Commanding officers are always human. Automen are intelligent enough to follow orders, but can't function without a mission objective or a commander. You'll occasionally find one wandering around the hills, leftover from a fight, lost in his looping thoughts. I come along and scoop them up, convince them to join my mission. That's how I built up this company."

"We're nothing but scavengers," another soldier said with a wide grin as he approached from the camp. Like Sarge, he also appeared uniquely human. "Everything we have is salvage. Equipment, vehicles, weapons, even our grunts."

Lieutenant Albert Dixon joined Sergeant Furst, dismissing the entourage to return to maintain camp. In contrast to the burly Sarge, Lieutenant Dixon stood tall and thin, with an angular, clean-shaven face and slicked back red hair.

"Dot, this is Lieutenant Dixon, the brains of this outfit."

"Does that make you the brawn?" the lieutenant asked with a sly grin. He offered Dot a handshake. "Friends call me Dix."

"Hello, Dix," she said, happy to see another friendly face, or any face that wasn't a walking, talking military drone.

"Dix and Dot, what a pair we make."

Dot shook both men's hands, feeling a little more comfortable with her new guardians, though she never let her loyal dog stray too far.

"Sarge thought we'd find your body somewhere in the hills," Dixon said, "or maybe floating in the Miracle, but I had a feeling you were a survivor."

"My friends are the real survivors," Dot said. "They were, I should say."

"That's an oxymoron, don't you think? A dead survivor."

Dot didn't appreciate the lieutenant's crude joke.

"I want to hear all about how you made it this far," Sarge said. "But first, let's get you some proper food and a fresh change of clothes."

Though her oversized blue fatigues were still intact, Dot realized the dress she wore underneath was torn and badly stained, its original blue color now completely gray from hiding in the dirt, sprinting through brush, and sleeping on a dusty mattress in a barn.

The night air was chilly, clear, and silent except for the metal clatter of the Automen servicing their weapons and fortifying their camp. Sarge sat her beside a fire and draped a flannel blanket over her shoulders. Dix brought her a thermal tumbler of hot soup and a small loaf of stale bread, a feast compared to the tainted half-fish she ate hours earlier.

An Automan set down a metal plate for the dog, an unusual sight after fleeing his brethren in Wellspring. Both the soup and Gypsy's dish contained strips of meat cooked well, almost burnt.

"That's rabbit," Sarge said, taking a seat by the fire across from the girl. "Don't worry, Little Miss, it's safe. Not a red or blue vein anywhere."

"The Worm," Dot said.

"That's right. We're pretty careful around here. Small game seem to be the safest prey, especially when they're young, not yet infected. Since the Automen don't need to eat, we only hunt enough for the human officers."

"Why do you call them Automen?"

"It's short for Autonomous Artificial Manual Serviceman."

"Artificial?" she said, suddenly fascinated by them. "You're saying they're robots?"

"Yes, but that seems like such a simple word to describe them. Dix refers to them as our grunts as if they were just cheap labor, but their synthetic flesh is actually the most advanced tech on the planet. They can repair themselves and each other like any intelligent machine, but they're biologically modeled clones of an artificial master soldier first made in the east."

Drone clones.

Dot sipped her soup and chewed on a strip of rabbit meat. She turned to see Dix and three Automen enter the camp with a most morbid haul.

"More salvage," Dix said. "Found it near where the girl was recovered."

To her horror, Dot saw the soldiers carrying the remains of her friend Vincent, his green-and-yellow body draped over them in tatters, his lifeless black eyes staring up at the stars.

"What are you doing with him?" Dot asked with a gasp.

"Easy now," Sarge said, nodding to his men to take the body out of her sight. "We just needed to clear the area. We can't have anything leading to camp."

"That 'thing' is my friend!"

"We'll take good care of him."

"He's dead! What kind of good care can you..."

Several of Vincent's withered vines fell off, making Dot drop her soup onto the dirt. Before she could protest further, she was startled by a deep moan from the plant-man.

"He's... alive?" Dot asked.

Vincent turned his head toward the girl's voice and spotted her by the fire next to Sarge. He turned back, surprised to be carried through camp by soldiers. He slithered off of them like a den of snakes pouring onto the ground.

"Dot!" Vincent said as he crawled awkwardly toward her on his hands and knees, propelled forward by newly grown vines, lengthening impossibly before her eyes. "You're not dead! Again!"

"I was thinking the same thing about you," she said.

"We were going to put your body in a tank of water," Sarge said. "Are you going to be okay?"

"Tank of water sounds good, actually, and some of that soup I smell."

"You knew he wasn't dead?" Dot asked the sergeant.

"We had a pretty good hunch."

Dot ran to Vincent and threw her arms around him in a warm embrace. It felt like hugging a thick bushel of leaves wrapped around a standing log. "I thought they killed you!"

"I told you, Dottie, I don't die."

"Veggies are pretty hardy," Sarge said. "But despite his bravery and bravado, he certainly can die, though it's pretty tough to take him down. His regenerative properties are a peak achievement of science."

"Too bad about his smarts," Dix said, "or lack thereof. He makes the grunts seem like scholars."

"Easy, Dix. He's our guest."

"Sure, and I'm his concierge."

"That's right," Sarge said, turning to look his subordinate in the eyes. "You're his concierge, cook, security, and transport. So am I. Let's not forget that."

"I won't, sir," Dixon said. "But I'm sure you'll remind me if I do."

Sergeant Furst disapproved of Lieutenant Dixon's curt remarks, especially in front of the girl. He understood his subordinate's poor attitude after weeks of heavy losses and setbacks, but didn't want to address it in front of others.

"Prepare the tank like we'd planned," Sarge said. "Vincent looks like he still needs a good soak."

"Already being filled," Dixon said.

Lieutenant Dixon left the group by the fire, where Sarge offered a seat and a cup of soup to the plant-man.

"I apologize if Dix seems a little grumpy," Sarge said. "All my human officers are. Things have been difficult lately."

"It's okay," Vincent said. "I'm used to folks not liking me too much. I'm just grateful that Dixie is our con-see-arr-gee. Sounds important!"

"It's probably best if you don't call him Dixie," Sarge said with a laugh. "The man is overworked, on edge."

"We're all on edge, in our own ways," Dot said. "But the fact that your company is helping us is more than we could ask for."

"I wish all my soldiers were as mature and understanding as you, Little Miss," Sarge said. He turned to the plant-man. "Dot says you were protecting her. I must admit, I was surprised to hear that."

"Well, I'm not much in a fight," Vincent said, "not like Gypsy, but I figured I could draw their fire while she ran away."

"You're very brave for a Veggie."

"Don't do that again," Dot said. "Sarge says you can still get killed. Promise me."

"Okay, I promise," Vincent said. "The bullets sting pretty bad, anyway."

"I envy you, Veggie," Sarge said. "I've been shot many times, and I can tell you not once did they ever just 'sting.'"

"His name is Vincent," Dot said. "He doesn't like being called 'Veggie.'"

"It's okay," Vincent said. "They also call me Vinny Greenblood, Veggie Vinny, Dim Vin, the Green Fool, Vincent Vines..."

"But you hate all those other names," Dot said, "because they used to poke you and tease you with those names, right?"

"But they're not poking or teasing me, Dottie."

"What people call you is important. Your name is Vincent."

"My name is Vincent," he said, realizing it was fine to affirm what he preferred to be called.

"Vincent it is then," Sarge said. "Now that we're all acquainted, perhaps someone can tell me how you all managed to travel this far south? And why?"

"Don't bother asking Dottie," Vincent said. "She don't remember nothing. Her memory is full of holes, you know, like cheddar cheese."

Sarge looked at the girl, curious. "Is that true? Is your brain 'cheddar' cheese?"

"I remember enough," Dot said, still unsure how much she should reveal about the past few days and about her memory loss.

"I reckon you were likely hidden during the fight by the bridge," Sarge said, "and I reckon you came out after everyone fell in the struggle. You don't have to hide anything from me, Little Miss."

"Vincent's right. I don't... I don't remember much before that. After coming down the hill, I saw the dead soldiers. I found Gypsy. We ran when we heard more coming."

"When they radioed you were still alive." Sarge thought about her plight for a moment, until the truth finally dawned on him. "Someone blessed you."

"That's what Father told her!" Vincent said. "I'm still not sure what that means."

"Neither am I," Dot said.

"You received The Blessing. It means someone injected you with a psychotropic drug that targeted specific memories and either blocked or erased them."

"What memories? What did I forget?"

"The Story of The World."

"Father told her that, too!" Vincent said, slurping his soup. "You really should meet him, though it's not really good timing because he's dead."

"Will you tell me?" Dot asked. "Father Young was going to tell me everything, but he didn't make it to morning."

"My condolences," Sarge said. "But it's not that easy. To undo a Blessing is to risk brain damage. I've seen folks go mad from it."

"I must know why everyone's fighting and dying for me."

"Yeah, I wanna know, too," Vincent said, petting Gypsy at his side.

Sergeant Furst set down his dinner and looked at his new companions. Though he didn't want to harm the girl, he had a feeling that revealing the truth wouldn't affect her in the usual manner, knowing who – and what – she really was.

"Alright then," he said, succumbing to the girl's pleading eyes. "A fireside tale seems about right. I suppose The Story of The World started about two hundred years ago..."

* * *

Lynn Harrod

The world had reached its zenith of science and technology, and in the pride and arrogance and greed that came with it so, too, came a crossroads for humanity.

Every breakthrough discovery meant for the good of all can be, – and always is – exploited for financial gain at the cost of many. Every powerful new tool created for the benefit of mankind can be – and always is – bent and broken down into a weapon to be wielded in the name of territory, religion, or legacy. Evolution is not without resistance, and though humanity's greatest enemy seemed to lie within, the world itself proved a far greater threat.

History has shown that no matter the achievements of advanced medicine, no matter how many diseases have been conquered, no matter how far life is extended, nature always has something else behind its back. At the dawn of the twenty-second century, when sickness and hunger were a distant memory and everyone from all corners of the Earth lived long, healthy lives with ample food and medicine, "The Lizard's Tongue" licked the globe, unleashed on the masses by a dimwitted fool.

First contracted by popular internet daredevil survivalist "Devon Devours" in the depths of the Australian outback after eating a small, raw lizard, a young Sand Goanna that had lived mostly on carrion, the rapidly mutating pathogen – classified LZ99 – caused lethal fevers and proved highly contagious. Devon sought attention through zany stunts, competitive eating, and bizarre foods, but ended up making his mark in history as Patient Zero in the worst viral onslaught the world had ever seen. Within an hour, one casualty grew to over a hundred. Within a day, the numbers climbed into the thousands. By week's end, Devon's fateful discovery had crossed continents and infected millions.

As the human body fought The Lizard's Tongue, it rapidly mutated into different strains, making immunity next to impossible even with its source identified. With global death rates skyrocketing weekly, a genetically engineered recombinant virus classified WN1M – better known as "The Worm" – was created to counter the initial attack in an effort to create an environment suitable for a traditional vaccine.

It worked too well.

The Lizard's Tongue was no more, but the cure turned out to be worse than the sickness. The man-made virus that was to be the savior of Man, made aggressive enough to combat any illness, was created so hastily that it didn't have an "off" switch. After taking control of one's immune system, it lay dormant in the body, resurfacing years later with old age and newborns, altering human physiology forever. To ensure its complete dominance, The Worm spread to livestock and crops, turning most meat and produce into carriers of concentrated death. A cut of steak or a bite of apple could end a man's life before he could slide his chair from the dinner table.

The crossroads came a decade later when – for the first time in human history – death rates surpassed birth. With far more people dying each day than were being born, it was a mathematical certainty that humanity and most other animal life on Earth would be extinct before the next century. Desperate, unthinkable measures were needed, and petty arguments regarding the moral ramifications of such actions split the world's nations apart, throwing them headlong into a New World War.

"The Loyalists to Man" sought survival of the species through research and science, while "The Purists of Earth" clung to their personal beliefs and faith, choosing to ride out God's storm and face its consequences with sacrifices they deemed necessary for "the purity of our race."

* * *

Lynn Harrod

"We were dying faster than we could make babies," Sarge said to a mesmerized Dot and confused Vincent by the fire. "After generations of fighting this thing, The Worm had burrowed itself in us all, ingrained in our DNA. Everyone's born with it now, usually dead before adolescence. Some live a little longer, a few reach middle age like me and Dixon, but no one sees their golden years any more. So, the brilliant minds that came up with The Worm in the first place gave up on trying to fix human beings and decided to create a new race of people."

"The hybrid humans," Dot said.

"Some plants and animals were unaffected by The Worm, so it was thought that if we somehow merged with them, we'd also be free of the disease. The Loyalists were willing to pay that heavy price to keep us going. The Purists didn't want 'abominations' roaming the Earth. They felt confident that God would sort it all out, sparing the devout, of course."

"How old are you?" Dot asked. "You look way past adolescence."

"I just turned thirty," Sarge said, though he looked much older. "My ancestors lived to be close to a hundred in their time. Today, I'm considered one of the oldest humans you'll likely meet, and I probably won't live to see forty. One day, maybe next week, maybe a few years from now, I'll wake up with a terrible fever. My arms and legs will feel like lead, and I won't have the strength to sit up or even talk. On that day, by sunset, I'll hardly be breathing. By midnight, I'll be gone, and that'll be the end of my story."

"I'm so sorry," Dot said.

"Don't be. I've come to accept it and actually feel somewhat fortunate. I've lived longer than all of my friends and family. My parents died shortly after I was born. My brothers died toddlers, my daughter a teenager." Sarge looked out at his company, largely comprised of artificial soldiers. "My human superiors went to sleep in camp and never woke up. Soon after enlisting with The Loyalists, I became their leader, surrounded by mostly Automen."

"How do you go on?" Dot asked. "How can you keep fighting this war knowing that no matter what you do, you'll eventually die?"

"We all eventually die, Little Miss. Every soldier is told that in Basic Training. What matters is what we do while we're still alive, how we fight, how we serve. Having a giant ticking clock hovering above you at all times can give you a sharp focus on your mission, and ours is to save the world. More to the point, our mission is you."

"Me?" The girl suddenly felt lost. "How am I your mission?"

"To our knowledge, you're the first human born without The Worm, and the first person immune to it."

There it was, the explanation that Dot had suspected all along, confirmed when she ate the tainted fish at Emerald Pond. The reason two armies chased her – one with rifles, the other with blankets and warm food – was because she represented a turning point for humanity, an end to the pandemic that clutched the world.

"I told you that fish was bad!" Vincent said. He turned to Sarge with a wide grin. "She ate a bass with the red and blue jagged lines in it. Didn't feel a thing! She even liked how it tasted!"

"How long ago?" Sarge asked with concern.

"Earlier this morning," Dot said. "Up at the pond."

"Emerald Pond?" He traced the lengthy distance in his mind. "Red and blue jagged lines? You saw them after you cut open the fish, didn't you? Branching across the meat?"

"Like electricity shooting through the sky!" Vincent said, dramatically spreading his vines out.

"If I had eaten that fish, Little Miss, I wouldn't be sitting here with you now. I'd be curled up in agony by that pond, and my men would have buried me there."

Dot's thoughts raced as she took in everything, overwhelmed not only by The Story of The World but by her unimaginable central role in it.

"Father Young said I wasn't born," she said, "that I was created like Vincent. I thought maybe he was wrong."

"He wasn't. You came from a long series of trials. They likely spent decades failing before making you. But you're no hybrid like your friend here. You're a bona fide human, just one with a bulletproof immune system."

"Wormproof!" Vincent said.

"Don't think any less of yourself, Little Miss. Everyone is born in some way. Some are 'Born Womb,' which means they came from natural childbirth, like Dix and myself. Others are 'Born Tomb,' created in a lab that they'll never leave alive. The hybrids were 'Born Boom,' created as part of a campaign to cure the virus."

"And what about the hybrids?" Dot asked. "What happened to them?"

"The hybrid programs were successful in weeding out the disease, but there were... drawbacks."

"Like what?"

"Veggies... plant hybrids... lacked intelligence. They were mentally stunted, often having the mind of a young child, even as they reached old age."

"I'm forty-one!" Vincent said proudly, not sensing the gravity of Sarge's story. "Almost as old as Father. My birthday was in June. He let me drive the Horse alone for the first time. He kinda had to, since he was dying."

Dot looked at her friend with fresh eyes, amazed at how youthful he looked and behaved for being as old as he was, and more understanding of his naive nature.

"Other programs had their own problems," Sarge said. "Beasties... animal hybrids... lacked emotional stability. They were prone to sudden aggression, deep depression, and suicidal thoughts. Turns out we mere mortals are bad at playing God."

"So, if I was Born Tomb, if I'm not a hybrid, what am I?"

"You're a new breed of human. I first learned about you through my superiors. I was told a child was being taken beyond the West Wall to a sanctuary, a fortified city for humans and hybrids."

"Kellan."

"You almost made it," Sarge said. "I regret not being there in time to protect you from the ambush."

"The West Wall is where the hope died," Vincent said, his voice turning somber as he recalled his father's words. "The North Woods is where the sickness lies. The South Lands is where the guns took over. The East Hills is where the bad men are."

"Where are we now?" Dot asked.

"The South," Sarge said.

"And where are you taking me?"

"West of the wall, to Kellan, as ordered."

"Where the hope died?" Vincent asked.

"All those things your father told you are myths. The truth is, there's all kinds of people in all parts of the world. Either way, I'd rather end up in a place with 'hope' in its name than those other parts."

"Now that I know where I'm going," Dot said. "Can you tell me where I'm from?" She felt nervous to hear the answer, imagining a sterile, heartless laboratory where people were mass produced as guinea pigs, destined to either die on the slab or live as a captive commodity to be fought over.

"I know you think your name is Dot from the tattoo on your hand, but it's not."

"Who am I then?"

"I don't know your real name, Little Miss, but I can tell you that 'Dot' is actually..."

BOOM!

Dot quickly ducked down under her oblivious plant friend.

Sarge looked across the camp to an arriving squad of his Automen. The loud noise came from an immense crate being unloaded from a truck, landing on the ground like the footstep of a giant.

"Special delivery!" Lieutenant Dixon said, calling out to Sarge from in front of the crate as his men pried its sides off. "It's just as you asked, sir. I never thought salvage crews would actually find one intact, but here it is."

The crate laid on the ground, lit by the full moon. At twenty feet long and six feet wide, it looked large enough to store a vehicle. The entire platoon gathered around as the salvage crew continued to remove thick wood beams from the crate's sides.

Sarge stood and left the fire, abandoning the Q&A with his new companions. His weathered face betrayed a slight smile at the sight of his new acquisition.

"We'll talk more later," he said to his guests. "I've been waiting a long time for this. Come."

"What are we doing?"

"We're going to say hello."

12

Abraham

Lieutenant Dixon guided the salvage crew as they pulled the cover off the crate, removing packing material and braces. What remained was a monstrous twelve-foot mechanical humanoid robot lying on its back as if it were a sleeping metal monster, its thick, long arms at its sides and two massive legs extended at rest. Thick armor covered its body. Its "head" resembled an assembly of cameras and antennae, with five large lenses for eyes, like an immense insect.

"Now *this* is a robot," Sergeant Furst said with pride. "An advanced artificial intelligence wrapped in 10-inch plate steel armor and an arsenal of weapons, all bound to a set of directives dictated by me. No organic material in its autonomous neural mass. No hive mind, no lab-grown cerebellum, no doubt or fear or misjudgment."

"This is an A1900," Dixon said. "It does have organic tissue in its fusion cortex, in its limbic system and frontal lobe."

"You're telling me it's got fleshy meat brains?"

"Partial fleshy meat brains, yes sir."

"Well, no one's perfect," Sarge said, "not even old Abraham here."

"Abraham?" Dot said.

"It... he... has a name?" Vincent asked.

Dixon groaned at their referring to the robot as "he."

"No name," Sarge said. "He's an Abraham-class combat mech. Think of him like a walking tank."

"Also, think of it as heavier, slower, and less efficient than our Automen grunts," Dixon said, failing to hide his contempt.

"Take it easy, Dix. We went over this."

"We did, Sarge, and I still don't know why this thing is here. No disrespect, sir, but the crew and I could have rounded up twenty more wandering grunts in the time it took to track down this two-ton tin can."

Sarge noticed the curious look on his new companions' faces. "What do you two think of him?"

"He looks amazing!" Vincent said, enthralled by his first sight of a mechanical soldier. "Father talked about these, said they fought in the war when he was a little kid."

"He's... intimidating," Dot said, also fascinated by the robot, perhaps a little fearful.

"Once it's up and running, sure," Dixon said, "but it can't hurt anyone before its initial charge. Unlike our grunts that don't need to eat or rest, this 'walking tank' needs to charge daily."

"Is that all, Lieutenant?" Sarge said with a sigh. "Come on, speak freely, Dix. Get it all out."

Dixon felt eager to oblige, to seize the opportunity to vent his frustrations. The two commanding officers faced Dot as if they wanted the girl to settle their long-running argument.

"Automen are scaled to use any weapon," Dixon said. "The Abraham unit can only use its onboard guns. Automen can run reconnaissance, enter any structure or operate any vehicle a human can. The Abraham is limited by its size and weight. It's meant mostly for open field combat, lumbering about, sticking out like a sequoia instead of taking cover. Automen can be easily replaced. The Abraham unit cannot. They're rare for a reason. I could go on, but all you need to know is that the thing lying lifeless in this crate has a whole mess of disadvantages for a company always on the move, a company looking to gain any edge in a fight."

"So, why did you want it?" Dot asked the sergeant. "Lieutenant Dixon makes a pretty strong case."

"Everything Dix pointed out is true," Sarge said. "Abraham's bulky, loud, slow, and limited in many respects. A lot of disadvantages, to be sure. But there are three reasons I wanted him. First, he has vastly superior firepower. One combat mech can face off against an entire platoon of grunts. Second, he's nearly indestructible. Even a direct hit from a Doom Cannon can't knock him off his feet. Lastly, he has unquestionable loyalty, or will have in a moment."

"Aren't all your soldiers loyal?" the girl asked.

Dixon stopped himself from a quick response. The two veteran commanders glanced at each other before turning to look at the many Automen working in camp alongside a handful of humans, satisfied that none were within earshot.

"How can I put this?" Sarge said. "The Automen can be a little too human at times. They constantly assess their surroundings, the status of a conflict, the odds of defeat, even the aptitude of their superiors, and it all influences their problem-solving protocol."

"I'm sorry, gentlemen," Dot said, "but I don't know what all that means."

"He's saying they can be turned," Dixon said with a dismissive glare, "unlikely as it may be."

"It is unlikely, Little Miss," Sarge said. "Dix is right. But it's possible. I won't lie to you."

"They can be turned to what?" Vincent asked, confused.

"They can be convinced to switch sides," Sarge said, hesitant to admit it. "It's how we recruited ours in the first place. Nearly every grunt in this company used to serve the Purists. When they're left behind after a rough conflict, we patch them up, sell them our cause, and add them to our numbers."

"You have to convince them?" Dot asked.

"That's right, and we have to keep convincing them daily. Automen need to believe in their cause."

Dot looked around at the dozens of identical artificial men around camp and suddenly felt less safe. Since these cloned soldiers were capable of defecting to the opposing militia at will, she couldn't bring herself to completely trust them, and she wondered how the sergeant and lieutenant could. Perhaps they simply had no choice.

"That brings us back to the Abraham mech," Sarge said. "He utilizes indissoluble imprint loyalty. Once I activate him, he'll serve only me for the rest of his operational life." He checked the time on his watch and turned to Dixon. "Speaking of which, is he ready?"

"It charges much slower by moonlight," Dixon said, "but it should have enough power to imprint by now."

Sergeant Furst walked to the dormant robot, now fully uncrated. As it laid still on the ground, its five insectoid "eyes" staring up at the night sky, Sarge used a power tool to remove its chest plate, revealing a red gel pad the size of his hand. He pressed his palm into the gel, looked into the mech's camera eyes, and recited his credentials.

"Benjamin Furst, Acting Sergeant and Lead Commander of the Loyalists 13th Company. Serve and protect."

Three quick beeps and a bright glow of the gel pad completed the brief ceremony, confirming the machine's undying loyalty. Dixon moved closer to the robot and pressed his palm to the gel pad.

"Albert Dixon, Acting Lieutenant and Second Commander of the Loyalists 13th Company." Dixon winced at naming himself "second," despite his rank being technically above a sergeant's. "Serve and protect."

A low buzz sounded in place of the three beeps, and the gel pad failed to glow, signaling a failure to imprint.

"Albert Dixon," he said again, frustrated. "Acting Lieutenant and Second Commander of the Loyalists 13th Company. Serve and protect."

Another low buzz. Dixon's imprint failed again.

"What the hell is wrong with this thing?" Dixon asked.

"If I remember correctly," Sarge said, "he can only imprint one person a day, part of his security protocol."

"That's just as well. It's your new toy, sir, not mine."

"He's ours, Dix, and we can try again at midnight. That's when the limit resets and..."

"Recommend we try again in the morning, sir," Dixon said firmly. "I plan to be dead asleep till sunup."

Though Sarge considered it urgent that their new combat mech imprint on the two senior commanders as soon as possible, he didn't want to push his lieutenant's thin patience in front of his guests and soldiers. Tomorrow morning would do fine.

"Morning works for me," Sarge said. He nodded and reattached the mech's chest plate, bolting it back into place. "How long before he's up and ready at full power?"

"A few hours at this rate."

"I noticed his central storage is vacant. Where are the Lotus bombs?"

"It didn't come with any, sir. They're kept separate during storage, but we had to move fast before the Greens showed up."

"I'm sure we'll find some out there," Sarge said, as if to assure the unmoving mechanical man. "Tell the grunts to strike camp at sunup. We'll head out after we've eaten, packed, and imprinted you. Our sleepy friend here will be awake and ready for the world by then."

"I can't wait," Dixon said with a huff, walking away to delegate tasks to the others. "I'll also tell them we'll be moving at half-pace from now on. I'm sure they'll love that news."

Sergeant Furst intended to ignore Dixon's flippant remarks but issued as petty last-minute order as he walked away.

"Inventory the munitions shed before you fall 'dead asleep,' Lieutenant."

"Now?" Dixon asked in frustration. "By flashlight?" He shelved his anguish upon seeing the sergeant's stern eyes fixed on him. "Yes, sir. I'll get on it, sir."

"Good man."

Sarge regretted venting his disapproval publicly but felt the need to address his second commander, to order the menial task as a reminder of rank and respect. He turned to Vincent.

"Let's get you to that water tank, my friend. And you, Little Miss, it's time we get you to bed. My guess is you need some sleep."

"You guess right," Dot said with a yawn.

"You'll sleep like a log with this beast protecting you."

Sarge knelt and rubbed Gypsy under his collar. He took Dot and her dog to a nearby tent before escorting Vincent to a water tank across camp. Dot laid on a cot and buried herself in blankets while her faithful dog stood watch at the tent entrance, as always.

"It's going to be okay now, Gypsy," Dot said. "I think it's going to be okay."

13

The Promise

Dot lay in her cot, comfortable at rest for the first time that she could recall. In her limited memory, she could remember every moment she went to sleep, none of which completely put her body or mind at ease...

Sitting upright in the dark hollow of the oak tree...

Curled up in the tall grass near Brandywine Falls...

Sprawled across the floor of the Wellspring library...

Ducked down in the dirt of a mutant cornfield...

Bundled on an old dusty bed in Father's Young's barn.

Sergeant Furst's military cot, covered in fresh wool blankets and plush cotton pillows, felt like opulence in comparison. She turned over and felt a sudden chill, as if the tent's canvas walls and roof had been yanked away, exposing her to the frosty night air. Looking up at the sky, not a star could be seen.

She sat up, rested her hand on Gypsy's head, and realized she was no longer in the Loyalist's camp. For a moment, she thought she'd been abducted, but the sight of the twin stars along the invisible horizon came into focus.

"You're going to die... you're going to save us all..."

Dot stood up in The Void, the endless expanse of darkness that now strangely felt like a second home rather than a bizarre intersection between reality and dream. The glowing stars once again held silhouettes of young girls wearing gowns and pointed hats, their details more pronounced as they floated closer with each encounter. Squinting at them, Dot tried to place their faces but only saw vague expressions within their intense glows.

"Keep running to the west... come back to the east..."

The conflicting words started as advice, guidance, but now had the tone of commands, the two mysterious figures sounding almost frantic in pushing Dot one way or the other.

"This place is weird," said Vincent as he wandered into view directly in front of Dot and Gypsy. "Not a single tree."

"Vincent?" Dot said, surprised. "Are you really here?" She already knew the answer.

"I was about to ask you that! People don't normally pop up in my dreams. I figure they didn't want to help harvest the crops."

"You dream about farming?" Dot asked.

"Not tonight I'm not."

"What should I do, Vincent?"

"What do you mean?" he asked. "It's a dream. You do anything you want! You can plant carrots or feed the chickens or trim the rose bushes..."

"Do I go west or east?"

"Oh, that," Vincent said. He scratched the small beard of moss on his chin. "Sarge was talking about taking you to that city where you'll be safe."

"Kellan."

"Isn't that west?" Vincent asked. "Isn't that still the plan?"

"I'm not so sure. One of those girls wants me to go east to find her."

"She needs our help?"

"Yes," Dot said, "but the other girl says I'll die if I go to them."

"Ask Sarge to take you!" Vincent said, proud of his smart idea. "With his soldiers protecting you, it'll be a breeze! Tell the glowy, floaty girls you have an entire company of soldiers with you."

"They would do that?"

"I get the feeling they'll do whatever you tell them. Sarge said you were special, important to saving his mission, I think."

Vincent was right. With one of the specters of The Void urging her to flee while the other begged for help, how could she continue on to the sheltered city without them? It seemed doubly cruel to abandon the twins while she had a militia at her disposal.

"You've got me, too," Vincent said. "I'll follow you east, west, even further south. Probably not north, since we just came from there."

"You don't have to," Dot said, remembering the sight of Vincent being shot to pieces hours before. "While the Loyalists come with me to find the Star Girls, I'm sure Sarge can have some of his men take you to Kellan. We'd both be safe."

"I can't go anywhere without you, Dottie. I made a promise! Father would be disappointed with me if I left you, even though he's dead. Plus, who would play with Gypsy? He loves it when I break branches off my body and throw them for a game of Fetch."

"They're both right," a familiar voice said, "but you have to follow your heart."

"George!" Dot turned to see her friend standing behind her in The Void. She ran to hug the boy, her smile beaming. "Please tell me it's really you."

"Well, I know I'm really me," George said. "I'm not so sure about you guys."

"My name is Vincent! They also call me Vinny Greenblood, Veggie Vinny, Dim Vin, the Green Fool, Vincent Vines..."

"His name is Vincent," Dot said, "and yes, we're really here. Somehow. Are you asleep in the camp with us? With the Loyalists?"

"You're with the Blues?" George said, glad that the girl was no longer on her own. "Last I recall, I'm asleep in a camp, but not yours. He travels fastest who travels alone. Remember?"

"I remember. Well, wherever you are, I hope you're safe." As overjoyed as she felt seeing him again, she couldn't shake the feeling that he abandoned her. "George, why did you leave me in the library?"

"I'm sorry, Dot. That wasn't the plan. I heard the night raiders and went out to count their numbers. I might've been able to handle a small squad, but when I saw how many there were, I had to lure them away from Wellspring."

"Away from me, you mean."

"I put out the fire, gathered my things, and made sure they spotted me as I ran off."

"West, to the river."

"Right. They lost my scent when I waded through the water and nearly broke my neck down some rapids. I backtracked and took out nine Greens surrounding the town, but by the time I returned to the library, you were gone. Frankly, I'm not sure how you pulled that off."

"It turns out you were right about Gypsy," Dot said. "He's a walking weapon, made quick work of some soldiers."

George glanced at the plant-man. "I suppose you met this Veggie after you got out of Wellspring."

"His name is Vincent," Dot said. "He doesn't like being called 'Veggie.'"

"She met Father, too," Vincent said. "I bet he'd love to meet you, Georgie, but he's dead, and he's not growing back."

"Sorry for your loss... Vincent," George said in a more respectful tone. "I know what it's like to lose a father." George looked at the dark horizon, at the twins beckoning in the distance. "I guess all that's left is to decide where to go. That's what you were discussing before I so rudely interrupted."

"I go where you go," Dot said. "You can't leave me again, George."

"I'll stick around, even it's just in dreams for now. But east versus west, that's not for me to decide. These girls are reaching out to you, Dot. It's your decision, not mine or Vincent's."

Dot took inventory of her allies – old and new – and estimated how long of a journey lied ahead. Though she had no idea exactly where the twins waited or even who they were, she felt they were closer than she could know. Most importantly, she felt the obligation of taking the twins with her to the west. Regardless of who accompanied her into the unknown East Hills, she had to find them.

"I'm coming back!" Dot yelled at the twin stars, her words echoing across the expanse. "I promise, my friends and I will save you!"

"Ouch!" Vincent said, clutching his arm. "That stung!"

"What stung?"

"I dunno. It felt like when the Greenies shot at me."

Vincent suddenly disappeared. George also vanished before Dot could make sense of it.

Gypsy turned and barked at the darkness behind Dot, as if he saw surrounding enemies she could not.

"What is it, boy?" she asked, kneeling beside him.

"Wake up, Little Miss!"

Sarge's voice boomed in the darkness.

14

Minimum Safe Distance

Dot awoke from Sergeant Furst shaking her by the shoulders, nearly knocking her out of her cot.

"We need to move!" Sarge said in a hushed, urgent voice before turning to the German Shepherd. "Quiet, dog!" Still disoriented as her dream faded back to reality, Dot barely made out the sergeant's words over the sound of Gypsy barking at the tent's open entrance. "Tell him to keep quiet! He'll give us away!" Sarge lifted the girl from the cot and set her on her feet.

"Down, boy!" Dot whispered. "We must be quiet!"

The dog instantly heeled and returned to her side after ignoring Sarge's orders a minute before. With his incessant barking stopped, the thunderous noise of the night raid overcame her. Gunshots rang out all around. Shouts of soldiers, their identical monotone voices coming from every direction, sounded frightening and surreal, as if one man was seemingly everywhere.

"They're here for you," Sarge said. His tone remained calm and focused, even as chaos consumed the surrounding camp. "I think they took some of my Automen, maybe most of them."

"What about the human soldiers?" Dot asked.

"Gone," Sarge said in a long exhale. He shut his eyes and took a deep breath, struggling to stay strong for the child. "They don't want humans. Just my synthetic grunts."

Before Dot could understand what he meant, before she could remember how an Automan's loyalty could be turned through mere persuasion, Sergeant Furst wrapped her in a blanket, flung her over his shoulder, and carried her out of the tent and across the camp. If the invasion seemed overwhelming within the tent, it grew sharp and deafening outside as they fled through the undergrowth of the trees.

"It'll be dawn soon," Sarge said. "If we're not a good distance down the road before light, we won't make it a mile before a Doom Cannon wipes us off the map."

"Aren't there reinforcements coming?" Dot asked.

"Little Miss, we are the reinforcements."

Sarge breathed heavily as he hurried the girl away from the tents and sheds, many of them burning as two armies clashed in the twilight. Still unable to distinguish the colors of their uniforms in the waning moonlight, all she saw were clones killing each other as they spread out in search of her.

"Sarge, how did they find the camp?"

"I've been racking my brain trying to figure that out," Sergeant Furst said. "Maybe we didn't get them all when we found you and your friend. All it takes is one to report back to the Greens. Automen rarely die since they can repair each other. That takes a lot of time, takes them out of the fight. But if just one got out unharmed..."

"Wait, where's Vincent?" Dot asked, bouncing as Sarge carried her across rough terrain. "And where's Gypsy? He was just with us!"

"All I know is where you are, Little Miss. That's all I can focus on. I need to get you out of here." He looked around as he continued through the woods. "Where is that damn jeep?"

"But we can't leave them behind!"

"There it is." Sarge ignored his ward's impassioned plea and took her around a boulder to a small utility vehicle waiting in a pasture. "Once I get you a safe distance away, I'll radio my men to retreat. They'll return to look for them after..."

"It'll be too late!" Dot said.

"That could be, but right now, we have no choice."

Sarge set her on the ground behind the isolated vehicle, a two-person off-roader that hadn't yet been discovered by the Purists. He reached into the rear cargo bed and pulled out boots, socks, gloves, pants, and a jacket, gesturing for the girl to put them on. Her simple night shirt and shorts wouldn't be enough for the arduous journey ahead.

"Sarge, we have to find them," Dot said as she put the fatigues on over her shirt. The thick, oversized clothes felt awkward on her, and she missed the frilly, soiled dress she left behind, tucked under her cot.

"Listen to me," Sergeant Furst said, kneeling down to look her in the eyes. "If they catch you, if you die, all of this will have been for nothing. You must understand that. And if your veggie friend is smart..."

"His name is Vincent," Dot said, her defense of the innocent plant-man a reflex now.

"If Vincent is smart, he'll stay in the water tank, out of sight until this hot zone cools off."

"You know he's not smart!"

"I know," Sarge said, his tone betraying his apprehension. "But he might be just smart enough to make it out alive. Now I need you to get in the jeep, Little Miss."

Sarge sat at the steering wheel but paused upon seeing its hood popped open while an Automan in blue ran away. Sarge cursed to himself, instantly realizing the situation.

He jumped out of the jeep, grabbed Dot, and hurried her away from the vehicle.

It exploded behind them, destroyed by the bomb planted by one of his own men a moment before. The force of the explosion sent them tumbling to the ground, its pillar of fire lighting up the pasture like a grand beacon for every clone soldier in the area.

"My Automen are compromised," Sarge said, struggling to catch his breath as he knelt at the base of a tree. "Perhaps all of them by now." He laid the girl down on a mossy patch, readied his rifle, and looked around for anyone approaching. Dot saw the defeat on the commander's face and feared the worst. With his soldiers dead or defected, and her friends missing, it felt like the end.

"Where's Lieutenant Dixon?" Dot asked. "Maybe he can help switch your clones back..."

"Dix is dead," Sarge said, trying to wrangle his quivering voice.

"How can you be sure?" Dot wanted Sarge to second guess himself for it would feel like their allies might all still live.

"I told Dix to inventory the munitions shed before bed-down." He pointed to a burning structure in the center of the camp, its monstrous flames rising above the treeline. "I gave him that task as petty payback for his poor attitude earlier. That shed... it was the first thing they hit."

"Sarge, you can't blame..."

"Dix was following my orders!" Sarge said, "and now he's dead because of me."

"Maybe he saw them coming and..."

"Don't you understand?" Sarge's eyes welled up, the burden of their plight squarely on his shoulders. "I gave Dix that fool's errand in the shed for being insubordinate, but I never saw him come out. I left Vincent in the water tank unguarded, but I never saw him come out. My flesh-and-blood officers went into their tents, your war dog ran into the fight..."

"But we never saw them come out." Dot suddenly felt alone again.

Sarge lowered his rifle and gently took Dot by the shoulders. He leaned in to be sure she heard his dire words clearly. "Everyone we trusted is gone, Little Miss. All we have is us."

As the gunfire grew louder, coming closer, Sergeant Furst was cornered into a drastic decision. He plunged his hands into the damp ground and pulled up fistfuls of mud. To Dot's shock, he smothered her face and hands with it, her only exposed skin.

"What are you doing?" she asked, the ice cold mud sending shivers through her.

"Automen use thermal vision at night. They can spot body heat when they're close. The mud might render you invisible while it's still dark."

"Might?"

"It's my running theory." Sarge considered his options, playing out scenarios in his mind until he came to a stark conclusion, the only line of action he had left. He turned to the girl with a disarming, sudden calm. "Do you trust me, Little Miss?"

Dot hesitantly nodded, having no choice but to follow her one remaining friend.

Child of Imago

"Good, because to save you, I must first put us in harm's way. When the time comes, I'll need you to close your eyes."

Sarge held Dot's hand and guided her through the brush, keeping low and in shadow. Her heart raced when she realized they weren't fleeing the camp but rather heading deeper into it, to the center of the "hot zone." She thought Sarge had lost his mind until she saw the combat mech come into view, still laying flat on the ground surrounded by the wood beams and metal braces that once encased it.

With shaking hands, Sarge used a small power tool to remove the robot's massive chest plate, once again exposing its central red gel pad. He grabbed Dot's hand and firmly pressed her palm into the gel.

"State your name," Sarge said. "State the name of my company. You remember how it goes?"

"My name is Dot," she said, unsure of the rest.

"Ward of the Loyalists 13th Company."

"Ward of the Loyalists 13th Company," Dot repeated.

"Child of Imago." Sarge stared at the girl, her face frozen, confused, scared. "Child of Imago! Say it!"

"Child of Imago."

"Serve and protect!"

"Serve and protect."

Three simple beeps and a bright red glow confirmed the mech's newly imprinted loyalty to the girl.

"Take care of Little Miss," Sarge said to the dormant war machine. "You're her guardian now. You'll be all she has left in this wretched world."

"Wait, Sarge, what do you mean?"

Sarge bolted the mech's chest plate back in place, scrambled to unplug power cables, and quickly pulled Dot away, but the desperate move proved a moment too late as dozens of Automen – both blue and green – encircled them.

"I'm so sorry, Dot," Sarge said softly, knowing what was about to happen.

He'd known since the moment the jeep was destroyed.

He flung his rifle across his back and picked up the muddy girl, cradling her in his arms. "I'm sorry I failed you. If you make it out, tell him I remained true to the mission, always his servant. Tell him I was devoted to the end."

"Tell who?" the girl said, nervous. "Sarge, you're scaring me."

"Close your eyes now, Little Miss."

Dot tried to make sense of what would be the commander's last words, tried to think of something to say or do that could return the clones to their side. Before anything came to her, Sarge threw her behind him as far as he could, aimed his rifle at the surrounding soldiers, and pulled the trigger.

Sergeant Benjamin Furst of the Loyalists 13th Company, the de facto leader of the greater human-hybrid movement and one of the oldest human officers still active in the field, took down seven of the hostile Automen in a wide arc of his rifle before a rain of gunfire annihilated him.

"Sergeant Furst!" Dot screamed from the mud as his mutilated body fell fifteen feet away, her tiny voice rising to a banshee cry in the night.

Her quivering shrill grabbed the synthetic soldiers' attention.

The Automen pointed their weapons toward her but did not fire, unable to visually place her. She realized the icy mud caked onto her skin did indeed keep her invisible to their thermal vision, just as Sarge had hoped, if only for the moment. With nowhere to run and the sunrise fast approaching, they would soon discover her, and they'd open fire just as they had with her friends. Even though she trembled from having just witnessed

Sarge's grisly death, she obeyed his last command and shut her eyes to avoid witnessing her own.

Bracing for a bullet, she winced and looked up as an intense, bright light flooded the area, throwing most of the decimated camp into view. But it wasn't the glow of the coming dawn, nor the gun-mounted flashlights of the many soldiers.

To the horror of the Automen, the combat mech let out a loud hydraulic groan over its lengthening of steel and titanium and chromium alloy as it rose to its feet, towering over them. Twelve feet tall, it stood nearly three times the height of the clones.

"Identification," the robot said in a calm, synthetic male voice as it reached its full height. "This unit is an A1900 Abraham-class combat mechanoid designed by the Humanist Global Consortium and constructed by the Loyalists To Man paramilitary union."

The frightening mech looked down at Dot with its spotlight and five insectoid camera eyes. It tilted its head almost as if curious, recognizing her, before turning to the sea of Automen and their raised weapons.

"Directive: Serve and protect the ward of the Loyalists 13th Company."

The mech positioned itself between Dot and the soldiers, its footfalls booming against the ground. A scan of the enemy identified 37 short-burst semiautomatic firearms aimed at its frame.

"Command: Surrender," the robot said to the platoon, its tone now stern, ominous. "Surrender or die."

The Automen backed away and unloaded their rifles at the war machine. They may as well have been firing at a granite mountain as the robot extended its arms, grabbed ten of them like rag dolls, and slammed them to the ground with the force of a runaway train. With two sweeps of its arm, it obliterated eight more, their gray blood spattering across its thick plate armor.

More soldiers ran into the melee, blasting the mech without pause. The Abraham mech turned and crouched down to shield Dot from the onslaught, picked her up in its wide palms, and opened its chest cavity.

"Request: Get in, Little Miss," the robot said, its calm, digital voice calling her by the nickname Sarge last uttered.

Dot quickly slid into its hollow chest, the vacant bomb compartment Sarge spoke of earlier. A small opening with bulletproof glass allowed her to see the soldiers rushing toward them, and she'd soon see how futile their attack would be.

Wide-gauge guns unfolded from the mech's arms as it returned fire, mowing down the Automen five at a time, sending them to the mud in a hail of bullets. The robot lurched forward through the masses, spraying them with gunfire as it advanced west through the trees.

"Where are we going?" Dot asked.

"Projection: The minimum safe distance is one kilometer west."

Dot could only trust her new guardian, whatever its strategy was. The sound of bullets ricocheting off its armor nearly drowned out her thoughts, but she sat up and alert upon seeing Gypsy ripping into a soldier ahead. The dog fought a pair of Automen at the base of a large tree. In that same glance, she spotted Vincent high in its branches, trying to reach Gypsy with his slithering vines. Her brief renewed hope of saving them dwindled as the robot continued past them, traveling deeper into the woods.

"We need to go back for them!" Dot yelled over the ongoing fire. The mech didn't seem to hear what it deemed an illogical order. "Robot, are you listening to me?"

"Directive: Serve and protect the ward of the Loyalists 13th Company."

"Robot... Abraham... those are my friends!"

"Directive: Serve and protect the ward of the Loyalists 13th Company."

"Go back for them, Abraham!"

"Assessment: The canine and the hybrid are not essential to the mission and are expendable."

"They are not expendable! Do something!"

"Statement: Calling for assistance." Abraham scanned the area ahead and plotted a course through the woods toward the Miracle River in the distance. To aid Dot's friends, it broadcast an automated distress signal, a last-resort call for help that it didn't know would never come. "Status: Reinforcements are not responding."

"We are the reinforcements!" Dot yelled, remembering Sarge's words. "I command you to obey! I command you to serve! Serve and protect! Remember? That includes our friends! Our allies!"

The mech stopped and scanned the area behind it. "Correction: Serve and protect allies."

With relative safety just ahead, Abraham turned and headed back into the hot zone, to the shock of the Automen. It opened fire on the soldiers as it returned to Vincent's tree, where Dot saw that he'd successfully pulled Gypsy from the ground and hid him in its foliage, fortified by a tight ball of his vines.

Abraham grabbed the protective ball, clutching it in the crook of his arm, and made an about face back to its original path away from the camp.

"Status: Another hostile company approaches from the west." Abraham scanned farther ahead. "Course Correction: Safe minimum distance is now one kilometer south."

With the extra weight of Dot and her friends, the robot's pace slowed. As it proceeded south, its sensors read the speed of the oncoming enemy and calculated that they wouldn't evade them fast enough. Though it moved onward, it continued to scan the area in all directions until it located a munitions shed not yet destroyed. It crashed through the shed's corrugated steel walls like tin foil and picked up four crates of IEDs – improvised explosive devices.

"Abraham... what are you going to do?" Dot asked in fear after seeing the crates marked "Danger Explosives" in large red letters.

Abraham hurled the crates into the thick of the soldiers and ignited them with wide arcs of fire from twin flamethrowers built into its arms. The explosion wiped out nearly all the remaining Automen, with the few survivors retreating to join the approaching platoon. Alone for the moment, it would give Dot and her companions enough time to distance themselves from their circle of sight before they had a chance to regroup.

"Status: Proceeding south to the minimum safe distance," Abraham said. "Projection: We shall be beyond their reconnaissance before they merge companies."

"Good robot," Dot said, catching her breath. "I mean, good job, Abraham."

"Dottie?" Vincent blindly called out from within his dense ball of vines, his high-pitched voice cracking, exhausted. "Are you okay?"

"I'm fine. What about you and Gypsy?"

"We didn't die! I'm so glad you didn't die either! But... how'd you get up in the tree?"

"We're not in a tree, Vincent."

"It feels like we are." He peeked through his vines. "I can see the ground way down below."

"Trees don't walk, Vincent." Her friend's innocent confusion felt comforting, as did the sound of Gypsy's barking.

"Request," Abraham said. "The canine must remain silent. Sensors may identify its distinct organic audio signature and locate its position."

"Gypsy is a 'he,' not an 'it,' Abraham."

"Correction: Sensors may identify his distinct organic audio signature and locate his position."

"I guess you're a 'he,' too," Dot said, unsure of what she was saying, rambling in shock. "That's what Sarge called you."

"Clarification," the robot said, continuing through the woods. "This unit has no gender."

"Well, I'm calling you 'he' in honor of Sergeant Furst."

"Acknowledgment, Little Miss."

"You call me Little Miss," Dot said with a sad smile. "I guess we're both honoring him, in a way."

"What did all that gobbledygook mean?" Vincent asked. "Gypsy's organic something signature?"

"It means they'll hear a dog and know where we are."

"Oh, I gotcha. Father said there's not many dogs left. I suppose Gypsy's yapping would stick out."

"Easy, boy," Dot said. As always, the dog obeyed the moment the order left Dot's lips. "We're okay now, boy."

"Where are we going?" Vincent asked, unable to see anything other than the ground from inside his protective ball. "Are we going to meet up with Sarge and the lieutenant?"

Dot thought about Lieutenant Dixon trapped in one of those munitions sheds as it exploded, much like the IEDs Abraham set off. She thought about the human soldiers asleep in their tents, never to awaken. Above all, she thought of Sergeant Furst's last stand, the sacrifice he made to buy her time to flee.

"Sarge and Dix aren't coming," Dot said. "All we have is us."

"So then, where is 'us' going?"

Dot had no idea where they were headed and doubted the mech did either. The invasion threw off any plans of traveling west to Kellan or heading east to the twins in her dreams. Abraham simply marched on, taking them as far from the Purists as possible before daybreak. The plan ended there.

"The safe minimum distance is one kilometer south, Vincent," Dot said, suddenly feeling completely spent. "That's all any of us know for now."

15

Welcome to Colt

The sun crested the distant East Hills and rose into the low clouds, casting long shadows amongst the trees and emitting a warm glow. From within Abraham's chest, an ovoid compartment of heavy steel lined with thermoplastic insulation, the welcome sight of the dawn did nothing to counter the biting chill across Dot's body. The mech's sensors spotted a large village ahead, and the shivering girl immediately thought of the spoils of civilization, like lost treasures yet to be claimed. She and her friends might salvage clothing and blankets, sit beside a wood stove or fireplace, or perhaps find a comfortable shelter for a day.

The girl imagined such creature comforts, for she assumed the village would be long-abandoned like the forsaken town of Wellspring, the burnt out tourist center at Emerald Pond, and the caravan of rusted travel trailers they passed as they trudged through the trees.

Abraham had reached his one-kilometer marker and continued another five, as instructed by Dot. After witnessing the onslaught at Sergeant Furst's camp, which included feeling the blood spatter from his execution, the girl felt uneasy at having only the minimum safe distance between her and the unfeeling, fanatical Purists. She didn't want to stop and reassess their situation until no sounds from trucks or guns or boots on the ground were heard for an hour. The sight of the village felt like a sign that they were safe from harm, being both literally and figuratively out of the woods.

Vincent had untangled his protective ball of vines and now walked beside their armored guardian, as did Gypsy, bringing up the rear. Dot remained inside Abraham's central storage compartment, something the robot insisted on while they were still moving. Though he explained the logic and rationale behind the decision, citing safety protocols and the probability of a strategic subsequent attack, Dot felt it was simply a kind gesture on his part and thanked him.

"Dang, this place looks familiar," Vincent said, as they reached a perimeter of sharpened posts jutting from the ground at odd angles. "I've seen these big pencils before."

"What are they for, Abraham?" Dot asked.

"Identification," the mech said. "These posts are security bollards, defense measures meant to counter hostile forces. They collectively form a crude barrier designed to impede military vehicles."

The Broken Road, with its faded yellow centerline, cut through the village, running west into the settlement and east away from it. A cluster of houses surrounding a tall church steeple lay ahead, beyond a grove of apple trees.

"It looks lived in," Dot said, unsure if that was a good thing. "Still, I don't see anyone."

"Population," Abraham said. "There are 81 life signs in this township. Within the complement, 45 are human, 27 are livestock."

Dot noticed his numbers didn't add up. She did some quick math.

"There's 81, but you only identified 72," the girl said. "What are the other nine? Dogs like Gypsy?"

"Unknown." With a hydraulic hiss, the mech extended his legs and easily stepped over the barrier.

"Nah, not dogs," Vincent said as he gently squeezed between the sharpened posts. "Father said there ain't many dogs left. Maybe the mystery nine are trees?"

"Look around, Vincent," Dot said with a laugh. "There's a lot more than nine trees in a forest."

"Big trees, I mean. The old trees. They have the most personality, you know. You can learn a lot from an ancient white oak, I mean, if he's in the mood for conversation."

"Clarification: My sensors are currently set to detect living animal biological signatures. The unidentified nine only have partial human homology."

"Hybrids," Vincent said with a tone of hope. "Abe's talking about hybrids!"

"Nine hybrids?" Dot said. "Sarge said the Purists killed them all."

"They killed all the plant hybrids, Dottie... except me, of course. There's still a few animal hybrids scattered around, but they're usually alone, like me. Nine in one place is a lot!"

"So why would so many be gathered here?"

"Corollary Speculation: The mission of the Purists of Earth is to track, locate, and contain hybrid humans. They do not always terminate them."

"What do they do with the ones they spare?" Dot asked.

"Possibilities: Scientific experimentation. Entertainment. Involuntary servitude."

"Slavery," Dot said with a sense of dread. The seemingly tranquil village suddenly felt foreboding. "Nine hybrid slaves outnumbered five-to-one."

"Alternative: They may simply be part of the township's citizenry, Little Miss. We do not have enough information to warrant alarm."

"Not yet."

"The town's citizen-whatsis?" Vincent asked.

"He's saying the nine hybrids might just live here with the humans," Dot said. "I certainly hope so."

"Nah, Father said the South Lands don't like hybrids."

"Is that where we are? The South Lands?"

"Abe said we were going south, right?"

A short distance past the barrier stood wooden frames with animal pelts stretched across them. Gutted rabbits, raccoons, quails, and pheasants hung to dry in the morning sun.

"Recommendation: The canine should remain from view as we enter the township." The mech stopped, throwing the area into an eerie silence as the sounds of his body's servos and actuators halted. "He should remain behind cover near the perimeter."

"Why?" Dot asked as she searched his compartment for a latch.

"Assessment: This township appears to be a hunting village. Although the canine is..."

"Gypsy," Dot said, correcting her metal companion. "Abraham, I'm glad you're now calling him a 'he' sometimes, but it's even better to use our names."

"Correction: Although Gypsy is a military asset, he will be viewed no different from other animals harvested for meat."

Abraham opened his chest, its concave cover pivoting upward, and helped Dot to the ground. After sitting with her knees pressed to her chest for over an hour, it felt good to stretch her legs and stand on soft grass.

"Why would anyone want to eat Gypsy?" she asked.

"Explanation: His German Shepherd mix breed is one of the few that have shown resistance to the WN1M pathogen."

"He's saying Gypsy can't get The Worm," Vincent said. "See, Dot, I can translate for the metal professor, too!" He knelt down and stroked the dog's fur, sad that his friend had to wait behind.

"Stay, boy," Dot said, knowing he'd obey her without question. "Keep near the defense posts."

"Abe, what village is this?" Vincent asked as he carefully looked around.

"Status: My localized region map has not yet downloaded from failure to connect to the network."

"Sorry buddy," Vincent said. "Maybe you'll connect to your network thingy later. Right, Dottie?"

"Of course he will," Dot said, smiling up at her guardian. "Don't worry, Abraham."

"Interpretation: Your efforts to assuage my failed assessment are noted and appreciated, but unnecessary."

Dot's attempt to comfort Abraham was futile, not only because the mech had no emotions and therefore needed no solace, but because his disconnection to the greater world could never be mended.

Having no knowledge of computers, Dot and Vincent had no way of knowing about Abraham's blindness. He was constructed many decades before, during an era when a global satellite network still functioned to provide him with detailed information about his environment, including a world map and up-to-the-minute wartime socio-political evaluations of each settlement. With those server farms all destroyed during the New World War, Abraham's impressive sensors were limited to his immediate surroundings.

"This path leads to the town square," Vincent said, suddenly recognizing the creek that ran alongside it. "I think I used to swim here."

"This is Colt?" Dot asked, scared to hear the answer. After hearing Father Young's tale of his devastating last night in that village, she hoped her friend was mistaken.

"Yep, this is Colt alright."

"You're absolutely sure?"

"I'm pretty sure, though I don't see the six baby birch saplings that were up against the creek."

Dot turned and spotted six tall trees along the creek, ominously leading them deeper into the village. Their white papery bark contrasted with the elm and oak all around them. She had a feeling they were the birch Vincent spoke of, but before she could ask Abraham to identify them, a voice called out from the distance.

"Tell your gear-head to stand down!" an old man shouted. "We have a Doom Cannon pointed at its head!"

"Assessment," Abraham said. "The village has no such countermeasures. Weapons are limited to small firearms and explosive projectiles."

"You mean they're bluffing," Dot said.

"Correct."

"It don't matter, Dottie," Vincent said. "Sarge told us one of those cannon things can't hurt Abe, remember?"

"From what I've seen, nothing can hurt him."

"Incorrect," Abraham said. "Though odds are minimal, anti-tank artillery such as Doom Cannons and Lotus Bombs can immobilize this unit with a direct hit if fired with precision at close range. However, as previously stated, this village is not equipped with such countermeasures."

"He won't fire!" Dot yelled, though she couldn't see anyone around. "We're not armed!"

From a distant barn, a pot-bellied old man with cascading gray-white hair, dressed in thick full-body leathers, emerged with five other men in similar attire. They carried long rifles and wore bandoliers decked with grenades. The old man, apparently their leader, approached the intruders alone, satisfied that they meant no harm. The sight of a child surely helped ease his mind.

"Like Hell you're not armed," he said, his deep voice grunting out a laugh. He kept his eyes on the combat mech. "I know for a fact this thing is a pre-packaged apocalypse prepared to level a village like ours."

"He's my friend," Dot said, meeting the old man halfway as a gesture of goodwill. "He'll do no such thing."

"Gear-heads ain't no one's friends, little girl. Ain't got no heart nor soul. He's just a giant gun with legs, the Grim Reaper in armor." He looked past her to the plant hybrid curiously scouting around the village. "Lord Almighty, is that... Vincent?"

"Senior Wainright?" Vincent said, his deep set black eyes fixed on the stout man now standing beside Dot. "You grew back!"

Dot recognized the name. George's stories from growing up in the South Lands painted Wainright as an honorable man and natural leader.

"You two know each other?" Dot asked.

"Francis Young was an old friend," Senior Wainright said, slinging his rifle behind his back. "We practically raised Vincent together from when he was just a hyperactive twig running around the creek. I thought you were dead, boy!"

"And I thought you were dead, too!" Vincent said. "It's good when two not-dead friends meet again!"

Vincent wrapped his arms and vines around the old man in a tight embrace, the sight of which caused the men at the barn to tilt their heads in confusion even as they held their guns at ready.

Abraham stood his ground, arms at his sides, careful not to alarm the apprehensive villagers.

"Where is that old coot you call Father?" Wainright asked. "The man still owes me a chess rematch!"

"We planted him on the farm," Vincent said. "We planted him because he's dead. Not not-dead like us, but dead-dead."

"I'm so sorry, boy. How did he die?"

"The Worm finally got him."

"As it finally gets us all, I suppose."

"Not Dottie! She's special. Wormproof!"

Dot felt uneasy with Vincent telling someone – even an old friend and father figure – about her resistance to the virus, a special trait that made her the target of two armies.

"Wormproof?" Senior Wainright looked at the girl again, this time in awe. "Is that so?"

"Vincent exaggerates," Dot said. "I used to live in Wellspring. I got out while everyone else became sick."

"That was quite a long time ago from what I hear, longer than you've been alive."

"There were still survivors there when I left to live with Father Young." Dot spoke her lie with a trace of truth, enough to convince herself and the old man. "Vincent, you know there's nothing special about me."

"Sorry if I don't make no sense," Vincent said, realizing his slip-up. "I do that sometimes."

"Oh, I certainly know that," Senior Wainright said as he slapped Vincent on the back. "Come on now, let's all get something to eat. We have some Hasenpfeffer simmering, enough for everyone."

"Hasen-what-faffer?"

"Identification," Abraham said. "Hasenpfeffer is a traditional German stew. Rabbit or hare meat is marinated and braised with onions and wine."

"Hellfire, that thing talks!" Wainright said.

"I told you, he's my friend," Dot said. "He's not some agent of the apocalypse, as you say."

"Little girl, wormproof or not, you will come to know who your real friends are, and it ain't synthetics or war machines, ain't Purists or Loyalists. You'll know who to trust because you're with your own kind now."

"Good to know, I suppose."

"It's alright!" Senior Wainright shouted to his confused men still stationed by the barn. "Put your damn rifles away! Vinny Greenblood is here! And he brought guests! Everyone can come out!"

One by one, 45 humans stepped out of the houses and sheds where they'd been hiding since the towering Abraham combat mech was spotted through guards' telescopes ten minutes earlier. At a distance, they stood all around Dot and her friends with smiles and waves. Though the greeting was meant as a warm welcome, Dot faced the fact that she was surrounded by strangers in the infamous South Lands and couldn't shake the feeling that coming to the place that both George and Father Young fled might have been a bad idea.

* * *

The feast comprised much more than rabbit stew after the villagers brought dishes to add to a long central table permanently installed between their semi-circle of houses, the church steeple looming above. All about the old "cul-de-sac" – a strange name Dot somehow knew – theirs were the only homes still occupied and maintained, revealing that the "village" of Colt was actually just a small portion of a larger town that had long since been destroyed by airstrikes during the New World War. The twelve houses and the church spared from the attack sat on what was considered hallowed ground, their residents seen as recipients of divine intervention. The villagers who lived in them now were descendants of those lucky few, as dictated by a strict doctrine that arose during the rebuilding. Colt's reputation as a religious sect of hunters and builders grew over time, with outsiders speaking of them as zealots awaiting their messiah's return, for He would surely grace the small protected neighborhood He deemed worthy.

The well-appointed table stretched down the center of the main street, easily accommodating all 45 human citizens and their mashed potatoes, corn, fruit salad, platters of quail, and pots of Hasenpfeffer. A young woman pushed a cart loaded with bottles of cherry wine and cask ale. Two young men carried a roast boar that the elder explained had been expertly butchered to circumvent tainted meat. A teenage girl hauled baskets of warm bread fresh from the ovens.

Senior Wainright escorted Dot and Vincent to one end of the long table, seating them beside him like guests of honor, while Abraham remained at the entrance to the village with Gypsy still hidden in the treeline just beyond the security barrier. Dot wondered if they knew about her dog after spotting the mech and his wards from afar, but was afraid to ask for fear of revealing him. Instead, she addressed the village leader's advanced age.

"Mr. Wainright," Dot said. "May I ask, how old are you?"

"I turned forty in January. Why?"

Dot traced the man's many deep wrinkles, uneven skin tone, and long strands of gray hair, somehow aware that they didn't normally belong to a man of forty.

"Everyone else seems much younger. How is it you've staved off The Worm for so long?"

"I stay out of the sun whenever I can," he said. "Sunlight seems to exacerbate the virus, or so I've been led to believe. I guessed it must be true. When I do venture out, to supervise the field harvest and what not, I slather myself with a poultice of crushed walnuts and aloe, an old Colt recipe. The stuff also makes for a nice dessert topping in the summer!" The old man laughed for a moment before his face dropped to a more serious expression as he looked up at the iron cross atop the church steeple. "Above all that, I have faith, little girl. That's the open secret to living in this or any world. You must have faith."

Dot had more questions for the elder, to be worded carefully so as not to reveal her memory loss or her wanted status. Before she could utter her next thought, Wainright outstretched his hands, prompting the others to do the same. The villagers held hands and bowed their heads. Dot nodded to Vincent to follow their lead, but was surprised to find him already bowed in prayer.

"Let us pray," Senior Wainright said, taking one more look at the cross before shutting his eyes. He held Dot's hand to his right and Vincent's long, leafy fingers to his left. "Lord, we thank you for the bounty we're about to share, for the shelter where we raise our kin, and for the harvests that continue to defy disease and drought. Most of all, we thank you today for bringing us our new friend Dot and for delivering our brother Vincent back into our family. All of this, you have graced us with, and for all of this, we are grateful. We continue to hold you high in worship, oh Holy

Serpent, for you have granted us life while you smite all others with divine death. We continue to be your warriors and your children. Amen."

The rest of the villagers muttered "amen" and released hands, eager to start the evening feast. Vincent dug into a platter of roasted vegetables. Senior Wainright started with the stew, pouring a splash of his cherry wine into it as seasoning.

Dot replayed the last part of the prayer in her mind. Senior Wainright thanked the "Holy Serpent" for sparing them while killing countless others with what he saw as a deserved death. She realized that the villagers of Colt were lorded over by The Worm itself, that the townsfolk viewed the virus's widespread destruction as God's will.

She spooned potatoes and carrots onto her plate, accompanied by a tall stein of spring water. She felt repelled by the sight of the rabbit's legs sticking out of the stew pot, recalling the sight of the animals stretched out near the barrier. Though she was certainly hungry, she didn't feel famished like she did at Emerald Pond, and didn't favor meat for now.

She looked at the villagers around the table, content with their supper, and found it odd that not a single child sat among them.

"Where are the children?" Dot asked the elder. "Don't they eat with the adults?"

"These are all my children," he said.

"I mean, children like me."

"It's been a rough year," he said, unable to look her in the eye. "The few littles we had were taken by The Holy Serpent these past three winters. He clearly needed more angels under His wings."

"Are there any more like Vincent?" Dot considered not asking about hybrids, for she feared Abraham's many grim scenarios for them, but felt comfortable speaking with the elder at the moment.

"There's never been anyone like him," Senior Wainright said, placing his arm around the plant-man's waist. "And there never will be again. Vinny Greenblood is one of a kind."

"His name is Vincent."

"Of course, it is."

Three women sat up from the table and pulled long silver and black musical instruments from behind the wine cart. They sat on stools at the other end of the table and played a lively tune.

"You ever heard such melodies before?" Wainright asked.

"Not so lovely."

"You ever seen musical tools before?"

"That's a flute," Dot said, pointing to one of the women. "And those are clarinets."

"Is that a fact? I didn't know that. We always called them wind tools of grace. How did you get to be so bright?"

"I read about them once." She immediately regretted identifying the instruments, not wanting to appear gifted or special. She certainly wouldn't share the fact that she could expertly play those instruments, nor that she knew the melodic tune they played was Tchaikovsky's classic "Dance of the Sugar Plum Fairy."

"So, you know how to read?" Senior Wainright asked.

"A little," Dot said. "I'm sure most of these folks can read better than..."

"I'm the only one here who can interpret the old books." He put down his knife and fork and turned for a good look at his young guest. "I told you there's no one like Vincent. It seems the same is true for you."

"Thank you, Mr. Wainright." She tried to hide her regret and apprehension behind a polite smile.

"Dot, you continue to be full of surprises. After dinner, I may have a surprise or two of my own."

16

The 23rd Wife

After having her fill of root vegetables, fruit pie, and the crude yet pleasant entirety of the Nutcracker suite, Dot was taken to a house just outside the main village. Senior Wainright left her in the care of Clara, the flutist from dinner, a woman seemingly in her early-twenties with long blond hair and a flowing sundress to match, a thin outfit hardly befitting a cold night.

"Did you enjoy the feast, girl?" Clara asked.

"You folks know how to cook," Dot said. She spotted goosebumps on Clara's exposed arms. "Shouldn't you wear a coat? You might catch a cold."

"It's chilly at night," Clara said, "but Senior prefers us in our summer dresses year round. I find the night air refreshing, and I don't fear sickness, for I pray to the Serpent nightly. His love, and the Senior's love, help keep me warm."

"Must be nice," Dot said. "I need these fatigues to keep me warm."

"But they're so ill fitting, girl. They're meant for a man, a soldier."

"Well, right now they're meant for me."

"Don't worry, girl, we'll get you some proper clothes. We have some in your house. It's just ahead."

Dot still felt unsure about staying at the village, especially with Gypsy out in the woods alone, stationed at the perimeter, but felt some comfort in having her combat mech following close behind.

"Your guardian is impressive," Clara said. "Where did you acquire it?"

"We found him abandoned on the side of the road," Dot lied. "We managed to power him up and..."

"And it now follows you? How extraordinary! It must give you some comfort having it protect you out in the wild. I grew up hearing about the old walking war machines. I never thought I'd see one."

"Abraham is more than a war machine to me. He saved my life. He saved us all."

"That may be true, but its service to you doesn't change what it is. It has no life force like us, like the Serpent. It's normally tasked with taking precious life, not preserving it."

"So I've been told."

"Know that it is a machine and nothing more. Synthetics have no heart, girl."

"His name is Abraham, and my name is Dot."

"And my name is Clara," the woman said, sensing the girl's defensiveness. "Clara, 22nd in His Name."

"You sound like royalty."

Lynn Harrod

"I feel like royalty at times, but it's simply a feeling of pride... and gratitude."

Dot heard the pointed tone in her voice and stopped herself from starting an argument, retreating to placating this devout woman until she could figure out the situation.

"You played so well tonight," Dot said.

"Thank you. Senior says you're familiar with music. You knew our wind tools of grace. Did you recognize the piece we performed?"

"No," Dot lied again. "Where did you learn to play?"

"Alice taught me when I married the Senior."

"You're his wife?" Dot asked.

"I'm his newest wife. We married when the spring flowers arrived. I wore them in my hair."

"How many wives does he have?"

Clara looked at Dot with curiosity, as if she asked a nonsensical question.

"We're all his wives," Clara said.

"All of you? That means he has..."

"Twenty-two wives. He has a grand family."

Upon reaching the house, Clara opened the door and allowed Dot to enter first. The girl glanced back at her mech, relieved to have him always near, though she was still hesitant to step across the threshold.

"Go on," Clara said. "You need to get some sleep."

Being one of the homes that bore the bombings of the New World War, it appeared burnt and derelict from the outside. Upon entering it, Dot was surprised to see it freshly painted and brightly lit with candles, elegantly furnished with dainty wooden furniture, a small bed, and landscape paintings adorning the walls.

"I hope it's all to your liking," Clara said, gesturing for the girl to sit in a rocking chair beside a crackling wood-burning stove that warmed the room.

Dot slid into the rocking chair and noticed how small it was, as if made specifically for her size. The rest of the room's appointments were similarly customized. Most adults would have a hard time relaxing there.

"Perfect fit," Dot said.

"That's good. And don't worry, we'll build anew as you grow older."

"This is all very nice, but I'm not staying long."

Once again, Clara looked at the girl as if she made no sense. Dot rose from the chair to punctuate her decision.

"I'm heading east to search for my... friends," she said, unsure of what else to call the twin star girls in The Void, or the community hopefully awaiting her in Kellan.

"Spring is only a few months away. Can't you wait until then before you resume your search?"

"What's so important that I'm here in the spring?"

"That's traditionally when we marry the Senior," Clara said. "You'll be moving in with him for a time."

Dot suddenly felt alarmed, realizing in horror that she'd been treated as the guest of honor, complete with a feast and entertainment, because she was expected to become the 23rd wife of the elder. She read the blank, almost stern expression on Clara's face and didn't bother disagreeing with her. She realized there was no point in arguing against their strict beliefs while standing in the middle of their isolated village. Such heresy might even prove dangerous.

"My apologies," the girl said, smoothing her tone. "I didn't realize the importance of spring, but it makes sense. It's the season of new beginnings."

"Senior said you were bright," Clara said with a renewed smile. "Vincent isn't leaving, either. Senior is to task him with the gardens again, where he will toil the day long, every day, in the Lord Serpent's name as he did before Father Francis stole him from us."

"Is that what you think he did?" Dot heard the edge in her voice and quickly adjusted. "I haven't yet learned your history."

Clara looked out the window at the scorched landscape that made up most of Colt. "I was just a child, younger than you, but I remember the night Father Young betrayed us all. When the Purists came, he abandoned us, stole our gardener, and spit on the doctrine of the Holy Serpent. Senior made a vow that nothing and no one would ever be taken from us again." She leaned in close to whisper in Dot's face. "We have guardians capable of taking precious life, too."

"You're right," Dot said, feigning a yawn. "I do need to get some sleep."

"I'm sure you've had a long day, but I'm so glad you're here now. We all are."

"I'm honored, Clara."

"I know. Senior says you're the perfect addition to our family."

"He's as kind as he is generous."

"His words are more than kindness," Clara said. "His words are wisdom. You're perfect for Colt because you'll have babies born without The Worm, and we will rise again to people the world. Good night, girl."

Clara walked out, shutting the door behind her. Dot waited for the sound of a lock but heard none. Her act must have been convincing.

She stood frozen in place, her fake smile and forced courtesy still stuck with fear even as she heard the woman walk away. She stared at the room, its small scale created just for her, as the dire situation finally unfolded.

Dot was to marry Senior Wainright, becoming his 23rd wife.

The villagers know she's immune to The Worm.

Vincent will once again become a slave to the village.

Dot's immediate and singular thought was to wait for everyone to retire to bed, leave the house in the wee hours to find Vincent, and leave the village during the dead of night.

17

The Old Barn

Senior Wainright walked with Vincent, arm in arm, his lantern lighting the way as they approached the barn by the creek where they first encountered each other earlier. Vincent was happy to be back with friends he'd long forgotten and thought he'd never see again. The familiar trail, the birch trees, and the sound of the creek brought him back to a time when Father Young cared for him in the barn's hayloft.

"You remember the barn?" Senior Wainright asked.

"I remember it very well. Father used to read to me on rainy nights, and stay when electricity fell from the sky."

"The storms scared you, didn't they, boy?"

"Only when I was alone."

"You'll never be alone again, Vincent. That's the beauty of Colt. You're back home now."

"I'll never be alone because I have Dot and Abe and Gypsy."

"Gypsy?"

Vincent looked away, remembering that Gypsy was supposed to remain secret, hidden from the villagers.

"Gypsy is what I call the ghost of Father," Vincent said, surprised at how easily he lied. "He died and won't grow back, so I imagine his spirit watching over me."

"His spirit does watch over you, boy. Always remember that."

"Yep, I always do."

"And you call him 'Gypsy'?"

"Yep, I always do that, too."

"Francis always was a wandering soul," Senior Wainright said as they reached the barn.

Vincent's smile fell away as the dark barn's open double doors suddenly looked like an awaiting maw in the night.

"Go on in, boy," Wainright said. "Vinny Greenblood is home again."

Upon entering the barn, Vincent's mind flooded with days and nights that had been blocked by his idyllic memories for years. He felt the exhaustion of the long hours he worked in Colt's fields, the pressure to produce more food for the village, the torment of the children and their endless abuse, both verbal and physical. He remembered being tied to the walls of the barn with his own vines and whipped for not working hard enough, always berated for not being human enough. They called him stupid, lazy, unworthy of living in a human village, lucky to be alive, and ungrateful for the villagers' mercy. Father Young alone defended him, and in defying the Holy Serpent's will, he willingly suffered whips and canes alongside his adopted son, their blood pooling together in the hay strewn on the barn floor.

Vincent had been in the safety of his North Woods farm for so long, he'd forgotten the personal Hell that Colt truly was. There were many moments in his life when he felt dumb, but that moment of realization stung, and he felt like the complete fool so many had called him.

Senior Wainright walked to the back of the barn. His lantern revealed the plight of the nine hybrids Abraham detected when they first arrived just after dawn, seemingly a lifetime ago.

Nine adult animal-human hybrids lay on the floor, their bodies weak and spirits broken, ankles chained to the wall.

Three men in farmer's coveralls were clearly dog-human. Two women in sundresses like Clara's appeared to be part chimpanzee. Beside them sat three teenage girls in smocks, their pointy ears and short yellow fur covered in leopard spots. The largest of them looked like an actual bear with only his coveralls and timid expression giving him away.

Vincent knew who they were but hardly recognized them, having last seen them as children.

"Why are they chained up?" Vincent asked. "Did they do something wrong?"

"Wrong? Their existence is wrong. These Beasties are in chains because they're wild animals masquerading as men and women. They're not innocent, gentle Veggies like you, boy. They're abominations. We can't have them walking around, living in houses, breaking bread at our table like they're members of our flock. Your father and I never saw eye-to-eye on that, but he left them behind while The Lord remained, always watching."

"So why are they here? If they're abomin... abominshuns... what you called them. Why not let them leave?"

"Oh, I wish I could," Senior Wainright said. "How I want nothing more than to let them walk away from this hallowed ground, never to return. But what kind of holy servant would I be if I let them leave to overrun another village? That would be wrong, wouldn't it?"

"I thought... I remember the Greenies shooting them, taking them away."

"We had a few dozen of these animals living here under your father's protection by the time the Purists arrived, but even their big truck couldn't hold them all, and Francis didn't want them killed, so I made a deal with their captain. I keep the world safe by holding them here on this sacred land, and the Greens can come take them for their own purposes whenever they see fit."

"They just come and... they take them away?"

"Not every day, just sometimes. They take one, come back a month later, take another two. It's why I keep them alive and healthy in this barn. That's why there's now nine when there used to be thirty-nine. That's why the soldiers left our village standing. Everyone wins. Am I right?"

"Everyone?" Vincent said, surprised at his own defiance. "Senior, I can't stay. I need to be with Dottie to protect her. I promised Father."

"I understand, boy, I truly do. I knew the kind of man your father was, and I know what it means to be on a mission, to be true to your word. The good news is the girl is staying, so if you need to protect her, if you need to keep your promise, this is where you must be."

"Dottie said she's staying?" Vincent asked, incredulous.

"Absolutely! You saw her at dinner. Everyone loved her! And she loved them! She's with her own kind again. Why would she ever want to leave? Am I right?"

"But those two girls in the darkness need her..."

"We need her, boy!" Wainright said, dismissing his comment as a fool's gibberish. "We're out here in the dark, too! And there's a whole hell of a lot more than two of us. Am I right?"

"I guess so," Vincent said, unsure. "I guess it'll be good for her here."

"Just as it will be good for you, too." Senior Wainright pulled a key from his jacket pocket and placed it in Vincent's hand. "Now that I'll have you running the fields again, I can pull my men out and put you and these nine to work. You see, my men could never stomach being around them, but with you in charge, there'll be no need for these terrible chains. Am I right? We can take them off? Please say we can take them off. The key is literally in your hand, boy, not mine."

"Yes," Vincent said, helpless. "Let's take off the chains."

"I knew you'd see things my way. Your strong vines can keep them in check if they get out of line, but hybrids always look out for each other. They won't think of defying you. As I said before, everyone wins."

"It doesn't feel like an everyone-wins." The key felt hot on his palm.

"Think about it, boy." Senior Wainright closed Vincent's long fingers over the key. "You don't want to see them get hurt, and they don't want to see you get hurt. It's pure harmony."

"Harmony is good," Vincent said, his fate sinking in.

"You get to work the crops, which is your passion in life. You get to be with your own kind where you belong, and you'll always know that the girl is safe from harm, just across the village."

"Safe is good."

Senior Wainright walked out of the barn, leaving Vincent in the dark with the nine hybrids.

"My boy," Wainright said as he started to shut the barn's double doors. "When you said you called Francis Young's spirit 'Gypsy,' I confess, I was relieved. For a moment, I thought you were referring to that big beast of a dog we caught earlier by the treeline. I'd hate it if we ended up eating something you had an affection for."

"That wouldn't be good."

"Sleep well, boy. Be grateful that the Lord brought you back to us. I can tell you I am."

As Senior Wainright shut the barn doors, locking it with a heavy chain, Vincent felt around in the dark with his vines and unlocked his hybrid brethren's chains.

18

Dot Alone

After lying awake atop the covers of her little bed for two agonizing hours, Dot slowly opened the door to the brisk night air, relieved to see Abraham still standing nearby. The giant mech stood silent and motionless, staring at the distant trees. She found it odd that he didn't turn and look down at her when she stepped out of the house, but soon discovered why.

Two men armed with machetes and rifles circled the robot, poking him and climbing up his legs to peer into his chest, into the empty central compartment Dot had been traveling in.

"Jonah, what is this?" one of them asked.

"Keep your voice down, Micah," the other man said. "The girl is sleeping."

"Why's its chest empty like that? That little space right there. What's that for?"

"The girl was riding in it earlier," Jonah said, keeping his voice low. "It normally holds the biggest weapons, mostly bombs."

Dot hid behind a shrub and eavesdropped as the two men – Micah and Jonah – kept prodding Abraham during their whispery exchange.

"Damn, so this thing actually used its bombs?" Micah said.

"Probably nuked an entire town. It's what they do."

"So why did it keep the girl and the Veggie alive?"

"Use your head," Jonah said. "It was taking them to the Greens. They've been out for her."

"What do they want with a kid?"

"Science thing. She's special. Could be a hybrid."

"A hybrid that passes for human?" Micah said. "Now that is special! I bet Senior's gonna rework their arrangement, trade her for a truckload of canned goods, weapons, maybe some liquor. Could be the best deal he's ever made with them."

"No, she stays," Jonah said. "Senior says the Lord brought her here to bear children without The Worm, make the world right again for the right people."

Dot wondered how Senior Wainright knew about her unique condition. The only explanation was that he learned it through his regular communications with the Purists.

"So, there's no way she's no hybrid," Micah said. "Senior wouldn't marry no hybrid, much less have kids with it."

"It doesn't matter. The Lord Serpent has willed it."

"So, it's true. He's gonna make her Wife 23."

"It makes sense," Jonah said. "Giving them the Beasties week after week is one thing, but letting the Greens take our best chance at survival, spreading the word to all four corners, that'd be foolish."

"What about the Veggie?"

"Senior says he belongs here."

"So we're keeping them both for ourselves?" Micah asked.

"It's the right move. The stupid Greens will never know."

"Stupid or not, they'll get a little suspicious when they see this war machine standing here like a statue."

"By then it'll will be ours to command. We just need to figure out how to work it."

"Yeah, well, until then, it might as well be an actual statue."

"It's nighttime," Jonah said. "Power source is drained. These things recharge in the sun. We'll get it running tomorrow. No sense in standing around out here. It's not like some passing raiders can steal it."

"Senior will be disappointed that we failed to power it up tonight." Micah dreaded the elder's wrath.

"He'll understand, but he probably won't know. By the time he wakes up, the machine will be ours."

The two guards walked away, back to the central village, down the Broken Road. Dot continued to listen to their chatter and waited for their voices to fade out before emerging from behind cover.

She walked up to Abraham, dismayed that her sentinel would be a motionless drone until he'd absorbed a full morning's sun, by which time her chances of fleeing the village with her friends would be slim. She climbed the mech and sat on his shoulder for a bird's-eye view of Colt and wondered where Vincent could be.

To her surprise, Abraham's left arm raised. He opened his palm, revealing a small electronic device the size of a walnut. He held it up to Dot. She took it, not understanding what it was.

"Request: Place the cochlear implant in your ear."

Abraham's voice sounded distant. The words repeated, and Dot realized it came from the small device. She placed it in her ear and heard her mechanical friend's voice with clarity, sounding as if all the world could hear it as well.

"Request: Use the cochlear implant to communicate with this unit."

"Abraham?" Dot whispered. "You can hear me?"

"Correct."

"From the device in my ear?"

"Status: The cochlear implant is a continually operational two-way communications implement only we can discern. No one else can hear me address you."

"Smart thinking," she said. "Is it true that your power is drained?"

"Status: This unit's reserve power is at 35 percent."

"Is that enough to get us out of here?"

"Projection: Reserve power is sufficient if we reach the minimum safe distance by sunrise."

"We need to be away from here so you can recharge with no one around, with no interruptions."

"Correct."

"That means we need to be gone well before the sun comes up."

"Correct."

"Can you help me find Vincent?" she asked.

"Status: To conserve power, this unit must remain here until our time of departure."

"So, it's up to me," Dot said. "It's just as well. With you walking around, we'll be heard or spotted pretty quick. Can you at least tell me where he is?"

"Location: Vincent is presently located in the barn at the northern limit of the township."

"That's way across the village, near where we came in." Dot suddenly felt overwhelmed. "Okay, I think I can make my way without being seen. Gypsy can join me. He isn't far from there."

"Incorrect," Abraham said. "Gypsy is no longer at his assigned station at the northern perimeter."

"Where is he?" Dot asked, concerned.

"Location: Gypsy is now in a commercial structure at the eastern limit of the township."

"How far is that from where we left him?"

"Location: His current position is 1.7 kilometers from his assigned station."

"Something's wrong," Dot said. "He'd never stray as far as that. Is he patrolling the area?"

"Negative. His position has not changed for 3.9 hours."

"Abraham!" Dot said, fearing the worst. "Tell me what's going on!"

"Probability: Gypsy is likely in danger, discovered by the citizenry. Because of his breed's resistance to the WN1M global pathogen, there is a high probability they took him to the township's mess hall to be harvested for meat."

Dot became light-headed from the dire news. Barely holding back her welling emotions, she looked out across Colt and spotted the barn to the north and a lone building to the east, one that looked more utilitarian than the villagers' houses. She wanted to run to her friends but didn't know who to search for first.

"I know where the barn is," Dot said, her heart racing. "But what would a mess hall look like?"

"Speculation: Given the town's limited number of functional structures, the mess hall would likely double as an abattoir. It would be an outlying building because of its pungent odors of butchered meat, a single-story structure equipped with a large commercial kitchen and ample seating."

"An old restaurant."

"Correct."

"I think I see it. I hope my good boy is okay."

Abraham sensed the girl's heartbeat rising above 120 bpm along with a sudden spike in her levels of epinephrine and norepinephrine. Her pained expression and elevated stress triggered his assistance response.

"Assessment: Gypsy is a German Shepherd, a canine breed known for strength, courage, and perseverance. He has extensive military training and displays above-average intelligence for his species. He is disciplined, loyal, and fearless. There is a notable probability that Gypsy will prevail, Little Miss."

"Abraham, are you... trying to comfort me?" Dot asked.

"Clarification: This unit is listing the factors of the situation in order to deduce an optimal strategy."

"I'm pretty sure this is your way of being sweet and kind."

"Clarification: This unit is incapable of empathic processes and emotional gestures."

"If you say so," Dot said knowingly. "I could have sworn for a moment that you were worried about my feelings."

The war machine stood silent for a moment, as if confused, rifling through its many possible responses.

"Strategy: You must seek our allies alone to allow this unit time to conserve power..."

"Yes, Abraham, we covered that."

"Recommendation: Locate Vincent first."

"Why Vincent first?" the girl asked.

"Status: Vincent is being detained with the nine missing unknown lifeforms."

"The hybrids."

"Correct."

"Why go there first?"

"Projection: The nine hybrids haven't moved since our arrival. They are likely being held captive. There is a high probability that Vincent is similarly imprisoned."

Dot's mind raced from the task that lay before her. "Anything else I should know before I leave you?"

"Analysis: The citizenry consumed tainted meat at evening's meal. The larger animals served showed signs of the WN1M pathogen."

"Tainted meat?" Dot asked. "But Senior Wainright said they cut around the bad bits."

"Analysis: Though they were prepared to minimize threat of exposure, the citizenry consumed mild portions of tainted meat, which has been known to compromise mental health."

"You mean it's driven them mad," Dot said. "They didn't eat enough to kill them, just enough to scramble their brains."

"Correct."

Dot recalled Sergeant Furst saying that only some small game, like rabbits and squirrels, were safe to eat. She thought back to dinner, to the many villagers that feasted on wild boar and deer. If they unknowingly infected themselves with low levels of tainted meat, altering their minds, it might explain why the honorable man George described, the kind-hearted elder that Father Young remembered, was now a heartless despot, a tyrant who regularly traded hybrids with the Purists as if they were merely commodities. It would explain why he demanded that every woman and girl join his harem, wearing thin sundresses year round for his pleasure.

"We can't save the villagers, can we?" Dot asked.

"Analysis: The citizenry's compromised mental health is irreversible and coupled with their zealous devotion to their invented faith."

"All we have is us," Dot said, once again thinking back to Sergeant Furst's last words.

"Correct."

Dot climbed down the mech. Upon reaching the ground, she shivered from both the night air and the perilous task ahead.

"Wish me luck," she said. "Don't move a muscle until I get back."

"Request: Do not die, Little Miss."

"Thanks, Abraham. I feel better already."

19

The Last Nine

Using the key from Senior Wainright, Vincent unlocked the chains of the nine hybrids imprisoned in the back of the dark barn. With the double doors shut and locked, moonlight streamed in through missing shingles in the roof high above. With his bioluminescent eyes, Vincent could see them on the floor while they could only see his curious, glowing stare looking down at them.

"My name is Vincent." He gathered up their chains and piled them in a corner. "They also call me Vinny Greenblood, Veggie Vinny, Dim Vin, the Green Fool, Vincent Vines, but I like to go by Vincent and Dottie says that's okay."

The nine hybrids remained silent, still not sure if Vincent was one of the villagers, though his fluorescent gaze gave some reason to think otherwise.

"You ain't one of them," one of the dog-men said. "You ain't human, are you, Vinny?"

"Am I human?" Vincent said with an amused grin. "Now that's new! No one's ever asked me that before! Except Dottie. She asked me that when we first met."

"He can't be no human, Ephraim," another dog-man said. "He wouldn't have freed us if he was."

"We may have gotten these chains off," a chimp-woman said, "but we ain't free. Senior locked those doors for a reason, and ain't nothing ever gettin' through them. Lord knows we tried. He's stuck in here just like us."

"I can see you, but you guys can't see me?" Vincent realized the darkness hid his features.

"The women can," the third dog-man said. "Monkeys and cats see real good in the dark."

"We ain't no monkeys, Elijah!" the second chimp-woman said with a low howl. "You remember that!" She turned back to Vincent. "If you ain't no human, then what are you?"

"I'm me!" Vincent said proudly.

"That's ain't very helpful, Vinny." Ephraim grunted and looked up at the gaps in the roof. "Apphia's right, you're stuck in here with us, whatever you are."

Vincent got the impression that the dog-man named Ephraim was their leader. "Boy, you sure are grumpy," he said. "I guess I would be, too, if I was trapped in a barn."

"He's not too bright, is he?" Elijah said with a snort.

"Sorry if I seem 'grumpy,' Vincent," Ephraim said with a dry tone, "but it's hard to trust a man I can't see."

Vincent looked around and spotted a lantern and a hammer on a shelf across the barn. He grabbed them from their resting spots with two of his vines, the silhouette of which startled the confused hybrids. To them, it looked like a tall man flung long snakes across the room. With a single powerful whip of a vine, he struck the hammer across the head of a nail protruding from a wall, creating a spark to light the lantern.

"There we go," Vincent said, slowly turning up the light, exposing himself to his brethren. "Now we can get to know each other!"

"So, you are a hybrid," Ephraim said, barely believing the sight of the bizarre green creature. "But what animal are you?"

"I'm a plant-hybrid. Human-plantae-liana if you wanna get scientifical. Father says I'm the last one."

"Great big guy over there is the last bear," Ephraim said. "I'm sure we'll all be the last of our kinds soon enough, Vinny."

"I said my name is Vincent. What are your names?"

"Speaking of something's no one's ever asked, I'm Ephraim." He pointed to the two other dog hybrids beside him. "These are my brothers, Ezekiel and Elijah."

"Apphia," the first chimp-woman said. "My sister is Ahlai."

"What about you girls?" Vincent shone the lantern on the three teenage leopard-hybrids huddled together.

Ephraim answered for them. "Their names are Sapphire, Sherah, and Salome."

"Such beautiful names!" Vincent said. "Nice to meet you all. How long have you girls..."

"They can't talk," Ephraim said. "Cat hybrids never do."

"What about the big guy in the corner?" Vincent nodded toward the bear-man, looking down at the floor.

"Tell him your name," Ephraim said to the bear, his firm tone akin to an order. "Go on."

The bear-man looked up at Vincent but offered no response, as if greetings were pointless in their seemingly hopeless situation.

"That's Solomon," Ahlai said. "He can talk but chooses not to."

"I understand," Vincent said. "I don't always talk either. A few years ago, I didn't talk for almost 20 minutes! I was trying to remember a joke about a chicken trying to cross a road. Still can't remember it. Maybe it was a goose."

"The reason Solomon doesn't talk," Apphia said, "is because the villagers whipped him last time he spoke out of line, something he used to do a lot."

"He also tried to run a lot," Ephraim said, "but his talking and running days are over. You won't hear a peep out of him…"

"What are you going to do with us?" Solomon said in a deep growl, surprising his peers. "Speak truth, tree man."

"You heard Senior Wainright," Vincent said. "He wants me to work you in the fields."

"Ain't no field work to be done at this hour," Apphia said.

"That's true," Vincent said, "so we're gonna do something else."

"And what's that, Vinny?" Ephraim asked, defiant. "What do you have planned for us in that little cabbage of a brain?"

Vincent flung his many vines at the immense, locked double doors and yanked them from their hinges with incredible force. The heavy oak doors flew violently toward the group. Solomon quickly reached up to catch them before they could crush his friends, but nothing landed in his giant paws.

He looked up and saw the barn doors hanging in the air above him, suspended by Vincent's vines.

"Damn, Vinny, not even Solomon could ever do that!" Ephraim said, astonished by the plant-man's strength.

"The fiercest storm could never do that," Solomon said, realizing he misjudged the tall, spindly creature. He helped Vincent place the doors gently on the floor to avoid alerting the villagers.

"Last of your kind?" Ephraim said, eyes wide with hope, the first to rise to his feet. "What the hell did you say you were again?"

"I'm Vincent!"

"I ask again," Solomon said. "What are you going to do with us?"

"You mean, what are we going to do? We're going to get out of here."

"But we can't," Ahlai said, her chimpanzee tail curling around her in fear. "Doesn't matter if the doors are open. They'll catch us, offer us to the Greens."

"Trying to run always gets you with the Greens," Elijah said.

"Not this time, brother," Ephraim said. "Not with Vinny... Vincent... with us now."

20

A Dangerous Plan

Dot lurked in the shadows of the central houses. Most of the villagers had retired for the night, leaving only a handful of armed guards patrolling the Broken Road that ran between them. Her eyes traced the yellow line that ran down the middle, extending east into the distance, to their escape.

Timing the guards' movements, she sprinted and ducked behind trees and under abandoned vehicles, just as she did in Wellspring. Except this time, she didn't have her trusty dog to defend her. If any of those men spotted Dot, it would doom her and her friends to remain in Colt at the whims of the deranged elder and his poisoned flock of devout followers.

Emerging at the northern edge of the neighborhood, she could see both the barn ahead and the lone utility building far to the east. For a moment, she considered searching for Gypsy first, for she desperately needed him, but the thought of Vincent and the imprisoned hybrids brought her back to focus, back to Abraham's plan.

With one last guard to pass, she ran to a barrel and jumped in, hoping it wouldn't topple over as she fell awkwardly inside. Landing on her head against a pile of spoiled berries, she froze upside-down and held her mouth shut, trying to control her heavy breathing. After a long, tense minute, she heard footsteps approaching and regretted her decision to hide there.

The footsteps sounded louder, closer, until they suddenly stopped. Dot prepared to shove the barrel over and scurry out. She couldn't fight the guard, but perhaps she could outrun him, make it to the barn, and free the hybrids while he went for help.

Two hands reached in and grabbed her, and in that frightening moment she fought his grip and swayed the barrel, but it proved too heavy to tip. The man grabbed Dot by her oversized coat and pulled her out, kicking and swinging her arms wildly. The hands felt strange, as if their fingers were topped with small blades, scratching her skin.

Out in the moonlight, Dot saw that the man's face bizarrely resembled Gypsy's, but with short, black hair. She knew immediately that he was an animal hybrid, just like the ones in Father Young's idyllic paintings.

"Quiet!" the dog-man said in a whispered shout. "Are you the girl?"

"Yes," Dot said without thinking, without knowing if she could trust him. She turned, startled to see two other dog-men with him, wielding garden tools like weapons.

"Take it easy," the dog-man said, seeing the fear on her face. "They won't hurt you. These are my brothers."

"Your brothers?"

"We don't look alike, but yes, they're my brothers. You can trust them."

"But can I trust you?"

"Vincent sent us. My name is Ephraim." He turned to his brothers. "The shaggy one is Ezekiel. The large one is Elijah."

"Gentlemen," Dot said with a nod. She still felt unsure about these men, despite the mention of her friend's name. As if to help process the shocking sight of such strange creatures, Dot identified their animal breeds.

Ephraim was a sleek black Doberman hybrid.

Ezekiel was a tall white-and-black Newfoundland.

Elijah was a muscular brown Mastiff.

"You know Vincent?" she asked.

"We know him now," Ezekiel said. "He told us to find you."

"It's all part of his plan," Elijah said.

"Keep it down," Ephraim said, peering out from behind the barrels for any movement. He'd heard a faint sound coming from behind one of the houses. Though the howling wind cloaked it, he trained all his senses on its cadence.

"Vincent came up with a plan?" Dot asked.

"A plan to get us out," Ezekiel said.

"He's as smart as he is strong," Elijah said.

"He's also brave."

"Yes, Vincent is very brave for a walking tree."

"No claws or fangs, but a strong spirit and a stout heart."

"You speak like a poet, Ezekiel."

"Thank you, brother. It's from something Apphia said."

"Ah, of course. She's always had a talent for words."

"How I envy her gift."

"Brothers!" Ephraim said in a hushed shout, still scanning the area. "I told you to keep it down."

"Yes, brother," Ezekiel said.

Dot knew the plant-man better than the dogs, and she didn't feel completely at ease knowing that strangers were following Vincent's instructions. Her innocent, naive friend always had the best of intentions but without foresight or strategy, and she doubted his little black book covered their current predicament.

"How did you know where to find me?" Dot asked.

"We could smell you across the village," Elijah said.

"Human youth has a distinct scent," Ezekiel said.

"I believe 'odor' is the right word."

"Perhaps 'stench' is better."

"Yes, that is better, Elijah. An odor hangs in the air while a foul stench leaves a trail like the one we followed..."

"Okay, gentlemen, I got it," Dot said, oddly embarrassed. "Yes, I stink. I confess, I haven't bathed in... never."

"Believe us, we know."

"Quiet!" Ephraim said in another soft shout. He gestured for the group to stay low as the last guard walked away behind the homes.

Sensing no one else for the moment, Ephraim stood up and looked sternly at the group. "No more idle chit-chat, brothers. And you, girl, your little barrel stunt almost gave us away. Clumsily leaping in like that, what were you trying to do?"

"I thought you were a guard," Dot said, brushing crushed berries off her fatigues. "I didn't want to be captured."

"A Colt guard wouldn't try to capture you. He'd run to sound the alarm."

"Even with a gun in one hand and a blade in the other," Elijah said, "no human would dare face us alone."

"Cowards all, if you ask me," Ezekiel said.

"Agreed, brother."

"No claws nor fangs, no spirit nor heart."

"Brothers!" Ephraim felt frustrated with his younger siblings. "Please stay focused."

"My friend said you were being held prisoner," Dot said. "How did you get out?"

"Your plant friend freed us," Ephraim said. "He asked us to find you, to keep you safe, and to search for another like us. A man named 'Gypsy.' We think he's in the mess hall."

"You can smell him too?"

"We can smell everyone and everything, girl."

"Well, Gypsy's not a man," Dot said. "Can't you smell that?"

Confused, Ephraim looked to his brothers. Before another word, he quickly led the pack farther away from the homes, out of sight of two approaching guards whose scent he'd barely caught seconds before.

"You're saying this Gypsy isn't one of us?" Ephraim asked once they were safely alone to talk. "Then why do we care what happens to him?"

"He is one of you, but not a man."

"Impossible," Ezekiel said. "There are no more true dogs."

"Well, Gypsy is."

"A genuine, true dog?" Elijah looked at his brothers in awe. "Another last of his kind."

"Vincent said you're special, too," Ephraim said, puzzled. "He said both the Greens and the Blues hunt you."

"Maybe she's dangerous?" Ezekiel asked, alarmed.

"Calm yourself, brother. Does she look dangerous?"

"No, but maybe she's a witch?" Elijah said.

"I don't think so."

"Maybe she's the last witch," Ezekiel said. "Could be she created the last true dog and the last remaining Veggie?"

"But who created her?" Elijah asked.

"That's a good question, brother."

"How I envy her gift."

"Gentlemen, I'm no witch," Dot said with a dismissive glare. "I don't even believe in the supernatural." She sounded unconvinced given the fact that she could apparently pull her friends into her nightly dreams and was on a quest to seek two mysterious figures made of light.

"Then who are you people?" Ephraim asked firmly.

"I'm not the last anything. I'm actually the first... it doesn't matter."

"Whether or not it matters, we deserve to know. The only reason we're not running to the river right now is our promise to Vincent."

"Where is Vincent?" Dot asked.

The three brothers looked at each other before revealing Dot's friend's risky strategy.

"He went to talk with the elder," Ephraim said.

"He's going to Senior Wainright?" Dot said, alarmed. "And you let him?"

"He wouldn't listen to us. He thinks he can reason with him, convince him to let us all go."

"That's his plan?"

"Now that it's been said out loud," Elijah said, "perhaps Vincent's plan isn't as good as we'd thought."

"Strong and brave," Ezekiel said, "but perhaps not very smart."

"Plant hybrids never are," Dot said. "At least, that's what others have said."

"Brothers, we need to go to the mess hall now!" Ephraim said with a growl, halting their discussion. "If Gypsy really is a true dog, they may be harvesting him as we speak! Senior believes pure canine meat is rare because it's divine."

Dot felt torn, with both Vincent and Gypsy in danger on opposite ends of the village. As safe as she felt with Ephraim and his brothers, and their determination to save her dog, she was more concerned with her gentle plant friend. Unlike these tough hybrids, Vincent wasn't a powerful fighter. Once again, the memory of seeing him shot to pieces flooded her thoughts.

"Which house is the Senior's?" Dot asked.

"He lives in the church," Ephraim said, hoping Dot wasn't planning what he imagined.

Dot spotted the steeple in the distance. "You go find Gypsy. I'm going to stop Vincent."

"You're delusional, girl. Vincent may not change Senior's mind, but he'll live. The Senior seems to like him. They have history. Meanwhile, Gypsy may already be dead while we stand here arguing."

"Then one of you come with me."

"There are guards between here and the mess hall," Ephraim said, growing impatient. "I can smell several from here, more than usual. It may take all of us to save the last true dog in existence. We can't leave him to chance. No, you must come with us and leave Vincent to his choice."

"Then you all go," Dot said, not once considering leaving her friend behind. "Save Gypsy. Please. I'll stay out of sight. They can't smell me like you can."

"Don't be so sure," Elijah said. "You already smell of rotten human. Now you smell of rotten berries."

"Just do as I ask. I'm special, remember? They'll come for me while you run to the river."

"We won't leave you alone, girl," Ephraim said.

"I won't be alone. I have another friend helping me. A powerful friend."

"Where is he?"

"He's... in my ear," Dot said. "He'll be able to talk to me once I'm back on that side of the village. It's hard to explain."

Lynn Harrod

Before any of them could protest further, Dot made her way toward the church near the circle of houses. To her surprise, the three dog-men obeyed her wishes and headed east to search for Gypsy, leaving her alone to locate Vincent and convince him to abandon his foolhardy idea of reasoning with a madman.

21

The Dark Chapel

Dot circled the church twice, keeping low, crouched in bushes, looking for a way inside. On her third trip around, she heard a familiar voice through a lit window.

"Why would I lie to you?" the male voice asked someone. "When have I ever tried to deceive you?"

Though it sounded faint, under duress, Dot recognized the tired, grizzled voice and forced charm as the elder's.

"Alert," Abraham said through Dot's earpiece, startling her. "There is a man inside the church." She was once again within range of the mech's communication.

"I know, Abraham," Dot said in a trembling whisper. "Thank you." She had to remind herself that no one but her could hear him despite his voice sounding so loud.

"Location: He is 6.5 meters west of you."

"I can hear him. Are there any guards coming?"

"Reconnaissance: The night patrol is focused on your designated house, the central neighborhood, and the mess hall. Based on observed patterns, four guards normally patrol near the church. However, they have consumed large amounts of intoxicants and are returning to their quarters in uneven paths."

"They got drunk," Dot said.

"Correct. Strong pear cider and cherry wine appear most present."

"Good. Let them sleep it off. Four less for us to worry about." Dot stepped onto a pile of firewood under the window, ensuring a firm stance. "I need to be quiet now, Abraham. You're free to talk, but I won't be able to respond."

"Acknowledgment."

Peering in through the window, it surprised Dot to find Senior Wainright alone, seated in front of a large desktop machine. He held a seven-inch metal rod that was tethered to the machine and spoke into it.

"I told you, I have seen no girl," Wainright said. "If I had, I would have radioed you immediately."

"Give us the girl and our pact is complete," a voice from the machine said, the same monotone male voice Dot heard repeatedly in Wellspring and on the Broken Road. Whoever spoke with the elder employed the voice of all Automen.

"We're getting our wires crossed," Senior Wainright said with a little laugh. "No pun intended to you and your synthetic comrades. Let's start over. What does this girl look like?"

"She looks like a fifteen-year-old human girl that isn't part of your congregation, draped in the enemy's uniform."

Dot could see the predicament on the elder's face. He wanted to keep Dot – and Vincent – to himself for the supposed betterment of his village but didn't want the full force of the Purists invading Colt after sensing his deception. It often proved difficult to lie to an Automan.

"You mentioned her companions," Senior said into the metal rod. "I don't know about a plant-man or any dogs, but I have the war machine. It's a big one. It's powered down, not far from me."

"The Abraham-class combat unit has imprinted on the girl. If it's there, so is she."

"You don't listen very well, my artificial friend. I told you, the machine is powered down. The girl likely ran off when it drained. Why would she stay with a lifeless robot?"

"We're sending a squad to investigate. They'll arrive by sunrise."

The news sent a chill through the elder. Despite his precarious agreement with the Purists, he never fully trusted them, not since the night they raided the village and nearly burned everyone alive. They were capable of anything when they didn't get what wanted.

"Sunrise, got it," Senior Wainright said, fearing the worst. "I'll be sure to roll out the red carpet for you boys."

From the corner of his eye, he saw a shadow move across the wall and knew he wasn't alone. Either a Purist scout had infiltrated his village or...

"One of my men is reporting in right now," the elder said. "Looks like they just secured that girl you're looking for."

"Then our pact is complete. We'll retrieve her upon arrival. The plant hybrid is yours."

Senior Wainright didn't believe them for a moment.

"Look, I told you, I don't know about any plant..."

The transmission ended before he could finish his lie. The Automen had long been wise to his secrets and devotion to his agenda, having analyzed the timbre and inflection of his voice many times.

"It seems they're immune to my charms." He turned to face the open door to the chapel and called out to the darkness beyond. "It seems you are, too. You can come out now, girl."

During the elder's communication with the Purists, Dot had snuck in through a side door and hid in a corner of the chapel, near the entrance to Senior's office and bedroom. She'd been looking for Vincent but found only rows of empty pews facing a pulpit. She'd made her way to his open doorway when he spotted her shadow.

"If you're looking for Vincent," he said, "he's with me now, back where he belongs."

"You're lying," Dot said from the dark chapel, having given up her charade. She heard her voice echo against the chapel walls and angled ceiling. It would help hide her position in the vast church. "Vincent's not with you in any way."

"He's out picking me some fresh sprigs of mint for my tea. I didn't want him around while I was on my business call. Why would I lie to you?"

"You must say that to everyone you meet," Dot said. "You've been lying all along. At dinner, you said you were against technology, but you have a two-way radio to talk with the soldiers while your men try to operate my mech."

"Just because I loathe technology, the same arrogant science that ended the world and threw us last remaining few into a race for survival, doesn't mean I'm above exploiting it. I despise guns, too, but we've stockpiled plenty of those."

"You said you were all about family, but you've enslaved the hybrids that used to live among you."

"Them living with us like ordinary folk was always Francis's mission, not mine," Wainright said. "He abandoned us to the

Greens, and I had to do whatever was necessary in order to keep Colt alive and in order. My men are brave, but they can't fight an army. Decisions had to be made."

"What decisions? You're not making sense, Senior."

"We give the Greens a hybrid now and then, tell them we found it wandering the woods or breaking into our food supply. It helped us create a mutual trust."

"Didn't sound like a mutual trust during your 'business call.'"

"You know nothing, girl," Senior Wainright leaned forward in his chair. "You aren't responsible for dozens of families. I give the cursed animal folk to the Greens to keep the Lord's chosen flock alive."

"Such drastic action. I thought your lord provided?"

"The Lord Serpent does provide, child. But that doesn't mean we sit on our hands, eyes shut, hoping to see tomorrow. We must act in His name."

"Do you hear yourself?" Dot asked, kneeling in the dark between the pews. "The tainted meat has poisoned your minds. It's warped your spirit, your sense of right and wrong."

"Did your robotic demon tell you that? Did his dazzling computer brain spot traces of the virus in our supper? What is that supposed to mean?"

"It means you've lost your way. You've surely disappointed your lord because you're not the upstanding, honorable man Father Young remembered."

Enraged, Senior Wainright stood from his desk, stepped out of his office and into the dark chapel, his sinister silhouette backlit in the doorway by the many candles on the shelves.

"Don't you dare speak to me about my way or my lord!" he shouted. "And don't you ever mention that Judas 'Father Young' again! Not in this church, not anywhere!" Senior caught his breath, returning to his eerie calm and charm. "Tell me, girl, what do you think you're going to do now?"

"I can tell you what I'm not going to do," Dot said, crawling between the pews to further obscure her position. "I'm not staying here, I'm not marrying you, and I'm not going with the Purists."

"I'm confused, because those are precisely your three options."

"It sounded like you left me with no options."

"So you heard that, too," Senior Wainright said. "You were eavesdropping longer than I'd realized."

"You promised them 'the girl.' You shouldn't make promises you can't keep."

"I don't. I'm very much a man of my word." Wainright rested his hand on a wall-mounted lever. "I'd prefer to take care of you here in Colt, believe me, but I put the village above any one person. Even me. Even you."

Senior Wainright pulled the lever, flooding the chapel with lights from banks of electric bulbs hanging from the ceiling. Dot remained crouched between the pews, out of the elder's view, but with nowhere to go. She didn't dare move, for it could now instantly reveal her location.

"The candles are mostly ceremonial," Senior said as he stood at the pulpit, "but for midnight mass and other church events, I throw open the electric stars. It's yet another way this old tech Luddite is a hypocrite, I suppose. I rather enjoy looking up at them, like bringing the night sky into this holy house."

Vincent stepped into the chapel through the front entrance, surprised by the brightly lit room. He stood at the back of the pews, with Dot hidden between him and the elder.

"Senior, I'm back!" Vincent said, holding up a small bottle. "I couldn't find a good mint leaf for you, sir, but I found this peppermint oil in a supply shed. A few drops in your tea will make you see reason, and also help with your digestion."

Vincent trotted down the center aisle past Dot, bringing the peppermint oil to the senior. The girl's heart broke when it seemed that Wainright hadn't lied – Vincent had rejoined his former "family" as if the horrors of their shared past never happened.

"Such a good boy, Vincent." Senior Wainright pocketed the bottle and placed his hand on the plant-man's shoulder. "I could always count on Vinny Greenblood. Good to have you back, son."

"Status," Abraham said through Dot's earpiece. "Vincent has entered the church." Dot couldn't respond for fear of revealing herself and her communication to the supposedly drained mech. "Query: Are you in peril, Little Miss? Should I intervene?"

"But I told you, sir, I'm not staying," Vincent said. "I'm leaving with Dottie. I promised Father."

"Of course you're staying, boy. Father couldn't have known that I was still alive after the stormy night he took you from us and left everyone to die. He couldn't have known that you'd reunite with me to help run the village crops once again. If you truly want to honor his memory, you'll stay here with me. I know you will."

"Sorry, nope, I gotta go with Dottie."

"We went over this, boy. 'Dottie' is staying, too. She's with her own kind now. She'll be happy here in Colt with her fellow humans, not evading artificial soldiers hiding behind every corner, not chasing silly ghosts from her absurd dreams. She's wisely choosing to join our flock."

"Then why is she on her knees between the benches?"

Dot stood up, seeing no point to hiding now that her friend was here for her. She felt relieved to learn that Vincent hadn't bought into the elder's plans as he'd laid out.

"You heard him," she said. "We're both leaving."

"Why leave?" Senior Wainright said as he walked up to Dot in the center of the chapel, his arms outstretched. "Why venture into the wild world where everything, including the very air, wants to kill you? Why not stay in this blessed paradise to be protected by the Lord Serpent?"

Dot felt disgusted by the elder's willful ignorance. Abused slaves maintained his "paradise," and he brainwashed his followers into believing they were a superior people, rewarded for their worship and contempt for outsiders. She had ready responses for the old man but knew none would land, blocked by his greed, his zealous views, and his madness.

"You'll have to figure that out for yourself," she said. "When the Purists come, you'll have to make up another story for them. This time, make it more convincing."

Senior Wainright now stood before the defiant girl near the back row of the pews while a confused Vincent watched from the pulpit across the chapel.

"You and your mech were wrong about the meat," the elder said. "It's not tainted, it's anointed. It doesn't weaken or cloud my mind. Quite the opposite, it makes everything clear. My Lord. My purpose. Right now, the Purists are on their way and they'll expect you waiting for them."

"Like I told you," Dot said, "you shouldn't make promises you can't keep. I hope that's understood."

"When I radioed them this morning, shortly after your arrival, they made themselves understood, too. They want the little girl untouched by The Worm, a special child protected by the last true dog, the last known plant hybrid, and the last surviving combat mech. Such a circus you all are. And as much as they'd prefer you alive, they'll also accept your cold corpse. In fact... perhaps that's how it should be."

The old man grabbed Dot by her coat sleeve, pulled a small silver pistol from his pocket, and pressed it to the back of her head.

"Let her go, sir!" Vincent said.

"I also would prefer her alive, boy," Senior Wainright said, his eyes teary and face torn with grief. "I didn't want to kill anyone. But her defiance brings death and misery wherever she goes. While I don't want the Greens to slice her open and study her insides while she screams, I also can't let her go only to have Colt burn behind her. Not again. Either way, she must die."

"Query: Should I intervene?" Abraham asked Dot over her earpiece. "I can be present in 4.7 minutes."

"Don't hurt her!" Vincent said. "You can't!"

"Why can't I, boy?"

"Because I'll kill you, sir."

"Intervene," Dot quickly said in a low voice. "Intervene now."

Senior Wainright dismissed the girl's nonsensical words and turned her and himself around to face Vincent across the chapel, still standing at the pulpit. The elder laughed at the notion of the naive, pacifist plant-man – a foolish, simpleton mutant he'd bossed around for years – hurling such a violent, final threat.

"Vincent, when you came to me earlier," the elder said, forcing calm, "you said you wanted to make things right. This is how we do it."

"This isn't what I asked," Vincent said, confused, overwhelmed.

"You asked for mercy. You begged me to let the hybrids go, to release the girl from her obligations, and to allow you to abandon us yet again, just as your 'father' did. Now, you're talking about killing me? Do you even know what you're saying, boy?"

"It's alright, Vincent," Dot said, hoping her mech would arrive soon. "You don't have to kill anyone."

"I think I do, Dottie," Vincent said, looking around the chapel, its bright lights sure to attract village guards at any moment. "I think it's the only way we're getting out of here." He turned to the elder with a determined look. "Sorry sir, but I told you, I made a promise to Father."

"How I wish you'd stop saying that!" the old man yelled. "It annoys me when you bring him up! And we both know a gentle soul like you couldn't even kill a daisy."

"I could kill all the world's daisies if it meant protecting Dottie, and I could kill you if I have to."

"Vincent, don't do anything," Dot said, her words unheard.

"You disappoint me, boy," Senior Wainright said. "Typical veggie. You often disappointed me when you were a short, scrawny twig of a child messing about when there was work to be done. It's why I had to whip you so many times. Surely, you remember those days? Am I right?"

"I surely do remember, sir," Vincent said. "But I ain't a scrawny twig no more."

Senior Wainright shoved the pistol to Dot's temple. "I meant it when I said I despise guns. But I know what they can do, and I know a stupid, clumsy farm boy like you standing across the room isn't faster than a bullet."

"Then I suppose I'll kill you afterward."

"You don't need to go with her, boy! Take back your threat right now and all is forgiven! You can remain here in Colt, safe and happy with me where you belong!"

"Safe and happy does sound good, but..." Vincent reached into his overalls and pulled out his little black book of Father Young's life instructions. He flipped through the pages until he found the confirmation he sought. He nodded. "Yep. I have to kill you, sir. Father says so right here. You can read it if you want."

"No, Vincent," Dot said, fearing for her friend's well-being more than the elder's threat.

Vincent slid the book back into his pocket and looked at Senior Wainright, his secondary father figure, for what he knew would be the last time, one way or another.

"You really think you'll do it?" the elder asked with an incredulous, mocking smile covering his shaken nerves.

"I need to make things right, sir."

"Intervene," Dot whispered again, glancing at the large front window. "Intervene, intervene, intervene..."

"I'm sorry, boy," the elder said. He pointed to a large cross on the wall with his gun. "There's no arguing with the Lord Serpent. I know you'll see I'm right..."

Senior Wainright's eyes widened in shock as he dropped his silver pistol, sending it tumbling to the wooden floorboards. He looked down to retrieve it and saw a long spear running through his body.

One of Vincent's snake-like vines – thirty feet long – was thrust deep into his chest.

The plant hybrid had stiffened his vine like hardwood and sharpened its tip like obsidian, an ability that surprised even him, for he'd never been called on to kill before. He'd flung his vine like lightning over the tops of the pews, striking the old man square in the sternum. Blood trickled out of the wound, out of his mouth, spotting the floor at his feet.

As Senior Wainright collapsed dead between the pews, Vincent drew back his vine and cut off the bloody, fatal tip with a quick swing of a knife.

Dot ran to a disoriented Vincent with open arms. "Don't look at him," she said as she held him. "Turn your eyes away."

Despite her plea, Vincent couldn't take his sight off the old man's body. "He won't grow back either, will he?"

"No, Vincent."

"Maybe some folks shouldn't grow back."

"Maybe not," the girl said, wiping a single tear from his face.

"I wish Father had mentioned all this in the book. I hated doing that, Dottie."

"I know."

"But I hated what he did, what he was going to keep doing, even more."

The two friends embraced in the brightly lit chapel, their tender moment interrupted by the sound of guards running and the floodlights of a 12-foot tall combat mech arriving outside, ready to raze the church – perhaps the entire village – to its hallowed ground.

22

Save The Pure Dog

Two centuries before brothers Ephraim, Ezekiel, and Elijah approached the lone utility building on the east side of Colt, the ancient ones knew it as Mr. Piper's All-Nighter Diner, a popular truck stop along the old interstate highway that became the Broken Road. Looted and torched during the riots of the New World War, its basement alone remained intact, with its short-order kitchen and walk-in freezer. Descendants of the town's original survivors made it their community mess hall, and they limited entrance to the elder's wives. Though the village's men hunted and killed animals, the women prepared them for supper or cloth.

The three dog-men knelt hidden in tall weeds in front of the former restaurant's sign, having no clue who Mr. Piper was, what a diner could possibly be, or what "Home-Cooked Quality Family Fare" meant. Ephraim assumed the words were a quotation from the village scripture. Elijah imagined they were rules about food rationing and penalties for theft. Ezekiel couldn't even read what little his brothers deciphered but viewed the stained, faded words as a warning, a sign that they should have fled the village the moment Vincent tore down the barn doors.

From their hiding spot, they peered through the building's doorless rear entry down the long, empty hallways. They could smell Gypsy, still alive, trapped somewhere within the cinderblock walls, while four guards patrolled outside.

"They should be asleep in bed," Elijah said with a snort.

"They normally would be," Ezekiel said, "but the Senior is no fool. He posted more guards tonight because he figured these new folks might be trouble. Looks like he was right."

"The villagers are the trouble," Ephraim said in a scolding tone. "Vincent and his companions just want out, free from bondage as we've always wanted. Recognize your enemies and allies."

"Yes, brother," Ezekiel said in shame, bowing to his alpha.

"We owe Vincent a great debt, and our pack always honors our debts. If Gypsy dies, the blood of the last true dog will be on us."

"That won't happen, brother," Elijah said, holding up a paw. "I swear it."

"I swear it," Ezekiel repeated.

"As do I," Ephraim said.

The oldest dog hybrid led his brothers low through the tall grass, up to the first pair of guards. In silent unison, they took down the men, smothering their faces until they laid unconscious.

"This is dangerous," Elijah said. "We should kill them. They'd show us no mercy if they saw us first."

"Sleep is too good for these men," Ezekiel said. "When they wake up, their first thought will be to put us down."

"We gave our word to Vincent," Ephraim said.

"The plant man is no killer, but we are. "

"I agree with Ezekiel," Elijah said. "What do words matter if we end up dead?"

Ephraim understood their confusion and their eagerness to slaughter their slavers, but the scent of the imprisoned dog reminded him of their promise.

"Dead or alive," the alpha said, "our word is all we have left in the world. They've taken our lives, our family's lives, till this night. Don't let them take our honor from us, too."

His brothers nodded with a renewed conviction. They gagged and bound the unconscious guards with rope from the barn and hid them in the grass as they continued toward the awaiting doorway.

Though Ephraim was determined to keep his promise to Vincent, he couldn't help but think of the chimp-women, Apphia and Ahlai, now far and away from that cursed place, likely sticking to the tallest trees. He imagined the leopard-girls, Sapphire, Sherah, and Salome sprinting across the forest floor while he and his brothers faced the entire village guard who were likely discovering their escape from the barn at that moment. Like his younger brother Ezekiel, Ephraim briefly wondered if perhaps they should have fled to the treeline with their hybrid family instead of entangling themselves in the plight of a human girl and her strange friends.

Entering the rear doorway of the mess hall, Ephraim shrugged off his doubt, dismissing it as fleeting cowardice unbecoming of an alpha. Without question, it was his leadership that helped keep everyone alive and hopeful, even as their brethren were taken from that forsaken barn one at a time for years, given to the whims of the Greens. So long as he led the fight, no hybrid nor pure animal would be betrayed that night.

The three brothers sniffed the air, pinpointing the two remaining guards and another three approaching. Ephraim waited for them to walk by before signaling his brothers to continue down the dark halls of the building, descending into the basement. He cherished his uncanny canine sense of smell, but how he wished he had the others' gifts – Apphia's nocturnal vision, Sapphire's blinding speed, Solomon's great strength, even Vincent's long reach. The only advantages the alpha dog-man always had over the others were his keen intelligence and sharp instincts, both of which told him the humans could soon trap him and his brothers in the old diner basement with armed guards blocking their exit.

Within the pit of his doubt, he reached the bottom of the stairs and saw a dozen skinned rabbits and deer, plucked cranes and turkeys, hanging lifeless from the ceiling. Their flayed bodies painted the humans as cruel savages with no love for the animal world. Beneath them all stood the last true dog, crouched in a defensive posture in the center of the basement. His bared teeth and low growl faced the brothers, stopping them cold, and they stood in awe of the pure animal they'd only imagined in dreams.

"Gypsy," Ephraim said, eyeing the chain around the dog's rear leg. "We're here to free you. We're here to take you to the girl."

Ezekiel carefully crawled past the dog on edge and located the large lock that kept him tethered to the wall. His long claws failed to pick the mechanism.

"Can't do it," he said. "I told you we can't."

"Yes, we can, brother," Ephraim said. "It just takes time."

"Time we don't have."

Ephraim also tried picking the lock, to no avail. A hard yank of the chain proved equally futile. Though he found comfort in

Gypsy's newly relaxed stance, he fought panic as he smelled more humans nearby, their stench mixed with the oil and powder of their infernal rifles and the odor of the hanging animal carcasses.

"What do we do now?" Elijah asked, also picking up the enemy's scent, his docile eyes betraying his fear.

"We take out our claws," Ephraim said with a snarl, hoping to put the fight back in his younger brother. "They'll be coming inside, but they won't be coming out."

"But you said no killing..."

"That was out there, Elijah. We can be merciful out in the open air. Deep in here, behind brick walls, we either kill or we die."

The three dog-men and the one true dog between them stared at the dark stairwell door, their only exit.

"Anything that comes through there gets ripped apart!" Ezekiel said.

"Death by dog!" Elijah said.

"Remember, they'll come in rifles first," Ephraim said. "Once we strike one, they'll all start shooting."

Footsteps came down the stairs, their echoes masking their numbers. Their scent was also undetermined, the raw meat hanging all around numbing their sense of smell. They'd know how many guards they faced only once they stepped into the basement.

"I'll pounce alone," Ephraim said. "Whatever happens to me, kill the others. Protect the dog."

A large man entered the basement in shadow and Ephraim leapt onto him with a vicious growl, only to be caught like a rag doll.

Solomon, the bear-man, standing eight feet tall, held him in his paws. Though Ephraim felt relieved to see his friend rather than the village guards, he quickly realized the escape plan he'd carefully laid out for his family had been abandoned.

"You were... supposed to lead the women... to the trees!" Ephraim said, his throat choked. "You were supposed to protect them!"

Solomon dropped Ephraim to the floor and stared curiously at Gypsy, who once again held an attack stance.

"We leave together or we die together," the large bear-man said in his deep, grizzled voice. "You always told us that."

"And you actually listened to me?"

"Might not have always 'listened' to your bluster, Mr. Alpha, but I always heard every word."

Solomon shoved his way through the dog-men, grabbed Gypsy's chain, and pulled it from the wall like dried out rope. He clutched the dog's steel collar and easily popped it open with his fingers, dropping it in a corner.

"Why bother pulling it from the wall?" Ephraim asked.

"Long heavy chain like this could come in handy."

"Yes. I like the way you think."

Solomon coiled the chain and draped it over his shoulder. The sight of their immense friend arming himself prompted Elijah and Ezekiel to search the kitchen for makeshift weapons.

Ephraim snatched a cleaver and a chef's knife from his younger brothers' hands, once again staring shame into them. "Remember, once we're back out there, no bloodshed."

"Yes, brother," Elijah said. "Outside, no bloodshed."

"I think I'm going back to not listening to you," Solomon said. "What's this nonsense about, Ephraim? No bloodshed?"

"We promised Vincent."

"You promised that beanstalk, not me."

"That beanstalk freed us," Ephraim said. "He said to spare the villagers, so that's what we'll do. We'll keep our word. All of us."

"That word might end up being our last."

"We keep our word!"

Solomon glared at their leader and bared his teeth, unable to strike fear into the alpha dog hybrid as he could any other man. He snatched a hare from a ceiling hook and bit into its dead flesh. The bear-man's breath reeked of bloody, rotten rodent meat as he grunted in frustration.

"Alright, I'll follow your damn rules," Solomon said. "Here in Colt, I'll spare the humans, but once we leave this forsaken place, those rules don't mean nothing. Pacifist survivors aren't survivors very long."

"Agreed," Ephraim said. "Out in the wild, beyond the village, we do what we must, if it ever comes to that. You have my permission."

"How very comforting."

Solomon devoured the hare, bones and all, as he accepted the illogical rules of their escape.

"You should have stuck with the plan, Solomon."

"Apphia made me look for you. We made it to the trees, but she felt it wrong to leave you to die. That old chimps's always had a soft spot for you, Ephraim."

"Dammit, Apphia!" Ephraim said with a snort. "That hard-headed monkey-woman listens even less than you!"

"I'm gonna tell her you called her a monkey," Solomon said with a grin.

"If we get out of this village alive, by all means, tell her." The alpha dog knelt beside Gypsy to check if the hunters had harmed him and was relieved to find no wounds. "Please tell me you came alone."

"Four humans outside. I think one of them saw me."

"Hard to miss you, big bear," Elijah said.

"Then be ready, little pup."

"I wasn't talking about the guards," Ephraim said. "Where are the women now?"

"Last I saw, they were making their way to the church."

23

Breakout

A dreadful horn blared across the village as Dot and Vincent ran out of the church to find Abraham standing in the center of the circle of homes, the long supper table crushed underneath his feet, while seemingly every man in the village ran outside with rifles in hand. The mech quickly scooped up Dot and placed her in the safety of his chest compartment again, which unfortunately had no room for the lanky plant-man.

"Status: The village is aware of our attempted flight."

"Dang, Abe, you don't gotta report what we can already see!" Vincent said, clinging to the 12-foot-tall robot's back.

"Clarification: They are also aware of the nine hybrids you freed from captivity."

"Good thing they're long gone."

"Correction: The nine hybrids are still within the township's limits."

"So, you did free them," Dot said, looking out through the mech's chest. "I don't see them."

"Me neither," Vincent said, confused. "Why didn't they run? That was part of the plan!"

Bullets bounced off Abraham's armor as he turned to face the villagers while unfolding weapons from his arms.

"Don't kill them!" Dot said.

"Assessment: The citizenry are a threat. We cannot reach the minimum safe distance while they actively pursue us."

"It's bad enough to shoot the clones, but they fix themselves. I will not watch the last humans die!"

"Because they don't grow back," Vincent said sadly. "Just like Father and... just like Senior."

"Query: Do you require zero fatalities?"

"Yes!" Dot said. "Zero fatalities! That's what I require!"

"Strategy: Non-lethal countermeasures."

Abraham sheathed his long twin guns. He extended a tube from his shoulder and shot smoke grenades in every direction, enshrouding the village in a thick green fog. The lack of visibility didn't deter the gunfire, which continued to pepper the robot as he marched forward.

"Is that poison gas?" Dot asked the mech.

"Negative."

"Let's get out of here while they're blind!"

"Assessment: The optimal route is northeast."

"So let's head northeast!"

Abraham's sensors and thermal vision enabled him to see the villagers surrounding him, which now included women holding torches to guide the guards. Careful not to harm them as ordered, he had difficulty leaving the cul-de-sac of central homes and found himself stuck near the church.

"Status: We cannot travel without harming the citizenry. Does the zero-fatality order still stand?"

"Yes, it still stands!" Dot said. "Zero fatalities!"

Before Abraham could form another assessment, Vincent's bioluminescent eyes spotted several villagers in the dense smoke falling unconscious to the ground.

"Umm, you said this ain't poison-death gas, Abe?" Vincent asked.

"Correct."

"Is it poison-sleepy-time gas?"

"Clarification: The gas is neither toxic nor somniferous. It is inert and harmless, meant only to obscure visibility."

"Then why are folks falling down like wilted flowers?"

Dot saw the villagers fall one by one before getting dragged out of the street. Within the green fog, she and Vincent saw the faint outlines of what looked like giant chimpanzees clutching the humans and choking them to the ground.

"It's my new friends from the barn!" Vincent said.

"The other hybrids?" Dot asked. "I hope they're not killing them."

"Assessment: The hybrids are merely rendering the human unconscious. We are still at zero fatalities."

"Move, Abraham! Move!"

The combat mech lurched forward, passing the church as he proceeded northeast, away from the homes. The chimp-women took out the guards while the leopard-girls sped around the neighborhood, knocking rifles away with cunning speed.

"Status: The remaining guards are equipping larger weapons behind the residences."

"They're breaking out the big guns," Vincent said. "I seen 'em earlier when I was out looking for the peppermint oil."

"Status: This unit's reserve power is at 12 percent."

"We need to get out of here now, Abraham!" Dot said. "You can't shut down on us! Not here!"

"Recommendation: Reinstate allowance for fatalities."

Dot wanted no further deaths on her hands, but didn't see any other way out before Abraham's power ran dry, leaving them helpless in the chaos. As she considered giving her mech the green light to fire at will, hopefully keeping casualties to a minimum, she saw several figures running into the neighborhood from the east.

Gypsy and the dog-men joined the foray, running into the fog, their sense of smell guiding them through the melee to the mech. Their arrival inspired Dot to stick to her morals.

"Zero fatalities, Abraham," she said.

"Revised Strategy: Instruct the hybrids to retreat and hold position behind this unit."

"Barn people, get over here!" Vincent shouted. "Get behind the big robot guy!"

Within a minute, all nine of the formerly enslaved hybrids made their way behind Abraham as he backed away from the cul-de-sac.

"This smoke is going to clear soon," Dot said.

"Strategy: Their path will be blocked momentarily."

With the villagers scrambling in the street, Abraham backed further away and unfolded his twin guns again. Dot's eyes widened, thinking he was about to violate her order to refrain from killing, until she saw him aim upward at the church steeple above.

With two powerful shots, the mech blasted the steeple with explosive rounds, sending the tall structure down in a fireball that rocked the village. Still blind in the smoke and now behind a wall of flame and debris, it trapped the villagers in their own neighborhood as Abraham led his entourage northeast, away from Colt, his armored body shielding them from the wild gunfire.

"Status: This unit's reserve power is at six percent."

"Abe's gonna fall asleep on us before we can get out of this place!" Vincent said.

"Just keep going as long as you can, Abraham," Dot said from within the robot's chest. "One step at a time."

"Acknowledgment, Little Miss."

Their chances seemed to dim further when they reached the mess hall where Vincent spied an arriving Purist transport coming to a stop, the first of many to come with the new dawn. Abraham readied his twin guns to destroy it, but Vincent's vines stopped him, yanking his arms downward.

"Don't kill the big truck!" Vincent said, thinking quickly. "We're gonna need it!" He turned to Ephraim and pointed out the Automen emerging from the transport. "Go get 'em! Now! These clone guys, you can kill!"

"You heard him!" Ephraim yelled to his brothers. "Death by dog!"

"Death by dog!" Ezekiel and Elijah echoed, extending their claws.

The three canine hybrids charged on all fours at the soldiers as they opened fire, pulling the clones out of the large vehicle for Solomon to slash apart. The hybrid women leapt from the mech onto the roof of the transport, grabbing the Automen's rifles and wrestling them to the ground, where leopard claws opened their throats.

"What are they doing?" Dot asked.

"I told 'em that clone guys are fair game," Vincent said. "They'll spend all day fixing their bodies while we get outta here! That was also part of the plan!"

"That's quite a plan you put together!"

Dot turned away from the carnage, reminding herself that "killing" an Automan ultimately meant nothing, as they would eventually repair themselves and each other to continue pursuit, as Vincent said. It would buy them time.

"Sapphire!" Apphia yelled out in the frenzy. "Sapphire!"

Dot hoped the leopard-girl was unharmed, that her lack of a response was only due to her being mute, as all cat hybrids were. To her horror, within the chaos of the enshrouding green smoke, she realized the truth. The shrill cry of the elder chimp-woman's motherly agony amidst the gunfire told Dot if they somehow survived the night, not all of them would see the sunrise.

"Status: This unit's power supply is depleted. Preparing to cycle down."

"Abraham?" Dot said, running her hands on the walls of his inner chamber as if to find a miracle button or switch that would grant him another few minutes of life. "Please, Abraham! You need to keep moving!"

To her shock, Abraham retracted his arms and shortened his legs as he backed into the cargo bed of the transport.

"Request: Vincent, please operate the transport vehicle."

The plant-man quickly complied, hopping in the driver's seat and starting the engine. Gypsy sat beside him in the front seat while the nine other hybrids clung to the truck's canvas top. Within moments, they emerged from the smoke and reached the Broken Road, barreling away from Colt, leaving the village burning behind them just as Senior Wainright had prophesied.

As they sped away, Dot peered out of her mech's chest and saw the lifeless body of Sapphire, the silent leopard hybrid among the remains of the Purists.

"Status," Abraham said. "The township's citizenry has abandoned pursuit." He could still communicate despite his spent body sitting folded and dormant. "Reconnaissance: Another troop of Purists will arrive from the north in fifteen minutes."

"We're gonna make it!" Dot said, hopeful, still sitting within Abraham's chest.

"Correct, Little Miss."

"You sure, Abe?" Vincent asked, now driving east down the old road. "Will we be gone by the time they get here?"

"Projection: At our current speed, we will be at the minimum safe distance in 7.1 minutes."

For Dot and her many companions, it felt like the longest 7.1 minutes of their lives.

24

Save Your Wishes

Though the road extended east to the rising sun with no obstacles in sight, after a solid four hours of driving, Vincent parked the troop transport in the seclusion of an old irrigation ditch. With his powerful, long vines, he covered the truck with fallen trees and thick shrubs, hiding it from view, leaving only a small section of the vehicle's hood-mounted solar panel peeking out through the foliage.

"You sure you guys don't want to come with us?" Vincent asked as he set down two more trees, to everyone's astonishment. "Once the truck's recharged, we'll be on our way."

"We swore we'd never return to the East Hills," Ephraim said. "And I swore I'd take my family west beyond the wall."

"What's the big deal behind that wall? What's over there?"

"A city that welcomes our kind, if it's not just a myth."

"Kellan," Dot said as she climbed out of Abraham's opened chest. Every time she spoke the name of that place, it felt more real. "I was on my way there, too."

"You can't go back down this road, girl," Ephraim said. "They'll find you if you're anywhere Colt again."

"Don't worry, we're not going back yet. Kellan will have to wait."

"Vincent mentioned you're looking to save others, too." Ephraim recognized her torn expression. "You're a brave child, maybe foolishly so, but braver than most."

"How will you all make it east? Like you said, they'll be waiting if you go back that way."

"We'll stay off the roads, stick to the high trees, to the rocks along the ridge. We'll forge paths no Automan would dare."

Apphia and Ahlai, the two chimp-women, stood on the side of the road with Sherah and Salome between them as if to protect the remaining leopard-girls. The mute teen sisters looked to the ground, still grieving after losing Sapphire during their final brutal push out of the zealots' village.

"I'm sorry for your loss," Dot said, realizing no words could comfort them. "I wish she were here."

"What is that worth, the wish of a child?" Solomon said with a grunt, removing his tourniquets. Dot winced at the sight of his wounds.

During their escape from Colt, Solomon had been shot three times: twice in his right arm and once in his left leg. Though the bear-man's hide was thick enough to help him endure, his wounds still needed attention. When they reached the minimum safe distance, Vincent pulled over and tended to the surly hybrid's wounds. He dug out the shrapnel, stopped the bleeding with tourniquets made from duct tape, applied a poultice, and wrapped the wounds with gauze. When the bleeding was under control an hour later, Vincent offered to remove the tourniquets, but he had touched the stubborn bear quite enough. It furthered his foul mood, a wrath felt by Dot.

"Hush yourself, Solomon," Apphia said, slapping the bear-man across the back of his head. "The girl is paying her respects."

"I understand, Apphia, but wishes, respects... they change nothing."

"You're grumpy from your wounds, old man, so I'll let it go this time. Don't dishonor our friends again."

"I don't mean to offend," Dot said.

"And I don't mean to be harsh," Solomon said, eyeing Apphia's stare. "Sapphire was taken from us and she can't be taken back."

"Can't be grown back," Vincent said sadly.

"I spent most of my life in that damn barn making wishes. It took me years to realize they helped no more than the villager's prayers or the elder's sermons, jibber-jabber we heard carried on the wind every night. They helped no more than our cries and pleas for mercy. So save your wishes, girl. Save them for things than could be. Just know we lost a good one today."

"We've lost a lot more over the years," Apphia said, struggling to stay strong for the teens who always looked up to her like a mother. "I always told these girls to be grateful for those we haven't lost yet, and now I'll tell them to be grateful that Sapphire died quickly while saving them, not slowly in the bowels of the Purists' labs. For that, we'll remember her well."

"I know wishes don't help," Dot said, "but I still wish I could have known her. She helped save us all."

"She was always brave," Ephraim said, bowing his head along with his brothers.

"She used to have seven siblings," Apphia said, swallowing the pull to weep. "The youngest was a cheetah, a child, barely cut her teeth when they snatched her from my arms. Sapphire fought them. She fought every time they took one of us away to give to the Greens."

"We'll remember her well," Ahlai said, following her older sister's example.

"And we'll stay together," Solomon said. "It's our best chance to survive."

"It's what Sapphire would have wanted," Apphia said. "If we make it to this rumored city the dogs speak of, this supposed paradise of animal and man, she'll smile upon us from the trees in the sky."

"What about you, Vincent?" Ephraim asked. "Will you come with us to Kellan?"

"We could use your help," Apphia said, "and you belong with your own kind."

"Dang, that's how Senior Wainright talks," Vincent said. "He talked like that when he was pointing a scary gun at Dottie."

"I only meant that we..."

"Sounds good, but no thanks. Dottie already told you, Kellan will have to wait. We got people to wrangle together first."

"The girl has her war machine," Solomon said. "It's stronger than me, stronger than the rest of us combined."

During their roadside farewell, Abraham sat silently in the cargo bed of the transport, his solar panels absorbing energy from the new day. None of them knew that he'd been recording their every word and would replay them within his digital mind as a remembrance of the sanctity of life Dot had instilled in him.

"I promised Father," Vincent said with an apologetic tone. "I ain't never broken a promise and ain't never gonna. But hey, after we find the spooky girls in the stars, we'll see you guys again in that nice city of yours. I got a feeling that place is for reals."

"You promise?" Apphia asked with a faint smile.

"Yep. I do."

Apphia turned, placed her long arms around the leopard girls, and guided them to the nearby treeline. Ephraim nodded goodbye to Vincent and Dot. He knelt down and rubbed Gypsy under his collar.

"Goodbye, Gypsy," the alpha said. "I wonder if you can ever know how much of an honor it was to meet you, to fight with you, the last true dog."

Without another word or glance back, the eight hybrids, former slaves of Colt, waded uphill through tall grass and disappeared beyond a cluster of rocks, the protective woods and rocky ridge waiting above them.

"How long before we can leave?" Dot asked her remaining companions.

"Truck's drained pretty low," Vincent said. "Gonna take most of the day to get it running again. Maybe we stay the night? I ain't in no hurry to be out in the open anytime soon."

"You sure they won't find us here?"

"Assessment," Abraham said. "There is no other humanoid life within a 10-kilometer radius."

It surprised Dot and Vincent to hear the calm, synthesized voice coming from the back of the transport.

"Abe, you're awake?" Vincent asked. "I wasn't sure how long you'd be knocked out."

"Explanation: Other than the unlikely event of my total destruction, I am never fully inactive. My motor functions are currently offline, but my sensory processor requires minimum power. This unit can never be 'knocked out.'"

"So, you heard everything we said just now?" Dot asked.

"Correct."

"You know about Sapphire?"

"Correct."

"How does that make you feel?"

"Assessment: Given the terrain, projected weather, and patrol routes, the eight hybrids have a 72.5 percent chance of successfully reaching their destination despite their loss in numbers."

"I didn't ask for an assessment, Abraham," the girl said. "I want to know how it makes you feel."

"Clarification: This unit can only provide strategic assessment based on event patterns, employed military tactics, distance traveled, and observed behavior. Further, my disconnect to the global network prevents me from..."

"Do you feel sad?"

Abraham sat folded in the cargo bed of the truck and processed Dot's seemingly simple question. Each moment in Colt, each word uttered, every bullet and flame and drop of blood replayed in his synthetic-organic composite mind as he considered the girl's query. The gravity of her words and the delicate tone of her voice looped in his brain with an illogical swirl. If the giant war machine could shed tears, he would have surely wept with his companions and embraced them in his powerful arms.

"Correct," he said.

"Yeah, I'm sad, too."

"I'll start a fire!" Vincent said, oblivious to the tender moment shared between the child and the robot. He started gathering kindling from a nearby dead oak. "I spotted some peach trees and wild carrots a little ways back. I'll put together a cobbler. We'll call it 'Sapphire Cobbler.' We can think of her while we eat it."

"That's very thoughtful, Vincent," Dot said. "And cobbler sounds good."

"Sometimes, Father would let me eat dessert before supper, if I worked hard that day."

"I bet you always worked hard."

"Correct," Vincent said, mimicking his metal friend.

Dot laughed for the first time in days. "I saw tents in the back of the transport. I'll set them up."

"Strategy: This unit will continue monitoring the environment, Little Miss."

"Let us know if you pick up anything."

As Vincent and Dot set up camp, Abraham continued to sweep the area with his sensor array while filling his batteries with sunlight. Gypsy stood guard, as he always did, on the side of the Broken Road.

* * *

With her eyes shut, Dot laid across the front seat of the transport, half asleep, her head resting in Vincent's lap as the rhythm of the wheels on the cracked pavement calmed her. She could still taste the sweet cobbler her friend made from wild fruit, shredded carrot, and raw flour from barley that grew near their camp. They'd started the next day early, packing up camp and leaving no trace of their night in the ditch.

"Vincent, how long have we been driving?" she asked in a sleepy voice. Hearing no response, she opened her eyes and sat up to look out the windshield, only to be startled by the complete darkness that surrounded them.

"Go back... come closer."

Dot turned and realized she no longer sat in the transport but was now standing in The Void, its total silence unnerving. Across the dark dream expanse, the twin stars remained distant, but their silhouettes of two young girls with pointed hats, flowing dresses, and contradictory commands floated ever closer. She felt she could almost reach out to them.

"You're heading to your death... you must save us all."

So close were the shadowy figures that Dot could discern anger on the Dark Girl's face and sorrow in the Light Girl's eyes.

"We're coming," Dot said, calling out to them. "No use in telling me to turn back. We've been on the road for a long while. By now, we're probably deep in the East Hills. I can feel we're closer than before."

"It's not too late to run... don't run, you're almost here."

"I'd listen to the doomsayer," George said from behind Dot. He stood in the darkness, lit from above by an unseen light.

"George!" Dot said. "Where are you now? I mean, in the real world? Did you find me?"

"I've been at Beacon Hill a few days. A lot of Purists wandering around here. Hopefully, they'll move on soon, but if I suddenly blink out of this bizarre nowhere you've pulled me into, it's because they found me asleep in the basement of an old farmhouse."

Dot felt Gypsy beside her, looking up at George without his usual mistrust.

"Do you agree with him, boy?" Dot asked her dog.

"Assessment: Your companion's advice is sound."

Dot felt startled to hear the familiar synthetic voice and looked around for her mechanized friend. Though his metal body was unseen at first, the robot's words boomed across The Void as if he were its overlord. His large armored frame soon appeared, which seemed strange even in such an impossible, metaphysical place.

"Abraham?" Dot asked, bewildered. "How can you be here?"

"Unknown."

"The rest of us, I think our minds are linked somehow, but how can yours be also?"

"Hypothesis: My neural net is compromised of both inorganic and organic material. Your ability to mentally connect with others

Lynn Harrod

has recruited the latter portion of my artificial intelligence, and your cognizance of my being has fashioned my visual presence."

"So, you really are here? Mentally, I mean."

"Correct."

"What's going on?" George asked, cautious and confused, as he stood in front of Dot, his bow and arrow at ready as if to protect her from the towering war machine.

"Put down your bow, George. That's Abraham."

"Who or what is Abraham?"

"Identification: This unit is an A1900 Abraham-class combat mechanoid designed by the Humanist Global Consortium and constructed by the Loyalists To Man paramilitary union during the final surge of the New World War."

"It's a mech?" George asked, dumbfounded. "You mentally linked... with a robot?"

"Explanation: Little Miss has imprinted on this unit."

"And it calls you 'Little Miss'?"

"Abraham's my friend," Dot said.

"Friend?" George shook his head at her naiveté. "Machines have commands and directives, Dot. They don't have friends. That goes double for giant walking weapons of mass destruction."

"You've befriended a lot of mechs, have you?" the girl asked.

"I've never befriended a Lotus Bomb, but I know they destroy entire towns. What if the Greens sent it to track you? The thing has no heart, no soul."

"Well, I promise you, this one does," Dot said in a firm tone. "He's special, one of a kind, just like me, just like Gypsy and Vincent."

"Sure, four one-of-a-kind wonders traveling together," George said with a smirk. "We should sell tickets."

"You're the second person to call us a circus."

George realized his cold take and attempt at humor landed wrong with the girl. He regretted his hurtful, judgmental words. "Look... I'm sorry, Dot. I didn't mean it."

"Abraham and I are friends, George."

"I believe you, and I'm thinking that might be the one factor that brings people in here. There's a short list of folks you trust completely, folks you form a connection with, and they show up in this place, in your dreams."

"I'm glad we finally agree."

"I feel honored to be on that list," George said. "Now I know how you feel about me."

"Let's not get carried away," the girl said with an embarrassed smile. "I mean, I like you, George, but..."

"I only meant that this is clearly your Friend Zone," he blurted, nervous. "I wasn't suggesting you and I... what I mean is..."

"Yes, of course. You're in my Friend Zone."

"Exactly. Yes. That's what I meant." George looked across the expanse at the twin girls aligned with the distant stars. "I guess that means those two hovering over there are also your friends?"

"I think so."

"You don't know so? Can we be sure?"

Dot understood George's default instinct to mistrust. Having survived alone in the wild for years, he encountered far more enemies than allies.

"One of them is asking for help," she said, pointing to the Light Girl.

"The other one is urging you to save yourself. That's the one who makes sense to me."

"I need to find them both. I'm not sure why."

"This gets more nuts with each minute," George said. "Where are you right now? I mean, in the 'real world'?"

"We were traveling east from Colt, probably eight or nine hours from it now..."

"You were in Colt?" George asked, his eyes wide. "So you got help from Senior Wainright?"

"The Senior isn't the man you remember, George."

"What do you mean? How else could you have made it so far unless he helped you?"

"He only wanted to help himself."

"Explanation," Abraham said. "The elder of the village and his devout followers have developed early onset dementia from consuming virally tainted animal meat."

"He enslaved hybrids," Dot said. "He tried to enslave Vincent like he did before."

"That can't be true!" the boy said.

"He called the Purists on me, George. He sacrificed the village hybrids, surrendered them for years to keep the soldiers from burning everything down."

"No. I don't believe it. Not Wainright. He'd never do that. Never."

"I'm so sorry, George."

"She's right, Georgie," Vincent said, appearing beside him. "The Senior lost his marbles. He was even gonna force Dottie to marry him! That was before the Greenies figured out she was there."

"Vincent?" Dot said. "How can you be here?"

"The same as before, I guess. Our brains are connected, remember? Just like the roots of trees planted side by side."

"Yes, but who's driving the truck?"

"I am," Vincent said, curious. "I've been driving all day."

"But you can't be driving now. You have to be asleep to be in here."

"Hmm, that's true, isn't it?"

"Turn back... you're getting closer..."

"Really, Vincent, who's driving the truck? Did you fall asleep behind the wheel?"

"You're all going to die... don't die on us..."

"You know, now that you mention it," Vincent said, "that long yellow line in the road started to get to me. I was feeling pretty sleepy, and no one else was awake to keep me focused on the..."

BOOM!

25

Monsters Ahead

The violent crash started in The Void and continued in the real world as everyone awoke. Dot fell to the floor of the transport's cab while choking dust filled the air. She looked up to see Vincent at the steering wheel, groggy, ripped from their shared dream as she had been. She pressed her cochlear device to her ear, both to ensure that it hadn't fallen out and to check on Abraham in the cargo bed.

"Abraham, are you guys okay back there?" she asked.

"Status: This unit remains functional and at full power. Gypsy is unharmed."

"That nice guy, Georgie, was with us again," Vincent said. "I can't wait to meet him in person, you know, and not inside your head."

"Me, too," Dot said. "I wish he were with us now."

"But Solomon said wishes don't help."

"He's right, but it doesn't change how I feel."

Vincent opened his door and stumbled out of the transport, which had veered off the road and plowed into an orchard. Sizing up their predicament, he quickly surmised that while he drifted to sleep, the massive truck left the road and took down three peach trees before being halted by a fourth, its roots upending and lifting the vehicle's front end by its ruptured transmission case.

"Nope, the truck ain't going nowhere now," he said. "The frame is crooked real bad, the wheels are all busted up, and the gears are spread out like puzzle pieces."

Dot jumped out of the truck cab to find Gypsy already waiting for her, ever the reliable guard dog, while Abraham slowly unfolded his armored body to full height as he emerged from the cargo bed.

"Abraham," Dot said, "what do you think?"

"Assessment: This transport is now non-operational. The forward chassis, front axle, and transmission are beyond our repair capabilities."

"Yep, just like I was saying," Vincent said. "The truck is dead."

"Correct."

As the dust cleared, Dot could see beyond the old orchard. Under the midday sun, the Broken Road ran a short distance away, continuing east. The charred remains of what used to be called a "shopping center" were within walking distance. A pair of peeling billboards flanked the storefronts, faded advertisements for a long-shuttered family restaurant and a travelers' inn. They stood adorned with smiling faces of satisfied patrons, their joy at odds with the sudden danger Dot's friends found themselves in.

As disturbing as the silence and isolation felt, and as eerie as the former businesses looked, it was the crude graffiti sprayed across the billboards in thick red paint that gave Dot a feeling of dread, words hastily scrawled across the old ads by terrified people fleeing the area many years before.

"TURN BACK," read the graffiti on one billboard.

"MONSTERS AHEAD," read the other.

The billboards brought the star girls to mind, with the signs' original comforting promises of food and rest contrasted by grim warnings to anyone unlucky enough to find themselves so far east. Dot assumed it was simply more rhetoric from the warring factions whose prejudice either supported or admonished human hybrids, survivalist encampments, or military occupations. Still, she wondered what "monsters" the signs referred to. In their desperate, divided world, everyone was a monster to everyone else.

"Hey Abe, is there another truck nearby we can borrow?" Vincent asked.

"Reconnoissance: There are 27 motor vehicles in the area, all non-operational and non-salvageable."

"Looks like we're walking for a while."

"Are there any people?" Dot asked.

"Reconnoissance: There are no humanoid life signs in a 10-kilometer radius."

"What about Greenies or Blues?" Vincent asked as he stood atop the transport and looked around. "Are your sensors sensing any of those Automen guys?"

"Reconnoissance: There are no artificial life signs within the radius."

"All we have is us," Dot said, recalling Sarge's final words again. She couldn't help but feel they might eventually be her last words one day. "What's up ahead? Are you still disconnected from your network?"

"Status: Network connection is still inactive."

"That's too bad," Vincent said. "Try again later, big guy."

As before, no one in the group could know that Abraham's network reconnection would forever be impossible, and that the mech's blind spot would always remain. However, despite being lost in the wild, Abraham continued to reconstruct a map of the greater world.

"Projection: Based on the evacuated communities we have passed and the commercial property adjacent to our present position, I ascertain through triangulation that a research facility is located 14.4 kilometers further down this road."

"Maybe they got a truck or two?" Vincent said.

"What kind of research facility?" Dot asked.

"Identification," Abraham said. "Dominion Research Vivarium."

"That sounds familiar," Vincent said. "Then again, everything sounds familiar to me. I wish I was better at remembering things I need to remember."

The plant-man's faint memory of names and places stemmed from the fact that his group had been unknowingly retracing a path he and Father Young took long ago, the Broken Road leading from his birthplace, on to the village of Colt, ending at his beloved, sheltered farm in the North Woods.

"I think we should stay away from this Dominion Research," Dot said. "Isn't it outside your radius, Abraham?"

"Correct."

"So we don't know who or what is over there."

"Status: This unit's power supply sustained damage during the conflict in the hostile township. Charge retention is currently compromised with an accelerated drain."

"What does that mean?"

"Explanation: This unit requires maintenance, Little Miss. My operation is limited at present, and I am at risk of shutting down indefinitely. Dominion will likely have necessary tools and a replacement power module."

"They also likely got monsters, Abe," Vincent said. "You read the big, scary signs, right?"

"You want to keep going down the road, Abraham?" Dot asked.

"Strategy: Our optimal course of action is to reach the research facility, locate and install a new power module, and scavenge for food and supplies."

Dot turned to Vincent and saw fear in his deep, black eyes, a fear that he couldn't explain but was firmly there. She didn't want to force him to revisit old haunts, not after enduring the trauma at his former home of Colt, but she also didn't want her mechanical friend to break down.

"Vincent, if you're not comfortable..."

"Nah, let's not make a decision on any nagging feeling I got," Vincent said. "My memory is shot, Dottie, kinda like Abe's network disconnect thingy."

"Kinda like me."

"I suppose so, but I could be worried over nothing."

"So, you are worried?" Dot said.

"Not with you and the big guy and Gypsy with me."

"Well, if you're sure, then it does look like we're walking for a while."

26

Dominion

After a three-hour, 13-kilometer hike through the woods, across rocky and muddy terrain parallel with the Broken Road to avoid being spotted, Dot and her companions caught sight of a building so large it dwarfed both Wellspring and Colt. Eight stories tall and a half-kilometer long, the Dominion Research Vivarium seemed to occupy the entire horizon, with the peaks of the East Hills beyond. To Dot, it looked like several airplane hangers connected end-to-end, whatever airplane hangers were.

"That must be the place," Vincent said, scrutinizing the roofline like a cityscape. "How much further, Abe?"

"Estimation: The facility is 1.4 kilometers ahead. We should arrive in 6.1 minutes."

"Dang, it looks like 6.1 hours to me."

"We're all exhausted, Vincent," Dot said from within the mech's chest. "We'll rest when we get there."

Though Vincent had clung to Abraham's back during their cross-country trek, wrapping his vines around the lumbering robot for so long took its toll. He looked down at Gypsy ahead of them, scouting their path, and wondered where the dog got his stamina.

"Gypsy is such a trooper," Vincent said. "I wish I had his strong legs, even though wishes don't help."

"Despite what Solomon said, I believe wishes can help," Dot said. "They keep your goals in mind, keep you focused."

"So true. I need to focus on staying focused."

"But you don't need to wish for Gypsy's legs, Vincent. You're stronger than you think."

"Me? Strong?"

"We've all seen what you can do."

"I suppose so, but hanging on to the big guy while he bobs up and down can make anybody tired. Still, it beats walking."

The group reached a tall chain-link fence that surrounded the immense property and was greeted by a metal sign on an unmanned guard booth – "Dominion Research Authorized Personnel Only." The rust on the sign, and the cobwebs and weeds in the small booth, suggested that no guard had stood at that post for decades.

A second sign hung on the fence – "Danger High-Voltage Electric Fence Stay Back 5 Feet."

"Electric fence?" Vincent asked, his voice quivering. "High voltage?"

"It means you'll get shocked if you touch it," Dot said.

"You mean dead shocked?"

"Correct," Abraham said.

"What does five feet mean again? My feet are much bigger than Dottie's, and Abe, yours are even bigger."

"Explanation: A measurement of one imperial foot has a metric equivalent of 0.3 meters. The electrical field's five-foot radius extends 1.5 meters from the fence."

Abraham's conversion math made no more sense to Vincent than the old sign, but he figured it was best to stay well away from the fence, far more than just five footsteps.

"Request: Please exit my frame with caution, Little Miss." Abraham opened his chest canopy.

"What's wrong?" Dot asked.

"Explanation: This unit's construction contains electrical insulator buffers comprising alloys of tungsten, bismuth, lead, and titanium. Humans do not have such protection."

"Abe don't want you to get zapped dead," Vincent said.

"The fence can't still be charged after all this time," Dot said as she climbed out of the robot and onto the ground.

"Incorrect. The security measure remains active with a continuous current of 8,000 volts."

"That sounds like a lot of volts," Vincent said.

"Correct. It is a potentially fatal level, particularly for Little Miss."

"We still need to get inside," Dot said. "We haven't much choice."

"Warning: Please remain behind this unit."

Abraham approached the main gate and forced it open, sliding it aside, snapping its badly rusted padlock. The electrical current crackled as his armored frame absorbed the fence's voltage. A moment later, the open gate awaited them.

"Dang, that lock looks old," Vincent said. "Older than the rest of the fence."

The girl realized he was right. While the padlock looked as ancient as the guard booth, the fence appeared nearly new.

"Good observation, Vincent," Dot said. "That's so smart."

"Thanks, Dottie! I think being around you and Abe makes me smarter!"

Dot liked to encourage the plant-man to think through situations, to scrutinize his surroundings, proving to the world that he wasn't just a simpleton to be dismissed. During their cross-country trek, Vincent had chattered on about his good and bad days in Colt, blocked memories newly exposed by the elder's cruelty. Dot hated every detail. She hated the fact that her friend endured years of daily abuse – both physical and mental – in that heartless hunting village before fleeing to the sanctuary of his beloved farm. So long as she was his friend and companion, she vowed that no one would speak harshly to him or look down on him ever again.

"Abraham, how is that possible?" she asked. "Why does the lock seem so much older than the fence as Vincent pointed out?"

"Explanation: The fence comprises a Class-40 galvanized wire mesh with a zinc-aluminum composite coating. Coupled with its uninterrupted electrical current, it has been largely protected from oxidation. The lock has no such protective material."

"Kinda like Dottie," Vincent said.

"Status: The lock's internal mechanism is seized from advanced rust."

Vincent picked up the large padlock and shook it. "Feels heavy and solid, like its insides are all frozen together."

"Correct."

"So, the lock has rusted shut," Dot said, "and the fence is still charged. That means no one has gone in or out in a long, long time."

"Agreement."

"Good observation, Dottie!" Vincent said. "That's so smart!"

"You pick up anything inside?" the girl asked her mech.

The robot looked up at the intimidating building. "Assessment: There are no organic or inorganic life signs within a 10-kilometer radius."

"If it's abandoned, why the electric fence and the locked gate?"

"Extrapolation: The facility's internal structure consists of iron alloy supports and lead wall coverings, supplemented by polymer-based material, the combination of which is known to interfere with conventional sensor arrays."

"Sometimes I get dizzy hearing Abe explain stuff," Vincent said. "He's the smartest war robot I know!"

"He's the only war robot we know," Dot said with a laugh. "Abraham, what are you saying? About the walls?"

"Possibility: The structure is blocking my scans. My assessment of life signs within is likely flawed."

"You mean there could be people in there?" Vincent asked. "Lots of people?"

"Correct."

"Why build something so big that can't be scanned?" Dot asked. "Not even by Abraham?"

"Why else, Dottie?" Vincent felt a chill run through his vines. "To keep folks from knowing what or who is inside! A scary, giant shack like this can't be hiding warm and fuzzy things! Monsters ahead, remember?"

"Theory," Abraham said. "The science facility was fled in such haste that some self-sustaining experiments may have continued after the human staff abandoned them. Such experiments are often networked with security measures."

Dot walked across a strange, cracked, paved field with white lines painted in a grid pattern protruded by weeds. Derelict cars – similar to those on the streets of Wellspring – sat neatly between the lines, as if they were meant to remain there forever. The girl imagined the immense grid once filled with hundreds of such cars, the personal vehicles of the Dominion staff. As she looked about her, only about two dozen remained, their windows busted out, their rusted frames now serving as homes for insect colonies and birds' nests.

"It's a parking lot," Dot said, recalling something she was taught before being "blessed" with specified memory loss. "This was a storage space for cars."

"I don't see a lot," Vincent said. He counted the vehicles, using his fingers and leaves to keep track. "I only see 14."

"At one time, there were a lot of cars. That's where the name comes from."

"Why did humans need to keep their cars here, Dottie? Didn't they have barns or stables like Father?"

"I'm not sure," Dot said, trying to piece together the property's history.

"The humans who left their cars here, they came to work, right? They weren't running."

"In the end, they all ran."

Dot and her friends crossed the parking lot and reached the front wall of the massive building. There were no doors in sight.

"Statement," Abraham said. "The nearest entrance is 22 meters south." He turned and led them down the windowless wall.

"The world wasn't always at war, Vincent," the girl said, still picturing the facility's old life. "People weren't always fearful for their lives. They had jobs, like you had on the farm and Abraham had with the Loyalists. They worked in places like this but lived next to each other in towns like Colt, along with their families."

"Families?"

"You know, a family, a group of people that lives and travels together."

"Like us?" Vincent asked.

"Like us." Though Dot surely saw her companions as an odd assembly of family, Vincent's strange question made her think of any blood relations she might have had prior to her Blessing. Sadly, her memory offered nothing to fill her need for a history, one worth fighting for.

Dot spotted the entrance Abraham spoke of, a simple door two meters tall and one meter wide that nearly blended in with the light gray brick wall extending in both directions, seemingly as far as they could see.

"Abraham, is that the only way in?" Dot asked. "It's too small for you."

"Assessment: There are six other accessible doors, all identical in dimension to this one."

"You'll have to wait outside, big guy," Vincent said. "We'll just go in, get your power thingy, get some supplies, and pop back out before dark."

"Agreement."

"That's twice we think alike, Abe! You guys really do have a way of making me feel smart!"

"Strategy: This unit will remain outside for surveillance while you infiltrate the facility. Through your cochlear device, I shall inform you when you are near the necessary equipment."

"I thought you couldn't scan inside the building?"

"Explanation: Once the structure is breached, this unit should have limited sensor access of the interior."

"He means he can peek in through the open door!" Vincent said. "Again, me and Abe think alike!"

"Very good, Vincent," Dot said with a smile.

Dot twisted the doorknob, to no avail. Like the perimeter fence, it was secured well. Abraham poked the knob with one of his massive fingers, easily forcing the door open with the buckling of splintered wood. The girl opened the door and peered inside. A dark stairwell descended into shadow.

"Will you be okay out here?" Dot asked the mech.

"Him okay?" Vincent said with a laugh. "No one is gonna mess with an Abe Class combat guy like him. The ones I'm worried about are us!"

"I was asking about his battery."

"Status: This unit's reserve power is at 63 percent."

"We'll be back before it's 62!" Vincent said.

"Projection: If you are in danger, command me to extract you and I shall immediately level the building if necessary"

"Whoa, not necessary, Abraham," Dot said, as if to calm her anxious friend. "But I definitely appreciate it. No need to worry."

"Statement: This unit cannot worry."

"Uh huh."

"I'll worry for both of us, Abe," Vincent said, unsure about stepping foot on the spiral stairs leading down into darkness.

"Request: Be alert at all times when exploring the unknown interior and maintain open communication."

"You sure sound worried," Dot said.

"Confirmation: This unit will be ready and waiting for your exit, Little Miss, and will expect your prompt return."

"I'll miss you too, Abraham."

"Let's just get this over with," Vincent said, nervous. He wrapped his vines on the stairwell's railing and started the descent ahead of the girl. Gypsy took three steps further down, the German Shepherd poised to defend his companions.

Abraham watched the trio disappear down into the dark. He widened his sensor array, taxing his corrupted power supply further, hoping to identify life forms within the building now that the door was open, but there were none.

He knew his readings were surely false.

27

The Walled Jungle

To Vincent's surprise and delight, the shadows engulfing the stairs came from the thick canopy of a massive rainforest – palm trees, kapok, and rubber trees stood over a dense floor of orchids, lilies, cacao, and coffee. Their combined scents were pungent, fragrant, almost overwhelming. After several minutes of making his way down the spiral stairs, he stared open-jawed at avocados, bananas, coconuts, dense clusters of guavas, bursting grapefruit, budding pineapples, and tree nuts of all varieties.

"Forget Kellan!" Vincent said. "We could just live here!"

"It is beautiful," Dot said, in awe of the spectrum of color before them.

"Sure, it's pretty, but look at all this food! It's like the ultimate farm! Think of the things I could grow here!" He ran his long, spindly fingers across a giant palm frond. "Euterpe precatoria. I've seen them in my picture books, but I never thought I'd see them up close. They're quite chatty if you stop and listen."

While her friend stood enamored by the abundant plant life, Dot heard the calls of different birds and the rustling of leaves, the occasional wild animal crossing the terrain under them. She theorized Abraham sensed no humanoid life because the animals here were "pure" like Gypsy, unadulterated, born of the land – be it a man-made habitat – rather than laboratory cages.

"These are animals," she said. "Real animals."

"Father said they were all gone, except for the little critters in the woods."

"I just saw two elephants," Dot said, unsure how she could identify them. "Over there are toucans, tapirs, and sloths."

"You sure know a lot about animals, Dottie. I guess you know a lot about a lot of things."

"I guess I do."

"If I'm stronger than I know, then you're smarter than you know!" He saw a large animal from the corner of his eye. "What's that big one over there with the stripes?"

"That's a tiger," Dot said, recalling that some animals were carnivores. "Stay away from him."

"But he's walking hunched over, on his hands and feet. They all are."

"That's because they're pure animals, Vincent. Aren't they amazing?"

"Yeah, but are you sure about him? The mean-looking tiger, I mean. Are you really sure?"

"Pretty sure."

"No wonder the walls are scan-proof," Vincent said. "If the Greenies knew about this place, they'd take it over right away."

"Why would they do that?"

"To eat everything, of course," Vincent said. "The Greenies are run by humans, and humans eat all plants and animals, Dottie."

"I know, but I'd like to think they wouldn't eat these wonderful creatures."

"They don't just eat fish and rabbits, they eat everything, even if they're pure and pretty. They kill 'em and eat 'em up."

Gypsy was the first to reach the bottom of the stairs, his paws treading upon soft, damp soil covered in ferns. Vincent and Dot joined him, overwhelmed by the immense, contained ecosystem.

"I'll start gathering food," Vincent said. "There's plenty of it! Ask Abe where the power thingy is."

"Location," Abraham said over Dot's earpiece, having heard Vincent. "The nearest maintenance shed is 15 meters north of your position."

"Good place to start," Dot said, though she couldn't see any shed through the dense foliage. "Abraham, I think I know why you didn't sense any humanoid life. All I see are pure animals roaming..."

"Revised Reconnaissance: There are 315 human hybrids within the facility."

Dot froze upon hearing her friend's startling update.

"Abraham, are you sure? You didn't detect any earlier."

"Explanation: I have widened the open doorway by an additional three meters and therefore widened my sensor sweep. It was necessary in order to guide you."

"You widened the doorway?"

"Correct."

"In a brick wall?"

"Correct."

Dot imagined the crashing sounds of cracked cement, bent rebar, and buckled iron support beams at the thought of Abraham widening a doorway within a reinforced cinderblock wall. She was surprised to have heard none of it. The overpowering sounds of the rainforest wildlife and the thick canopy overhead must have muffled his actions.

"That was dangerous, Abraham, but I don't think anyone heard you. I certainly didn't."

"Explanation: I measured internal decibel levels and calculated the risk of the destructive measure. It was a drastic course of action necessary in order to guide you."

"But you're not worried," Dot said with a knowing smile.

"Statement: This unit cannot worry."

"If you say so."

Judging from the mech's willingness to annihilate anything that posed a threat to her, his openness to learn from her, and the fact that he occasionally called her "Little Miss," Dot had long suspected that Abraham had perhaps a modicum of emotion, even if he didn't realize it. His recent revelation that portions of his wondrous computer brain comprised organic gray matter convinced her he indeed had the capacity to feel. Whether that was a good thing for a powerful war machine remained to be seen. She just felt relieved to have imprinted on him the night they met. A combat mech can make for a comforting and loyal friend, but also a nightmarish enemy.

She looked across the peaceful rainforest floor, which seemed spacious before but now felt alarmingly dense after learning of the many wild creatures lurking in the bush.

"So, there are hundreds of hybrids living in this rainforest?" Dot asked.

"Hybrids?" Vincent said. "Hundreds?"

"Correct," Abraham said. "Proceed with caution."

"He said to be careful," Dot said to Vincent.

"If Abe says to be careful, I'm going to be double-extra-careful."

While Dot and Gypsy ventured deeper into the rainforest in search of the shed, Vincent picked fruit and nuts as fast as his many vines could handle, bundling them in tarps he found draped across abandoned utility vehicles.

"Heliconia," Vincent said, as he plucked a bunch of bananas from the top of a tall tree. "Nice and ripe. These will make a fine pudding tonight."

He paused upon hearing movement behind him and turned around slowly.

A young girl with features of a fawn – light brown fur spotted and underlined with white – watched him from behind a tree with a timid doe-eyed expression. He snapped off a few bananas and offered them to her at the end of one of his snaking vines, but the little hybrid girl ducked into a bush, afraid of the strange plant-man now staring at her.

"Don't be scared, little deer," Vincent said. "The trees like you. This kapok says you're a sweet girl."

Seeing the fear in her big brown eyes, he dropped the fruit and stretched a vine to a nearby pond. He picked a large water lily, pink and yellow, and offered it to her. The fawn-girl emerged from the bush and took the delicate blossom from his long, leafy vine with a hesitant smile.

"See, I'm not gonna hurt you," the gentle plant-man said. "My friends and I like hybrids. The trees say your name is Ama."

"I'm Ama," a female voice firmly said from behind the child. "Who are you?"

The fawn-girl's trepidation fell away as her mother, a tall elegant caribou-woman with powerful legs and majestic velvet-skinned antlers atop her head, stepped out into the open as if daring Vincent to accost them. She relaxed her stance upon seeing the innocent, curious look on his wood-grained face, her sharp instincts telling her that this strange man posed no threat.

"I say again, who are you?" Ama demanded.

"I'm Vincent! They also call me Vinny Greenblood, Veggie Vinny, Dim Vin, the Green Fool, Vincent Vines, but I prefer Vincent, and Dottie says that's okay because..."

"I've never seen you before," Ama said, interrupting him with a commanding tone. "And I'm familiar with every predator and prey here. Which are you?"

"Me? Oh, I'm a vegetarian. Father let me try a bite of fried squirrel once, but I felt nauseous swallowing it. I cried all night, not sure if it was guilt or indigestion. Maybe both. I used the chamber pot twice. What a mess. I drank a gallon of honey tea to help..."

"So you're prey?" Ama said.

"Vincent is no one's prey," Dot said, entering the clearing with Gypsy. "And he's not a predator, either. He'd never kill anyone."

"I killed a bunch of those Greenie Automen guys," Vincent said with regret.

"Automen don't really die, Vincent, remember? They fix themselves. They fix each other. You even reminded us back in Colt."

"Oh yeah, I forgot," Vincent said. "You mean they grow back?"

"Yes, in a way."

"I ask a third time, who are you?" Ama said, confused and frustrated. She stepped forward to get a better look at the newcomers.

"I'm Vincent, but I guess I already told you that. This is Dottie and that's Gypsy."

Ama leaned forward and sniffed the tall, thin plant-man. She touched the leaves on his arm, unlike anything in her rainforest. "Were you born here?"

"Actually, I think I was."

"This is The Great Domain?" Dot asked, piecing together Vincent's life from his many stories.

"Hard to say. I was in a greenhouse, a big lab above a rainforest... like that one up there!" He pointed to a long glass-walled room suspended above the forest's canopy. "I remember the view. This might be the giant indoor rainforest I came from. I'd have to see other giant indoor rainforests to be sure."

"I have a feeling this is the place, Vincent. Do you want to go up there and look around?"

"Yes, I think I do, but... I'm kinda nervous."

"We may never come here again," Dot said. "If you ever wondered about where you're from, now is the time to find out. I have problems remembering, too, and I'd want to know the truth." She turned to the tall hybrid woman, now at ease with them but still alert, always watching the perimeter of the clearing with her ears perked and antlers held high. "Don't you agree, Miss Ama?"

"Perhaps it's best you don't remember," Ama said. "Sometimes, I wish I didn't."

"Trust me," the girl said, "you don't want to wish for that. Maybe you can help us?"

"Can the little deer girl come with us up to the lab?" Vincent asked, smiling down at the fawn-girl with the water lily now resting atop her head like a tiny hat. "I bet she never saw this place from up top."

"No one goes up there," Ama said. "I'll never go up there, which means Ameri won't."

"Ameri? That's her name? What a pretty name for a pretty deer girl."

"My friend told us there are hundreds of hybrids here," Dot said. "Are they dangerous?"

"I'd like to see them," Vincent said. "I want to meet every one of them!"

"Then it's true you aren't prey," Ama said. "Only a predator seeks other clans. Prey stay with their own kind and avoid the hunters, especially at night when they hunt in packs."

"They can't be that bad! We made friends with dogs and leopards, even a bear!"

"We aren't predators," Dot said.

"You're human," Ama said, still unsure about the visitors. "Though you're not yet grown, girl, you're the apex predator, worse than any tiger or panther here."

"Dottie doesn't kill no one," Vincent said. "Neither do I."

"You said you killed 'Automen'."

"Dottie reminded me they don't die."

"Maybe not, but you still attacked them, and a moment ago, you *thought* you killed. Now you want to meet others. My Ameri isn't going anywhere with you."

"Miss Ama," Dot said. "We don't need to meet anyone. Right, Vincent?"

"I suppose not," Vincent said, deflated. "We just need to find a power thingy for our big robot mech guy and we'll be leaving."

"You make less sense with each word, plant," Ama said.

"Sorry if I don't make no sense. I do that sometimes."

"They're machines," Dot said, realizing the caribou-woman in her long-sheltered world might not know about artificial soldiers or combat mechs. She might not even know the Story of The World. Living behind the walls of this sealed ecosystem for generations was akin to receiving a Blessing. "Machines and synthetics are like the equipment in the lab above us and that old utility truck over there. Some are creatures with arms and legs. They can walk and talk, but they're not alive. They were made during the war."

"Now those guys are definitely predators," Vincent said.

Ama looked down at young Ameri as she plucked petals from her water lily and watched them float down onto her little hooves. The child's innocence always strengthened her mother's vigilance.

"I may not know 'Automen' or 'mech'," Ama said, "but I know what a machine is, and I definitely know war. We fight to survive every day."

"But you said..."

"I say you make no sense because you speak of leaving. Whether or not you find what you're looking for, and whether you're human or animal or plant, no one leaves The Great Domain."

28

A Little Curious

Gypsy led Dot and Vincent to the maintenance shed as Ama and her daughter Ameri retreated into the forest. Dot replayed the caribou-woman's last words with dread. The predators she spoke of were likely watching them from afar. Dot could practically feel their eyes on them.

Vincent pulled the shed's corrugated steel door from its rusted hinges, allowing Dot to enter the small storage room. She found sealed sets of tools, shelves lined with batteries and parts, and wall hooks holding firearms. Everything was untouched and covered with decades of dust.

"Why are there guns in a rainforest?" Dot asked.

"Predators," Vincent said. "The humans who used to live here must have used them for protection."

"But none of them have been used. Their activation pins are still in place."

"Dang, you sure know a lot about a lot of stuff, Dottie."

"I'm starting to see that, too."

"Maybe folks left before they needed these guns?"

"Instruction," Abraham said through Dot's earpiece. "Search for power modules labeled A1000, A1500, A1900, or A2120."

Dot spotted a rack of small metal devices, cylindrical and fitted with some kind of electrical port. They were labeled "PM-A2120."

"I think found the power modules," Dot said into her earpiece. "PM-A2120. About the size of a soup can?"

"Correct," Abraham said over their two-way link.

"Are you sure this will do? You're an A1900."

"Clarification: The power module you hold was designed for a later model but is compatible with this unit. It will theoretically double my output capacity, increasing my strength and speed."

"Amazing," the girl said, examining the miraculous "soup can" in her hand. "It's hard to imagine you any stronger, Abraham. How many do you need?"

"One."

Dot gave the module to Vincent. He rolled it in his palm before tucking it in the front pocket of his overalls.

"How can something so small power up a big giant robot like Abe?" he asked.

"Clarification: This unit's solar collectors and battery bank absorb and retain power, respectively. The module merely regulates energy flow and routes it to different systems."

"Like a heart pumping blood," Dot said.

"Correct."

"No wonder you can't fully function without it. Let's take two just to be safe."

"Gratitude."

"What next, big guy?" Vincent asked, pocketing a second module.

"Instruction: Search for toolsets labeled similarly."

"Got one," Dot said, spotting a small plastic case. "Toolset for A2000 Series."

"Instruction: Keep the power modules and toolset dry and bring them to me immediately."

"We're going to explore the lab first."

"We are?" Vincent said in his confused, cracked voice. "But Abe said we gotta go..."

"It's now or never, Vincent," Dot said. "There may be answers for you up there."

"Answers to what?"

"You have questions, just like me."

"I do?"

"Vincent, haven't you ever wondered why you left this place? Why Father Young took you away? He used to work here. He and his friends helped create these hybrids, only to leave them contained to fend for themselves. Don't you want to know why?"

"Father took me away because... he wanted to protect me."

"Yes, but protect you from what?"

"The predators?"

"But you were safe up in the lab," Dot said.

"I suppose that's true."

"And what happened to the scientists? Why did they leave? They made you. They raised you. Aren't you curious?"

"A little. But why is this such a big deal to you, Dottie?"

Dot thought about why she felt the need to dig into her friend's roots when he clearly didn't share her urgency.

"I may never learn about my history," the girl said, "but I can at least help you learn about yours. I know you'd do the same for me if you could."

"Yep. I would."

"We'll see you shortly, Abraham," she said into her earpiece.

"Recommendation: Abandon your exploration and return to the surface to install my replacement power module. I will be unable to protect you if I experience a sudden power failure."

"Abraham, don't you want Vincent to learn about where he came from?"

"Conclusion: It is illogical to risk one's life and the lives of others in pursuit of extraneous knowledge."

"Knowing who you are is not extraneous," Dot said.

"Conclusion: Vincent's history does not benefit our current mission."

"And what is our mission?"

"Statement: Our current mission is to locate your associates in jeopardy and relocate them to safer ground."

"And why am I doing that? I don't know who they are, and their safety doesn't affect us."

"Speculation: You cherish all life and wish to safeguard theirs."

"It's more than that," Dot said. "I need to know why so many people died for me, why they wiped my memory, and finding those girls is the key."

"Query: Do you refer to the spectral individuals we encountered on the metaphysical plane?"

"In our shared dream, yes, those girls."

"Maybe Abe is right, Dottie," Vincent said. "We should get out of here before those predator guys get some ideas. They might not want to eat a walking salad like me, but you probably look like a girl-shaped sandwich to them."

"Vincent, Sergeant Furst said you were the last remaining plant hybrid in the world. He assumed the others were killed in the wild by the Purists, but something tells me there never were any others out there. I don't know why, but I think there was ever only one of you set free. Father Young felt the need to take you away, but he couldn't have done it alone. He probably had help. You saw the security outside."

"I was a little curious before," Vincent said, "but now I'm extra-super-curious."

Dot pressed the cochlear device in her ear and spoke with a forced tone of authority, knowing that her mech would protest. "Abraham, we're going to investigate the lab over the rainforest."

"Recommendation: Abort and return to this unit immediately for optimum safety."

"I already know how you feel, but I've made my decision. Will you guide us?"

"Projection: Sunset will occur within the hour. Night raids are possible now that the security fence and exterior wall have been breached."

"I promise we'll be out before then. Will you guide us?"

Standing in the maintenance shed, with Vincent's bundle of food sitting just outside, Dot waited for a response. She feared she either lost communication with her guardian above or lost his confidence in their revised mission. Either way, without his help, they'd be practically blind roaming the facility.

"Abraham, will you guide us?" Dot asked again.

"Location," Abraham said after a long, tense minute. "Proceed to a ladder seven meters north of your position."

29

The Velveteen Rabbit

Gypsy remained at the foot of the intimidating caged ladder. It rose 50 meters above the rainforest floor, with landings every 10 meters. Dot and Vincent carefully climbed the rusted steel rungs, many of which had rotted like splintered wood. The suspended greenhouse lab was the size of a sprawling suburban home. Its walls were made of reinforced glass supported by curved beams and covered in an active wire mesh, an ominous amount of protection for an area so high above the trees.

Stepping onto the floor of the brightly lit lab, Vincent's mind flooded with memories of running between the many workstations when he was barely tall enough to see over them, mashing buttons on computer keyboards, all while holding a large plush rabbit in his hands.

"Velvie," he said, imagining the doll with him. "I wonder where she is."

"Who's that?" Dot asked.

"She was my bunny rabbit. Such a cutie pie. She had big black marble eyes, brown velvet fur, a bow, and a little red dress. She could be a little sassy sometimes, but she loved me. Velvie was with me wherever I went."

"She was your toy," Dot said, enamored by the thought of a little plant boy clutching his plush doll. "Did you take her with you?"

"No. I left her on my cot. I remembered her too late, after we ran up the stairs and made our way outside. Father said to leave her behind, that the others would take care of her, but I don't see anyone here."

Though the workstations were mostly intact, many of them still running with monitors observing areas of the rainforest, no scientists remained to operate them. The dust and cobwebs told Dot that the last of the humans fled – one way or another – many years ago.

Dot stepped through the exit hatch, back outside onto the catwalk at the top of the ladder. She looked up at the banks of skylights above the facility and realized they were the only source of light. Abraham said sunset was approaching, soon to be followed by nightfall. The rainforest would be cast into total darkness, making their departure ever more perilous.

"Abraham, how soon before it's dark?"

"Estimation: Zero visibility in 38 minutes."

The mech's many warnings replayed in her mind in shouts, like two hands grabbing her by the shoulders, trying to shake some sense into her. While Vincent explored his past, they might die, eaten alive by the predators. Ama said they came out in packs at night. The sun was setting soon, and it was a long way to the spiral staircase.

Dot stepped back into the lab. "Vincent, let's give ourselves ten minutes tops and then head out..."

She looked for her friend and nearly fell over in fright upon seeing an old man in a white overcoat standing in the middle of the main room. He stared at the girl through cloudy eyes behind thick glasses, his long gray hair resting on his shoulders in rope-like strands.

"Who are you?" Dot said, keeping sight of the exit hatch.

"A proper introduction starts with your own name first," the elderly man said in a tired yet friendly voice.

"I apologize. My name is Dot."

"You're a human and a child, two things I thought I'd never see again."

"My friend's name is..." Dot looked around to find Vincent gone, likely lost in one of the lab's many adjacent rooms. "He was just here a moment ago."

"I know your friend well. HPL-VNCT-001."

"What kind of cold name is that?"

"It means he was the first hybrid case study of human-plantae-liana in vivaria chloroplastic nucleosidic transition. HPL-VNCT-001. Cold labels aside, child, we simply called him 'Vincent.' It came from his biological classification, of course, though I like to think we named him after my grandfather. They had a lot in common, if not their species. They both had an overabundance of energy and a plethora of bad jokes."

"What did you do with him?" the girl asked.

"I merely pointed my finger to the door behind me when he mentioned Velvie. He's in his old bedroom now."

Dot wanted to join her friend but still didn't trust the curious old man, who simply stared at her in awe.

"A proper response to a proper introduction continues with your name next," Dot said.

"Quite right. Dr. Iziah Blum at your service, child."

"You know a lot about Vincent."

"I know everything about Vincent."

"You created him?"

"Oh, Heaven's no," Dr. Blum said. "I'm only 42, less than half Vincent's age."

As with Senior Wainright, Dot somehow instantly knew that Dr. Blum was much younger than he appeared, though she still felt surprised by his actual age, even more so with Vincent's.

"You're saying Vincent is 90?" Dot asked.

"He's 89, if memory serves."

"He thinks he's 40."

"That's because his long-term memory didn't fully form until about that time in his life."

"I don't understand."

"Do you remember anything from when you were a toddler?" Dr. Blum asked. "Vincent had an extended early childhood, to put it mildly, and he will likely outlive us all."

Dot had more questions, but wanted to check on her friend. She walked around Dr. Blum and placed her hand on Vincent's bedroom doorknob, turning to the old man before opening the door.

"You won't disappear on me, too, will you?" she asked.

"I've been in this lab all my life, child, and will continue to be in this lab for the rest of it. No one leaves The Great Domain."

"We'll see about that."

Dot entered the small bedroom and stood overwhelmed at the layers of plant life adorning wall shelves, hanging in baskets, and overflowing from box containers lined with gardening tools meant for tiny hands. Decades of childhood wonder sat in an oak toy chest in one corner, a rainbow-colored bookshelf in another. Between them sat several watering cans with tiny handprints in blue, green, and yellow, along with the name of their owner scrawled with crayon – "VNCT."

"Vincent," Dot said. "This really was your room?"

His unique body nearly lost in the dense foliage, Vincent sat on his old cot next to "Velvie," a chubby plush rabbit in a little red velvet dress.

"She never moved," Vincent said, his voice barely above a whisper. "She's still in the same spot where I left her. It makes me sad."

"But you found her again. You should be happy."

"No one played with her all this time. She got lonely, went back to being a doll."

"Wasn't she always a doll?"

Vincent stretched out a vine to the corner bookshelf and grabbed one of his many children's stories. He handed the thin, illustrated book to Dot.

"The Velveteen Rabbit," Dot read. "I know this story."

"Then you know what happened."

"My memory is kinda fuzzy," she lied. "Why don't you tell me?" She sat beside him on the cot and handed him the book.

"The velveteen rabbit loved the boy," Vincent said. "She wanted to be a real bunny for him, but the boy was sick, always poked by doctors, always taking tests, stuck in bed all day with tubes sticking out of him. They were trying hard to make him normal. One night, the Flower Fairy visited the velveteen rabbit and made her real, but by then the boy had moved away. She never played with him again."

"I see," Dot said. "That little boy had it rough."

Vincent flipped through the pages of his favorite childhood book and gazed at its elegant artwork. "If only the rabbit went with the boy when he was taken away, they would have played together every night, and she would still be real."

Dot picked up the plush doll, the first to touch it in years. She patted off its layer of dust.

"She's looking at you right now," Dot said. "She's right here beside you, smiling at you. She'll always be your friend, and she'll never leave you again."

Vincent looked at Dot with a breath of hope.

"You promise?"

"I promise, and it doesn't get more real than that."

"Everyone else left," Vincent said.

"Yes, they did. They had to. But she'll leave you."

"Okay."

Dr. Blum stood in the doorway, having just heard their tender conversation. Vincent looked up at him.

"What about you, Dr. Blum?" he said. "Will you leave?"

"Like I told your friend, I will never leave," Dr. Blum said. "I told her no one leaves The Great Domain. But you, my son, you must leave. This is no place for a boy as special as you."

"This time, I won't forget Velvie."

"I'll make sure you don't."

* * *

"Estimation: Zero visibility in 19 minutes."

"Thank you, Abraham," Dot said into her earpiece. She spoke with a mouthful of the spinach omelette Dr. Blum had quickly prepared for her and Vincent. The eggs came from hens kept in the next lab, fried in chicken fat and mixed with herbs and vegetables from Vincent's bedroom. The doctor had long maintained the room as his personal garden, which provided more than enough food for the sole remaining member of the faculty.

"This was your favorite," Dr. Blum said. "I must've made it for you hundreds of times. I used butter back then."

"You made me omelettes," Vincent said, imagining his former caretakers' smiling faces. "Dr. Artemus made pies and cookies. Dr. Wellington made pancakes. Dr. Imago and Dr. Young... Father... made soup, stew."

"Dr. Imago?" Dot asked. "You remember him?"

"I remember them all now, sitting with me at this table, eating with me, teaching me how to talk and how to read. Father taught me all about gardening, which is like farming, but smaller. Sometimes they'd let me play down in the forest. They carried guns to keep me safe, but they never had to fire a shot. The others liked me, I think."

"The other hybrids."

"Yes." Vincent took the last bite of his omelette. The faces of the doctors faded with the remnants of that final taste. "What happened to them, Dr. Blum?"

Velvie sat on the dining room table between them all, the only one still smiling, as Dr. Blum recalled the fate of his comrades.

"When I was a child about Dot's age," Dr. Blum said, "my father said fifty men and women of science ran Dominion when it first opened, back when he was also a child. The newly formed global government pooled their resources and technology to create this marvelous place, the largest and most advanced contained ecosystem ever built, and the first to be completely self sustaining. Compatible plant and animal life from every corner of the world was brought here, and it all worked together with perfection. Our mission began in harmony."

"What went wrong?" Dot asked.

"The mission itself. None of us had the foresight to see that it was critically flawed from the start."

"But you said everything was perfect," Vincent said.

"This place was perfect, every detail of its design, every root and leaf, every dragonfly and woodpecker and mouse and elk. Perfection and pure genius. It's what we did with it all that was foolish, arrogant, simply wrong. While my father and grandfather and their peers patted their own backs and celebrated the creation of this miniature world, it never occurred to them that the beings they worked so long to produce would undermine it all."

"The hybrids?" Vincent asked. "They ruined everything?"

"To be clear, I'm not saying your fellow hybrids had any malice. I love them all like my children and I can honestly say they never intended to drive out their creators. We just didn't factor their incompatibility with the very environment made for them. How could we? Our mission was equally ambitious and unprecedented, to reshape humanity through a fusion of animal and man. The world was desperate for a solution to The Worm, and in our hubris we looked to leapfrog over millennia of evolution. That was our first mistake."

"You said this place was self sustaining," Dot said. "It seems like it still is. What kind of mistake do you mean?"

"We had only studied the known animal kingdom before entering these halls, and we discovered later that our centuries of knowledge were pointless in the new age. The sum of all human knowledge, of all biologic, zoologic, and botanic studies, didn't prepare us for the unique needs of our hybrid offspring. As has been said many times before, humans are terrible at playing God."

Dr. Blum stood from the table and looked out through the glass walls at the man-made rainforest, the only world he'd ever known, a world he equally loved, hated, and feared.

"The hunting grounds in this vivarium were painstakingly designed to accommodate wolves, but not wolf-men. The trees were perfect for gorillas, but not primate-hybrids. The food and shelter we offered may have been ideal for deer and sloth and tigers, but not for their half-human counterparts. And so, as we released our beloved hybrids into our walled garden, paradise quickly fell."

"I still don't understand," Dot said. "Why are hybrids so different from the animals they come from?"

"The animal half is logical and rational, taking only what it needs from nature day to day, forming an equilibrium with its environment. But the human half cares nothing for balance. It plans ahead, stockpiles meat, trades with others, forms alliances only to betray them for personal gain. The human half gives in to paranoia, greed, and a lust for power. Soon after populating these woods, predators formed cross-species packs to hunt in large numbers. Their prey formed survivalist factions, striking hard and fast when cornered, exacting revenge after heavy casualties. This rainforest became the battleground for bloody, eternal war. Our grand solution to The Worm turned into another crisis."

"What happened to the staff?" Dot asked, afraid of the answer.

"They weren't taken by the packs, child," the doctor said, having seen the dread on her face. "They fled a few at a time over the years, choosing to take their chances out in the wild rather than face the hell we created in here. In time, fifty brilliant scientists dwindled to a courageous five: Artemus, Wellington, Young, Imago, and Blum."

"Where are the five now?"

"My grandparents died of old age, my parents of disease. Artemus and Wellington left soon after. Young fled with Vincent. That same night, Imago left and sealed the facility behind him."

"Why?" Vincent asked. "Why not just allow the hybrids to leave like I did?"

"Imago sealed the doors and gate because I asked him to. Vincent, my son, with your kind heart and innocent mind, you've always been an anomaly. The other hybrids weren't ready for the real world, and the Purists can't know of their existence. They would exploit them, do unspeakable things to them on behalf of their unholy faith."

"That's why the walls block scans," Dot said.

"How do you know that?"

"Our big mech buddy is waiting outside for us," Vincent said. "Say hi, Abe."

"Estimation: Zero visibility in 10 minutes," Abraham said over Dot's earpiece.

"Abraham says hi," Dot said, "in his own way."

"You have an Abraham combat mech?" Dr. Blum asked, astonished. "It actually obeys you?"

"Oh yeah, big guy, taller than me!" Vincent said. "He's real nice for a killer robot."

"Then you have a fighting chance out there. If you leave now, you can make it to your mech before dark. I'll light your way from this workstation."

"Perhaps we could stay the night?" Dot said.

"Your mech must have forced opened the gate. That means the facility is vulnerable. Leaving now is your best option if you want to stay ahead of the Purists."

"What about you, Dr. Blum?" Dot asked. "Will you come with us?"

"I must stay here, child. Someone has to maintain the habitat. I run everything from this lab. Without me, the balance would tip and this world would devour itself. I can't let my children suffer while I run away. I owe it to them."

Though Dot and Vincent could no longer fathom anyone spending the rest of their lives behind those walls, they understood Dr. Blum's reasoning and had to respect his decision. They stood from the table and nodded thanks for the meal and the memories. Before they could reach the door to the ladder, a loud howl filled the room.

"OWOOOOOOO!"

"What was that?" Dot asked, shaken by the sudden fright.

"That's the sound I fear," Dr. Blum said. "That's the sound of this world devouring itself."

"OWOOOOOOO!"

Dr. Blum rushed to the nearest workstation and changed channels on the monitor, switching between 30 closed-circuit cameras installed throughout the rainforest. He pressed a button rapidly, searching the live video feeds for the crying creature.

"OWOOOOOOO!"

"I see him!" Vincent said. "Go back a few!"

Dr. Blum switched back to a channel he'd flipped past and was startled to see a lone wolf hybrid chained to the front bumper of a derelict truck in a clearing below. Artificial rain came down from hundreds of sprinkler pipes in the ceiling, drenching the poor beast. Though the gray-and-white wolf-man appeared powerfully strong, his body covered in fur and muscle, he made no effort to escape his entrapment. He merely looked at the rising moon through a skylight and howled in agony.

"OWOOOOOOO!"

"Oh no," Dr. Blum said with dread. "I've been watching him for a while, but I didn't think this would happen so soon."

"Who is he, Dr. Blum?" Dot asked. "Is he hurt?"

"Not yet."

"Why is he chained up and howling like that?"

"His name is Cezar, and he's not howling because he's in any pain. He's crying out in shame, he's about to be killed, and he's standing in the middle of your path."

30

Cezar

Dot climbed down the long ladder to the rainforest floor. Gypsy stood waiting at the ladder's base, his eyes and ears pointed toward the incessant, guttural howl coming from the nearby clearing.

"OWOOOOOOO!"

"Estimation: Zero visibility in eight minutes." Abraham's voice sounded loud and urgent in Dot's earpiece.

Vincent made his way down slower, partly because of his fear of heights and partly due to his cargo of the power modules, a plush rabbit, a bag of egg sandwiches and fresh fruit, and two loaded pistols, all coiled within his vines behind his shoulders.

"Sorry I'm being a slowpoke," Vincent said as he hopped off the ladder.

"It's okay, Vincent. You're carrying everything."

"It's not that, Dottie. I'm nervous about these guns. I've never used one before. What if I use mine wrong? What if I drop it and someone takes it? Someone could get hurt."

"Dr. Blum made sure their handles recognize only our fingerprints, and only when we're holding them right. Otherwise, they're just L-shaped bricks."

"I get it, but I'm still nervous. I've seen what guns can do, seen it up close."

"Me, too," Dot said, remembering when Sergeant Furst fell dead to the mud in front of her and when Vincent was shot to pieces beside his father's work truck.

"Do we really need these things?" Vincent asked, unfurling his vines to reveal the twin pistols, one marked with a "D," the other with a "V."

"OWOOOOOOO!"

The heartbreaking howl answered the question.

"We just need to hold them," Dot said. "It's only a deterrent."

"Detergent?" he said. "The guns have soap in them?"

"Deterrent. It means just having them around for everyone to see will keep anything bad from happening."

"Like a scarecrow."

"That's right. The hybrids are smart enough not to take chances with guns around. That's why the scientists never had to fire one. Neither will we."

"What do we do about the moaning wolf guy?" Vincent asked, afraid to even glance in the beast's direction.

"We keep our distance, make our way back to the stairs."

"Can't Abe just come down here?"

"He's too big to use the spiral staircase," Dot said, looking up at the steps rising high above the forest floor. "And if he jumped down, I don't think we could get him back up top."

"Okay, we keep our distance."

"Estimation: Zero visibility in seven minutes."

"You're really going to count us down minute by minute, Abraham?" Dot asked.

"Correct."

Dot took her "D" gun from Vincent and gestured for him to ready his. Clutching their firearms with both hands, they ventured ahead and into the clearing with Gypsy leading them through the brush.

The silence and the growing darkness overcame them as they caught sight of the wolf-man chained to the abandoned truck. Standing on level ground with him, he seemed even larger, more menacing. The tormented creature met their stare with a blank expression. Though he'd never seen a human child or a plant hybrid, he showed no trace of curiosity, no plea for help in his sad eyes. He simply awaited his fate, as Dr. Blum said.

After passing the chained beast in a wide arc and making it across the lit clearing, Dot couldn't bring herself to step onto the spiral staircase. The supposedly feral creature didn't swipe his claws or snap his fangs, as Blum had warned. There was no rage or ravenous hunger. Instead, Dot sensed intelligence, regret, and despair – shame – and felt the need to reach out to him, to make it known she felt for him in his plight.

"Dr. Blum says your name is Cezar," Dot said as she stepped away from the stairs. "But he didn't tell us why you're chained up like this."

"It's best you leave Cezar," the wolf hybrid said, referring to himself in the third person. "The hunters watch us now."

"Who put you here?"

"Cezar chained himself," the wolf-man said. "Caffar demanded it."

"Caffar?"

"Caffar is the alpha. Caffar speaks, Cezar obeys."

"Alpha means he's the first!" Vincent said. "Ephraim is an alpha! The doctors used to call me alpha when I was a little twig!"

"The plant is right," Cezar said. "Caffar is first, Cezar is last, so Cezar chains himself to the old machine."

"But why?" Dot asked. "They're coming for you, aren't they? They hunt only at night, and night is about to fall."

"Cezar doesn't matter to you."

"That's not true. Speak to me. I may be the last person you'll ever have time to talk to."

Cezar looked down at Gypsy standing beside the girl. Like so many others, he'd never seen a pure dog before, even in a biological wonder like Dominion. The sight of the canine's trust in the human girl encouraged him to speak, to confide in her.

"Cezar is a pathetic weakness to the pack. Better Cezar fights for his life and dies for their meat."

"Estimation: Zero visibility in six minutes."

"Not now, Abraham," Dot said into her earpiece.

"Cezar is ready to die with his claws out," the wolf said. "Cezar will die so that the pack may become stronger."

"Dottie, the man has his own mission," Vincent said. "I don't want to see him get hurt, but it seems important to him."

It also felt important to Dot.

"I'd be the pathetic one if I didn't offer to help you," she said. The pistol felt heavy in her hand when she spotted him eyeing it. Trust between two people is impossible when one holds a loaded gun. To Vincent's surprise, she tossed it away into the bushes.

"Dottie, you gotta pick that up!" Vincent said. "Dr. Blum told us these guns are our only way out! It's detergent, remember?"

"The plant is right again," Cezar said. "The hunters will let you pass if you hold a human weapon."

"I know what Blum told us, Vincent," Dot said, "but we both know the weapon is a lie. I won't kill anyone, and I won't trick them into thinking I would. They may look like wild animals, but they're people."

"Estimation: Zero visibility in five minutes."

By that point, the mech's regular updates through the girl's earpiece were unnecessary as the sunlight had changed to orange, then to dark amber, as filtered through the dense canopy. The skylights now resembled large black squares mounted to the ceiling high above, leaving only the scattered lampposts Dr. Blum had activated along their path, their small circles of light positioned every 10 meters.

Despite Abraham's estimation, zero visibility had already arrived.

"Toss your gun away, Vincent," Dot said.

"But Dr. Blum said..."

"Trust me, we need to toss the guns."

Vincent swallowed his fear and flung his pistol into the trees as they approached the restrained wolf-man.

"I can't let you die with a chain around your ankle," Dot said.

"Cezar says you can, and you should."

"I had a chain around my leg once. I don't remember why, but I know I felt hopeless and alone."

"Senior Wainright always used a rope with me," Vincent said, recalling the times he was punished for not working hard enough for the villagers of Colt. "But I guess I felt the same way."

Walking up to the wolf hybrid, Dot saw how powerfully built he was, how his arms and back were layered with muscle, how his claws were long and sharp like ivory sickles. She wondered how anyone could view this intimidating beast as weak and deserving of a lonesome death, and she wondered how someone so strong could feel pathetic and worthless.

"Where's the key to the lock?" the girl asked. "If you're going to fight for your life, we're going to at least make it fair."

"Three-on-one was never meant to be fair," a deep grumbling voice said from the complete darkness beyond their circle of light.

Dot and Vincent turned to see three hybrids emerge from the woods. Two wolf-men, larger than Cezar, were followed by the tiger-man they saw earlier.

The girl quickly calmed down her dog, who crouched ready to pounce, as she faced the surrounding hunters.

"Caffar," Cezar said. "They're not part of this."

"Caffar is not so sure," the alpha wolf hybrid said, sizing up the newcomers. He was easily the largest of the wolves, with only Juma, the tiger-man, standing taller.

"Tell Calah and Juma to stay back," Cezar said. "Let them pass."

"Mr. Caffar," Dot said, stalling for time. "Why would great hunters such as yourselves need to chain your prey?"

"This isn't a proper hunt," Caffar said. "This is Cezar's last chance at redemption."

"Let them go!" Cezar said, seething, baring his teeth. "They don't know our ways. They don't know Cezar's disgrace."

"They're about to learn."

"What are we to learn?" Dot asked.

"That you should have kept your guns."

In a flash, the two wolf hybrids sprinted at Dot, with the tiger-man tramping across the clearing at Cezar. Dot screamed in terror as she ran to the abandoned truck and leaped through its open window.

Caffar rammed the truck door and reached in for the girl. She kicked at him, backing away to the rear compartment.

Gypsy growled and latched onto Juma, the tiger-hybrid, his fangs piercing the beast's neck. Juma grabbed the dog with both paws and struggled to rip him from his jugular.

"The pup has some fight in him!" Juma said, amused yet unable to remove the dog's clamped jaws.

Vincent flung vines at Calah, the other wolf-man, twisting them tight around his neck and slamming him to the ground. Calah leapt to his hind legs, ignoring the pain.

"Query: Shall I intervene?" Abraham asked.

Dot was ready to summon her mech, who could clearly hear the commotion, but feared the deep sunken rainforest would forever be his tomb. She kept the spiral staircase in her sights as she fought off the alpha wolf's clutches through the truck's window. She opened the driver's door, stumbled out onto the dirt, and scrambled through the dark for the stairs. Dot could feel Caffar's breath behind her as he pursued her through the underbrush.

"Leave her be!" Cezar screamed as he pulled at his chain, buckling the front bumper of the truck.

Dot reached the spiral staircase but felt the firm grip of Caffar's paws around her legs as she fell hard on her face. The alpha spun her around for a good look before the killing blow, and Dot stared up into his wild eyes.

As she screamed, Caffar's body was shoved aside by a blur in the darkness.

Ama, the caribou-woman had sped past him, thrusting her long legs deep into his ribs, sending him tumbling against a kapok tree. Her hooves took the wind out of him as she ran circles around the three predators, striking powerful blows with each pass. So blindingly fast were her sprints that the wolves could barely track her movements.

Dot felt vines wrap around her torso. They raised her high onto the staircase, safe from the melee, while her plant friend remained on the forest floor.

Lynn Harrod

"Vincent!" Dot yelled from above. She saw her friend fending off Calah and Juma, his long vines hovering in the air like pythons, while Ama flanked them, landing kicks, avoiding their claws.

At the base of the kapok tree, Caffar clutched his ribs in pain, caught his breath, and noticed a water lily blossom near his feet. He caught a pair of doe's eyes fixed on the flower and saw movement in the bushes. The wolf-man reached in and pulled out the young fawn-girl.

"Ameri!" Ama screamed, coming to a halt in the center of the lit clearing beside Vincent.

Cezar howled with rage. He ripped the truck's bumper from its frame and ran to the hybrid child. Wielding the steel bumper like a massive club, he brought it down hard onto Caffar's head. Caffar slashed at his brother, missing him by inches, but severing the chain.

The two wolf brothers grappled in the dirt, lunging their fangs at each other's throats.

"Where was this ferocity before?" Caffar said, laughing. "Where was this bloodlust during the hunt?"

"Cezar's bloodlust is meant for you!"

"You thirst for your brothers' blood while you kneel to the caribou and the little fawn! You pity them, defend them, but the truth is you're afraid of your nature!"

"Cezar is afraid of becoming a heartless, mindless maw, afraid of being like you!"

"That is one thing you never have to fear!"

Dot helplessly watched the long-pent conflict from the staircase when she felt the buzzing of her earpiece.

"Status: This unit is preparing to level the structure."

"No!" Dot said. "Abraham, hold your fire! There are hundreds of people down here!"

"Projection: This unit can limit damage to perimeter areas to minimize casualties."

"I said no! Zero casualties! Remember?"

"Statement: I remember everything, Little Miss, but my directives compel me to protect you."

"Protect us all, Abraham! Hold your fire!"

"Alternative: This unit is preparing to enter the structure."

"No! It's too far down! You'll be damaged. You'll never get out!"

"Assessment: This unit's functionality is irrelevant. Your safety is paramount."

"Listen to me, Abraham! You are not irrelevant! I won't make it a day out there without you! I command you to stay where you are and hold your fire!"

"You're no wolf!" Caffar said to Cezar as they fell to the dirt, their arms and legs entangled. "Look at you defending our prey! Defending the new meat!"

"Cezar was your prey! Not them!"

"You're all our prey now! And you're to blame, brother! Everyone knows you're always to blame!"

"Then let them blame Cezar for your death!"

Cezar grabbed the chain that held him prisoner moments before and wrapped it twice around Caffar's neck, silencing the alpha wolf as he struggled to breathe.

"Cezar is sorry, brother," the scared wolf said, stifling tears as he tightened the chain. "Cezar is sorry he was made this way..."

BOOM!

BOOM!

Everyone froze when the gunshots rang out across the rainforest. From her vantage point on the stairs, Dot saw Dr. Blum standing at the base of the laboratory ladder, shotgun in hand. He walked into the lit clearing with his weapon pointed at Caffar.

"Caffar says stay out of this, human," the alpha wolf-man said.

BOOM!

Dr. Blum fired another shot into the forest, shattering a dead log to splinters, establishing dominance.

"So, that's what it's like," Dr. Blum said. "This is the first time any gun has been fired in our home. May it be the last." He looked up at Dot on the spiral stairs. "Go child! Take your friends with you."

"Status: I detect a Purist squad within a five-kilometer radius. They have likely heard the gunfire."

"Dr. Blum!" Dot yelled. "Everyone! Soldiers are coming! With more to follow!"

"There's always more to follow, child. We'll be okay."

"You don't understand! It's not just the gate, the door above me has been ripped away, and the walls around it..."

"I know," Dr. Blum said. "The security breach was detected immediately, but I just now saw it."

"So you know they're coming."

"Let them come."

"Yes, let them come," Caffar said, eager to confront the full force of the vile Purists he'd heard about all his life. "My brothers and I will be ready."

"No, you won't," Dot said. "They'll bring an entire company, maybe two or three companies, hundreds of Automen, tons of firepower. They'll kill or capture everyone here."

"Your combat mech can defend us," Dr. Blum said.

"Abraham will defend *me*. Even if he somehow beats the odds, I'm afraid others will get hurt in the fight. They've burned down entire cities. This rainforest will mean nothing to them. Doctor, you must run."

Dr. Blum looked up at the rainforest canopy as he'd done every night of his life. He looked at the nervous and scared expressions around him, the anxious and uncertain eyes of the predators, and little Ameri hiding behind Ama's legs.

He looked down at the smoking shotgun in his hands, a powerful weapon that would soon be useless against overwhelming odds.

"You're right," Dr. Blum said. "Even if we repair the doorway and shield ourselves from their scans again, they've likely targeted this facility by now."

"I'm so sorry, Doctor."

"This was inevitable, child," Dr. Blum said as he gestured for Vincent and Gypsy to join Dot on the spiral staircase. He waited for them to reach her before turning to his habitat hybrids who hadn't seen him emerge from the lab in years. "Whether or not we're prepared for the wild world, the time has come for us to leave Dominion. My children are no longer safe at home." Blum lowered his weapon and turned to Caffar. "From what I know about the Greens, you have until sunrise to get the clans out, both predator and prey."

"You must do as he says," Cezar said.

"Why must Caffar do anything a human commands?" Caffar asked, defiant, determined to fight the coming enemy.

"Some in the forest may remember the doctors," Cezar said. "Some may listen to this one. But they will all obey you, brother."

Being the oldest of the wolves, Caffar remembered the tales of the warring humans and their machines, their weapons, their staggering numbers. Though he welcomed the challenge of the fight, he had no intention of becoming their prey or allowing his fellow hybrids to fall to their invasion.

He looked at Ameri and Ama in the clearing. The fawn-girl's water lily blossom still laid at his feet. He gently picked it up and brought it to her cautious mother.

"There is much hunting to be done out there," the alpha wolf-man said. He looked to his brothers and cleared his throat for a new command. "Hunt resumes in seven nights! Until that time, we get everyone out and away from the humans!"

"So, we're free to go?" Vincent asked, coiling his vines. "Just like that?"

"If these soldiers reach us, the hunt will be over for us all."

"What about Cezar?" Dot asked.

Cezar also wondered about his fate. Their ceremony of his final fight was forever tainted.

"Caffar knows Cezar will redeem himself," the alpha wolf-man said. "It just won't be with Caffar or Calah or Juma. He's to face the wild world without his predator clan. Soldiers and starvation will grant him the honorable death he seeks. Caffar has made his decision."

"What about you, Dr. Blum?"

"I belong with my children," the doctor said. "I'll go with them. Hopefully, I can redeem myself, too."

31

A New Clan

At the start of another dark night in the woods, Dot, Vincent, and Gypsy emerged from the facility through the widened entrance to find Abraham positioned near the open gate. His spotlights blinded them as they met him, his sensors continually monitoring the area.

"We got that power thingy you need," Vincent said proudly. "We got two of them!"

"Acceptable," Abraham said as he started to install the new module. "Gratitude."

"Don't get so emotional on us, Abraham," Dot said. "Now lets get out of here."

"Reminder: This unit cannot feel..."

"Forget what I said," Dot said with a smirk. "Of course, we know you don't have emotions. Right, guys?"

Vincent nodded and smiled, still slightly confused. Gypsy pressed his head against one of the robot's armored legs.

"Correct," Abraham said. "This unit cannot feel or express emotion."

"Of course you can't, Abraham."

"We often deny our feelings in pursuit of our duty," a low voice said from the busted doorway.

Dot and her friends turned to see Cezar standing alone in the rubble.

"So, it's true," Dot said. "You've been banished."

"Caffar is the alpha, and Caffar's decisions are always final."

"Everybody is leaving The Great Domain," Vincent said, "but you aren't going with them?"

"They've already left."

Rather than use the narrow spiral staircase as Dot had done to reunite with Abraham on the west side of the facility, Dr. Blum had opened several hanger-sized doors on the east side, a grand escape more befitting the exodus of hundreds of hybrids. Cezar was there to bid a tearful farewell, not to his brethren, but to Ama and Ameri, the pair he often protected from nightly hunts. Such actions earned him a badge of cowardice amongst his fellow predators, a shame he'd been prepared to address through the Hunters' Sacrifice of Redemption before Dot and her friends intervened. Though he'd wished to die to strengthen his clan, his flesh to be consumed by the pack, he couldn't abide innocent blood spilt in his name.

"We often deny our feelings in pursuit of our duty," Dot repeated. "Caffar taught you that?"

"He said it every night from the day Cezar entered the hunt."

"But you never believed it."

"Cezar did believe it, girl. With my fangs and claws and heart, Cezar believed it. But a coward fails to follow his convictions."

"Where will you go now?"

"He could go to Kellan!" Vincent said. "He could make his way along the ridge like the others."

"Kellan?" Cezar asked.

"It's a city of humans and hybrids," Dot said. "I mean, if it exists."

"Cezar doesn't belong to any city. Cezar must roam the wild. Caffar made his decision."

"You could roam with us," Dot said as she climbed up into Abraham's chest.

"We're going to Kellan later," Vincent said. "But first, we need to find the floaty star girls from our dreams."

"It's a long story," Dot said.

"Cezar's dream has died," the wolf said. "It would honor Cezar to follow you into yours."

Dot and her companions looked at each other, seemingly all agreeing to the wolf-man joining their travels.

"So, you don't eat animals?" Vincent asked.

"Not always," Cezar said, ashamed of the curse of his pacifist nature. "Never hybrids."

"But... you do eat veggies... I mean..."

"Cezar won't kill you, plant," the wolf-man said. "You have nothing to fear from me. Another reason Cezar is a failure as a predator."

"I'd also be a failure as a predator," Dot said.

"Me, too," Vincent said. "And Abe here won't kill no one, either, even though the big guy could kill everybody if he wanted to. Welcome to the circus! That's what some folks call us."

"Clarification," Abraham said. "This unit will instantly kill the wolf hybrid if he ever harms Little Miss."

"Oh yeah, that," Vincent said. "He really, really means it."

"Cezar swears to never harm any of you," the wolf said.

"It sounds like you really, really mean it, too."

"Well then, in Vincent's words," Dot said. "Welcome to the circus. Right now, we need to leave."

As Dot and her group of friends left the Dominion Research Vivarium, walking out through the main gate, she realized something was missing.

"Where's Velvie?" Dot asked, noticing the plush bunny hadn't been in her friend's vines since the brawl in the clearing.

Ten minutes prior, when Dot and Gypsy climbed the staircase to the surface, Vincent doubled back and handed his beloved velveteen rabbit to Ameri before she joined the exodus. The fawn-girl smiled and placed the water lily blossom on the doll's head, pressing its stem under the rabbit's floppy ears.

"Velvie will be a real bunny to her," Vincent said. "The story book said the love of a child makes her real."

"But what about you?" Dot asked.

"Me? I'll be fine. I have the love of another child."

"That's not quite what I meant," Dot said, touched by her friend's sentiment, "but I admire and respect your decision, Vincent."

"That's the first time anybody's respected and admired me! Thanks, Dottie!"

"Reconnaissance: A number of humanoid life forms are within a 10-kilometer radius, approaching from the southwest."

"Where does that leave us?" Dot asked her mech.

"Strategy: The minimum safe distance is one kilometer north."

Careful to avoid the Broken Road for now, Abraham lurched forward through the thick woods, heading through the East Hills, his new companions close behind. During his sensor sweep of life forms, the combat mech failed to mention that one humanoid he detected sat a half-kilometer away, perched on a high cliff.

George Reed had been watching Dot and her friends from above as they left The Great Domain. Though he was too far to shout to her, he kept her in his binoculars. If he could have somehow spoken to the girl, he'd have warned that she and her entourage were unknowingly trekking across the hills north toward the forbidden town of Beacon Hill.

32

The Pain of Love

When Dot woke up to the sight of a river at dawn, she briefly feared that she and her friends had taken a wrong turn. After crossing dark countryside all night while she slept in the robot's chest, they may have inadvertently doubled back and returned to the Miracle River in the west. The gentle, rhythmic sound of the passing water was identical to the river she and the Loyalists were about to cross before a brutal ambush by the Purists took their lives, leaving only a lost girl and her scattershot memory. For a moment, she felt alone and helpless again, just as she did before she crawled out of the hollow of that ancient oak, before she learned The Story of The World.

Dot was jolted back to the present upon seeing Cezar laying on his back on a boulder while Vincent tended to his wounds.

"You sure this don't hurt, Cezzie?" Vincent asked as he applied a herbal poultice to the wolf hybrid's shoulder and thigh, their flesh ripped apart by his older brother's claws. "I used this same paste on Father once. He said it felt like termites eating him from the inside."

"Cezar knows pain well," the wolf-man said. "Some pain is like knives of fire, makes Cezar howl, but most pain can be ignored, controlled, even relished."

"Relished? That means you like some pain?"

"It means Cezar loves some pain." The wolf was amused by his companion's curiosity and confusion. "Not all of it is bad."

"Father said it's good to get hurt sometimes because that's how you learn things. But why would you love it?"

"Some pain shows your courage, shows you how strong you are. But all pain reminds you that you're alive, prepares you for more, and that is always good."

"I suppose so, but even though I can't die, I try not to get hurt. I don't like getting cut or shot."

Dot stood behind Cezar's boulder and listened to the odd conversation. Hearing Vincent say he didn't like getting shot sent a shiver through her, the image of his "deaths" still fresh in her mind. Despite her friend's insistence that he could never die, she couldn't depend on that, and she wanted to forget those horrible moments.

She saw Abraham standing to her left, further down the river, his solar cells absorbing the sunlight of the new day. Gypsy stood along the river to Dot's far right. Together, the combat mech and the German Shepherd guarded their camp.

"Where are we?" Dot asked as she stepped out from behind the boulder. She knelt down by the river's edge and splashed icy morning water on her face. Though she still wore her cochlear communicator, the towering robot replied aloud for all to hear.

"Location: We are next to the Regal River in the East Hills region, 49.1 kilometers north of the Dominion Research Vivarium."

"For a moment, I thought we went back to the river that passes Wellspring," the girl said.

"Clarification: You are referring to the Miracle River, which parallels the West Wall, in close proximity to the region where we first met. Beside us now is the Regal River. The confusion is understandable. The two bodies of water have similar widths, currents, and riparian plant life. "

"The Regal River is prettier," Dot said, relieved to be far from that distant, haunted place. "It feels more peaceful."

"Agreement."

"How was the trip here?"

"Kinda scary," Vincent said.

"Summary: The terrain was technical with elevation ranging from 12% to 30% grades, comprised mostly of..."

"I meant... how are you guys doing?" Dot asked, interrupting her mech's report. "I fell fast asleep, but you must have been walking all night."

"Status: This unit's primary power is at 80.5 percent. Reserve power is at 100 percent."

"So, the new part is working well?"

"Status: My upgraded power module has increased capacity and efficiency by a notable degree."

"Abe's doing fine," Vincent said. "He was our first patient! The power doohickey wasn't sitting right, but it turns out Cezzie here is a whiz with tools."

"You're a mechanic, Cezar?" Dot asked.

"Cezar spent much of his life working on the old machines in the rainforest," the wolf said, wincing at the pain of the stinging poultice. "Caffar hated how Cezar often avoided nightly hunts, but the trail lamps, atmosphere generators, and water filtration pumps needed daily maintenance, tasks usually more than Dr. Blum could handle alone. Cezar crafted parts, upgraded the filters, improved the system."

"You chose to create," the girl said, "to build and repair instead of destroy."

"That was Cezar's contribution to the clan, but when Cezar came of age, Caffar made it clear it wasn't enough."

"Caffar may be your 'alpha', but he isn't always right. No one is."

"Yes. Cezar realizes that now."

"And how are you doing?" Dot asked, nodding to his treated injuries. "It looks like Vincent's taking good care of you."

"Cezar never dreamed that a plant would save his life."

"What do you mean? How serious were your wounds?"

"Cezzie's doing great," Vincent said, smothering more poultice on the wolf's leg, wrapping them tight with gauze. "He don't heal as quick as me, don't fix up as clean as Abe, but he sure can take the pain. He even kinda likes it, which is strange to me. I'd be blubbering like a little sprout if I was him!"

"Cezar's cuts were long and deep," the wolf-man said, "but the plant is a miracle man. Cezar is grateful for the care."

Vincent had spent much of the night gathering herbs and roots for Cezar. He collected turmeric, wild onion, dandelions, aloe vera, walnut, and chili pepper, and pounded them against a rock to form his all-purpose medicinal paste. The natural healing properties of the poultice were accelerated by the addition of Vincent's wondrous mutant blood, a bright green bioluminescent goo that had only been used to grow impossibly large crops – and prolong his surrogate father's life – before the wolf's injuries demanded attention.

When Cezar mentioned that Vincent saved his life, it proved more true than Dot could have known. During their escape from Dominion, while the girl slept inside her marching mech, the wolf-man was slowly dying. He wouldn't have seen his first sunrise at the edge of the Regal River were it not for Vincent's help. Had he not joined Dot and her friends, Cezar would have died alone in the night.

"You got a little bit of Vinny Greenblood in you now," Vincent said to the wolf as he finished tending to his wounds. "A lot, actually. Hey, that makes us blood brothers now!"

Cezar laughed at the realization, a sight that both startled and delighted the girl.

"What's funny?" Dot asked with a curious smile.

"Cezar is the shame of his clan because Cezar refuses to kill prey."

"So that's why you were chained up. That's why you were having the redemption ceremony."

"Caffar and Calah mocked Cezar for eating mostly fruit and roots. Juma often said if Cezar kept eating vegetables, Cezar would eventually become one. So now the cowardly predator sitting before you is literally kin to a plant. If only Juma knew, the mighty tiger would fall to the ground in hysterics."

"You keep calling yourself a coward," Dot said, "but I find you very brave. That mother and daughter must have been terrorized by the predator packs for years. You helped keep them alive."

"No, Ama is the brave one," Cezar said. "After her mate was taken by the hunters, Ama was forced to fight Caffar many times. She even faced Juma once, and no one had ever dared meet him in single combat before. Cezar knew then that her grace and elegance were matched by her determination and tenacity."

"She does sound brave."

"Indeed, she was brave and much more," Cezar imagined Ama standing by the river, her long legs and velvet antlers contrasted by the gently flowing water, as he continued down his memories. "During Winter Solstice, she met with the predators to request armistice on behalf of her child. For a caribou widow, an exquisite woman of prey, to enter a den of beasts alone to ask for respite from the nightly hunts, there was no braver act in the rainforest. It was her courage, her love of her child, and her pure heart that inspired Cezar to defy his clan's traditions."

"You love her," Dot said, feeling the beast's swelling emotion.

Cezar had never dared speak the words aloud, but had whispered them in his sleep many nights.

"Ama is a bold beauty that would never have a pathetic creature like Cezar," the wolf said, lying on his back across the boulder. "Cezar couldn't join her clan, so Cezar vowed long ago to protect it."

"I met her," Vincent said, "and I don't think she knew you'd been looking out for her people."

"Protecting prey is a disgrace for a predator. She would've thought even less of Cezar."

"Nah, I don't think so, Cezzie. She seemed pretty smart to me. I think she would have understood."

"Perhaps you are right, Vincent," the wolf said. "Vincent, my new blood brother. Though you are but a plant, you are wiser than Cezar."

"Aw, thanks! I ain't never been called wise before! Folks usually call me a fool."

"You? A fool?" Cezar asked, incredulous.

"Yep! All my life! Ever since leaving Dominion a long time ago when I was just a twig, everybody always made me feel kinda sad, kinda small. Everybody except Father, Dottie, and Abe."

The wolf hybrid looked astonished and enraged, prompting Dot to back away a few steps. He ignored the pain of his wounds as he struggled to sit up on the boulder, to look his new friend in the eye.

"Hear me now, Vincent," the predator said. "Cezar saw you fight, saw you risk your life to save the girl in the rainforest. You helped Cezar repair the war machine, cooked our meal, crafted medicine for my care. This wolf's pitiful corpse would be rotting in the dirt and weeds were it not for your quick thinking, your cunning and skill. Any man who deems you a fool, who dares to disrespect you, to make you feel sad and small, that man is blind and ignorant and unworthy of your grace. From this day forth, such scoundrels will answer to Cezar's unforgiving wrath and pay for every insult with a quart of their blood."

"Aww," Vincent said. "That's the sweetest thing anyone's ever said to me!"

The wolf-man's fearsome vow came from the depths of his heart, for he was incapable of anything but sincerity and truth. More than a "blood brother," he saw the plant-man much as he did the girl, an angel whose pure goodness glowed like a flame whose embers must never fade. With what little honor Cezar he had left, he felt determined to uphold theirs.

"I feel the same way about Vincent," Dot said. "But let's skip the bloodshed, Cezar. Someone once taught me that insults are best left to wither away. You're right when you say ignorant folks aren't worthy of Vincent. They're not worthy of you, either."

"As you wish, girl," Cezar said. "Clearly, your teacher was noble and wise."

"Yes, he was," she said, another blocked memory dislodged.

Cezar leaned against the boulder, shut his eyes, and breathed deeply. His thoughts drifted back to the enclosed rainforest, to Ama running through the trees and outside into the wild, leading the elk and antelope and deer hybrids, with little Ameri in her arms. How he longed to run beside her, to hold her hand in one paw, the little fawn-girl's in the other. He'd shield them from pain, suffer on their behalf, and ensure that they never felt frightened again.

Dot also thought about Ama, Ameri, and her wolf companion. Everything suddenly made sense. She realized how hard it must have been for Cezar to refuse to hunt out of love for a woman who feared him and his brethren. After many agonizing years of defending them in secret, he succumbed to his sorrow and shame and loneliness, offering himself for the Sacrifice of Redemption. The final act would have restored his honor, provided meat for his clan, and ended his torment of unrequited love.

"Thank you for sharing your heart," Dot said, placing a hand on the wolf's massive paw.

"Thank you for listening to Cezar's drivel. Cezar is embarrassed to confess his weakness and sin."

"You are anything but weak, Cezar, and I don't see your actions as sins. From what I've heard, you've lived a life of redemption."

"Perhaps one day Cezar will see it your way," the wolf-man said, "but not today."

"Status: This unit's primary power is at 100 percent." The mech folded in his solar collectors and walked toward the group.

"Looks like Abe's all set to go!" Vincent said. "Cezzie's heart-sharing must have gotten to him, too."

"Extrapolation: The wolf hybrid evidently shares Little Miss's value for all life, a rare and noteworthy trait for a pack predator."

"You know, for a metal man with no emotions," the girl said, "that sure sounded like respect and praise."

"Clarification: This unit was merely observing the wolf hybrid's psychological profile, Little Miss."

Dot always liked it whenever Abraham called her "Little Miss," as if Sergeant Furst lived on within the war machine.

"And his name is 'Cezar'," she said.

"It should be easy to remember," Vincent said. "He says his name a lot."

"Correction: This unit was merely observing the psychological profile of the wolf hybrid known as Cezar."

"That's a little better," Dot said. "We'll work on that."

The girl rolled up her pants and walked into the wide river, the running water ice cold, the color of coffee, gentle like a brook. She stopped when the water reached her knees, which sent chills through her. She wobbled on loose rocks for a moment before collapsing into the shallow water, laughing at her clumsy fall.

Vincent helped Cezar up off the boulder and onto his feet before walking to the river's edge to help Dot. He smiled at the girl sitting in the water, playfully splashing as if she hadn't a care, if only for a moment. He reached for her with a vine and lifted her to shore.

"I'll go in next," Vincent said, "then Cezzie, then Gypsy..."

"It was nice for a minute," Dot said, "but it's absolutely freezing and the loose rocks make it hard to stand. Believe me, it's no fun."

"Nope, it won't be no fun at all! I don't like cold water either. It makes my roots tense up." Vincent held up one of his long feet, revealing the many roots protruding between his toes. "It really stings, but we gotta do it."

"Cezar also hates the water," the wolf hybrid said, "but the combat mech insists we must ford across, and Cezar trusts his judgement."

Dot looked out over the expanse of icy water, the river seemingly calm but no less treacherous than any other crossing they'd encountered.

"Wait... we really need to cross the river?" Dot asked. "Here?"

"Correct," Abraham said. "The nearest bridge is 9.6 kilometers to the west, which I estimate will likely place us within range of the Purists' last known location and therefore their reconnaissance. Currently, there are no humanoid lifeforms within a 10-kilometer radius. This entry point offers our greatest chance to continue undetected."

"How deep is the water?"

"Estimation: The Regal River ranges from three to five meters deep near its banks, descending to 22 meters toward its center."

"Did you say 22 meters?" Vincent said. "What is that in feet? I only know feet. Kinda."

"About 70 feet," Cezar said, drawing from his years of metric conversions while maintaining the facility's machinery. "Deep enough for a watery mass grave."

"How can we make it?" Dot asked her mech. "Surely, you can't float, Abraham."

"Correct. This unit weighs 4.1 metric tons and cannot float due to my mass, shape, and density."

"I don't understand. I thought we were supposed to cross the river here?"

"Strategy: My frame is waterproof at a rating of 30.5 meters. I can likely walk across the river bottom without incident."

"What about the rest of us?" Dot asked.

"We'll be the ones floating," Vincent said. "That's the best part! We worked it out while you were asleep. We'll be on a raft, and Abe will tow us across. It should be a piece of cake, which means it should be easy. Father used to say that."

"It certainly doesn't sound like a piece of cake."

"Can the girl travel in the machine's chest as she did last night?" Cezar asked. "The raft may fail. Cezar won't place the child in jeopardy."

"Estimation: Travel across the river will take approximately 28 minutes. With this unit's ventilation system sealed underwater, the girl's oxygen supply within my central compartment would be depleted in approximately 12 minutes. The strategy of our joint union would fail. Unacceptable."

"The raft won't fail, Cezzie," Vincent said, "because nature built it!" He whipped his vines through some nearby shrubs and dragged a fallen tree toward the group, its trunk roughly the size of a canoe.

"Do we have tools to craft this into a proper vessel?" Cezar asked.

"No, but there's no need! We'll just sit on this tree and sail across! It's two pieces of cake!"

"The current will spirit us away."

"Nah, I'll be holding on to the big guy while he walks down below with the fishes."

"The deepest part of the river is 70 feet," Dot said. "How long can you stretch your vines?"

"32 feet. I checked once on the farm."

"32 is not 70," Cezar said.

"Abe says the deep part is in the middle. I'll hang onto him as long as I can, let go for a little bit, and grab him when he's farther along."

"Could that work, Abraham?" Dot asked, hoping for a resounding "yes."

"Projection: At the moment Vincent releases his vine from my frame, I can alter my path to match yours as the current pulls you downriver at 5.2 kilometers per hour. However, given the change in elevation of the riverbed, I may be unable to match your accelerated speed. Chance of success is 65.3 percent."

"I like the sound of 'success' and a big number like 65-something," Vincent said.

"That's a 34.7 percent chance that we'll float away helpless," Cezar said. "34-something is also a big number."

"Look at Cezzie and the quick math! You're the smartest wolf I ever met, smart like Dottie."

"If we lose the mech," Cezar said, "we'd be lost for hours."

"Correction," Abraham said. "In such a scenario, you would travel less than one kilometer, approximately five minutes, before reaching an area with Class Five rapids."

"Class Five?" Vincent asked. "Now, that's a low number. Five don't sound so bad."

"Definition: Class Five river rapids are long and violent, following each other in consistent succession with rocky obstructions, potentially lethal drops, and an extremely steep gradient."

"We'd be smashed to pieces," Cezar said with a snort. "Maybe not the plant, since he apparently can't die, but surely the rest of us."

"What do you all think?" Dot asked, hoping someone would come up with a better plan. "We risk getting spotted by the Purists if we take the long way around west, or we risk drowning if we cross the river here. It sounds like we're stuck."

"We can do it, Dottie," Vincent said. "Abe and Cezzie are real smart, and I hear what they're saying, but I know we can make it. You gotta trust me."

"Cezar will follow you either way," the wolf said to the group. "Whether we cross the bridge to the west or cross the water here, either death would be honorable."

"Honorable or not, no one's going to die," Dot said. "What do you think, Abraham?"

"Projection: Our two options have nearly equivalent chances of success and failure."

Dot's unique friends all looked to her for a decision. As she pondered each path, the choice was made for her by the sounds of Gypsy's sudden barking and the rumbling of several approaching motor vehicles.

The Purists had found them.

* * *

"That sounds like trucks," Vincent said. "Big trucks."

With a single bound, Cezar leaped high onto a nearby tree, scrambled to the top in seconds, and searched the woods behind them. "Three troop transports approach from the south!" he shouted to his friends below.

Alarmed, Dot quickly turned to her mech. "I thought you said there was no one in ten kilometers. How did they sneak up on us?"

"Unknown," Abraham said. "Commencing diagnostic."

"Is that new power doohickey not working right?" Vincent asked.

"Diagnostic Complete. Sensor array is fully operational."

"So why didn't you pick them up on your sensors?" Dot asked.

"Unknown."

With no time to wonder how the soldiers got the drop on them, Dot yelled at the wolf atop the tree. "Are you sure those are troop transports? Abraham didn't see them coming!"

"Cezar sees guns!" the wolf shouted. "Dozens of men in green uniforms! All with the same face!"

Three trucks loaded with identical, armed Purist Automen.

From what Sergeant Furst told her about their tactics, Dot knew they were just scouting squads, and she knew they'd likely already communicated with their company back at base.

"We need to hit the water now!" Dot called out. "We worry about the rapids later!"

"Negative," Abraham said. "Your makeshift raft will not be out of their weapons' range in time."

"They probably told the others about us!"

"Correct."

"What do we do?"

"We fight!" Cezar howled with the terror of an entire wolf pack as he jumped from the tall tree, landing on the roof of the first transport. With his claws out and fangs exposed, he shredded his way through the soldiers, seething with rage upon each fatal blow.

As the three trucks burst out of the woods, Dot worried that Cezar, who was still recuperating from his wounds, would succumb to the soldiers' greater numbers.

The Purists poured out of their trucks and immediately opened fire on the group.

Abraham lurched toward the clone troopers and unfolded his twin barrels, blasting the two trailing trucks with an incessant blaze of gunfire that ripped the vehicles and their passengers to pieces.

"Gypsy, you stay with me, boy!" Dot said. "Vincent, get Cezar out of there!"

Vincent sprang into action. He grabbed two trees with his vines and flung himself high into the air, directly into the brutal melee of the first truck. He landed atop the cab and quickly wrapped his vines around the wolf-man.

"No!" Cezar said. "Release Cezar!"

"Nope, can't do that, Cezzie. I can patch up cuts, but not bullet holes!"

Cezar took down five soldiers before Vincent shielded him, absorbing the gunfire from the remaining seven.

"Dang it, I hate getting shot!" Vincent said as he yanked Cezar out of the transport and brought him back to the river.

The surviving soldiers ran for cover in the trees and continued their barrage, firing mercilessly at the group. Dot and Gypsy hid behind the riverside boulder while Abraham marched up to the truck and crushed its engine with his monstrous feet.

"Instruction: Avoid the treeline."

"Don't worry," Vincent said. "Ain't no way we're going back in there!"

"Release Cezar!" the wolf-man said. "Let Cezar fight!"

"Sit this one out, big guy. Let Abe handle this. You still got more healing to do before you can take on the Greenies."

Vincent and Cezar joined Dot and Gypsy behind the boulder, leaving the combat mech to deal with the scattered squad in the woods. His warning to avoid the treeline puzzled Dot until she saw him extend a wand from one arm and ignite the trees with arcs of fire. His flamethrower lit the woods ablaze, forcing the Automen out from cover. In seconds, he mowed them down with automatic fire until none were left standing.

"Did the mech kill them all?" Cezar asked, breathless, as Vincent loosened his vines from around him.

"Automen repair each other," Dot said. "With enough time, they seem to recover from almost anything. They'll be back up on their feet by tonight."

"We'll be across the river by then," Vincent said.

"Or crushed against the rocks in the Class Five rapids," Cezar said.

"It's a risk we have to take," Dot said. "There's more coming. A lot more. We have to move."

Abraham returned to the river. He picked up the fallen tree and tossed it onto the shoreline.

"Status: 36 casualties. Threat eliminated."

"For now," Dot said with dread.

Without further discussion, the combat mech walked into the river. Vincent climbed onto the tree and shot his vines onto Abraham's back. Instantly, the tree slid away from the shore and into the icy water. Cezar helped Dot and Gypsy onto the canoe-sized log, and the four of them rode it out onto the Regal River. The current, which seemed so deceivingly calm before, suddenly felt like a thousand hands pulling them downriver. It took all of Vincent's strength to hang on to Abraham as he continued onward.

Within minutes, the mech was completely submerged while the makeshift tree-raft floated far from the river's edge, their camp now a distant refuge.

As Dot clung to the dead tree, her feet dangling in the freezing water, her fears of the river were equaled by a new paranoia.

The Purists were now somehow able to appear out of nowhere.

33

Crossing The River

Cezar held Gypsy down beneath his body in the middle of the tree while gripping its trunk with his long claws. Dot sat behind him at the rear of the tree, holding his tail to help balance her as the current gently swayed their raft. The northern bank of the river looked impossibly far from her low vantage point, her legs wrapped tight around the trunk.

Vincent sat at the front with two of his vines stretched to their limits, tethering them to the combat mech walking along the river bottom 30 feet below. He barely held on, surprised at how much farther they needed to go. He'd hoped they'd be much closer when he eventually let go of his lumbering friend.

"It's almost time!" Vincent said. "I can't hold on much longer!"

"We're not even a quarter of the way across!" Dot said.

"Dang, this really hurts! I feel like I'm about to pass out!"

"Let go if you must!" Cezar said. "We'll brave the rapids together!"

"Pretty sure we'll die down there, Cezzie. I saw those Class Five-something rapids when I searched for herbs last night. They're pretty rough."

"Don't push yourself too far, Vincent," Dot said.

"It's my fault, Dottie. I figured we'd make it a lot closer. I'm sorry."

"Don't apologize, just let go..."

Dot's voice trailed off as she watched Vincent's body fall into the freezing river. She gasped in shock upon realizing that he held his grip literally until he became unconscious.

"Vincent!" Dot screamed into the water, her voice cracking in the wind. "Vincent!"

"Hold on, dog," Cezar said as he stood from his crouched position over the animal. "Cezar must leave you now." He balanced on his hind legs for a moment before diving into the water.

"No, Cezar!" Dot quickly shimmied up the trunk to Gypsy and held him down against it, as the wolf had done. For two terrifying minutes, the girl and her dog clung to the floating tree alone, their hybrid friends lost under the water's surface.

As she started to cry, a loud splash woke her from despair. Cezar climbed back onto the tree and clutched its roots at the rear.

"He's okay!" Cezar said. "Vincent extended his reach! He's still holding on!"

Moments earlier, Vincent realized that his vines' 32-foot limit wasn't enough for the little distance they'd traveled. In order to hang on to Abraham longer, he entered the water and held the tree with another stretched vine, doubling his reach to 64 feet –

Lynn Harrod

nearly the full depth of the Regal River – all while he held his breath.

"He said to tie him to the tree," Cezar said, wrapping one of his friend's strong vines around a branch.

"When did he tell you that?" Dot asked.

"Before we departed."

"What for?"

Cezar hesitated to answer. "It's just a precaution."

Confused, Dot thought about the times she'd seen Vincent grab objects ten times his size, holding them in the air with ease. His strength was greater than even he knew. Knowing that, she realized there was only one reason his vines needed to be physically tied to the tree.

"He's going to drown," Dot said in horror. "He can't hold his breath long enough, so he's going to drown and leave his vines tied to Abraham for us."

"Yes," the wolf said. "He said it was a possibility."

"And you knew..."

"He made Cezar promise to keep it secret."

"Make him let go!" Dot said. "Untie him! We might survive the rapids..."

"Cezar is sorry, girl," the wolf said with a pained face. "Cezar made a promise, as a blood brother. The plant is as brave as he is wise. His plan will succeed... even if he won't. Cezar is proud to be in his clan."

"There must be another way! We just need to think..."

Dot's frantic thoughts aloud were muffled by the river as the tree dipped below the surface. Vincent's vines held tight as Abraham marched on, but weren't quite long enough to keep them above water. The girl struggled for gasps of air as the tree slowly descended, bobbing up and down with the current. During the brief moments she poked her face up, she heard the distant rushing rapids for the first time. They sounded like a thousand beasts roaring, waiting for their helpless prey to float into their den.

Cezar clutched the rear of the tree and kicked his legs as hard as he could, hoping to help their crossing along.

A moment later, Dot and her friends were completely underwater, clinging to the tree ten feet below the surface.

Within the murky depths, with barely enough strength to keep hold of the tree, Dot could only watch as Gypsy floated upward, paddling hard to stay close. Cezar gave up kicking, reached up, and grabbed the German Shepherd by his tail to keep him from being swept away to his death.

Below her, Dot spied Vincent's lifeless body far below, his outstretched vines keeping them all together.

In the quiet of the deep, she considered letting go, her lungs ready to burst, and her arms and hands afire as she scrambled to keep hold of the tree. She knew she'd soon release her grip, either from fatigue or drowning, and she looked around at her desperate friends one last time. She thought of George out there somewhere, looking for her, the villagers of Colt who felt elated to add her to their flock, and the Automen whose single purpose was to track her down and capture or kill her.

Sergeant Furst's kind face appeared before her in the dark depths, encouraging and comforting. Father Young sat in his chair by the fireplace, delighted to see a child once more before leaving this world. The twin girls of The Void floated alongside her, silently calling to her with their hollow eyes. Perhaps they were dead all along, and her visits to their vast expanse in dream were glimpses into the afterlife. Senior Wainright wasn't completely wrong. There was more to life than what we saw in the daylight, and there was a chance to rejoin with those whose time had passed.

Lynn Harrod

Dot always knew she'd find the Light and Dark Girls, just not like this, not now.

As her lungs finally failed her, and her insides filled with river water, her head spun in delirium, and a chill scuttled across her back.

She felt the sensation of the tree ascending, of the morning breeze brushing against her backside, as they returned to the surface. She craned her neck and painfully coughed up the water that had filled her lungs. In her heavy, deep breaths, she saw a grove of elm trees ahead, within reach, and the upper body of Abraham as he climbed up the north bank of the river.

The robot turned and pulled the vines wrapped around the piping on his back, dragging Vincent and the fallen tree to shore. Cezar threw Gypsy to safety before crawling through the mud in agony, away from the pulling current.

Dot wanted desperately to run to Vincent but could only lie in the mud for a moment, her body nearly shut down, like the wolf's. Gypsy alone sprinted to the plant hybrid and barked into his sleeping face.

"Vincent," Dot said, wheezing, staring at her friend's unmoving body surrounded by elm trees looming over them. "You... were right. Your plan worked... again. Thank you... thank you for saving us."

"You're... welcome," Vincent groaned as he gazed up at the sunny sky.

The sound of his innocent voice startled Dot, and for a moment, she wondered if it was another vision, a merging of The Void and the real world.

"Vincent?" she asked, her face half caked in mud.

"Told ya," the plant-man said, panting. "Told ya it would work."

Slowly, he coiled his vines around his forearms as he vomited river water onto his chest. Dot crawled on hands and knees through the thick mud and collapsed beside him.

"You really can't die, can you?" she said with a tired laugh.

"Not today... I couldn't... but for a moment there, I kinda thought I might."

"You have the stout heart of ten packs of wolves," Cezar said. "You saved Cezar again. You saved us all. Cezar owes you his life twice." After taking in a gulp of air, he looked up to the sky and howled in honor of his brave friend, a ferocious sound that pierced the tranquil woods.

Dot sat up and looked down at Vincent, his huge black eyes still fixed on the morning sun.

"Why'd you do it?" she asked.

"Father said so," Vincent said. "He said to keep you safe. If I don't, he'd be upset with me, even though he's dead."

"You never let your father down, do you? That's what keeps you going."

"He died for me. A lot of people died for me. He'd want me to remember that."

"Well, do me a favor and don't you ever die for me," Dot said. "No one should die for me."

"I'll try not to, Dottie. Now, if you'll excuse me, I need to lie here and dry out for a while. I'm too waterlogged and exhausted to move right now."

Abraham scanned the area.

"Reconnaissance: I detect no humanoid life forms within a 10-kilometer radius."

"I'm not sure if that's a good thing anymore," Dot said. "They got to us somehow."

"Extrapolation: The Purists of Earth have found a way to circumvent my sensors, to hide their presence."

"Can you widen your sensor array beyond life sign signatures?" Cezar asked, tapping into his engineering prowess. "Add thermal imaging, movement, pattern recognition, terrain disturbance, metallurgical compositions, weaponry."

"Status: Widening sensor array now."

"Look at Cezzie's scientific talk!" Vincent said. "Pretty smart wolf we got."

"Dr. Blum was a good teacher," Cezar said. "He tutored Cezar when he was a pup."

"He's to you sorta kinda like Father was to me."

"Not 'sorta kinda,' my friend."

Gypsy licked Vincent's green-and-yellow wooden face. The plant hybrid laughed at the tickling feeling.

"No more talking, Vincent," Dot said. "You rest all you want while we make camp. Let us take care of you for a change. I think we're done for the day."

34

Vows in The Void

Dot looked out across The Void. For the first time, she stood in the dark expanse without confusion or disorientation. The curious sensation of adjusting to the sudden, strange new surroundings – like waking slowly and groggily from an intense dream – had been replaced with acceptance, perhaps even comfort. The Void now felt like a real, physical place familiar to her, though she was well aware she was actually asleep in the camp Cezar made along the north side of the Regal River, tucked in an alcove against a rocky cliff.

Vincent had spent the day drying out after being deep in the river for nearly half an hour. Abraham and Gypsy patrolled the area.

To Dot's surprise, Cezar hunted small game for supper, returning to camp with several hares. He explained that his refusal to kill was specific to humans and fellow hybrids, and that by no means was he a vegetarian like his tall plant friend. He didn't consume ten pounds of meat daily like his former clan brothers, but he still craved it, viewing his unfortunate hunger like a moth seeking flame. To accommodate Vincent's needs, Cezar also foraged for root vegetables, herbs, and wild berries, yet another act the predator never imagined he'd ever perform.

Cezar had to search for food and medicinal herbs because the ample supplies they'd taken from Dominion had either been destroyed in the brief conflict with the Purists or simply left behind when they quickly fled across the river on a fallen tree. Vincent appreciated the gesture. He knew how awkward it must have been for a wolf to harvest plants alone during the day, his former pack's nightly hunts a distant memory. Dot looked at the two unlikely friends in both astonishment and admiration. If only the world could come together like those two.

"You're very close... you're not far enough..."

The whispered voices took Dot by surprise. Lost in her recollection of the night's events and the bonds formed, she forgot she was in The Void, forgot about the Light and Dark Girls along the unseen horizon. Dot had become so comfortable in the dream expanse that it felt like home, even though she still had no memory of any home in her life.

"I know I'm close," Dot said to the glowing figures floating to her left and right, almost within reach. "I can feel myself drawn to you now." So close were the specters that she could see silhouettes of wires or string or straw protruding from their pointed hats, a detail that eluded her before.

"Run away... it's too late to run..."

"I'm not running. You should know that by now."

"Don't be afraid... Fear for yourself and your friends..."

"I'm not afraid!" Dot called out. "My friends and I protect each other! Together, we'll make it to you, and we'll free you!"

"We must be free... we can never leave..."

Though the conflicting twins still alternately urged her to find them or flee, still in their identical, monotone voices, Dot felt their respective hope and desperation ever stronger. She could now see the outlines of their faces within their glowing auras, their furrowed brows, their eyes wide and vacant like holes. Despite her undeniable connection to them, she suddenly wondered if they were actually alive or simply echoes of children she once knew, shadows of twins that now only lived in her twisted, perhaps manipulated imagination.

"I'm all dry now!" Vincent said, taking a moment to realize where he was. "Whoa, back in the weird, dark place again? I guess I'm asleep. Dang, I hope I'm not still passed out in that river!"

"You're fine, Vincent," Dot said. "You spent the day drying in the sun. We made camp while you rested, remember?"

"You sure that wasn't a dream?"

"That was real. You're in a dream now."

"Okay, I remember. Cezzie brought me some raspberries. Nice and juicy. I offered some to Gypsy, but he was busy on a rabbit leg, right, boy?"

The German Shepherd barked, seemingly in agreement, the dog now standing behind Dot.

"Reconnaissance," Abraham said in his synthetic voice, his armored body appearing behind Vincent. "Sensors detect nothing."

"Nothing in this place or nothing in camp?" Dot asked, oddly unsurprised by the apparitions of her friends, as if they simply walked through the front door of some surreal clubhouse.

"Clarification: Based on my upgraded sensor sweep, there are no humanoid life signs within a 10-kilometer radius of our camp. There are 78 native animals, 19 abandoned vehicles, and four derelict structures."

"So, when you said you detected nothing, you meant... in here."

"Correct."

"Nothing at all?" Vincent asked.

"Analysis: My sensors detect no chemical composition, acoustic propagation, or electromagnetic wavelengths. There is no carbon-based matter, no mass, temperature, or any other measurable dimension within this metaphysical plane, not even our own life signatures."

"I guess Abe can't scan dreams," Vincent said. "Too bad. I had a weird dream about catching fish, driving a truck, and picking berries I still can't figure out."

"You were dreaming about things you actually did," Dot said. "Normal dreams."

"Yeah, but I really had to pee in those dreams. What's that about?"

"Vincent, you probably had to pee."

"Dang, you're as smart as Abe!" Vincent said. "That's just what he said earlier, when we were still in the wide-awake world."

A snort came from behind the group as Cezar appeared in The Void. The wolf-man looked alarmed, as if he were about to be attacked from all sides.

"Feels weird, don't it?" Vincent said.

"It feels like Cezar has lost his mind," the wolf said, staring at the glowing figures in the distance.

"We all know the feeling, Cezzie. Your first time in a group dream, in a never-ending, empty space, with two bickering ghosts floating in the stars... yeah, it can feel a little strange."

"What is this foul place, girl?" Cezar asked.

"I'm not entirely sure myself," Dot said.

Cezar sprinted toward the spectral twins but got no closer to them, nor any farther from his companions, as if he were running in place with nothing below his feet.

"Your friends can come with you... your friends will all die..."

"These must be the 'Star Girls' you spoke of," Cezar said, "the ones who disagree about your path."

"The ones we must save," Dot said. "I can't give you a good reason. I just know it in my heart."

"Cezar respects that you follow your instincts, but are you sure they're deserving of your faith?"

"No, but we have to try. I hate putting you in any more danger, and I don't mean to get you involved if you don't feel..."

"Cezar vows to find them," the wolf-man said. "Cezar will keep them safe and escort them to your sanctuary city in the west."

"Kellan," Dot said, as if saying the name aloud made it more likely to exist.

"Yes. Even if Cezar doesn't make it through Kellan's gates alive, you will, girl. Nothing else matters to Cezar."

"Agreement," Abraham said. "This unit is similarly dedicated to completion of our joint mission."

"Me, too!" Vincent said, placing his hands on Cezar's shoulder and Abraham's arm. "I'm also similarly dedicated to what these guys similarly said. Father would be proud."

Gypsy barked as if to solidify their pact.

Dot turned to the distant glowing shapes with her arms outstretched.

"Do you see now?" Dot said. "Do you see it's not just me anymore? We've all decided to come for you! Whatever fears you have, we'll face them together! There's no need to be afraid because there's nothing we can't handle together!"

Lynn Harrod

"You don't know what waits for you... you don't know who's here with us..."

"Of course I don't, but together..."

"You do not know... you could never imagine..."

For the second time since they urged her to avoid towns, the two whispers seemed to agree. One wanted Dot to run for her life while the other wanted her to rescue them, yet in that moment they both warned her about some unknown threat ahead she couldn't conceive.

"Then tell me!" Dot said. "What can't I imagine? What stands between us?"

"Some of you will die... not all of you will live..."

"Why can't you tell me where you are? Who's with you? Why can't you tell me anything that can help?"

"They listen... they know everything..."

"Who's listening?" Dot asked.

"You must choose who goes with you to the west... you must choose who stays forever in the east..."

"Are they talking to you, Dottie?" Vincent asked.

"Of course..." Dot looked at her friends' confused faces.

"What are they saying?" Cezar asked. "Are they speaking now?"

"You guys can't hear them?" Dot asked.

"I never knew they talked!" Vincent said. "I always figured you were just saying your thoughts out loud. I do that sometimes. A lot, actually. I'm doing it now!"

"All the times we've been here, only I could hear them?"

"Correct," Abraham said.

"You've all been in this soulless abyss before?" Cezar asked. "Together?"

"Yep, we've visited Dottie's ghost friends many times," Vincent said. "Or maybe they visit us? I'm not for sure."

"They're not ghosts!" Dot said, unconvinced. "They're alive, and they need our help!"

Cezar took Dot's hand as he peered across the expanse, still uncertain if the Star Girls were to be trusted. "Living or dead, friend or foe, we will find them, girl."

"They're friends, Cezar, and they're alive. I can feel them just as I can feel you all next to me. I know we're getting closer each day."

Upon the realization that no one knew the Star Girls had been communicating with her, Dot felt ashamed of bringing them along on a mysterious mission that might prove futile, maybe even fatal, if the Dark Girl was to be believed. They made the dangerous journey with Dot, not out of concern for the Light and Dark Girl, but solely because she needed their help. For all they knew, Dot was indeed chasing ghosts, yet they pledged themselves to her cause. It was a leap of faith she never asked for and suddenly felt guilty for having.

"I love you all," she said, "but you don't have to come with me. In fact, I'm beginning to think maybe you shouldn't. After everything you've been through, you deserve better. You deserve to be safe at Kellan."

"We're not leaving you, Dottie," Vincent said. "Right, Abe?"

"Correct," the combat mech said. "We will complete our mission together as a unified front."

"Cezar will never break his vow," the wolf hybrid said.

Dot felt touched by everyone's devotion. She turned to the distant twins of light, then back to her circle of friends. "We don't even know if they're real or just in my mind. We could be running toward nothing, to an empty building or a forgotten grave."

"We might not believe in the Star Girls," Vincent said, "but we believe in you, Dottie."

Lynn Harrod

"Cezar agrees," the predator said. "The hunt is not about the prey, but the pursuit, the belief. It's the chase that drives us, not the catch."

"Abraham?" Dot said, leaning on the mech's logic and reason. "How do you feel about this?"

"Reminder: This unit cannot feel or express emotion."

"Yes, you keep saying, then make an assessment. Should you follow me east to an unknown destination that may turn out to be pointless, one that will likely put us in danger? Or should you go west to a city that will welcome you and keep you safe?"

"Clarification: Whether the City of Kellan exists, the risk-reward ratios you present are irrelevant. This unit has imprinted on you, Little Miss. I will follow you to any destination, known or unknown, high-risk or low."

"We made our choice, Dottie," Vincent said. "You're stuck with us jokers!"

"And I'm grateful," Dot said, "but I can't shake the feeling that you're the ones stuck with this joker."

"Some of you will die... not all of you will live..."

"I keep repeating their words in my mind," she said. "We don't know what's coming."

"I know what's coming," George said, suddenly standing within her group.

"George!" Dot said, taking him by both hands. "Where are you? I mean, in real life?" She brushed aside the long hair dangling over his face for a better look at his kind eyes. "Where have you been?"

"I've been following you, Dot. I barely missed you at the hybrid habitat, but I tracked you through the woods to the Regal River. I found your campsite and saw the aftermath of your fight with the Greens. Unlike you brave fools, I couldn't risk crossing it there. There was no way I'd make it."

"Who is this boy?" Cezar asked in a demanding tone.

"This is George," Dot said. "He's a friend."

"He's a ranger guy from the south!" Vincent said. "So far, I've only dreamt about him, but he seems nice, and Dot really likes him!"

"Vincent!" Dot said, side-eyeing her plant friend.

George turned away to hide his blushing face.

"A ranger?" Cezar said. He walked up George, his exposed fangs and claws uncomfortably close to the boy. "A woodsman ranger from the South Lands? Cezar has heard tales of your clan's bravery, your unmatched hunting prowess. If the girl considers you an ally, if my blood brother vouches for you, know you have Cezar's respect."

"That's... good to know," George said, intimidated by the monstrous beast looming over him. "You have my respect, too... umm.. Cezar."

"We should have waited for you, George," the girl said.

"You couldn't have known, Dot. From a high ridge, I watched you down in the river, saw what your friends did to get you to the other side. I believe them when they say they'll follow you anywhere."

"So do I," Dot said, wiping a tear from her cheek. The emotions of her friends' dedication and the reunion with the boy overwhelmed her.

"I also believe the girls across The Void when they say you won't all make it," George said.

"What's that mean?"

"I'm familiar with the East Hills, Dot."

"So you know what's waiting for us?"

"Only danger and heartbreak. Maybe you should listen to the girls in the lights, abort your mission, and take your new family west to Kellan."

"You... you can hear them," Dot said, realizing George had some sort of connection to the Star Girls just as she had. "Vincent, Cezar, even Abraham, none of them can hear the twins, but you know what they've been saying all along."

"Yes, and they're both right, as I said before. I also said the decision lies with you, Dot. It always has. But as much as I hate to tell anyone what to do, I must now insist that you run. Go west. Leave the girls behind."

"You know who they are, don't you?" Dot said. "Are they alive?"

"I don't know. It's hard to say."

"I don't understand..."

"Nothing I can say will make you understand. After you were Blessed, after you learned the truth of the world... I fear I'll break your mind forever. I fear I'll lose you."

"You're not making any sense!" Dot said, scrambling to piece together her remnant memories. "Tell me, please! I need to know!"

"I can't, Dot. A ranger is true to his word. Like your friends, I also made a promise. A vow."

"To who? George, what are you not telling me?"

"Reconnaissance," Abraham said. "A number of humanoid life forms are within a three-kilometer radius..."

* * *

Dot awoke to the combat mech's sudden warning without a chance to pinpoint George's location or even say goodbye for now. She expected to see intruders, their camp invaded, but was met with the relative silence of the woods ribboned by the crackle of their campfire and the gentle flow of the nearby Regal River.

"Abraham?" Dot said. "What was George hiding from me?"

"Unknown."

The girl sat up and looked around the camp. She imagined armed Purist Automen hiding behind each of the thousands of trees and shrubs surrounding them.

"Where are they?" she asked, calming herself. "The humanoids you spoke of? And how many?"

"Reconnaissance: 21 humanoids are located 2.9 kilometers northwest of our position."

Abraham stood at the entrance to their alcove, his 12-foot armored body cloaked in darkness, nearly blended into the woods. Gypsy paced just behind him, guarding the alcove's entrance. Vincent and Cezar continued to sleep. Dot wondered if the plant and wolf were still standing in The Void or if they shuffled on to their normal dreams of fishing, farming, and hunting.

"Yes, I remember now," Dot said. "In The Void, you said they were within three kilometers of us."

"Correct."

"But I thought your sensors scanned 10 kilometers around us?"

"Correct."

"So how did 21 humanoids suddenly pop up so close to us without your detection?"

"Unknown."

Concerned, Dot rose to her feet, walked between Abraham's legs, and joined her dog at his post. She examined the woods with him, hoping not to see anything shifting in the shadows.

"That's the second time your sensors missed something," Dot said. "Are you sure you're okay, Abraham? I'm worried about you."

"Commencing total system diagnostic."

"That's good. Let me know when…"

"Diagnostic complete," the mech said. "Sensor array is fully operational and functional."

"Maybe it's not," Dot said. "Maybe the river water did something to your sensors, or maybe you were damaged more than we thought back in Colt."

"Incorrect. My sensor array is waterproof to a depth of 30.5 meters and was unimpaired after the skirmish at Colt."

"Vincent said there was some trouble with the new part we found for you. Maybe that's interfering with your scans?"

"Clarification: The upgraded power module you scavenged for this unit is fully compatible with my sensor array. It was misaligned upon installation but was later reinstalled properly. The wolf hybrid, known as Cezar, is quite adept at energy panel repair and maintenance."

Dot still felt confused. During the group's shared dream, their safety bubble was breached, and Abraham offered no explanation.

"There's 21 humanoids?" she asked.

"Correct."

Dot found that number curious, familiar, but didn't know why. She thought of something Sergeant Furst had told her. "They're coming this way?"

"Incorrect. They hold their northwest position."

"Automen soldiers?"

"Identification: 16 are human, five are artificial."

"That's 21 altogether," Dot said, trying to figure out the puzzle. "But it doesn't make sense. A town or settlement would be all humans. A military troop would be mostly artificial soldiers with only a few human officers, according to Sarge."

"Extrapolation: Based on our travels and updates from your associate, George, the township you speak of is likely Beacon Hill."

Beacon Hill.

Damn, that also sounded familiar.

It sent a chill through her body.

Dot looked over at Vincent and Cezar, still resting peacefully around the campfire in the alcove. She wanted to confer with them but didn't want to rob them of their deep slumber, something that was increasingly rare.

"What can you tell me about Beacon Hill?" Dot asked her mech.

"Location: Beacon Hill is a former suburban community that served as an outpost during the first Purist occupations. Its current value as a military asset is unknown."

"Looks like your connection to the network is still down."

"Correct."

"Keep trying, Abraham. You'll get it back."

Since first discovering his severance from the global data network designed to govern his actions – around the time they first encountered Colt – Abraham had sent out 550 messages and tests over the course of their travels. Each outreach not only failed to garner a response but ended with a "lost signal" automated reply. He eventually came to a grim conclusion about his failure to communicate, realizing he was blind in the wild.

"Status: The world government global satellite network has been dismantled or abandoned."

"What does that mean?"

"Explanation: This unit has no geographic, cultural, or sociopolitical reference to draw from."

"There's no network? No one we can call for help?"

"Correct," Abraham said. "As you have proclaimed on occasion, Little Miss, all we have is us."

35

The Graveyard

By the time Vincent and Cezar woke up, Dot had doused the fire and gathered their supplies, bundling them in blankets from Dominion. Seeing no other path to take, the group ventured forth through the woods, toward the town of Beacon Hill and the 21 humanoids Abraham detected. With the mech's sensors continually sweeping the area, Dot's plan was to pass the town at a distance and hope the mysterious 21 didn't also have advanced reconnaissance that would reveal their presence, equipment that might be hidden from Abraham's sensors.

Emerging from the treeline, they stood on the gradual slope of a hillside and saw the town far below, a vast collection of homes around a central downtown, all enshrouded in an ominous darkness. With so many people supposedly there, Dot wondered why they had spotted none from their vantage point.

"It's still dark, Dottie," Vincent said with a yawn. "The moon is still out. Why'd we leave camp so early?"

"Abraham detected people in the town ahead," Dot said. "He picked up 21 humanoids."

"Human-ode?"

"Humanoid. It means they're shaped like humans. They have two arms, two legs, and one head, just like us."

"So, Abe is also a human-ode, too? He's like us?"

"Yes, Vincent. Abraham is like us. To answer your question, we left camp early because we need to keep moving. That surprise visit at the river has me worried and a little scared."

"I'm worried, too," the plant-man said, "but I'm not scared because we're all together!"

"You're not scared... yet," Cezar said as he stared at the dark, distant town. He looked up at Abraham. "That place at the bottom of the hill with the many structures. That's where you detected people?"

"Correct."

Cezar felt uneasy about entering any kind of 'human habitat.' Since he was a pup, he'd heard startling stories of the old cities with their imposing towers touching the sky, their streets overflowing with millions of people. Though they collapsed to ruin hundreds of years ago, he had nightmares of being trapped in a human city during its prime, overwhelming him with fear and confusion. More unnerving were the tales of the current villages and encampments, their humans territorial and bigoted, for such places still existed.

"How far are we from this... town?" Cezar asked.

"Location: Beacon Hill's municipal boundary is 2.4 kilometers northeast of our position, with the town proper another 1.1 kilometer beyond."

"How many souls do you see? What kind of people are down there? Are they well-armed?"

"Identification: 16 are human, five are artificial."

"Soldiers," Cezar said. "Perhaps a full troop."

"That's what I thought at first," Dot said, "but the humans outnumber the clones 3-to-1. That doesn't sound like any troop to me, blue or green."

"Cezar smells sulfur, polymer, tramp oil," the wolf said, keeping his nose alert. "Steel, iron, rubber. The scents are faint but all around. How do you feel about it, Abraham?"

"Reminder: This unit cannot feel..."

"Apologies," the wolf said, forgetting that his towering companion was an unfeeling war machine. After traveling with him for two days and seeing how much he seemed to care about Dot, Cezar started to regard the robot as an intelligent and emphatic being, even a genuine friend, as the others had. "Cezar just wanted to know if you agree with the girl, that the people in the town aren't soldiers."

"Clarification: This unit agrees with Little Miss. The detected 21 humanoids are unlikely to belong to any military company. They have not advanced on our position and do not carry firearms nor operate vehicles or heavy machinery. Their defenses are limited to steel blades."

"They could just be utility knives," Dot said, "for cutting meat or cloth."

"Or swords and spears for striking flesh," Cezar said.

"Or sickles for harvesting wheat," Vincent said, "or butter knives for making buttery toast and jam and Pain Perdu. That's French toast, you know."

"They could be any of those things," Dot said. "We don't know."

"If we don't know for sure, Dottie, why are we walking toward the blade people at night?"

Vincent posed a good question. The group would normally avoid large groups, especially after the chaos of Colt and the Purists' pursuit along the Broken Road. But Dot felt the pull of the Star Girls grow ever stronger. It pained her to feel closer to them with each passing day while having no way of knowing how much farther they actually had to go.

"We need to get around that town," Dot said. "We need to get past it and up into the east hills as soon as we can, hopefully before they know we were ever here. If we try to wait them out, they might discover us, gather their numbers, and force us back to the river. I don't know how you guys feel, but I don't want to risk crossing the water again."

"I also vote to not go in the river again," Vincent said, shivering from the mere thought of it. "Those fishes bit me a lot."

Dot looked down the rocky hillside, its many boulders and occasional trees lit by the waning moon, and saw no alternative path. "Guys, I think we may have to go down into the..."

"Oww!" Vincent said, hopping on one foot. "One of these rocks cut me!"

"Let me see." Dot knelt down to examine his ankle wound. She was stunned to the gash heal before her eyes. "What did you trip on?"

"That square-looking rock right there!"

Cezar picked up the "rock" Vincent pointed out and was startled to hold a metal helmet in his paws, one much larger than any man could wear. Its snapped antennae must have cut into the plant-man's leg.

"Who could wear such a huge helmet?" Dot asked.

"This is no helmet," the wolf-man said. "This is the head of a mech."

Cezar leaped atop Abraham and surveyed the dark hillside. From his vantage point, he realized the many boulders around them were actually the remains of combat mechs, and that the area once held a fierce battle. It explained the myriad of scents he caught moments before. Six mechs, most much larger than Abraham, laid scattered in the weeds, their bodies torn asunder from an unimaginable clash of giant machines.

"Abraham," Dot said. "What is this place?"

"Location: Based on proximity to the township and the presence of fallen combat mechs, we are standing at the site of the 'Founders' Last Stand,' a skirmish between the rebellious citizens of Beacon Hill and the combat mechs of the Purists of Earth."

"How did it end?"

"Conclusion: The historic event was meant to be a final confrontation that would decide the course of the township's continued progress but resulted in total annihilation on both sides."

"The townsfolk died here," Dot said, "along the machines they fought."

"Correct."

Abraham stood motionless as he constructed simulations in his mind, scenarios of hundreds of humans pitted against six war machines. From what he knew of the town's history, the desperate citizens were mostly farmers but had somehow found a way to take out the mechs, a bold strategy that ended up costing their lives.

As Abraham pondered the fates of the long-dead warriors – both man and machine – Vincent felt something brush against his leg. He looked down and saw two small animals running off with his supply bag.

"Those little critters took my stuff!" he said.

"What was in that bag?" Cezar asked.

"Food, herbs, tools, another power thingy for Abe..."

Cezar bounded after the tiny creatures. Vincent followed close behind, leaving Dot alone with the robot, who stood stuck in deep thought.

"Reconnaissance: There were six combat mechs on this hillside."

Dot sensed her large metal friend was troubled, something that should have been impossible. "What kind of mechs were they?"

Abraham looked around him, pointing to the fallen machines as he described them.

"Identification: To the north are the remains of two Ares-class A1000 units, remote-controlled by Purist officers. To the south is an Atlas-class A1500, automated through complex sets of 'if-then' commands. To the east is an Apollo-class A2120, fitted with a synthetic gravitonic brain. To the west is an Azrael-class A2500, the largest and latest of the series, also fitted with a synthetic gravitonic brain."

"What about the one at our feet?" Dot asked knowingly, careful not to step on the destroyed machine she suddenly recognized.

"Identification: This mech is an Abraham-class A1900, fitted with a synthetic positronic brain."

"Like you."

"Correct."

Dot was surprised to have understood his overly technical description. She replayed it in her mind and traced the brief lineage of the robots. "It sounds like the first two models had no minds of their own."

"Correct. The Ares-class and Atlas-class were rudimentary designs. They did not employ artificial intelligence beyond their immediate actions. They relied on operator input."

"So, the thinking machines started with you."

"Correct."

"They had feelings, didn't they?" Dot asked.

Abraham didn't answer her as quickly as he normally did. He looked about him, at the remains of the more advanced mechs.

"Incorrect. They did not."

"They?" She noticed his hesitant, specific response. "What about you? I mean, what about this other Abraham?"

Once again, the robot stood silent for a moment as if carefully considering the girl's query.

"Explanation: The Abraham-class unit's positronic brain, a composite organic-synthetic mind, was deemed a failure in the field. Its shortcomings compromised military strategy in the face of ethically difficult tactics. To address this issue, the gravitonic brains of the later Apollo-class and Azrael-class units eliminated organic matter, limiting decisions to results-based strategy and removing the hesitation of earlier designs."

"Abraham, I think I understand now." Dot translated his cold summary as easily as she could French or Spanish. "I think I'd rather have your positronic brain than their gravitonic ones."

"Query: Why, Little Miss?"

"You have a conscience. The Abrahams had a hard time killing people they thought didn't deserve it, so they replaced you with robots who wouldn't question orders, no matter what they were. In other words, the military felt they couldn't depend on you as a heartless killing machine because you had feelings."

"Reminder: This unit does not have the capacity for..."

"Yes, I know what you've always told me. But we're standing in a graveyard of humans and machines, and I can feel your despair. It's okay, Abraham."

"Request: Do not share this realization with the others."

"Why not?"

"Explanation: Their assessment of this unit will be unfavorable if they are made aware of my defects."

"Your feelings are not defects," Dot said. "The fact that you refuse to just simply point and shoot, the fact that you consider who or what you're fighting and might refuse to commit atrocities... it doesn't make you weak or broken or defective. I think it makes you thoughtful and brave."

"Disagreement."

"Abraham, I wouldn't consider you a friend if you didn't know right from wrong. You've always listened to me, even if it wasn't the logical strategy. Can we agree on that?"

"Agreement."

"I was once taught that the way you see yourself is important, maybe the most important thing. You might not realize it now, but you've just taken a step in the right direction. I'll be with you when you're ready to take the next step."

"Gratitude, Little Miss," the mech said.

"Still, I promise I won't tell the boys."

"Gratitude."

36

The Old Sloth

Vincent had a hard time keeping up with Cezar as he sprinted up the hill back to the treeline, returning to the dense woods in pursuit of the little thieves that snatched his friend's supply bag.

"Where are you, Cezzie?" he called out to the trees. "Dang, you sure are fast! Hey, I can hear the river again! We're getting too far from Dottie!"

"Get down!" the wolf said from a bush.

Vincent joined him in his hidden, crouched position. They spoke in hushed voices, though the plant-man didn't know why.

"What are we doing?" he asked.

"Cezar has found the fools who stole from us. Their herbal, musky scent is all around us now, so strong Cezar can taste it. Surely, you've picked it up, as well."

Vincent sniffed the air. "Hmm, smells like cloves and raspberries mixed with the stinky old chimp women from the barn."

"Monkeys," Cezar said, pointing to two creatures at the base of an elm. They looked like young boys with long black tails, their faces and shoulders covered in white fur. They rummaged through Vincent's bag which sat among many other pillaged sacks, boxes, and crates, unaware they were being hunted.

"Monkey boys?" Vincent asked, keeping his voice low. "Aww, they're so cute!"

"Cute, indeed," Cezar said in a whisper, eyes fixed on his prey. "Cute, mischievous little devil monkeys."

"Capuchin monkeys, actually," a grizzled voice said from the tree branches above. "A most crafty species."

"Rotten roots!" Startled, Vincent leapt high into the air, eyes wide like black saucers. His spindly legs flung him well above the treetops.

Cezar caught him and gestured for him to stay quiet, to look for the voice.

"Who was that, Cezzie?" Vincent asked.

"Cezar doesn't know," the wolf-man said. "Cezar can't pick up his scent."

"Maybe the monkey devil fruity smell covered it up?"

"Capuchin monkeys do have a most pungent odor," the drawling elderly voice from the trees said. "Garlic, cloves, berries, citrus. They rub them on their fur. It masks their numbers from predators. No offense to present company."

"Where are you?" Cezar asked. "Show yourself!"

"I am here, as you are here."

"He sure talks funny," Vincent said. "I kinda like it."

Cezar wished he could see the good in all as easily as his blood brother, but he could only look around in defense of the calm, worn voice neither of them could spot. Only when the twin monkey boys jumped from their loot pile and scrambled high up to a large, ancient sloth did the wolf and plant finally see him. The sloth moved so slowly he nearly appeared frozen, a unique method of camouflage.

"Unlike my boys," the old hybrid said, "sloths have no distinct scent, a most rare trait that saved my life on many occasions, I assure you."

"They're yours?" Cezar asked as the small thieves handed the sloth Abraham's spare power module.

"They are mine and I am theirs," the sloth-man said. "You are mine as well, Mr. Wolf. The pleasant Mr. Plant, I don't know."

"You guys are buddies?" Vincent asked, delighted. "Cezzie, are you going to introduce me? I'm Vincent! They also call me Vinny Greenblood, Veggie Vinny, Dim Vin..."

"Don't listen to them, Vincent," the wolf said. "Cezar has never met these trickster monkey fiends."

"Tricksters, are we?" the sloth said in his slow drawl, amused. "Fiends?"

"Cezar says 'fiends.' You've stolen something most precious to our companion."

"Your companion? You must mean the large walking machine. My sincere apologies, gentlemen. I didn't realize he was yours."

"He is ours and we are his," Cezar said, "to borrow your words."

"Abe's our friend," Vincent said.

"Curious." The old sloth examined the power module, rolling it in his hands, before tossing it to the predator below. "Most curious. I've never thought of befriending a machine."

"You'd like him," Vincent said. "He's the nicest killer robot you'll ever meet."

"As strange as it may seem, I believe you, Mr. Plant."

"His name is Vincent," Cezar said, following the girl's example of encouraging his friend's preferred name.

"And your name is Cezzie."

"Only Vincent calls this wolf Cezzie. You will say Cezar."

"It's easy to remember," Vincent said. "He says his name a lot."

"Greetings, Vincent and Cezar," the sloth said, "two most unlikely companions. Welcome to the graveyard." The sloth slowly climbed halfway down the elm before dropping the rest of the way. He extended his long, hairy arms, offering dual handshakes. "I am Saabir. My boys are Kondo and Kunto. We mean you no harm. We come from The Great Domain."

"So, that's how you know Cezar," the wolf hybrid said.

"You got out with the others!" Vincent said. "I don't remember seeing you at the big farewell, Mr. Sabb-berr, sir, but I'm glad you made it out of the rainforest before the Greenies showed up."

Still unsure about Saabir, Cezar circled the great elm tree that held the old sloth's Capuchin boys. He smelled another dozen monkey children elsewhere in the trees along with the felt linings of storage trunks, leather hides of satchels, and linseed oil from wooden crates, all bounty from decades of pilfered goods.

"No, Vincent," the wolf-man said. "They've been out in the wild for years. They've somehow found a way to come and go from Dominion, to live in the wild while scrounging for supplies from the rainforest."

"That's where all the stuff came from," Vincent said, proud of their deductive skills.

"How right you are, Vincent and Cezar," Saabir said.

The elderly sloth explained that they had lived in the woods north of the Regal River for decades, having fled the rainforest vivarium when he'd only been walking for a month. His parents placed him in the building's ventilation shafts before predators took their lives. The winter storms hadn't yet arrived, and the river was at its lowest point when he forded the water to the woods and the hallowed ground he called "The Graveyard," a leveled hillside littered with the bones and armored frames of a battle that left no survivors. After several years alone, the orphan sloth nearly succumbed to loneliness before devoting himself to helping other infants escape the facility.

One by one, he carried hybrid monkeys, raccoons, foxes, badgers, possums, and chipmunks to a sanctuary he constructed from the remains of mechs. Behind steel plate walls, they lived in safety until the night the dreaded "Gardeners" – masked and hooded night raiders – roamed the hillside. Saabir took his children to the treetops, to armored huts held up by the massive elms and oaks, where they've lived in isolation ever since.

"You gather supplies from Dominion?" Cezar asked after hearing his history. "Why not search the town below? It's a much larger habitat to uncover."

"We rarely go past the graveyard," Saabir said, "and we never venture into the town."

"Why not?" Vincent said.

"You've surely heard the expression, 'No one leaves The Great Domain'? Clearly, that's not true. Present company is proof of that." Saabir looked up and saw his many children gathered in the treetops, small woodland creatures of every kind standing on the little porches of their makeshift huts. "I invite you to stay with us, to live off the land and the lush offerings of the rainforest facility. After looking down at that cursed ghost town for nearly a century, after watching both lone travelers and caravans enter those abandoned streets, I can tell you with no uncertainty that no one leaves Beacon Hill."

Vincent and Cezar looked at each other before turning to the distant town at the bottom of the hill.

"What waits for us there?" Cezar asked.

"I can't tell you because I've never seen anyone."

"But you said folks go in but they don't come out?" Vincent said with a shudder.

Cezar realized Saabir had no answers other than his dire warning and dismissed it as long-held paranoia. It made sense that an old, slow-moving sloth and his young, defenseless children would cling to the treetops, limiting their supply runs to the familiar rainforest facility.

"It pleased Cezar to meet you, Saabir," the wolf-man said, "and we wish you worthy hunting and good luck, but we must return to our companions."

"The robot, the dog, and the girl," the old sloth said.

"Yes. We are a pack."

"They are yours, and you are theirs."

"Yep," Vincent told him. "What you said."

"Then I will be the one to wish you good luck, Vincent and Cezar, because you won't find it in that town."

37

Beacon Hill

After Vincent excitedly told Dot and Abraham about Saabir and his many "cute little" adopted children, failing to fully express the gravity of the old sloth's warning, the group continued down the hillside, past the old battleground, down to the streets of the dark town. With so many people supposedly there, Dot wondered why they hadn't seen a single soul from their earlier vantage point. Even under the faint light of the waning moon, within the town's limits, one of them should have spotting someone.

"Are you sure there's people here?" Dot asked her mech.

"Yeah, Abe, I don't see or hear nobody," Vincent said, his bioluminescent eyes and sharp ears picking up nothing.

"Cezar doesn't smell them, either," the wolf said.

"Correction: No humanoid life signs are detected within a 10-kilometer radius."

"How's that possible?" Dot asked in shock. "You spotted 21 people a little while ago, mostly human. Could they have left and covered that much ground so quickly?"

"Speculation: Based on their previous location and the density of this township, only a large vertical-takeoff aircraft could feasibly extract a group of humanoids and quickly transport them across 10 kilometers. However, such a scenario is unlikely."

"Impossible is the word, my metal friend," Cezar said. "A large flying machine could not be missed. Its engines would deafen our ears, its body would block the moon. But how could they have left the town otherwise?"

"Unknown."

"Creepy stuff," Vincent said, looking down at the dark streets. "That many folks can't vanish just like that... even though that's what Mr. Sabb-brr said happens here."

"Are we sure Abraham's scans are working?" Dot asked. "They didn't work at the river."

"Cezar thinks so," the wolf said. "Cezar checked the mech's systems himself, calibrated the sensors, aligned the power module, cleaned the array lenses. Cezar swears the mech is functioning perfectly."

"Abraham, think. What could have happened? We can't have any more surprises."

"Hypothesis: It is possible that this unit's sensor array detected trace evidence of a former occupation and misinterpreted it as a current position. The newly installed power module is rated as 90 Percent compatible with this unit."

"Cezar understands," the wolf said, though he still felt unsure.

"Well, I don't understand," Dot said. "I thought the new part fit and was better than the old one."

"Me, too," Vincent asked. "Can you translate that, Cezzie?"

"Abraham is an A1900 mech with an A2120 power module," the wolf said. "The device works, Cezar can attest to that. But it wasn't meant for him. He's suggesting his internal chronometer may not be synchronized with his sensors."

"I think I get it!" Vincent said, proud of himself for finally understanding technical jargon. "You mean his timing is off! Dang, Cezzie, I'm sure glad you're with us now."

"So am I," Dot said. "You're saying he might have seen 'shadows' of people who are no longer here. That still doesn't explain how we missed the ambush at the river."

"Agreement," the robot said.

"Cezar can correct his chronometer," the wolf said, further assuring the girl. He liked the fact that he contributed to her group, that he could put her troubled mind at ease. "However, the adjustment will take time."

"We'll have time for that later," Dot said. "Whatever the problem is, it looks like we're alone for now."

Beacon Hill was flanked by high cliffs to the east and deep marshes to the west, making it difficult to circumvent the town as they'd planned. At some point, they needed to travel through it, the central Broken Road being the clear path. With the sudden disappearance of the townsfolk, people who may have never been there to begin with, trekking through the ominous town seemed to pose no threat, but the girl learned not to take quiet moments for granted.

With Gypsy leading as always, and Abraham bringing up the rear, the group carefully continued down the streets, past neighborhoods and their countless abandoned cars, onward through the heart of the town. Dot saw schools, churches, a city hall, office buildings, restaurants, and shopping centers, all familiar sights from other stops on their journey. Though her memory still eluded her, she started to piece together what human cities used to look like before the world ended their reign.

"No people, but do you guys see anything else?" Dot asked. Under the crescent moon, Beacon Hill appeared long dead and in near total darkness to the girl, but to her friends and their enhanced eyes and ears, the town had plenty to offer.

"Cezar smells meat," the wolf hybrid said, pointing his sensitive snout to the east. "Not meat from a fresh kill, but meat that has been preserved. Meat, fish, grain."

"There's vegetables!" Vincent said, turning to the west. "The trees say there's lots of root and vine vegetables in that direction, still in the ground."

"Speculation," Abraham said. "The presence of perishable supplies suggests that the residents of this township may return."

"Should we investigate?" Cezar asked. "Or should we get through this dreadful place as quickly as we can?"

"How long before the sun comes up?" Dot asked.

"Projection: Sunrise will commence in approximately five hours."

"Five hours. That might give us time."

"Time for what, Dottie?" Vincent asked.

Dot wanted to pass through the labyrinthine town and back into the woods before sunrise, before anyone could surprise them like the Purist squad at the river, but the dense downtown called to her. She thought of the treasures of Wellspring and couldn't resist exploring for supplies and perhaps triggered memories. Most importantly, she also secretly hoped to allow time for George to track them, as he had mentioned camping in the same town days before.

Five hours seemed like plenty of time to sneak about the streets and through the many vacant buildings, but the clock would run out fast if they searched as a group.

"Cezar and Gypsy can look for the meat," she said. "Vincent and I will look for the produce."

"Produce?" Vincent asked.

"Fruits and vegetables."

"Huh. 'Produce.' I've never heard that word before."

"Neither have I," Dot said, her vocabulary surpassing her memory. "But I guess I actually did."

Abraham stopped walking. He focused his sensors on his immediate surroundings. "Strategy: This unit will remain in the township's central region for optimal, omnidirectional monitoring."

"Omni-direct-what?" Vincent said.

"Abraham wants to scan all around," Dot said, "and this is the best spot for him to keep watch over us."

"I don't know, Dottie. I'm not too keen on us splitting up."

"No one's here," Dot said. "No one will be alone except Abraham, and we all know he can take care of himself."

"I suppose you're right."

"Agreement," Abraham said. "This unit will remain in the central plaza to serve as both continual reconnaissance and as a marked location to regroup."

"Sounds like a plan," Dot said.

"Request: Be careful, Little Miss."

"I don't think any of us could not be careful if we tried."

Dot tapped her always-on cochlear earpiece to comfort the concerned robot. She held onto one of Vincent's vines as they headed west while Cezar and Gypsy followed their noses east.

If only they had been more concerned with the improbable failure of the mech's sensors and the impossibly sudden disappearance of the 21 people in the pitch black darkness of the abandoned town, perhaps they'd have sensed the grave dangers ahead.

38

The Victory Garden

Vincent peered down every side street he and Dot passed, his glowing eyes shining on alleys, driveways, corridors, and parking lots. Trotting from one side of the main thoroughfare to the other, he took solace from the girl clutching the end of one of his extended vines. So long as she remained connected to him, he found the courage to explore the creepy, abandoned downtown.

Dot kept to the middle of the wide street, out in the open, where she felt most vulnerable yet most alert, denying anyone the chance to sneak up on her. She kept her guard up though she felt certain they were alone. It seemed impossible that all four of her companions with their gifted senses could be wrong.

"Looks like the markets have been picked clean," Vincent said, emerging from his sixth storefront. "There's not even a can of sweet corn, not even a packet of seeds! When the old ones left, they must've taken everything."

"The old ones?"

"The folks who used to live here a long time ago, the ones who didn't go up the hill to fight the big robot guys."

"The ones who didn't end up in the graveyard," Dot said solemnly. "The ones who ran."

"I'm glad they got out, but they're probably dead now, and they're probably not gonna grow back, like Father."

"No, Vincent," Dot said, knowing it had likely been two hundred years since the town's prime. "The original humans will not grow back."

"I wish they were still here."

"Sometimes, wishes don't help," Dot said, recalling the earlier advice. "But to be honest, I'm glad they're gone. If they left in such a hurry, taking anything they could carry, they must have fled in fear. Whatever forced them out, it's good they got away when they had the chance, even if they're not with us anymore." She recalled the morbid scene in the Wellspring church.

"I guess that makes sense," Vincent said, unsure.

The downtown storefronts gave way to the start of the marshes and wide open fields underneath bordering silos and warehouses. Beacon Hill used to be a farming town, its west side now comprising withered vines, decimated groves, and dead orchards. Despite centuries of unchecked growth, most of the crops had been taken by weeds run amok and the appetites of pests and woodland creatures. It all seemed a wasteland until Vincent felt the presence of fresh, healthy plants.

"Over there!" he said, pointing to a cluster of eight-foot weeds. "It's a victory garden!"

"Where? I don't see anything."

The plant hybrid didn't see it either, but he felt it on the ground beneath his feet and smelled its myriad of scents wafting in the air.

"There!" Vincent said. "Behind the old fig trees! It's huge!"

A victory garden – also known as a war garden – was a government-mandated ordinance made during times of potential enemy invasion that provided rations of seeds, soil, mulch, and tools in order to grow small personal gardens. High-nutritional fare such as beans, cabbage, carrots, kale, beets, peas, lettuce, tomatoes, chard, turnips, and squash were provided to each citizen. With cities both great and small falling to their knees in the wake of the New World War, manufacturing facilities ceased operation, collapsing trade routes and killing nearly all marketplaces. For humanity to survive, it needed to turn back time and live off the land as its ancestors had centuries before. A single victory garden provided enough food for a common household.

The elected officials and community leaders of Beacon Hill – the "founders" as Saabir called them – envisioned life beyond the mandate, combining the citizens' rations and labor into one massive public garden west of Downtown. The noble effort grew enough food for everyone who chose to remain in their hometown under the faint hope that they could somehow outlive both the global pandemic and the international war. With the townsfolk now long departed, it seemed puzzling that an abundant, thriving garden meant to feed hundreds could still exist, let alone thrive. It seemed far more than enough for the settlement of 21 they assumed would return.

Wading through the marshes and weeds and rocks, Vincent came across the largest, most opulent garden he'd ever imagined. Thirty feet behind him, his little friend clung to his long vine, making her way to the pristine crops.

"Look at it, Dottie!" Vincent said. "It's ten times bigger than Father's farm ever was! And it's well kept, better than Dominion! The carrots and corn are a bit small for my liking, but they're strong and ripe for harvest."

"Where are you?" Dot said, trailing behind, lost in the tall, thick weeds. "I can't see you, Vincent!"

"Just follow my voice! You gotta see this! I don't know how this is possible. Maybe the marsh has something to do with it?"

Vincent would never know how right he was. The famous and ambitious Beacon Hill Joint Victory Garden was bioengineered, crossbreeding common farm produce with swamp plants like pickerel, bulrush, and horsetails. The resulting crops had robust roots that worked as filters for the marsh runoff water, blocking the muck and absorbing the rich nutrients. Complementing the human-hybrid trials, the mass garden was one of the most advanced crossbreeding science experiments of its time, a paradigm shift in agriculture.

Vincent picked a large tomato and bit into it, allowing its juice to run down his chin. The pulp was sweet, deep red, with a firm, crisp skin. "Dottie, you need to taste this! It's even better than the tomatoes we used to grow up north!"

In his excitement, Vincent failed to notice the lack of tension in his extended vine, which meant the girl no longer held its end. He reeled it in, hoping to wrangle her to his side but was startled to feel no pull through the weeds. In the night's silence, he fully coiled his vine only to find his friend gone.

"Dottie?" he called out, no longer afraid of being heard. "Dottie??"

He leapt to the top of a derelict tractor and looked around, his bright eyes casting light over the marsh and the rich crops. With a wide sweep of his arms, he flung his many vines in all directions like a giant spider, hoping to catch hold of the girl again.

Like the 21 people that vanished in the night, Dot was nowhere to be found.

39

Familiar Blood

Despite his uncanny sense of smell, Cezar let Gypsy lead him down the dark streets, down back alleys, to the pungent scents of both preserved and freshly butchered meats. Though he considered himself a seasoned hunter, he deferred to the one true dog as they prowled the town in search of the substance they both craved.

"Protein," Cezar said to the dog. "That's what we beasts need. It's what we demand. The living flesh of natural animals, their essence empowering us to continue our nightly hunts together. Cezar and Gypsy, roaming the night together, a mighty pack of two."

Their kinship extending beyond friendship, Cezar felt a bond with the German Shepherd as he realized their shared heritage.

Though the hybrid was borne of human intellect and predatory hunger, he remained half-man whereas the dog was a pure, untainted pack hunter, more worthy of the kill than his Dominion brethren. The wolf-man envied the dog – even admired him – for his dedication to the hunt, his sharp instincts, and his unbreakable loyalty to the girl.

In truth, Cezar wished he was a whole wolf or true dog with no traits shared with Man. He'd fit in better with the wild world, feeding from the last kill, thinking only of the next, living day-to-day with no burden on his mind other than survival. It would still be dangerous, still be an ongoing struggle, but it would be an honorable way of life with no self-doubt polluting his mind.

He growled and ripped himself from his wretched feelings of regret, cursing his pathetic self-pity. He saw it as a failing of Man he'd inherited through his unnatural creation.

"You are indeed a coward, Cezar," he muttered to himself. "Caffar always knew. You dream of another life when you should be focused on the present, on your new clan who now depends on you. The kind girl and your other new allies will never feel safe with such an unworthy wolf dragging them behind."

His bout of penance was interrupted when Gypsy stopped a short distance from a single lit doorway at the end of a long, narrow building. The smell of blood and entrails overpowered Cezar, and he had to fight his urge to tear the door from its hinges. The wolf in him wanted to rush in and feast on the game he'd smelled from afar, but the man in him wanted to pause, to circle the structure and consider if such a prize was actually a trap. It could easily be tempting bait for fools to uncover shortly before their capture. He resented his human need to survey the area before heading in, viewing it as another innate weakness, and entered the dark hallway, baring fangs and claws.

Cezar gestured for the dog to stay, to remain alert at the door while he ventured in to discover what lay ahead. Upon turning several corners, he found himself in a room full of hung meat, large carcasses of deer and elk surrounded by hares on hooks and quail in insulated coolers. If the dog had accompanied him inside, he'd have recognized it as identical to Colt's morbid mess hall, the former diner turned abattoir.

"What a bounty," Cezar said as he examined the expertly butchered flesh, their blood having dripped and drained onto the cement floor. "Such care was put into their preparation."

He'd never seen so much meat on display, all within reach, ready for the taking. There was no tainted meat, no trace of the virus. More importantly, there were no hybrids, which he refused to kill, just natural animals. Despite his immense hunger, he detected an odd scent in the room, a familiar smell he'd once caught long ago. It forced him to reexamine the riches before him.

"Cezar has smelled this blood before," he whispered to himself as he pulled aside the deer and elk hanging from the ceiling, revealing an open doorway he'd missed when he first entered the room. "It's not hybrid nor contaminated, but..."

Stepping into the second dark room, his nocturnal eyes saw the source of the strange, beckoning odor of dried meat and fresh blood. He stood revolted by the sight of several *human* corpses on metal tables, their innards picked apart and laid bare on wooden countertops and stuffed within stainless steel bowls and trays.

The current citizens of Beacon Hill – wherever they were now – had succumbed to cannibalism, an extreme solution to avoiding The Worm. The depraved, desperate act tested the wolf-man's resolve.

"These people butcher each other," Cezar said in horror. "No ceremony of honor, no redemption to speak of. They feed on their own. This town is the heart of humanity's Hell."

Cezar ran out of the macabre slaughterhouse, returning to his canine companion. As he led the dog back to the center of town, his only thought was to warn the others before it was too late.

40

The Pale Children

Dot awoke in a cavern lit by a single candle on a wooden shelf. Her dirty, oversized military fatigues were gone, replaced by a fresh, white cotton gown with intricate seams and stone buttons. Her boots were replaced by wooden sandals, and her long curly hair was bound in a bun.

The cavern was the size of a common room. Its long tables, down pillows, and crude artwork adorning the rock walls suggested it was some kind of community center that could accommodate a hundred souls.

Desperate to make sense of her predicament, she thought back to the moment before she found herself in the cavern. She remembered being outside in the night, her feet tramping through shallow mud, while Vincent excitedly rushed ahead through the tall marsh grass, calling out to her upon finding some unexpected treasure. Before she could respond or follow his voice, she felt an arm grab her from behind, shoving what felt like a small cushion into her face. She looked up to see dark, hooded men around her and smelled a strange chemical odor, followed by blurry vision and weakened legs.

She fell to the ground and realized she was alone in the cavern. With the rocky cliffs east of the marsh and across the large town, she wondered how much time had passed and how far she'd traveled after her mysterious assailants abducted her.

Dot's first instinct was to yell for help, but she quickly quashed that urge and crept to the cavern's exit, where she saw a long corridor stretching out before her, lit by occasional torches mounted on the walls. They exposed more artwork, some on canvas, some on paper, most scrawled onto the rock. Stick figures stood together in groups, tended plants and trees, and carried baskets of fruit, the illustrated history of whoever lived in such a dreary place.

Dot made her way down the corridor, passing many other cavernous rooms carved from the walls. She spotted beds, clothing, toys, tools, bales of grain, and crates of produce.

Continuing through the corridor, she encountered children in some rooms, most much younger than her, all with pale skin and wide, dark eyes. They put down their books and dolls and turned to her with curious stares. She smiled at them, but received no expression in return. They showed no fear, no trepidation, only curiosity.

"Where am I?" Dot asked.

The children looked at each other, unsure if they should speak with the girl. Though she was now dressed like them, she had none of their scars, and her skin had a warm color they'd never seen.

"What is this place? Are we still near Beacon Hill?"

Some of the smaller children approached Dot for a closer look. A six-year-old boy took her by the arm and gently touched the tattoo atop her left hand, rubbing it to see if it would smear like paint. He seemed puzzled when it didn't.

"That's my name," she said. "Dot." She had more questions about who brought her there, how and why they did it, but she had a feeling they didn't know, for she doubted young children had any voice in such a suffocating place. She instead stepped back and started over with a smile. "My name is Dot, like on my hand. What are your names?"

The oldest child, a nine-year-old girl, gestured for the others to step away from the stranger. Her thin, pale skin was nearly translucent. She stood among her many siblings, prompting them to retreat to the back of the room.

"Speak with the Widows," the pale girl said. "We're not allowed to talk to you."

"You're talking with me now," Dot said.

"Speak with the Widows."

"Where are they?"

The nine-year-old shook her head at the younger children, and everyone turned away from Dot. They stared at the floor until the strange, smooth-skinned girl left their room.

41

The Widows

Dot returned to the corridor and continued down its length, passing several more rooms of children playing, studying, and sleeping. She assumed they'd offer her the same unwelcome stares, all of them forbidden from speaking with her, so she passed them until she reached a large, round room where an argument between adults ensued.

"Bringing her here is madness!" a man said. "She has The Worm! You can see it all over her!"

"I saw nothing of the sort," another man said. "And you can no longer catch The Worm from people. It's not transmitted that way."

"Hogwash!"

"You ingest it from tainted food," a third man said, "or it's already within you from the day you come into this world."

"That's a myth!"

"The virus is still in the air up top!" a fourth man said. "You can still get it from reckless cretins wandering the wild! Don't let your hopes blind you!"

"We don't know anything for sure," the second man said. "That's why she's here. So we may learn."

"I say she brings the virus! She brings death! And when our garden dies, you can blame yourselves for allowing her to infect us all!"

Dot peeked into the room and saw thirty men sitting in chairs in a wide circle, all facing each other during their heated exchange. To her surprise, they appeared to be quite old, much older than Father Young or Dr. Blum. Their weathered, wrinkled skin was as thin and pale as the children's, and their eyes were completely black. Dot wondered if these people had ever seen the light of day.

Three ancient women, older still than the men who surrounded them, sat in chairs in the middle of the circle with ornate garden spades in their hands. Their long white hair blended with the albino skin of their stoic faces, and their flowery gowns – the only color of any clothing – suggested an air of authority. Their status as figureheads was confirmed when one of them held up her spade, instantly silencing the room.

"Dr. Felix examined her thoroughly," the old woman said. "If she had The Worm, he would have spotted the signs."

"Dr. Felix has been wrong before!" a man shouted.

"He said we'd one day see the sun!" another man said.

"He told me my daughter would live to become a woman! He said she'd bear grandchildren! Why should I ever trust his words again?"

The old woman pointed her spade at the angry men.

"The Worm is indeed still transmissible," she said firmly, ending their debate. "If the girl had The Worm, it would have killed every elder in this room by now, and I don't see a single corpse among you."

"Our scouts have heard rumors of The Exceptional Girl," another of the commanding old women said, her spade held high. "They spied on the Greens, heard that she defeated The Worm and was coming our way. Now the Gardeners have brought her here. It is done."

"If any Gardener falls dead tonight," a man said in a stern yet anxious tone, "if even one of them shows signs..."

"Careful, Alderman," the first old woman said. "Your tone sounds like the beginning of a threat."

"It is the middle of concern."

"Gardener Moon and his men are well," the second old woman said with a dismissive wave of her spade.

"Are we certain of that?"

"They are well, and the girl is here. It is done. Don't pray for a miracle only to question and fear its arrival."

As the third old woman lowered her spade, she noticed Dot at the entrance. She smiled at her and hushed the crowd, gesturing for the girl to come in for all to see.

"Don't be afraid," the first old woman said, pointing her spade at Dot. "Our debate never ends, but what my sisters and I say is rule and law. No one will harm you."

In her plain cotton gown, Dot stepped into the round room. As her eyes adjusted to the many wall torches and the wide candelabra hanging above, she noticed the group was flanked by silent guards in cloaks, hoods, and masks with creepy blank expressions. They stood in shadow along the walls, holding long spears and swords.

"Will *they* harm me?" Dot said, eyeing the guards and their intimidating weapons. After witnessing Sergeant Furst's troops betray him, she learned to mistrust soldiers, even those who appeared under control.

"The Gardeners do nothing we don't wish them to do. Come, child. Let us take a good look at you."

Dot entered the circle and stood before the elder women. The first of them took her by the hand and glanced at the Aldermen as if to prove the stranger posed no threat.

"You seem healthy, child," the old woman said.

"She's too small," a man said. "Too small for the town."

"She'll grow, you'll see. In time, she'll come of age."

"She'll still be too small," another man said.

"Maybe for the town, but not for the elders in this room."

Everyone in the circle nodded in agreement, seeing the logic of the old woman's strange statement.

"What's your name, child?"

"My name is... I actually don't know my name," the girl said, surprised by her candid response. "But I'm called Dot."

"My name is Margaret, but no one has spoken that name for many years. I'm called Widow Hawthorne. These are my sisters."

Still holding the girl's hand, the old woman stood and brought her closer to the two other women in the center.

"This is Judith. We call her Widow Baxter. Next to her is Laura. We call her Widow Sullivan."

The oldest child in the caves had told Dot to speak with The Widows, and here they stood, enthralled by her.

Widow Hawthorne seemed to be the leader. Widows Baxter and Sullivan also clearly lorded over their community, though they appeared to defer to their oldest sister.

"These men at the wall are The Gardeners," Widow Hawthorne said. "They protect us, go out into the wild for us under the cover of night. They serve us, therefore they now serve you."

"If you say so," Dot said.

"I understand your doubt. You have questions, as have I."

"Where am I? Who are you people?"

"We're the last of the garden folk, descendants of the Great Victory Garden."

"I was at Beacon Hill with my friends," Dot said. "I need to find them. How far are we from the town?"

"Not far at all," Widow Hawthorne said.

"How long would it take to go back?"

"Go back?" the widow said. "You never left, child. Beacon Hill is directly above us."

42

Unknown

Vincent ran from the marsh back to the center of Downtown where Abraham stood scanning the area. Along the way, he climbed nearly every building, no longer caring if he was heard or seen, in a frantic attempt to relocate Dot. The vast, astonishing garden he discovered had been wiped from his mind. All that mattered now was finding his little friend.

"She's gone!" Vincent said to the robot, nearly running into him. "They took her!"

"Query: Is Little Miss in danger?"

"Yes! Maybe? I'm talking about Dot! They took Dot!"

"Query: Did you identify the party responsible?"

"Query query query, no I didn't identificate anyone! I was really hoping you did, Abe!"

"Reconnaissance: I detect no humanoid life forms within a 10-kilometer radius."

"Not now, maybe, but what about a little while ago?"

"Negative."

"Nothing?" Vincent asked, exasperated. "You were scanning the whole time, right?"

"Correct."

"Not one blip on your sensor things since we got here?"

"Correct."

Vincent circled the plaza, jumping atop old vans and street lamps, hoping to spot the girl walking down the street.

"How could I lose her? I'm such a doofus!"

"Query: What was your path and location before she left your sight?"

"We looked around. I ducked into some doorways, through some windows, tried to find supplies. We went into the marsh, just over there at the end where the buildings stop. I walked through some mud and grass and ended up in a big vegetable garden." Vincent felt dumb, guilty. "I got so excited... dang, I should've never gone ahead of her. Any ideas? Maybe someone took her, or maybe she just left me to go snoop around some more?"

"Status: I detect no assailants nor the girl."

"Are you positive your sensing thingies aren't messed up? Test them! Scan for us! One of your really good, deep scans, Abe."

"Reconnaissance: I detect the one plant hybrid humanoid, HPL-VCT-001, human-plantae-liana, located 2.2 meters west..."

"I guess that's me?"

"...one wolf hybrid humanoid, HCL-CMZ-777, human-canis-lupis, located 804.8 meters west..."

"I suppose... that's Cezzie?"

"...one German Shepherd, ACF-452, animalia-canine-familiaris, also located 804.8 meters east..."

"That's gotta be Gypsy."

"...one warren of 16 rabbits, Oryctolagus cuniculus, and 27 wood mice, Apodemus sylvaticus, located..."

"Okay, Abe, I got it. Your scanners are working real good. That actually makes me more worried than if they weren't, 'cause it means we're totally lost."

"Agreement."

"So, what do we do now?"

"Recommendation: We search the wider area of the girl's last known location."

"Okay, but what about Cezzie and Gypsy?"

"Assurance: The wolf hybrid and the domesticated dog will easily find us with their heightened olfaction."

"You mean they can smell good."

"Correct."

"I guess you're right," Vincent said, briefly forgetting the urgency of their situation. "They'll find us. They got some good schnozzes, and no one else smells like corn and metal, like me and you, I mean."

"Correct."

"Course, those two kinda smell the same, if you ask me. Not sure why."

"Explanation: They both belong to the species canis lupus."

"Oh yeah. So true. You are wise, my metal friend. That's what Cezzie would say."

Vincent and Abraham left the plaza and headed back toward the marsh on the western edge of town, the mech's spotlights flooding the streets and vacant buildings. Though Vincent trusted that his two canine friends could take care of themselves, he still wondered if leaving their meeting spot was the right decision, and felt relief upon Abraham's next report.

"Update: The gray wolf hybrid known as Cezar and the German Shepherd dog known as Gypsy..."

"Get to it, Abe! Just say their names." Vincent felt bad for scolding the mech. "Sorry if I'm being impatient-ed."

"Acknowledgment."

"So, what about them?"

"Update: Cezar and Gypsy are in motion, quickly closing the distance between our parties at a speed of 16.5 meters per second."

"Dang, that sounds fast. Is that fast?"

"Correct. It is above average speed for both wolf and dog."

"Glad they're coming back. I'll feel a lot better if we stick together. Even though they can sniff us, let's wait for them."

"Agreement."

"Where are they now?" Vincent asked, getting excited.

"Update: They are 648.1 meters from our location."

"I wonder why they're running?"

"Unknown."

"Where are they now?"

"Update: They are 582.3 meters from our location."

"What about now?"

"Update: They are 565.8 meters from our location."

"Getting closer and closer. How about now?"

"Update: They are 532.5 meters from our location."

"Shoot, I'm sorry again if I'm being a pest, Abe," Vincent said, feeling as though he was annoying the mech, which was actually impossible. "I just wanna see 'em is all."

"Understood. You value their familiarity."

"Yep, I sure do. With them running like the wind, I hope they ain't in trouble. Maybe they're being chased?"

"Negative."

"Oh yeah, I guess you'd know if they someone was following them. Where are they now?"

"Update: They are 416.2 meters from our location."

"Dang, they really are fast!" Vincent imagined them in full sprints, side by side, speeding down the dark avenue toward them. As a thick fog rolled in, enveloping much of Downtown, he wondered how they kept up their pace without running into the many abandoned cars laying dead in the street. "I wonder who'd win in a race between them? What do you think?"

"Unknown."

"Oh, come on, Abe. Take a guess." Vincent wanted to lighten the mood after being so harsh with his friend. "Don't be so quick with the 'unknown' answer. Who's gonna get here first? You know, like if they was in a race? I say Gypsy will win."

"Prediction: Cezar would defeat Gypsy in a hypothetical race."

"Really? Why Cezar?"

"Explanation: The average speed of an adult German Shepherd on even terrain is 13.4 meters per second. By comparison, the average speed of a gray wolf in similar conditions is 15.2 meters per second."

"Ah, but Cezzie ain't no ordinary wolf. He's a hybrid, like me, stands on two legs. You gotta take that into your calculating thoughts."

"Clarification: Cezar stands on two legs but runs on four."

"Good point, but he's a big boy with a heavy build. I still think Gypsy will win. Where are they at now?"

Before Abraham could answer him, Gypsy emerged out of the fog. Vincent giggled and smirked at the robot.

"See, I knew it!" Vincent said. "My money was on him all along! That's something Father used to say, back when money was still a thing. Good boy!" As he rubbed Gypsy under his collar, Vincent's little celebration faded when he realized the dog had arrived alone. "Where's Cezzie? Hey boy, where's Mr. Big Bad Wolf?"

Vincent assumed his friend was close, within shouting distance, but couldn't see him through the dense fog.

"Umm, Abe?"

"Update: Cezar has stopped 102.3 meters from our location."

"What's that in feet? I only know feet."

"Clarification: Cezar has stopped 335.6 feet from our location."

"That's real close, ain't it? Why the heck did Cezzie stop for?"

"Unknown."

"You know, it always gives me the creeps when you say that word. I'm gonna go see where he..."

Abraham grabbed Vincent by the arm, stopping him from backtracking to the wolf.

"Recommendation: Do not attempt to intercept him."

"Why? What's wrong?"

"Update: I no longer detect Cezar within a 10-kilometer radius."

43

An Intriguing Piece of History

Dot sat at a long table within a great hall. The rock walls around her, adorned with more crude artwork, were supported by the same kinds of wood and metal beams as the adjoining tunnels she walked through. Judging from the beams' sleek design, reinforced rivets, and expert welds, Dot knew the winding cavernous passages were built before the pandemic and war, though she still hadn't figured out their original purpose.

A large bowl of chicken vegetable soup sat on the table before her. Beside it was a pitcher of water and a half-loaf of bread. The Widows insisted she eat and move to better quarters more befitting an honored guest, for that is how they viewed her. Despite the arguments about her presence, the Aldermen and

Lynn Harrod

their families bowed to the Widows' mandate that Dot be pampered and treated with respect.

The soup was spicy yet mildly fragrant with herbs, a comforting balance of flavors and textures that was meant to calm her. She would have preferred plain vegetable soup, but the presence of chicken broth was tolerable. It had to be, for her hosts insisted on it. This "Exceptional Girl" could have whatever food and drink she desired once her welcoming, mandatory, nutritious soup was finished.

Widow Sullivan, the third in line of the three old ladies whose words were "rule and law," entered the vast dinner hall, trailed by the curious whispers of children who'd been following her down the main passage that connected the many rooms. Like her sisters, she wore a decorative cotton gown, her regal spade tucked in a front pocket. After shooing away her entourage, she smiled and sat beside her guest.

"How's the soup?" Widow Sullivan asked.

"It's very good," Dot said. "It tastes fresh, like the carrots and herbs were picked today."

"They likely were. We only harvest what we need for the day."

"And the chicken?"

"It's actually quail. We keep a small cage of them for special occasions."

"Is this a special occasion?" Dot asked.

Widow Sullivan pointed to the artwork on the walls, depicting her clan's history in the tunnels beneath Beacon Hill.

"Many of us are direct descendants of the Founders, seven generations of the families, Hawthorne, Baxter, and Sullivan."

Dot thought back to her first glimpse of the town when she and her friends came down the hill after crossing the Regal River. She remembered many storefronts and tall buildings with those three names. Hawthorne School of Law. Baxter Bank and Trust. Sullivan

Medical Center. Of the many families that now lived within the passages below the town, the Widows belonged to the three most prominent.

"You asked if this was a special occasion," Widow Sullivan said. "My dear, you sit here with the proud honor of being our first welcomed visitor ever. Not everyone agreed to it, but I can assure you..."

"Your decision is rule and law."

"Exactly."

"Why?" Dot asked.

"Why?" Widow Sullivan said, confused. "I'm not sure what you're asking, my dear."

"Why does everyone follow your orders? And why did you bring me here? You call me a visitor, but I was drugged and carried here while my friends are up top wondering where I went."

"Don't be offended when I tell you this, but your 'friends' are not welcome," the widow said. "Please understand. We've been watching you since you first arrived. Two hybrids, a war machine, and a lowly dog? Such abominations have no place in The Garden of Humanity."

"Then neither do I," Dot said. "My friends and I take care of each other. I need to let them know I'm safe."

"You're only safe if you remain with us down here, and you know that. Out in the wild, there are many who hunt you. We know because we spy on the Greens, hear word from survivalist encampments, intercept communications between the Purists and the Loyalists. Unlike us, they won't take you into their families. They'll either want you locked in a cell, strapped to a steel table, or dead in the ground."

Dot put down her soup spoon, having had quite enough of the forced hospitality.

"Don't be offended when I tell you this," the girl said, "but with all the soldiers hunting me, I'd feel much safer with my abominations."

Widow Sullivan smiled and shook her head.

"I understand how you might feel," the old woman said. "A combat mech and three beasts would seem to be powerful allies, especially to a child, but can they be trusted? Artificial soldiers defect, hybrids look out only for each other, and pure animals merely seek survival. We humans must stick together else we die alone."

"So I'm here for my protection?" Dot asked. "You say I shouldn't trust my friends, but why should I trust you?"

"My people aren't warmongers or scavengers. We're gardeners. We toil in the Earth and care for our crops as we care for each other. Our clan isn't mad like the North, not violent like the South, not foolish like the West, and not heartless like the East. We want humanity to live on in peace. We can only achieve that with our own kind."

You belong with your own kind.

How exhausted Dot felt hearing variations of that insipid phrase.

"You never answered my first question," the girl said. "Why does everyone follow your orders?"

Widow Sullivan rose from her seat and approached a mural in the center of the room. The artwork told the story of three men against a legion of soldiers, fighting for control of Beacon Hill.

"It was two centuries ago," the old woman said, running her fingertips across the paint. "Two hundred years that seem like a millennia."

"When The Story of The World begins."

"Exactly. Our founding fathers built the mighty Victory Garden along the marsh, leading a joint effort on a massive scale. They united us, gave us hope, lifted our hearts and spirits while the world fell into chaos and despair. When the soldiers came, the Founders took us into these mines before facing the enemy, before leading them away from our families."

The Third-In-Line Widow told Dot the tale of the Founders, of Drew Baxter the Brave, Pete Sullivan the Strategist, and Rand Hawthorne the Wise. The three community leaders each took their seven best warriors – 21 loyal human guards in all – and stationed them throughout the city. They were known as "Gardeners," a sacred title with a double meaning. It referenced to the town's agricultural lifeblood but also came from its root word "guard," as a garden is ultimately just a protected, separated place. The 21 brave men and women, armed only with homemade spears and swords, willingly sacrificed themselves to the gunfire of the unfeeling Purist Automen and war machines while their families and friends took shelter in an abandoned mineral mine who composite rock walls somehow blocked reconnaissance scans.

A lengthy battle ensued that extended beyond Beacon Hill's borders, into the surrounding hillsides. Though the Gardeners brought down the combat mechs, they and the three Founders ultimately fell to the synthetic troops. After throughly searching the town for survivors and salvage, the clone soldiers repaired each other and left, convinced that the area had been cleansed of hybrids and rebels, and had been pillaged of any resources. With no need to eat, the artificial soldiers left the Victory Garden intact when they moved on, a hallowed field that would be maintained and harvested only at night.

Dot thought back to the graveyard, to the machines resting in pieces in the hillside, surrounded by the bones of the brave rebels.

"How did 21 humans with spears defeat six mechs?" the girl asked. "That seems impossible. They must've had some other weapon, a powerful one."

"That is an intriguing piece of history," Sullivan said. "One of their machines turned on the others. Some believe it was a defect on the part of the Purists, their engineers' hubris to blame. Others are convinced one of our Founders discovered a way to reprogram it, his genius to credit. Either way, the Gardeners were wise enough to exploit the flaw in its infernal programming. Our songs praise their wisdom."

"It was an Abraham mech, wasn't it?" Dot asked. "The machine that turned?"

"I'm not well versed with the technology of death, nor do I have any interest in it, but our history books remember the broken machine that went mad and attacked its masters."

"It didn't go mad. It sympathized with your cause and chose to protect the town. That old Abraham mech aided Beacon Hill knowing it would sacrifice itself, just as the Founders did. Your songs should sing his name as well."

Widow Sullivan laughed. "How I wish I had a child's naive view of the world, as if a machine could have a heart or even a name."

Dot imagined that historic final battle and drew from her foggy yet vast knowledge. No doubt that old Abraham deployed a bomb from its chest, likely an EMP – an electromagnetic pulse – that rendered itself and the other five mechs inert. It all made sense now, and it was clear that if the "defective" Abraham centuries ago was willing to die to protect the town's citizens, her Abraham would surely do the same for her. She didn't bother to explain herself, to expound on the ethical quandary of that misunderstood mech. She had a feeling the old woman would hear none of it if she had.

"Do you have any other questions, my dear?" Widow Sullivan asked, amused by her curious nature.

"Why harvest the garden only at night?" Dot asked. "And how have you grown so much older than the rest of the world?"

"The answer to both came from a brilliant woman who served as the town's chief doctor. She concluded that sunlight helped The Worm propagate, and that avoiding it could extend one's life. It's why we have so many elders in our clan, and why many of our children grow up to live full lives. We owe our heritage and way of life to Dr. Antonia Imago, the first of the Widows."

Dr. Antonia Imago.

Dot didn't dare reveal her connection to that family name, for she still didn't know her own history, and she had yet to fully trust the old woman beside her.

"Tell me more about the doctor," Dot said. "Did she have family here, too?"

Widow Sullivan explained that Dr. Imago was sent by GARD – the Global Allied Races Delegation – a division of the old nations' governments, to help facilitate the Beacon Hill Joint Victory Garden. She remained long past her mission out of love for her new husband, Richard, and the townsfolk she came to care for. She raised a family within the tunnels of the old mineral mine and insisted that sunlight be avoided in order to keep the virus manageable. In the wake of her death, her genius was passed down to her sons, who eventually left to further their late mother's work in search of a cure. Having no faith in the controversial hybrid programs which sought to rebirth humanity rather than restore it, they felt certain that the answer lay within humans, that a pure human would one day be born – or created – that could defy The Worm.

Dot wondered if the old woman knew of her unique condition.

"Have any of the Imagos returned with good news?" Dot asked.

"Sadly, no," Widow Sullivan said. "They returned every autumn with nothing to report until they stopped returning at all. But we've always held to the belief that their Exceptional Child would lead us into a new era."

"What happens when this exceptional person shows up? Are they to raise exceptional children immune to the virus?" Dot thought of the zealots of Colt and their plans to integrate her into their congregation through forced marriage to Senior Wainright.

"That would take another three generations," Widow Sullivan said. "It wouldn't help our people here and now. No, we have a more direct solution in mind."

44

Strange Scent

Cezar woke up in a small, dark room, a beam of moonlight shining down through the open hatch he'd fallen through. He hit his head while tumbling down and momentarily blacked out before realizing he'd been tracked and trapped. His four-legged companion wasn't with him, and he hoped the dog avoided the snare.

"Gypsy?" Cezar called out in the darkness. "Where are you, brother? Are you hurt?" He sniffed the air, detected no scent of the German Shepherd.

With his nocturnal lupine eyes, Cezar spotted the faint outline of a wall-mounted torch, snuffed out for the moment. He grabbed it and slashed the rock wall with his claws, lighting the torch aflame in the shower of sparks. The room seemed smaller, with its four walls now clearly seen, vacant chains dangling from the ceiling.

The open hatch was high above. Despite the great height, the wolf-man could've leapt through it.

A lone metal door stood behind him. Despite its thick steel, he could've torn it from its hinges.

Cezar dismissed any notion of escape, for he felt compelled to investigate his would-be prison before returning to the surface. He raised his snout and took in several quick sniffs, focusing on any deviation in the dank, musty room. He picked up a confusing trio of scents – humans, hybrids, and artificials, all mingling together in the unseen area beyond the reinforced door.

"What is this vile place?" Cezar muttered to himself. He wondered if he'd been unconscious longer than he'd thought. Perhaps he was taken far from Beacon Hill to a remote detention site. He wondered which army had set the trap and assumed it was the Loyalists, the "good guys," as Vincent called them. It would explain the mixed company he smelled.

He wanted to call out to the soldiers for aid, those who would be his allies, but kept silent until he felt certain who was behind his capture.

Cezar peered through a small window in the metal door and saw a long hall stretching out and away from his cell. It was dimly lit by torches, like the one he now held, and its rock walls were covered with crude chalk drawings. Ancient support beams of wood and steel held it all up.

He examined the sturdy door, looking for a weakness, a hinge bolt he could pluck out or a lock he could yank aside. If needed, he could gather his strength and rip the door away in one clean, loud jerk. Pulling on the handle, he saw no need for force.

The door was curiously left ajar.

* * *

Widow Sullivan took Dot down the hall to the girl's new quarters, a modest room with a down bed, a trunk of clothes, two bars of soap, and a shelf of books. One of the imposing masked, hooded Gardeners followed, making any notion of running impossible.

"What are you to do with me?" Dot asked.

"Right now, we're going to give you a warm bed, clean clothes, and hot food whenever you wish, things you may have never enjoyed before. There's an assortment of books to read with plenty of pictures, in case the words escape you."

"I can read," Dot said too quickly, revealing too much of herself. "I mean, I can read a few words."

"Of course you can read, and I'd wager much more than just a few words. No need to play the fool. I had a feeling you'd been properly educated, like my sisters and I."

"What makes you say that?"

"Even now, I can see it in your expression and hear it in your tone," Widow Sullivan said. "You have the confidence and maturity that only high intelligence can offer. It's in the way you carry yourself, the way you ask questions without hesitation, fear, or foreboding. It's in the way you follow your heart, my dear. You've likely been tutored, and you've most assuredly been Blessed."

"Blessed?" Dot said, feigning ignorance. "I'm not sure what you mean. I've never belonged to any church."

"My dear, you know exactly what I mean. An ordinary woman walks into a room full of spiders. She's frightened. If she's an expert on spiders, she may enter with caution and tread lightly. However, if she doesn't know what a spider is, she enters bold and unafraid."

"Please Widow, I don't know what you're saying." Dot knew her naive front was transparent.

"Only someone who'd received the Blessing, someone who had her memories erased and scattered like sand, would keep pushing into the East Hills, a forsaken place that all others avoid. You've been looking for something, or perhaps someone."

"My friends and I are just trying to survive, like anyone would."

"By crossing the Regal River near the clutching rapids? By walking straight down the center of Beacon Hill in the wee hours of the night? It would take either a complete idiot or an incomplete memory to entertain such things, and you are certainly no idiot, my dear."

Dot wondered how long the Gardeners had been watching them from behind their protective rock walls. She didn't attempt to deny the old woman's intel.

"We crossed the river there because we underestimated the current," Dot said, thinking quickly. "We entered Beacon Hill because we saw no one about. It looked deserted, like the many other towns and streets we passed through. My memory didn't matter."

"But it does," the Widow said. "If you knew the world as I do, you'd know this town is split in two."

Widow Sullivan told Dot about the two warring factions of Beacon Hill. She and her sisters belonged to the "Gardeners of The Moon," underground dwellers who ventured out only at night, keeping the virus in check by avoiding the sun's rays. They respected all races, natural or otherwise. They grew their own food, crafted their own tools and cloth, and reached a harmony with their environment.

The town proper above was occupied by their counterpart, the "Gardeners of The Sun," scavengers who roamed throughout the day and had long slipped into madness from The Worm's grip.

Like pack predators, they took what they needed from whatever or whoever was unlucky enough to cross their path, and what they needed most was meat.

"What do you mean, they take meat?" Dot asked.

"The Gardeners of The Sun butcher travelers and feed on their flesh."

"Cannibals," Dot said with a lump in her throat.

"They follow the original doctrine, the Founders' old ways," Widow Sullivan said. "They believe there's power to be had from consuming people who've been brave enough and strong enough to survive."

"The Founders believed that? They ate their own?"

"It was a dark time for the town."

"But you no longer believe that, do you?" Dot asked, knowing well that devout belief and desperation made folks capable of anything. "The Aldermen said I was too small, but you assured them I'd grow big enough for the Elders."

"In time, yes."

"Big enough for what?"

"Enough talk for now," the Third-In-Line Widow said as she stepped back into the hall. "Get some rest, my dear. You'll learn everything there is to know about us soon enough. You're going to be here a long time."

45

The Holy Gardeners

Cezar crept down the hall, using his sensitive nose to guide him through the overwhelming scents throughout the labyrinthine passages. After leaving his unlocked, unguarded cell – clearly an old trap that hadn't been used in ages – he snuffed out his torch and relied on his sharp senses. Whoever lived down there, regardless of their stance on hybrid life, would no doubt be horrified to see a hulking beast of a man lurking about in the shadows.

Passing a dozen quarters full of sleeping humans without detection, he approached a grand room alive with the scents of blood, hair, skin, fur, and polymer – humans, hybrids, and artificials. The seemingly important chamber comprised three tall chairs in the center of a ring of several dozen smaller chairs. At first, Cezar imagined an underworld king and queen, but the simplicity and odd number of the central thrones suggested a kind of government assembly room instead.

Cezar leapt onto a support beam seven meters high above him, gripping its hardwood with his long claws, and crawled along the ceiling like a giant gray spider into the grand chamber. Below him were the many vacant chairs, their important occupants away and asleep for the night. Still, the overpowering scent of different species flooded the room. He wondered if a row of prison cells was near, perhaps beneath that very chamber.

As he thought of his next move, he finally noticed the seven unmoving guards in shadow, standing along the walls like statues. They were outfitted with long red cloaks, large hoods, and black expressionless masks, each armed with long spears made from farming implements. Shovels, trowels, and rakes were sharpened and reinforced, turning ordinary tools into fierce weapons. Their posts were likely stationed over a vast dungeon that held the many species overwhelming his senses.

With no time to look for those poor souls, Cezar crawled along the ceiling beams with careful, silent precision, looking for any trace of the one distinct scent he picked up when he approached the chamber moments earlier.

The girl.

Cezar's gifted nose told him that Dot had been there a short while ago, surrounded by a room full of humans. Now the only presence was the mysterious hooded garrison flanking the central sunken area. With no sight of Dot, the wolf-man cautiously turned and headed back to the hall, his claws embedded into the wooden supports.

Nearly at the exit, he made the mistake of clutching a beam too close to its edge, chipping off a splinter of wood. He reached out but failed to catch it, sending it down onto a chair. The soft sound made the guards' heads turn, and in seconds, all eyes were on the wolf hybrid above.

As they readied their spears, Cezar dropped to the floor and swiped at them, ripping their cloaks to ribbons as they backed away and knelt in defensive stances. They rushed him in unison like the collapsing petals of a flower, and from his wild swings, he tore off the masks of several guards.

Cezar saw human men and women, a gorilla hybrid, a kind of predatory bird hybrid, and – most shocking of all – three Automen clones, all wearing the same red-and-black ensemble. Never had he imagined such an eclectic troop.

"The girl!" Cezar said, seething as he bared his teeth and spread his claws. "Where is the girl?" He looked around him at the silent guards, the blades of their spears at his sides. Though he feared a coordinated group attack, his thoughts focused on the child's well-being, fueling him with anger and determination. "Give Cezar the girl, unharmed, and no one need die!"

"You can't kill them all," an old woman said from the entrance. The guards knew her as Widow Baxter, the Second-In-Line of the three "sisters" acting as descendent wards for the townsfolk.

Cezar didn't know who she was, but her ornate gown of colorful trim and encrusted gems, along with her commanding tone, reeked of royalty.

"It may cost Cezar's life, old woman," the wolf hybrid said, "but Cezar promises you, this lone wolf certainly can kill them all!"

"This is not all of them," Widow Baxter said. "This is but seven of 21. My sister is summoning the others. You will never see the child again..."

Cezar jumped over the guards and landed behind her, his incredible speed taking them unaware. He grabbed Widow Baxter by her long, white, braided hair and clutched her throat with his right paw. For the first time in over a century, the commanding old woman feared for her life.

"Cezar doesn't need to kill 21. Cezar only needs to kill you. Understand, if the girl has been harmed in any way, Cezar vows to end your life first."

Widow Baxter's eyes widened, her body stiffened. Realizing that the outnumbered wolf was ready to die to protect the child, she nodded to her surrounding guards, gesturing for them to stand down.

"What... what exactly do you want, Wolf?" she asked, struggling to breathe.

"Cezar already told you, old woman, and Cezar demands an answer!"

"The girl... yes... I know she means a great deal to you."

"You know nothing!" Cezar gripped the woman's throat tighter. "She means everything! Cezar asks one final time before painting the walls with your blood. Where is she?"

"I'm here, Cezar!" Dot said from behind him. She'd heard the conflict from her nearby quarters, and though her nose was not as highly tuned as his, she immediately recognized his unique odor of blood-matted fur.

Cezar needed to keep the guards in sight and could not turn toward her.

"Have they hurt you, girl?" he asked over his shoulder.

"I'm okay. They won't hurt us."

"These creatures are savage!" the wolf-man said. "Cezar has seen their butchery! They cut up humans like livestock! Hang them to bleed out and dry in a vulgar abattoir! Say it so, girl, and I will slaughter their queen!"

"No! They've treated me well! Please, let her go!"

"No one harm this creature," Widow Hawthorne said as she entered, taking both Cezar and Dot by surprise and offering a welcome moment of relief for her restrained second sister. "Gardeners step away, tools to the floor."

"Margaret, no!" Widow Baxter said, trembling.

"Gardeners, do as I command!"

Cezar kept his grip on Widow Baxter's neck as he surveyed the room. The guards, now unmasked and no longer a mysterious faceless mass, held their spears at their sides and to the floor as ordered, allowing him a wide berth. Widow Baxter offered no resistance in his hold as she let her body fall at ease, as much as she could surrender.

Behind Hawthorne, no additional guards were summoned to the long hall, as he could not see or smell them. What Cezar could smell was the stark contrast in body chemistry between the two old women. He instantly sensed Hawthorne's higher authority.

"It appears Cezar is not holding the queen," the wolf said.

"No, you are not," Widow Hawthorne said.

"Perhaps it should be your neck in my claws instead?"

"You still wouldn't have a queen."

"Queen, President, Governess, Mistress, call yourself what you will!"

"The girl is right." Widow Hawthorne spoke without a trace of fear or doubt. "We've been good to her. There's no need for violence. You have my word."

"You must forgive Cezar," the wolf said with a snarl, "and you must understand if Cezar finds no comfort in the word of a human, especially one in command of her human colony. In my experience, they are the least deserving of trust."

"Look at my Gardeners," Widow Hawthorne said, pointing to her seven guards across the room. "They stand before you, unmasked by your hand. Do you truly believe such a mixed lot loyally serves a 'human colony' or any other place of intolerance? Ours is an integrated community, a tribe of many bloodlines."

"Cezar is a hybrid, trusts only his own kind. Perhaps Cezar should look past the queen and speak to her drones."

"You will speak with no one while you hold my sister," Hawthorne said, firm and direct.

"Please, listen to her," Dot said, preparing for the worst.

"She does not command Cezar!" the wolf-man said as he eyed the renewed grips on the spears. "No human does!"

"I command all down here!" Widow Hawthorne said.

"Release the girl!"

"Release yourself!" Widow Hawthorne raised her trowel in the air, readying her guards. "Release yourself from my sister unless it's indeed blood you want, for I will flood this chamber with yours!"

"As Cezar knew you would."

"I would do so only if all else failed," the First-In-Line Widow said, lowering her voice. "And I would do so in shame."

Cezar caught the scent of truth and determination, heard the timbre of sincerity in her voice. Fearing not for his own life but for the girl's, he reluctantly released Widow Baxter's neck. She resisted the urge to run from the enraged beast and caught her breath. To support her elder sister's diplomacy, she calmly nodded to him, straightened her gown, and joined Dot and Hawthorne at the doorway as if the tense confrontation was but a tepid misunderstanding.

"Are you hurt, Judith?" Hawthorne asked her sister.

"Just a scratch. He held his fingers tight but kept his claws out and away."

"The poor beast didn't want to hurt you."

Widow Hawthorne took a moment to examine Baxter's neck. Satisfied that she was unharmed, she turned back to the wolf waiting anxiously in the center of the room.

"You keep calling me queen, but I'm their queen no more than you are their enemy. And they're not drones nor slaves nor indebted in any way. The Gardeners are our warriors, our protectors, our spies. I'd prefer you respect their oath, their vow of silent service, and spare them your scrutiny. But if you must speak with a hybrid hoping to strike an accord between us, you may... speak with me."

To the shock of everyone in the room – including her sister's – Widow Margaret Hawthorne, the eldest of the Widows of Beacon Hill, Lord Commander of the Gardeners of The Moon, pulled down her collar to reveal her neck and shoulders. She slid up her sleeves to show her forearms and held out her right leg to expose her calf.

The bare, vulnerable skin across her body was covered with thick overlapping scales. Colored gray, green, and blue, some of them the size of a pea while others resembled great doubloons. They looked stark and painful against her soft cotton gown and delicate stitchings.

"What are you?" Cezar said, dropping all apprehension.

"Human-serpentes-pythonidae."

"A snake hybrid?" Dot asked.

"How fitting," the wolf said.

"A snake-human hybrid," the Widow said. "Don't dismiss my better half, as I don't dismiss yours."

Sensing the confrontation abated, Dot wrapped her arms around the immense wolf-man. He returned the embrace, never taking his eyes off the surreal group around him.

"We must go, girl," Cezar whispered. "It may be true that they haven't harmed you, but Cezar dares to add the word 'yet'."

"We shall never harm you," Widow Hawthorne said, having heard his warning. "Neither of you. This, I swear."

"Cezar saw your livestock on the east end of town," the wolf said, confused. "Cezar saw the humans hanging from the rafters."

"We are the Gardeners of The Moon. We live in harmony with our land and each other. What you saw was the cruel work of the Gardeners of The Sun. Many of those heartless savages, and many of those hanging bodies, were once our people."

"Why did you take her?" Cezar asked, still unconvinced. "If you're so unlike your monstrous cousins? Why snatch a child from her caretakers in the night?"

"To protect her. Those of The Sun will awaken soon, and they would also take her, but for a much more gruesome purpose."

"They'd eat her."

"They would," Widow Hawthorne said, dismissing her sister and the guards with a wave of her trowel. She waited for them to leave the chamber before taking her seat alone in the center of the ring. "Like us, they know about the Exceptional Girl, how the Purists hunt her, and they've concluded why she's so desperately sought."

"And why is that?" Cezar asked. He wanted to see how much the old woman knew, or assumed to know.

"The Worm has no hold on her. She's immune to the virus that ended the world. Any clan that captures her will look for some way to harness her power."

"I have no power to give," Dot said.

"Maybe not, but for seven generations, people have been desperate for a miracle, and you're as close as they may ever get."

"They've been watching us, Cezar," Dot said. "They thought I was in danger with you and the others."

"The others," Cezar said, realizing how long it had been since they were together. "We must let them know we are alive, that we are near."

"It would be dangerous to go up top right now," Widow Hawthorne said. "The surface dwellers are likely waking up soon."

"By which you mean your mad cousins?"

The senior Widow looked Cezar in the eye and dared to place a hand on his shoulder. "I understand why you protect her so fiercely, especially here. Daytime invasions have occurred before, and we've fought them back each time. Out of respect for your devotion, I honor you with a choice."

"Tell Cezar the choice and let this 'poor beast' decide if there's any honor to it."

"Remain as our prisoner and watch from a locked room as we care for Dot, or don a red cloak and become a much-needed addition to our Gardeners. For your service, you would be at the girl's side for as long as you're with us."

"And how long is that?" Cezar asked. "How much longer are we all to hide in these tunnels, like rats huddled in a sewer waiting out a storm?"

"You may liken us to rats," Widow Hawthorne said, "but we've outlived and outlasted most villages and towns. My people have been here since the end of their world, and you will be here until the end of yours."

"What about our friends?" Dot asked.

"Your friends above are likely dead."

46

The Elders' Feast

"Cezar must confess," the wolf hybrid said as he escorted the girl down the subterranean passages to her new quarters. "Cezar didn't want to kill anyone, even those who would do us harm."

"You have a big heart," Dot said.

"It is a coward's heart."

"Please, don't call yourself that."

"As you wish."

Cezar barely fit inside Dot's meager quarters, designed for one. Like a giant dog, he curled on the floor at the foot of her bed as she slipped under the blankets by the light of the bedside candle. A tense silence hung between them as she reached over and blew out the flame. The quiet of the deep cavern was unnerving in the wake of disturbing news.

"Do you think she's right?" Dot asked in the dark. "Are the others dead?"

"Outside, Cezar caught their scent just before reaching the Widows' trap. They were near, but Cezar was so focused on reaching them he clumsily tripped a wire, fell into an open hatch, and landed in an old cell. While Cezar looked for a way out, the scent of friends became distant. Are they dead? Captured? Either is possible. From what I've seen, this other clan of the daylight is vicious and clever. It's ever more reason we must find our way out."

"Clever?" Dot asked.

"Wherever the Sun people slept during the night, Cezar didn't pick up their scent, and the mech didn't read them on his sensors. They found a way to remain well hidden from both raiders and soldiers."

"Widow Sullivan said the Gardeners are the most highly trained soldiers of any town or city, any survivalist camp, any militia. She spoke of both clans."

"They are certainly highly trained in camouflage," Cezar said. "What else did the old woman tell you? Perhaps there's something we can use to our advantage when the moment arises."

Dot summarized the history of Beacon Hill as best she could. She described GARD, the global government's Victory Garden program, and how the three founders of the town rallied their citizens to band together to form an unprecedented community space that could feed hundreds. The hardy, bioengineered crops were resistant to the fiercest elements and resistant to The Worm, a rare trait in the wake of the vile pathogen that ended the world that was also known to decimate agriculture.

She told him about the Widow's ancestors and how the Founders led three troops of seven – 21 sacred protectors known as "Gardeners" – in a final conflict with the Purists that was lost before it started. Their sacrifice allowed time for the townsfolk to retreat to the caverns and passages of the old mineral mine, a grand shelter impervious to scans and weapons, its narrow tunnels resistant to a large-scale invasion.

21 Gardeners.

Dot remembered the moments she'd heard or seen that number, from their early recon of the town to the paintings on the tunnel walls to Widow Sullivan's tale of their storied history. The special number made her realize something curious about the offer made to Cezar.

"Widow Hawthorne said she wanted to add you to their ranks," the girl said, piecing things together. "I don't believe her."

"Why do you doubt?"

"If you joined them, you would bring them to 22. But from what I've seen, they have deep-rooted faith in their traditions."

"Cezar sees what you mean," the wolf-man said. "These people live on superstition and would never have more than that holy number of 21 protectors watching over their precious little monarchy. Three queens, each with seven elite guards. No room for a mistrusting lone wolf."

"Widow Hawthorne said we're here to stay," Dot said, replaying every conversation she'd had to that point. "She said they're not like the rogue clan, that they don't intend on eating me to gain my 'power,' but I wonder."

"What is it you wonder, girl?"

"I wonder how much time we really have."

Without another word between them, Dot and her large friend went to sleep in the dark cavern. Though the girl quickly fell asleep after such a tiring day, the wolf's nose and ears took much longer to join her.

* * *

Lynn Harrod

Within the dream space of The Void, Dot and Cezar once again encountered George. With no signs of Vincent, Abraham, or Gypsy, they feared Widow Hawthorne's dire prediction was true.

"It appears that the others truly are dead," Cezar said.

"It certainly seems that way," Dot said.

"They might just be awake," George said, taking the girl by the hand. "This dark and wondrous place you've built in your mind, it can only be visited in dreams. Don't count your friends out just yet."

Cezar nodded and groaned in despair as he stared out across the expanse at the Twins, floating closer than ever. Their faces had more detail, and for a moment, Cezar saw two adolescent girls who resembled his little friend, their identical faces topped with what looked like pointed hats.

"Witches!" Cezar said. "The twin girls of the stars are witches! They've taken your face!"

Dot couldn't see the level of detail her friend had and wondered what he was talking about.

"Right now, I'm worried more about Vincent and the others," she said. "If they're still alive, they might be stuck in that dreadful town, and those cloaked guards might hide in their gardens and tunnels, ready to attack in secret."

"Cloaked guards?" George said. "Gardens and tunnels? So, it's true. You really are at Beacon Hill."

"Yes," Dot said. "You mentioned you've been there?"

"I spent a few nights with them," George said. "I ran into one of their patrols during my travels. They reluctantly took me in, fed me, gave me a warm place to sleep."

"Reluctantly?" Cezar said.

"Why did you leave?" Dot asked.

"The Gardeners of Beacon Hill cannot be trusted, and I don't just mean the cloaked guards. They constantly argued about what to do with me, and some of their ideas were... heartless."

"Which clan?" Dot had a hard time believing her subterranean hosts would have harmed the boy.

"What do you mean?" George asked.

"The town split into two clans. Which one lost your trust?"

"I don't know, Sun, Moon, is there a difference? Each one will tell you the other has gone crazy. The truth is, they all lost their minds. They only care about..."

* * *

"Wake up, Child," a woman's voice said in a hushed tone.

Dot awoke in her down bed with Cezar beside her. Though the wolf-man's body still lay on the floor, he had moved about during the night and placed his long snout upon her bed like a large pillow. His deep snoring told her he was still in The Void, or wherever his dreams took him after she was pulled away.

"Widow Sullivan?" Dot asked through the haze of her abrupt awakening, her voice groggy and faint. "I thought we were to sleep through the day. It can't be evening already."

"I'm sorry, my dear," Sullivan said, keeping her voice low. "I know you're exhausted and that a couple of hours isn't enough, but it's a new dawn, in many ways. You've been summoned to the court."

"The court?"

"The central chamber where my sisters and I meet with the Elders and the Aldermen."

"The round room with all the chairs," Dot said.

"Yes. We must go now while the sun is still anew."

Dot reached toward Cezar to jostle him awake, but Widow Sullivan stopped her with a gesture for silence.

"Let him sleep," the Widow said. "We won't be long. You'll be back in bed beside him soon enough."

Dot nodded and rose to her feet. She took her bunched-up blanket and unfurled it across her friend, covering most of his body.

"Lead the way, Widow Sullivan."

"Please. Call me Laura."

The Widow's comforting words and tone had the opposite effect on Dot, given the odd situation and George's interrupted warning.

"I think I'd prefer to call you by your title," Dot said, unsure. "For now, anyway."

"Why, my dear?"

"It's more respectful."

"Laura," Widow Sullivan said again, with a smile. "You are to call me Laura, a privilege most don't enjoy. My eldest sister is Margaret, followed by Judith. Please, I insist, my dear."

"Dot," the girl said.

Widow Sullivan looked confused.

"If we're being informal, my name is Dot."

"Yes, of course. Dot."

Dot followed the old woman out of the room, into the long hallway, leaving Cezar behind to sleep. She noticed what looked like slight irritation on the Widow's face.

"I'm sorry, Widow... Laura... I just need to get used to it."

"First names are the least of your concerns, Dot. There are more pressing matters to 'get used to' today."

"I'll get it in time."

"Time, we have plenty of."

Dot's unease turned to guilt, for she had no intention to remain in Beacon Hill to be raised by the Widows, despite the warm welcome and safety offered her. As with the other communities she'd encountered, she would keep her plans secret until an opportunity to flee revealed itself.

Widow Laura Sullivan took Dot down the hall, back to the central meeting chamber – the "court" – where Senior Widow Margaret Hawthorne and Second-In-Line Widow Judith Baxter sat in their tall chairs surrounded by a dozen Elders in their designated seats. Seven hooded, masked Gardeners stood at their posts along the walls of the round room, silent and unmoving, spears in hand.

Unlike the earlier meeting, which felt like a routine gathering of controlled chaos, debates between the Aldermen and Elders, this quiet early-morning session seemed unusual. There were no background sounds of folks roaming the hall nor pattering of children's feet, for the rest of the clan were in bed, asleep for the day. There was no grumbling and shouting of a packed room, for only half of the chairs were occupied.

Looking at the men's worn and wrinkled faces around her, Dot realized they were the oldest of the clan, a group of twelve hand-picked for the clandestine meeting. Whereas the men argued with one another before, they now sat in united silence, facing the entrance, awaiting the girl's return.

Widow Sullivan guided Dot through the crowd, onto the raised central area, to join her regal sisters.

"The sun has just risen above the hills," Widow Hawthorne said to the men. She held her ceremonial trowel high, seizing the room. "After much deliberation, my sisters and I have heeded your concerns."

"Why aren't the Aldermen here?" Elder Wright asked in a demanding tone, a short man with a braid of long, gray hair.

"This meeting is for the Elders alone," the Widow said, "former Aldermen who have served their community, passed the torch, and now face the ends of their lives sooner than most."

"Nonsense! We decide nothing without a full congress!"

"We must wake the Aldermen," Elder Abernathy said, his stout belly shaking as he nodded with his own suggestion.

"Rather than wonder why they aren't here," Widow Baxter said firmly, "remember why you are here, and remember to be grateful."

"The girl is not yet fully grown," Elder Wright said.

"True," Hawthorne said, "but as many of you have pointed out, she is grown enough for the Elders in this room, and that is enough for a feast, the first of many to come."

"What feast?" Dot asked as she looked about the room. She kept her nerves in check as she saw no banquet, smelled no cooking, heard no servants.

"It's a symbolic feast," Hawthorne said, dismissing the girl's growing concern. "An actual feast will follow later tonight. A celebration."

"Please, someone tell me why we're here," Dot asked. "Let's not speak in riddles."

"You are the feast," Elder Stewart said, his freckled, bald head reflecting the candlelight. "No riddle to it."

"I think I need Cezar with me." Dot turned to the doorway, ready to call out his name. "He's supposed to be at my side at all times. That's what you said, Widow Hawthorne."

"Please. 'Margaret.'"

"I want Cezar with me now. Please. Margaret."

"Pay no mind to Elder Stewart's rude outburst," Widow Hawthorne said, shooting the old man a stern look. "He merely meant that you are the guest of honor."

"Cezar!" Dot yelled.

"Calm yourself, my dear..."

"You're going to eat me, aren't you? Just like the Gardeners of The Sun eat travelers! George tried to warn me. You've convinced yourselves that I'm some miraculous cure for The Worm. Cezar!"

"George?" Hawthorne said.

"He's been here before! He knows you people!"

"The Woodsman Ranger," Elder Wright said, recognizing the name. "She speaks of the disturbed boy we found in the farmhouse."

Widow Hawthorne also remembered the defiant young man and the trouble he caused before he fled the caves.

"Calm yourself," the Widow said. "The boy had the wrong idea. You won't be harmed."

"Then how do you plan to 'feast' on me?"

With a nod, Widow Hawthorne summoned a Gardener into the center. The tall, silent guard held Dot by her arms as Hawthorne held her trowel close.

"What are you doing?" Dot asked, her voice quivering. "Cezar! Cezar!"

"No need to shout. We want to assure your friend gets his much-deserved rest, so we've locked his door."

"Cezar!"

Widows Sullivan and Baxter gripped Dot's right arm and pulled up her gown's sleeve, forcing open her palm. Hawthorne placed the tip of her trowel into it and slowly slid it downward. Like the many other farm tools that were formed into weapons, the trowel had a sharpened edge that cut into her hand. Her curled fingers served as a cup to gather the blood.

Sullivan quickly produced an ornate crystal goblet and placed it under the wound. Keeping firm hold of Dot, she squeezed her palm, pushing forth a thin stream into the glass. Dot stared at the goblet – already half-filled with an ample serving of plum wine – and watched as her blood flowed into it, topping it off.

With the goblet now filled two fingers from the rim, Widow Hawthorne held it high and swirled it like a fine vintage. Her sisters released Dot and wrapped her hand with gauze.

"We aren't savages," Widow Hawthorne said. "We don't eat children."

"But you drink their blood?" Dot said, incredulous. "You and your sisters are insane if you think this will do anything!"

"This is for the Elders."

"You're lying! You only think of yourselves!"

"My sisters and I do not need to drink."

"Why should I believe you?" Dot asked.

"Believe us, child. Believe us because... we're hybrids."

The words left the old woman's lips with a sting for she hadn't referred to herself or his sisters as anything other than 'widows' for two centuries.

"*All* of you?" Elder Stewart said, rising to his feet. "Not one of you is a pure human?"

Widows Baxter and Sullivan looked at each other before nodding to the men, who now appeared shaken from the revelation.

Dot thought back to when Hawthorne exposed her reptilian skin to the Elders and Aldermen earlier, a startling moment that seemed to also take her sisters by surprise. She now realized the old women stood surprised, not from the secret, but from their oldest sister's decision to reveal it.

The men sat in shock and anger. By the Widows' decree, they long viewed hybrids and Automen strictly as servants, subhuman, abominations kept in check in service to the clan. Hawthorne found it easy to control the Aldermen and Elders by catering to their prejudices. With the men now facing their exposed queens, the notion that they'd been led by ancient hybrids proved a foul truth hard to swallow.

"The girl is right!" Elder Abernathy said. "You women are liars!"

"How can we trust you again?" Elder Stewart asked.

"What other tricks do you have planned?"

Widow Hawthorne answered by holding up the goblet of blood and wine meant solely for them.

"We've kept this clan together for nearly two centuries," the Widow said, "since the night our husbands led the 21 original Gardeners to their deaths in order to keep us safe and hidden. Don't play the fool now. Surely, some of you had your suspicions."

"Surely, we did not!" Elder Stewart said.

Over their many years underground, the Elders, the Aldermen, and their families never once thought of the three Widows as anything other than human. Though the caverns sheltered them from the sunlight, prolonging their lives, the townsfolk eventually succumbed to the pathogen before reaching middle age. Many died quite young, some during childhood. Each of the six generations of post-war Beacon Hill grew up with the old Widows leading them, and none questioned their nature for none knew of their unnatural, long life. It was always assumed the sisters were merely descendants of the original Widows.

"Then let today be a new dawn not only for a cure," Widow Hawthorne said, "but for truth, for a death of secrets among us."

"Remember all we've done for you," Widow Baxter said. "Remember what our husbands have done for you. Rand Hawthorne. Drew Baxter. Pete Sullivan. Remember their sacrifice."

To Hawthorne's dismay and the horror of her sisters, the honor of following the three Widows dissolved before them, leaving only the contempt for lab-born creatures and artificial soldiers.

"The Founders didn't die for us!" Elder Stewart said, rethinking their history. "They died for their unholy wives!"

Hawthorne raised her trowel high, prompting the cloaked Gardeners to step forth from their posts. The ominous gesture silenced the old men.

"We've brought you the Exceptional Girl!" Widow Hawthorne said. "We have her blood in this cup, ready to share among you, and now you choose to defy us?"

"The blood won't work!" Elder Wright said. "The girl made that clear. It didn't work with the ranger boy, and it won't work now!"

"George?" Dot said. "You mean you tried to..."

"My wife drank the ranger's healthy blood, and she still fell to The Worm last winter! My poor Maureen died a fool!"

"You promised us a feast!" Elder Abernathy said. "Your pathetic cup breaks that promise!"

Widows Sullivan and Baxter turned to their oldest sister, alarmed at losing the loyalty of their congress for the first time in the history of their reign. So sure was Hawthorne that the girl's blood was their answer, so sure was her resolve, that she felt it time to reveal her nature to the clan. She never expected their innate hatred of non-humans to eclipse what she believed to be a cure.

In her moment of doubt, she doubled down on the goblet in her hand.

"Shall I pour this out?" Widow Hawthorne said. "Are you so certain of failure that I should empty this goblet to the ground? Or are you willing to take a chance? Forget who we are. Forget your blind hate. This blood holds your future! The future of your families!"

The twelve Elders now stood in silent rage and confusion, surrounding the Widows, who were in turn supported by their Gardeners.

"Make your choice," Widow Sullivan said, feigning defiance and courage. "This moment is your destiny, a moment that may never come again."

After a minute of tense silence, Elder Stewart calmed himself and extended his open hand. As his peers watched in uncertainty, he accepted the goblet from the senior Widow. He clasped his fingers around the stem of the glass and looked into the bloodied wine within.

To the old women's shock, he loosened his grip and let the goblet fall to the stone floor. Shards of thick glass flew across their feet as the goblet shattered in a splash of the "cure" they'd long been promised.

"No more tricks," Elder Stewart said. "We spoke of a proper feast, and we're entitled to it."

Widow Hawthorne looked to her guards, to her sisters, and to the group of angry men. Her offering had been soundly rejected, and she was forced to make a grim choice.

"The girl is not yet fully grown," the Widow said with a heavy heart.

"As you sisters have pointed out," Elder Stewart said, "she is grown enough for the Elders in this room."

47

civil war

While Dot endured the horror of the Elder's Feast in the central court and the macabre turn it suddenly took, Vincent and Abraham roamed the marsh above. Even in the twilight of the coming dawn, they discovered nothing that could lead them to the girl. They returned to the Downtown plaza, to the spot they'd agreed to regroup. During their long search, Gypsy had wandered the town on his own, following his nose far from his friends until he, too, was missing.

"Where'd that doggy go?" Vincent asked after finally realizing his absence. He called out to him in all directions. "Gypsy? Where are you, boy? Gypsy?"

"Reconnaissance: Gypsy's last known whereabouts are 6.2 kilometers north of our position."

"You mean you aren't sensing him no more?"

"Correct."

"Dang, I knew this town gave me the creeps."

"Recommendation: Keep your volume low."

"Keep my what?"

"Clarification: Be silent, Vincent."

"Why?" Vincent said, lowering his voice. "What's going on?"

"Reconnaissance: I detect Purist movement 9.8 kilometers north of the township."

"Where Gypsy was heading?"

"Correct."

"Do they... detect our movement?"

"Unknown."

"There's that word again," Vincent said. "You saying 'unknown' creeps me out even more than this shady town."

"Agreement."

"What the heck do we do now?"

"Alert: I detect human movement within a one-kilometer radius."

"Where exactly? How many? Just a few, I hope."

"Reconnaissance: 23 humans are gathered 102.3 meters from our position."

"In feet, Abe. You know I don't know no meters."

"Clarification: They are 335.6 feet from our position."

"Wait, ain't that around where Cezzie disappeared?"

Abraham didn't reply. Instead, he readied his twin guns and turned east. Though the sun now shined upon Beacon Hill, the dense morning fog still hung thick in the air, obscuring their view of an oncoming enemy.

"Folks were disappearing. Now there's Greenies just popping up like this?" Vincent kept his voice near a whisper. "Let me guess, 'unknown,' right?"

"Correct."

With his towering friend ready to open fire on any oncoming hostiles, Vincent crouched low to the ground and prepared himself for a risky, perhaps reckless move.

"You stay here, big guy," Vincent said. "I'm gonna head over and check it out."

"Recommendation: Remain with this unit until safety is secured."

"Naw, I got a feeling if you start blasting, we're gonna be swarmed with people, and Dottie said no one is supposed to die."

"Clarification: That directive is void during self-defense measures."

"Well, we're gonna do our darnest to avoid that. Nobody dies. Just stay put, and keep your scanners open for anything unusual. You with me on this?"

Abraham took a moment to consider their limited options, calculating their chance for success and the diminishing odds of their friends' survival.

"Agreement." Abraham held out one of his arms and opened a small hatch, revealing a cochlear implant similar to the one he gave Dot. "Instruction: Place this device in your ear to keep open communication."

Confused, Vincent did as he was told and was startled to hear his friend's synthetic voice from the tiny device.

"Query: Can you hear my output?"

"Kinda weird," Vincent said, "hearing your voice through this little thingy, but not out in the open. Is this how you talk to Dottie?"

"Correct."

"Well, not now, I suppose."

"Correct."

"Let's see if we can fix that."

Vincent slithered across the ground, using his vines like long snakes to pull him forward. He continued on toward the area Abraham pinpointed, using the fog and weeds to hide his slender body, until he reached the hatch hidden in the ground that Cezar fell into.

Normally, the old trap hatch was covered in dirt and surrounded by grass, camouflaging it perfectly. It fooled the eye of both man and machine, for its door and frame were made of an iron-lead alloy reinforced by a polymer-based material designed to diffuse sensor arrays. Like the structural supports within the passages of the mineral mines below, the hatch was made to be invisible. The only reason Vincent could see it was because its door was currently swung open with nearly two dozen masked men in cloaks climbing down through it, long spears strapped to their backs.

"Rotten roots!" Vincent said. "Abe? You with me? Please tell me you're still with me, big guy." The plant-man hoped the little plastic thing in his ear picked up his whispers.

"Acknowledgment."

Vincent was relieved to still have his friend's company, even if it was just over their radio link.

"Abe, you seeing these scary guys?"

"Reconnaissance: The number of humans diminishes as we speak. Reason is..."

"Don't say 'unknown,' big buy, 'cause I think I figured it out. They're dropping down into some door hidden in the grass, into some room maybe, and for whatever reason, when they're underground, you can't see 'em no more."

"Hypothesis: There must be a subterranean facility designed or augmented to block sensors."

"Wonder what they're hiding?"

"Hypothesis: The wards of the facility have made efforts to hide their shelter."

"Father told me about these," Vincent said, still fixed on the cloaked humans entering the hatch one at a time. "When the big war was brewing way back, folks started building bunkers out of anything, like old irrigation ditches, basements, sewage tunnels. Anything like that here?"

"Negative."

"You ain't lookin' right! I tell ya, Abe, I see a bunch of spooky guys in masks hopping down through a small door and not coming back out, so the room or facility or whatever must be bigger than we think. Forget looking for the underground place. That ain't happening. Try looking for stuff that might give you some ideas. Father said it's the little things give you the big picture."

"Acknowledgment."

From his position in the central plaza, still hidden in the fog, Abraham scanned the town again, filtering for anything unusual, anything that didn't exist in the other communities they encountered. It took the mech 12 seconds to compile a list of factors unique to Beacon Hill.

"Reconnaissance: Sensors show derelict specialized industrial equipment and raw materials. Transport vehicles rated for 400-ton payloads, hydraulic and electric rope shovels, rotary drill rigs outfitted with hammer rock drills, wheel loaders, motor graders, processors filled with gravel and sand, and laced with gypsum and limestone..."

"Whoa, slow down," the plant-man said. "What's all that stuff mean?"

"Extrapolation: This township sits atop a vast mineral mine."

Vincent watched as the last of the Gardeners of The Sun disappeared into the hatch.

"I don't know nothing about mineral mines. How big is this underground place? How many folks might be down there?"

"Assessment: Given the projected size of the mine based on the surface support equipment, the subterranean shelter could house a complement of several hundred."

"Dang," Vincent said, as he realized what he had to do. "Abe, I told you to scan for anything unusual, but now I want you to be on the lookout for something very specific. It's just a few steps. You follow?"

"Acknowledgment. This unit shall follow your strategy. Proceed with the primary step."

Vincent slinked toward the open hatch, his heart racing as he got closer.

"Okay, first I want you to scan the plants, all of 'em, everywhere around town. Get familiar with every blade of grass, every leaf, every patch of moss..."

"Scan complete."

"Shoot, that was fast."

"Proceed with the secondary step," Abraham said.

"Next, keep scanning again and again, and look for a plant that weren't there a minute ago."

"Acknowledgment."

Vincent peered into the total darkness below the hatch, his bioluminescent eyes guiding him.

"I guess this is it," Vincent said, struggling to shake off his gripping fear. "Gotta do it. Gotta find Dottie. Then we find Cezzie and Gypsy and get outta here."

"Query: What should I do upon detection of a new, unique plant?"

"Dig it up," Vincent said. "Dig it up as fast as you can."

Without another word, he dropped through the open hatch.

* * *

Vincent stood in the long hall of the Gardeners of The Moon. After carefully entering the hatch and climbing down the shaft, he avoided a terrible tumble by bracing the rocky walls with his many vines. Landing gently on his feet in the small cell, he knew Cezar had been here hours before and hoped his friend had survived what was likely a sudden fall.

The cell and the hallway connected to it were lined with torches. Rather than use one to light his way as the wolf had surely done, the plant-man doused each flame with his leafy fingers, enshrouding him in darkness. With his enhanced sight, even more revealing that the wolf's, he didn't need light to see. What he needed was any advantage he could get if he were to face the troop of cloaked, masked soldiers he saw moments ago.

Vincent could see in total darkness.

The mysterious soldiers likely could not.

"Abe? You still with me, big guy?" Just as he had predicted – and feared – Vincent lost contact with the combat mech the moment he was underground, the minerals in the rock walls and their support beams blocking not only sensor sweeps but radio communications as well. "I guess it's just me then."

Vincent continued down the hall, keeping low and quiet, until he heard a commotion from a room ahead. Craning his neck for a better view, he saw one of the cloaked soldiers standing in the middle of a cave, outfitted as a family home. The masked man clutched a spear, one once used as a farming tool, to hold several human families at bay. Though the plant hybrid didn't know the nature of the conflict, didn't know friend from foe, he sided with the families, their children undeserving of such terror.

Vincent crept behind the hostile Gardener, intending to grab his weapon, but his stealth was thwarted by a scared young girl further frightened to see the bizarre green-and-yellow man with thin, spidery arms and snake-like vines.

"They brought monsters!" the little girl yelled.

The hostile Gardener spun around.

In an instant, Vincent wrapped his vines around the soldier, gripping him tight, making him drop his spear. He wanted only to restrain the masked man, but he fought like a tiger, and Vincent was forced to muffle his mouth and squeeze the air from his body. Within seconds, the guard passed out cold, his mask tumbling to the stone floor with a crack.

To Vincent's surprise, the Gardener's face was that of a teenage boy, no older than George Brook. With the fierce facade gone, he looked harmless as he plopped unconscious on Vincent's feet.

"He got killed by his own monster!" the little girl said.

"I'm not his monster," Vincent said. "I'm Dottie's monster... I mean... I'm just a garden variety plant guy. Hey, that's kinda funny..."

"Please, don't hurt my family," a man said as he grabbed the girl and scooted her behind him. He stepped forward, gesturing for the others to stay back. "If you must eat someone, eat me!"

"I'm not that hungry," Vincent said. "I had a lot of corn and squash in the big garden. But if I was hungry, I wouldn't eat any of you. I'm a vegetarian!" From their terrified faces, Vincent could see his words offered no comfort. All they saw was a hideous creature, a beast with big black eyes that accompanied the night invasion. "What I mean is, I'm not a monster. I'm Vincent! They also call me Vinny Greenblood, Veggie Vinny, Dim Vin, the Green Fool, Vincent Vines..."

"You're with them," the man said, extending his arms as if to offer himself as a sacrifice. "And I'm with you. Take me."

"No thanks. And I'm not with those guys. I'm looking for a girl. Her name is Dottie."

"The Exceptional Girl?" a woman asked, revolted by the sight of the tall plant hybrid.

"Umm, sure, I suppose. She's very nice, and she knows lots of..."

"The Exceptional Girl may be in her room, further down the hall past the court."

"That's better," Vincent said. "Very helpful."

"We aren't supposed to know this, but the Elders intend to feast on her tonight."

"Okay, not better. In fact, that's just about the worst thing I can think of."

"The Gardeners of The Sun are storming the tunnels! They're here to take our home! They'll take her, too!"

"Wow, it's really getting worse the more you tell me," Vincent said.

The family man lowered his arms. "You're not here to eat us?"

"No, sir, I'm not, though if I were into eating humans, I still wouldn't eat you. I mean, you seem like decent people."

"Stay with us," the woman said, realizing the odd creature could be an ally.

"Yeah, I'd like to stay and make sure you're alright, but I really need to go, now that I know about the whole feast thing."

With the trapped families begging him to stay and protect them, Vincent returned to the long hallway and continued onward into the chaos of the invasion.

Over the next ten minutes, Vincent saw other caverns of tormented humans and dispatched the soldiers blocking their only exits. One by one, he smothered the Gardeners of The Sun to the shock of the townsfolk, quickly returning to the darkness of the hall. He continued onward until he reached what he assumed was the "court" they spoke of, a large, round room full of old men, three old women, cloaked guards clashed in battle, and the grim sight of his little friend.

"Oh no, Dottie. What have they done?"

48

Bloodshed in The Court

Cezar awoke from his deep slumber in Dot's sealed quarters, not from the sounds of the melee, but from the scent of fear. He smelled the anxiety of humans and hybrids facing death, a distinct scent he'd fine-tuned during his lifetime as a pack hunter. In the many panicked breaths and desperate gasps, he singled out one.

Dot.

The wolf leapt to his feet and grabbed the door's handle, alarmed to find it locked.

"Girl!" he yelled. "Dot! Cezar is coming!"

Cezar cursed himself for failing to be at her side during the unseen commotion. Mixed with the smell of dozens of terrified people, he heard screams, the clashing of weapons, and the falling of bodies. Most of them sounded like the heavy weight of fully grown men and women landing on the stone floor. As he pulled at the large door, he kept an ear open for the sound of his ward.

He thought of the young fawn-girl Ameri and the time his fellow hunters had cornered her, forcing her to the dirt. The dread he felt was palpable, and in his revisited anguish, he ripped the door from its iron hinges and hurled it across the room with a loud boom.

Sprinting down the hall on all fours, he followed his nose to the central court and leapt into the violent melee of Gardeners, slashing at their spears, throwing them against the walls, in his search for the girl.

"Dot!" he called out again. "Give Cezar the girl or Cezar will kill you all!"

Vincent had reached the court mere seconds before Cezar pounced into the room. He looked past his blood brother entangled with a dozen soldiers, past the three old women standing helpless amid the struggle, and saw his little friend laying unconscious on a long table.

Rather than join the fight, Vincent ran into the room, jumped onto Dot's ceremonial table, and thrust one of his vines up into the ceiling. The hardy vine slithered through rock and soil until it protruded through the surface, where Abraham instantly detected it from afar.

"Stop this madness!" Widow Hawthorne bellowed as she stepped in front of Dot and Vincent, shielding them from the onslaught. "Gardeners, stand down and hear me now!"

The fighting stopped. All the Gardeners, of both The Sun and The Moon – human, hybrid, and Automan – lowered their spears and stood staring at the matriarch.

"For two centuries, my sisters and I have kept this town safe," she said to the warring guards, "and we did it with your help. Remember your beginning. We took you in after the world discarded you, gave you purpose while humanity condemned you, and renewed your honor when history forgot you. For these gifts, for your duty, and for the vows you swore, you will all obey me! My word is rule and law!"

The masked, hooded warriors lowered their spears, their foggy minds racing, revisiting their pasts. As the eldest Widow said, each of them came to Beacon Hill as a lost soul, a reject from another town or settlement, an escapee from a prison or work camp or laboratory.

Humans exiled, deemed obtuse and unfit to contribute.

Hybrids hunted, desperate, fleeing the hatred of their kind.

Automen abandoned, their bodies and minds torn asunder.

Each of these unwanted misfits was disturbed and in search of a home when they wandered into Beacon Hill a lifetime ago. Seeing the Widows as their new guiding lights, they soon swore an oath and donned the cloaks of the honorable Gardeners of The Moon. The hybrids and Automen among them proved loyal to the sisters, but many of the humans in their ranks had a driving hunger for meat and sunlight that led to a break from logic and reason. Obsessed, they seceded from the sacred guard, splitting them from their brethren, giving birth to the rogue Gardeners of The Sun.

Standing together in the subterranean central court for the first time in ages, hearing the inspiring words of the First-In-Line Widow, their feeling of union came flooding back, and for a moment, the elite guard of the township, current and former, remembered their place in the world's order.

The two clans once again became one, and though they still wore masks meant to visually and symbolically unite them,

Widow Hawthorne could see it in their eyes – the years of doubt, the fractures between them, were falling away.

"This girl's torment cannot unite us," Widow Hawthorne said to the room, to both guardians and Elders. "Her death would serve no purpose. I see that now. Her blood will not save you. Her flesh and essence will not deliver you. Only you can save yourselves. Only you..."

The Widow's inspiring words were cut short by the painful sting of a blade through her stomach.

Elder Stewart had grabbed her sharpened trowel and thrust it into her.

"You're right, Widow Hawthorne," the old man said as he shoved the tool deeper into her with seething anger. "Only we can save ourselves! Not trickery from hidden hybrids! Not empty promises backed by enslaved drones! We humans must fight to survive, to preserve our way of life!"

Vincent stood atop the table, over Dot's unconscious body. He eyed Cezar, standing alert between the soldiers, and nodded up to his extended vine, which still pierced the rocky ceiling high above. He hoped his mech friend would soon come and "dig them up."

As Widow Hawthorne slumped down in her regal chair and slid beside Dot's ceremonial table, leaving a bloody trail behind her, Elder Stewart pointed her trowel at the two remaining sisters.

"Tell them," the old man said to the second and third Widows, breathless, pumped with adrenaline. He'd always despised the senior Widow, always envied her control, and now allowed his contempt for hybrids and artificials to unleash his hatred of the matriarchy. "Tell these brainless monstrosities that you now command them all, and that we now command you! If you truly care for this town, if you don't wish your sister's death to be in vain, tell them the way things are. Tell them or join your sister!"

To Widow Baxter's surprise, Widow Sullivan nodded and repeated the old man's words.

"We do as Elder Stewart says," Sullivan said. "We can reunite and move forward together... under the lead of the Elders and the Aldermen. My word is rule and law."

Sullivan turned to her sister and gestured for compliance.

"We move forward with them," Widow Baxter said. "My word is rule and law."

"So it shall be," Elder Stewart said. He turned to his fellow men, looking for any signs of discontent. Though there seemed to be unease and doubt, the men's silence solidified a renewed stance behind their de facto leader.

"Kill the wolf and the plant thing," Elder Stewart said, "and let us continue with the feast..."

BOOM!

The room shook with the magnitude of an earthquake.

BOOM!

BOOM!

Dirt and chunks of rock fell from the ceiling as the air heated to an almost unbearable degree.

"Widows!" Elder Stewart said. "Tell your guards to..."

BOOM!

The ceiling caved in around them. Cezar quickly pounced onto the table beside Vincent, and together they shielded the sleeping girl from the debris.

BOOM!

The old men and the eclectic guardians scattered, clinging to the walls as sheets of shale, limestone, and precious ore tumbled to the floor, breaking apart in vast chunks, until the muggy air cooled as the sky opened above them.

Peering up at the morning light, diffused by the fog, the people of Beacon Hill were terrified by the sight of a 12-foot combat mech looking down at them with blinding floodlights and powerful armaments, the whirring of its mechanical innards a nightmarish cacophony of iron and steel.

"Command: Surrender," the robot said to the speechless onlookers, his tone stern, frightening. "Surrender or die."

The Gardeners of The Moon and The Sun dropped their spears and hugged the stone walls, never taking their eyes off the menacing machine. The Elders knelt underneath the disarmed warriors, unsure of their fate.

With the room now exposed to the elements and to the armored behemoth above, Cezar savored the moment as he turned to the helpless clan.

"Hear Cezar now," the wolf-man called out with a snarl. "You can 'move forward' with these foolish, frightened old men if you wish, but you will do so with no feast, with no ounce of flesh or drop of blood for any of you wretched fiends. And until we leave this cursed, forsaken pit, consider Cezar your new king!"

No one dared respond, not the guards, not the old men, not the arrogant Elder Stewart who sought to consume the girl in the fleeting chance of a cure. The entire town of Beacon Hill now cowered before the wolf hybrid standing high above them, a war machine at his command.

"Query," Abraham said, his synthetic voice echoing throughout the tunnels. "Shall I terminate the hostiles?"

Cezar knew it was a bluff. He knew his metal friend had no intention of harming anyone, not only because the girl strictly forbade it, but because his animal instincts finally concluded that the machine somehow had a soul. Like Dot, Cezar had replayed the historic Founders Last Stand in his mind, considered every possible strategy, and realized the original 21 human Gardeners must have been aided by the one Abraham mech on the battlefield. There was simply no other way a group of farmers turned soldiers could defeat such impossible odds.

The wolf turned to the quaking masses before him and shook his head. "No, Abraham. Let them be."

Satisfied that they were under his control, Cezar tenderly picked up Dot from her table, her long, curly hair dangling between his claws. The girl stirred as he placed her in Vincent's snaking vines and gestured for him to take her up to the surface while he remained behind for a final warning.

"There was a time when Cezar would have you all put down for your transgressions," the wolf said. "There was a time when Cezar would have snapped his fingers and told his mech to reduce this cavern to a burning crater. But the child you sought to kill for your selfish gain implored Cezar to cherish all life, even that which does not deserve such mercy. Always remember that you owe each new day to her, and that any defiance or pursuit will lead to your death."

Reaching the sunlit surface, Dot awoke and looked down at the three Widows, their faces pleading for forgiveness.

"Bring them up," Dot said, her voice weak. "Bring them to me."

Cezar held out his paws and helped Widows Sullivan and Baxter up into Vincent's vines' embrace. The plant-man pulled them up into the daylight.

"Bring her, too," Dot said, pointing to Widow Hawthorne's body sprawled across the court's floor.

"This queen is dying," Cezar said solemnly.

"She deserves to see the sun one more time."

Cezar lifted Widow Hawthorne from the floor and saw that she still clung to life, what little she had left. As he brought her to Vincent's many vines, he turned to the Gardeners along the walls.

"To my fellow deviants," Cezar said. "You don't have to follow any queen or king of any human who would treat you like a tool.

We're destined for the City of Kellen beyond the West Wall. I urge you to leave these pathetic fools to their precious Victory Garden and their self-imposed underground prison, and join your brothers and sisters across the Miracle River. Either listen to this wolf and meet us there, or remain here and never see us again."

With one powerful leap, Cezar bounded up the gaping hole in the ceiling and landed beside his friends, now joined by the former Widows of Beacon Hill, three hybrid sisters revealed to all.

Vincent carried Hawthorne away from the court's exposed hole to the town's Downtown plaza, the spot where they'd agreed to meet if trouble arose. Baxter and Sullivan followed, keeping their distance from the war machine. They looked up through the fog at the blurry sun sitting in its overcast sky, their first view of daylight in nearly 200 years.

Widow Hawthorne was not long for the world as she was placed gently down on a patch of damp grass. She met the girl's eyes.

"You were never going to let them, were you?" Dot asked.

"No," Hawthorne said. "You reminded me of my daughter, Elise. My husband, Rand, would have never forgiven me if I'd let those men take what they wanted."

"What did they want again?" Vincent asked, perplexed.

"It doesn't matter," Dot said. "Cezar encouraged your servants to go west, and I'm telling you the same. Now that you've revealed yourselves, you'll never reclaim your seats at their court. You should leave, just as we are."

Baxter and Sullivan looked at their eldest sister, whose eyes told them what to do, though they were scared to take such a risky venture.

"Do as she says," Widow Hawthorne said. "Our husbands' legacy is gone. The Elders and Aldermen won't accept you, no matter what they might say. The humans outnumber you 50-to-1, and you'd be their slave just as much as the Gardeners under your command."

Baxter and Sullivan heard their sister's words, but were not yet convinced. Only when they saw their former guards emerge from the ground and into the light of day did they realize what they must do.

"It's not really a choice, is it?" Widow Baxter said.

"I'm afraid choice is no longer a luxury for us," Hawthorne said. "Not here. Not any more."

The two guardian clans – the Gardeners of The Sun and the Gardeners of The Moon – gathered near the marsh, their numbers rising to 42, double the sacred 21. They heeded Cezar's words and abandoned their posts, determined to seek others like them in pursuit of some semblance of normalcy, freedom, and acceptance. A mythical city of tolerance sounded more appealing than the blind obedience of sadistic men who saw them as inferior.

"Maybe you can go with them?" Vincent said.

"Vincent's right," Dot said. "They were loyal to you once. They can protect you. Stick to the ridgeline, head west, and you'll avoid the Purists."

"Maybe that is the way," Widow Baxter said. "Maybe we should look for this city of theirs." She turned to Hawthorne. "Sister, is that what you'd have us do?"

Widow Hawthorne looked up at her younger sisters with vacant eyes, her lifeless stare the last thing they'd see in their longtime home. As the group discussed their options a moment before, she'd drifted off, never to awaken.

Sullivan turned toward the Gardeners making their way across the marsh and noticed seven of the masked, hooded men awaiting them, loyal holdouts still willing to serve their sacred Widows.

"Good journey, my dear," Widow Sullivan said to Dot. "We wish you well in the East Hills, and we hope you find what you're looking for."

"We will," Dot said.

"Perhaps we'll meet again in your city beyond the Miracle River."

"We will," Dot said again. "I promise."

One Gardener approached the group in silence. Without a word, he picked up Widow Hawthorne's body and carried it to his group, crossing the marsh. Sullivan and Baxter walked with him. A minute later, their figures disappeared in the morning fog.

"You okay, Dottie?" Vincent said. "We lost you for a while there."

"I'm not okay, Vincent," the girl said. "Not remotely. But I'm with you all again, and that means I'll be okay."

"Cezar will never leave your side again," the wolf said.

"Statement: This unit will also remain in close proximity at all times."

"That's... that's good to know," Dot said in a haze, still groggy from the mild drug they injected into her in preparation for the ceremonial feast.

Cezar delicately placed Dot in the mech's central chamber, and the odd group left Beacon Hill, heading north, away from the cursed town.

"Abe," Vincent said. "You weren't really gonna blow up all those folks like you said, were you?"

"Negative."

"It was a beautiful, grand bluff," Cezar said.

"Correct."

"I didn't know you could bluff!" Vincent said. "I thought you never lied!"

"Strategy: There are times when an empty threat can serve as a productive deterrent."

"Cezar is impressed," the wolf said, slapping his friend's armored leg. "Where are we going now?"

"Statement: We must travel north a minimum of 10 kilometers."

"Wait, where's Gypsy?" Dot asked.

"Umm, that's where we're going," Vincent said, uneasy about the bad news. "That's what the big guy's talking about, Dottie. We lost Gypsy a while back. He disappeared from Abe's scans. He was last seen up there somewhere, near some Greenie camp."

"Then that... is where we're going," Dot said, her voice trailing off as she rubbed her eyes.

"Rest now, girl," Cezar said, looking at Dot through the narrow window in Abraham's chest plate. "You've been through an unforgiving ordeal. We'll wake you up when we find him."

Dot thought back to her time in the caverns and how far hope had faded before her friends found her. "Down there, I thought I'd never see you all again. Thank you for saving me, for not giving up. Thank you very much."

"You're very much welcome," Vincent said with a smile, the people of Beacon Hill already out of his thoughts.

49

Q and A

Dot and her friends stayed off the Broken Road but kept it in sight as they tramped north through the woods under the late-morning sun. They kept to the shadows and the old growth of the trees, carefully moving forward through the thickets of the ancient woods that provided cover even for the giant war machine.

"How's the girl?" Cezar asked. He saw Dot turn over within Abraham's chest.

"She's awake now," Vincent said, "but still kinda fuzzy."

"What infernal potion did they give her?"

"Sleepy Pinkies, I think."

"What are Sleepy Pinkies?" Cezar said.

"Plante-Caprifoliaceae-Valeriana. Valeriana officinalis. You know, Sleepy Pinkies!" The plant-man sang a melodic poem...

408 *Lynn Harrod*

Sow 'em in the shade in the early spring!
Move 'em out in the sun when summer begins!
Soak 'em real good, let 'em do their thing!
Don't smell 'em though 'cause your eyes will sting!

"Cezar is confused." The wolf-man looked up at the mech. "Abraham, can you help explain?"

"Analysis: Little Miss was given a phytochemical bioactive compound oil of Valerenic and Acetoxyvalerenic acid, a combined anesthetic agent that includes a number of alkaloids and iridoids..."

"Cezar remains confused."

"You know, the little pink and white flowers," Vincent said. "They smell cheesy, like her stinky feet. I saw some in the rainforest."

"Valerian root," the wolf said. "Cezar recognizes the scent now."

"Yep. That's what Father called it. Those mean cavemen gave her a lot."

"I'm okay, guys," Dot said, slowly sitting up within the robot. "I'm still in a fog, and I still have my 'cheesy' feet, but I'm fine."

"Quick!" Vincent held up one of his hands to the girl. "How many fingers am I holding up?"

Dot focused on her friend's outstretched hand, saw all his fingers raised. "Seven?" she said, curious.

"Good! I used to ask Father that when he got fuzzy sometimes."

"Vincent, did you grow an extra two fingers just now?"

"Yep. I tried to trick you, but you passed the test!"

"Not good enough for Cezar," the wolf said. "Girl, do you remember your name?"

Vincent shook his head. "Nah, that's no help, Cezzie. She could never remember her real name, remember?"

"That's not what Cezar meant..."

"Ask her your name!"

"Cezar doesn't think that will help, either."

"Okay, you ask her something, Abe."

"Query: Can you recall your five most recent declarative statements in order of location, word count, and general import?"

"We are a useless lot," the wolf hybrid said.

"How about I ask you guys some questions?" Dot said. "They're kinda personal, but they've been swirling in my mind for a long time. One question for each of you."

"Ask me anything!" Vincent said. "I didn't have time to study, but I'll do my best!"

"Cezar is willing," the wolf said with some reluctance.

"Abe?"

"Agreement: A line of articulate inquiry from you, Little Miss, would satisfy our concern regarding your coherence."

"I'll start with Vincent," the girl said. "You mentioned several times that you don't die. What makes you say that? It certainly seems that way, but when did you first know?"

"When I lived in Colt, I got hurt a lot. The villagers were real mean, but I was also real clumsy. When we built the barn, I fell off the roof and cracked my head open like a rotten melon. It hurt bad and I couldn't move or talk. I heard folks say I was dead for sure."

"How horrible!"

"It was horrible!" Vincent said. "But Father knew what to do. Father always knew what to do. He planted me in the ground up to my neck and soaked the soil. Pretty soon, I was shouting, 'Hey guys! Can someone dig me up?'"

"That's amazing," Dot said with a laugh.

"Father said I can grow back from getting hurt bad. I figured everyone was like that until he died."

"I remember," Dot said, recalling her friend's unusual reaction to Fathers Young's death.

"Now do Abe!"

"Proceed with your query," the robot said.

"It's about your brain." Dot was careful with her wording despite it being impossible to offend or embarrass the mech. "You told us it's part organic, part synthetic."

"Correct."

"Where did the organic part come from?"

"Explanation: The donor of my cerebrum's outer layer is Animalia-Cetacea-Delphinidae."

"Dang, what the heck kind of plant is that?" Vincent asked.

"That is no plant," the wolf-man said. "Cezar recognizes 'Delphinidae.' Abraham's brain flesh comes from a dolphin, a docile creature that swims in packs in the open waters of the sea."

"Big Abe's got fish brains?"

"Clarification: My organic cerebral cortex was extracted from an oceanic mammal. Its spindle neurons include advanced perception and interpretation, pattern recognition, long-term memory, logic and reason, general communication, contextual comprehension, and sequential problem-solving."

"It seems your animal side claims the lion's share of your mind," Cezar said. "What does your machine side govern?"

"Clarification: My synthetic positronic neural net concerns military strategy, weapon deployment, damage assessment, and field-tactical analysis."

"War stuff," Vincent said sadly.

"Half of your mind is occupied with death," Cezar said to his mechanical friend.

"Correct."

Dot remembered how the combat mechs built before Abraham had no minds of their own, and the ones after him had their logic, reason, and communication removed, leaving only a focus on war. She sensed the change of mood in her friends, including the mech.

"You're more than just a weapon, Abraham," Dot said. "From now on, you're a big dolphin in a metal suit to me."

"Gratitude."

"Now you have a question for Cezar?" the wolf hybrid asked the girl, failing to hide his hesitation. "Cezar will answer as best he can."

"Why do you speak in the third person?" Dot asked.

"I don't understand," Vincent said, scratching his mossy chin. "I mean, he's talking to three people now."

"Speaking in third person means Cezar doesn't use pronouns like 'me' or 'I.' He always refers to himself by name. I noticed all the predators talk that way."

As the group continued through the woods, eagerly awaiting the wolf's response, Cezar fondly thought back to his early childhood in the rainforest.

"When we were pups, Dr. Blum taught Cezar and Calah how to speak, how to read. He was generous with his knowledge and wisdom. Calah quickly tired of the laboratory classroom, but Cezar enjoyed the man's company. Reading was always a struggle, but he continued tutoring Cezar in mathematics, science and engineering, culture and history. Together, we traveled the world, past and present, through his beloved photo books and video records. It was a wondrous time."

"I envy you," Dot said. "I wish I could remember my teacher."

"Our sessions were always in the morning, but for the rest of the day and night, Caffar was my guide and mentor. As Alpha, he was responsible for instilling a sense of honor and duty in not only us wolves but all the beasts of the Great Domain. To Caffar, we were the overlords of the rainforest. We didn't devour everything like a mindless locust swarm, as the humans would have you believe. We kept a balance between predator and prey. To maintain our station and our self-respect, Caffar insisted we refer to each other, and always ourselves, by name. We never spoke in the diminutive sense."

"I think I understand," Dot said. "It's similar to a troop using titles like 'captain' or 'lieutenant.'"

"Exactly. It helped us remember our place in the world, our responsibility, our connection to each other." The wolf-man stopped walking, looked at the girl, and chose his next words with difficulty. "However, if you prefer that Cezar... that I... speak in the diminutive sense, then I shall oblige. It's not Cezar's... it's not my intention... to confuse my friends or isolate myself with how I was raised to speak. Cezar knows... I know... it can sound cold and off-putting. I can talk as you do, if it pleases you."

"I love you the way you are, Cezar," Dot said, feeling guilty for inadvertently questioning his upbringing. "I was just curious. You don't have to change for me."

"I like the way Cezzie talks," Vincent said. "It helps me remember who I'm talking to!"

"If you are sure, girl..."

"I'm sure, Cezar. You have a unique way of talking. Don't let anyone tell you different."

"As you wish."

"I thought of a question for you, Dottie," Vincent said. "Were those mean cavemen really gonna eat you?" He hadn't thought about the Elders for hours, but the grumbling in his empty stomach reminded him of the selfish men's literal hunger for the girl.

"That was the idea," Dot said. "I'm glad they didn't get the chance."

Though Vincent had been in the middle of the clash between Beacon Hill's two factions, he felt confused about what they wanted with the girl and why they'd fought each other for so many years. It proved difficult for Dot to explain, for she also couldn't comprehend their little civil war or their rationale about finding a cure for The Worm within her.

"Would it have worked?" Vincent asked. "If they ate you, I mean. Would they be cured of the virus?"

"I don't think so," Dot said. "I'm pretty sure it doesn't work that way."

"Cezar's clan believed a hunter consumes more than just the flesh of his prey," the wolf hybrid said. "When a hunter eats his prey, he absorbs its life force, its station, a small part of its place in the world. Eat a lowly, slimy frog and you may feel small and weak. The lean meat of a gazelle gives you the agility to bound across the land. Rich oxen meat builds great strength."

"So, you really are what you eat," Dot said with a laugh.

"Cezar believes so."

"How about if you eat veggies?" Vincent asked the wolf. "Do they count?"

"What is it mothers tell their young ones?" the wolf asked. "Eat your vegetables so you may grow tall and strong. Growth and survival make up the essence of a plant."

"So true," Vincent said with pride. "But wolves are carny... carny... meaty-vores, right? They don't normally eat no plants, do they?"

"Of course we do. Neither wolf nor wolf hybrid is foolish enough to starve if there's no meat to be had, and the hunters in my old clan were intelligent enough to know the way of the world. The plant supports the animal."

"Like how I support you!" Vincent said, thinking himself clever.

"The same can be said of dogs."

"If you mean Gypsy, he'll eat anything! I once fed him wild fingerling potatoes, and he gobbled them up like sausages!"

Vincent liked learning more about his friends and had many more questions for them, but the mention of their missing companion made Vincent remember their current mission – to find the German Shepherd before something terrible happened.

50

The Honorless Apostates

"How much farther, Abraham?" Dot asked as the group ventured farther north through the woods across the afternoon. "It feels like we should've reached him by now."

"Reconnaissance: We passed Gypsy's last known location seven minutes ago, 1.3 kilometers southwest of our current position."

"So, what are you saying?" Vincent asked.

"He's saying he doesn't know," Cezar said. "He lost Gypsy's trail."

"Correct," Abraham said.

"None of us know, Vincent. We must face the possibility that we may never find our pure dog."

"Correct."

"Not correct!" Vincent said, shocked by his friends' grim view. "Of course, we'll find him! With my eyes, Cezzie's nose, and Abe's extra-sensing senses, how can we not find him?"

"Clarification: Gypsy's unique life form signature will not appear on my sensors if he has been dispatched and reached decomposition levels of active or advanced decay."

"What's all that mean?"

"If Gypsy is dead," Cezar said, perhaps too bluntly. "If he has been killed and eaten, Abraham will detect him as just another carcass, my nose will smell just a pool of blood, and your eyes will see only bones picked apart."

"That's not true!" Vincent said, growing nervous. "He's German! Just like Father's ancestors! And Germans are too tough to die without a fight!"

"German *Shepherd*, brother."

"Dang, that's right! He's a shepherd, too! And shepherds always take care of their pack. Cezzie says we're a pack."

"We are indeed." The wolf-man felt for his innocent plant brother who now struggled to hold onto hope. "Always remember that."

"That means we'll find each other for sure." Vincent turned to the mech. "Ain't that right, Dottie?"

From within Abraham's chest, Dot hesitated to answer her friend for fear of dousing his spirit. Moments earlier, she'd dozed off for a time and briefly reentered The Void alone. Her friends weren't there, for they were still awake, a factor George made clear. Gypsy may have been awake as well, or he may have been...

"Reconnaissance: Purist squad detected 9.8 kilometers ahead, directly north of our position."

"What exactly do you see?" Dot asked, hopeful.

"Identification: Six humans, three hybrids, and one pure canine in what appears to be a Purist encampment."

"Pure canine means dog!" Vincent said. "See, I told you guys! That's gotta be our canine up ahead!"

"Correct."

"Humans and hybrids?" Dot said. "No Automen?"

"Correct."

"Something's wrong," Cezar said. "The Greens mostly employ artificial soldiers."

"Sergeant Furst told us that, too," Dot said. "Abraham, if there are no clones, what makes you think they're Purists?"

"Extrapolation: Their complement of biometric weapons and proprietary mobile support equipment, all gathered in a militarily strategic optimal position, suggests a Purist encampment."

"Then that's the weirdest crew of Greenies I've ever heard of," Vincent said. "No clone guys? And I never heard of hybrids working with them."

"Theory: The hybrids and canine are gathered in a central area, away from the humans. They may be held captive."

Dot feared that was the situation. "Keep your sensors locked onto Gypsy."

"Acknowledgment."

"We need to reach that camp before he disappears again."

* * *

An hour later, after another nearly 10 kilometers of rough terrain, the Widows' sedative had finally run its course. A reinvigorated Dot insisted on climbing out from the mech and walking with her companions as they approached the camp. She told Abraham to stay back to avoid detection while she and the others scouted ahead. Though his many servos were minimized by internal sound dampeners, the silence of the morning offered no camouflage for his movements. If they were to investigate the area and locate their four-legged friend, they needed stealth, something a 12-foot armored combat mech was incapable of. Sergeant Furst's and Lieutenant Dixon's list of Abraham's pros and cons came to mind, useful wisdom she felt grateful to remember.

Parting ferns for a better look ahead, Dot was surprised to see humans in blue uniforms sitting at a large campfire.

"Those aren't Purists," Dot said. "Those are Loyalists!"

"Not bad guys?" Vincent said. "This is a camp for the good guys?"

"Looks that way."

"It doesn't smell that way to Cezar," the wolf said. "Cezar smells fear and anxiety."

"Everyone's afraid, Cezar, even Loyalist soldiers."

"The scent is not on them, girl. I smell it on their prey. The robot is right. Gypsy and the hybrids are being held prisoner."

In the center of the camp, a short distance from the fire, stood a steel shed large enough to contain several people.

"Can you guys tell what kinds of hybrids are in that shed with Gypsy?" Dot asked. "I want to know if he's okay in there."

"Not only can Cezar tell you their species, Cezar can tell you their names."

"You can smell names?" Vincent asked. "Dang, your nose really is good!"

"Cezar knows their scents well: Caffar, Calah, and Juma."

"From the rainforest?" Dot asked.

"Those great big hunter guys?" Vincent said with a shudder. He recalled the three predators well, the two wolf hybrids even larger than Cezar, and the tiger hybrid who dwarfed them all. "What are they doing way up here? Weren't they gonna head west with everybody else?"

"Maybe they came to help us after all."

"Cezar wishes that were true," the wolf-man said. "But Caffar believed we were well secured as a new clan, and it's not in his nature to protect anyone. As for the city in the west, he cares nothing for safety and shelter. He lives for the hunt, comfortable in harm's way. He clearly led my former pack out into the wild to seek proper sport, prey more worthy than rabbits and squirrels."

"Purist soldiers," Dot said.

"Yes. Caffar has always dreamed of hunting them. He surely smelled their armaments, just as Cezar did, and just as Abraham sensed."

"But Dottie said these guys are Blues, not Greenies," Vincent said. "Dang, I'm so confused."

"We aren't yet certain of anything," Cezar said. "Don't let the sight of humans in blue uniforms cloud your judgement." The wolf hybrid raised his snout into the air and took in several quick sniffs, focusing on his old brethren's distinct odors. Something smelled different, disconcerting. "Juma's scent has... changed."

"Assessment: The tiger hybrid's body chemistry denotes significant injury." Though he wasn't with them, Abraham spoke over Dot's and Vincent's cochlear earpieces from afar, having overheard their exchange. "Shall I intervene?"

"Abe says Juma is hurt bad," Vincent said to Cezar, who had no earpiece. "He says it's a... significant injury? He wants to know if he should go save him."

"Tell the mech there's no saving to be done," Cezar said in a somber tone. "Cezar can smell his 'significant injury.' Much blood loss, torn flesh, and shattered bone. Cezar is afraid there may be no more hunts ahead for the mighty Juma."

Dot saw great sorrow on her wolf-friend's face. As much as she wanted to save his tiger brother, she trusted his sharp instincts. She also didn't want Abraham's sudden presence endangering

Gypsy and the others. She knew their hidden position was the only advantage they had at the moment.

Cezar had other thoughts.

"We flank the humans," he said. "Surround, capture, interrogate. During our incursion, our trusted mech must remain behind. His loud motor functions will give away our cover too soon."

"There's not many of them," Dot said. "If they see Abraham, they might surrender."

"Or they might flip a switch and electrify the metal shed, killing all inside. That dishonorable deterrent was used at Dominion for many years."

"Dishorrible detergent," Vincent said. "You sure have a way with words, Cezzie."

"Thank you, but keep your focus, Vincent. Cezar will need your strength and resolve in a moment."

"You got it! I will focus on being focused."

"What's the plan?" Dot asked.

Cezar surveyed the area one last time before laying out his strategy. "Dot, you will advance to the west and attract their attention while Vincent advances east and prepares to rip the door, nay the walls, off that infernal shed."

"What about you, Cezzie?" Vincent asked.

"Cezar will strike from above."

"Remember, Dottie says no killing if we can..."

Without another word, the wolf hybrid climbed the nearest tree and leaped from branch to branch toward the six humans in blue fatigues huddled around their campfire, getting closer with each tree.

Dot crouched in the brush to the west of the camp, inching her way forward through ferns and sedges and wildflowers until she crept so close to the soldiers that she could hear their breathing.

She wished they were engaged in deep conversation to allow her more time to better position herself. Taking in the moment's silence and the clear meadow ahead, she hoped her spot would suffice as she awaited her companions.

"Location: The soldiers are gathered within 3.9 meters from your location." Abraham's voice startled Dot. Though only she and Vincent could hear him, she still felt uneasy, his voice loud and distinct in her head. "Query: Are you in peril? Shall I intervene?"

Dot didn't dare answer him so close to the soldiers, and she hoped he wouldn't take action without her consent. Though he remained a half-mile back, she knew he might storm the camp within a minute, disregarding their careful plan, if he felt her life was in jeopardy. The sight of a rampaging combat mech was every troop's worst nightmare, but such fear leads to rash action, and Gypsy and the imprisoned hybrids might suffer from the fallout.

She looked to the west and spied Vincent across the camp, slithering across the dense forest floor, his slender body nearly flat with the ground, taking refuge behind a stack of cut wood near the central shed. She looked up and spotted Cezar high in the redwood giants, clinging to the massive trees, his claws embedded in their bark.

Not knowing what to do, Dot stared up at the wolf, for it was his plan, and she awaited some signal to start her distraction. Indeed, Cezar pinpointed her and gestured to remain on standby while he readied himself. He turned to Vincent and nodded the same unspoken order, to hold position until he made his move.

The wolf-man spread his long, sharp claws and prepared to dive onto the six unsuspecting humans, but halted himself upon seeing his old brother Calah emerge from the shed with a tray of roasted meat. To Cezar's surprise, his fellow wolf hybrid served

Lynn Harrod

the charred meat to the humans around the campfire, a sight he'd never imagined.

As the soldiers in blue took large pieces of what Cezar's snout identified as roasted wild boar, he saw a smiling Caffar carry the carcass out of the shed, proud that he and his brethren had pulled every ounce of meat from its bones before tossing it onto the shed's makeshift barbecue, a grill crafted from mesh fencing.

Confused, Cezar quickly held out his open palms to his friends hidden in the brush below, gesturing for them to abort the planned attack. Dot understood the new order, having seen the wolves socializing with the soldiers, but Vincent laid on the ground behind the shed and couldn't see the unusual, peaceful scene.

Mistaking his friend's signal, Vincent unleashed his vines and pulled the corrugated steel walls from the shed. The buckling metal made a thunderous sound as he lunged forward to "save" Gypsy and Juma.

"Vincent, no!" Cezar shouted as he dropped to the ground, to the shock of the camp.

Upon reaching the destroyed, exposed shed, Vincent stood puzzled at the sight of an injured Juma resting on a cot, petting the German Shepherd at his side.

"Gypsy?" Vincent said. "We thought you were in danger, boy."

"Your pure dog is with six veteran soldiers and three predators," Juma said, "and you thought he was in danger?"

"Umm, Cezzie?" Vincent said, coiling in his many vines. "What's the heck's going on?"

"Cezar would also like to know what the heck is going on," the wolf-man said as he approached his former Alpha. "Caffar, Cezar apologizes for the intrusion, and for the shed. We thought you needed aid."

"We did, brother," the largest wolf said. "Caffar won't lie. We desperately needed help. We encountered a formidable Purist troop. Juma was gravely injured, and we faced our deaths, but the Apostates joined us and together we ended Greens' hunt."

"Triumphant as always," Cezar said. "Did you strike the final killing blow?"

"Of course."

"You always were the best of us."

Caffar looked into his younger brother's eyes and abandoned his stoic front, his judgement, his noble position as Alpha. Instead, the oldest wolf-man's smiling face made it clear he felt overjoyed to see his clan's exile again.

"It's good to see you alive and ready to fight," Caffar said. "Caffar is glad we didn't kill you at the redemption ceremony."

"Cezar has come to feel the same way."

"Caffar also wondered what you'd do when you saw us with these humans."

"You knew Cezar was here?"

Caffar nodded his head and tapped the end of his nose. "How quickly you forget your roots, brother. Caffar caught your scents ten minutes ago. They were impossible to miss. The human child has a distinct, foul odor."

"Yes, she is in dire need of a bath," Cezar said.

"And the plant hybrid is particularly pungent."

"Thanks!" Vincent said with a wide grin. "No one's ever called me pungent before!"

The Alpha looked at the dense woods behind them. "Caffar also smelled polymer, silicone, charge powder, and scorched steel. It lingers in the air even now. Caffar assumes it's the great war machine you mentioned."

"Abraham," Cezar said. "He awaits beyond the trees, half a mile south."

"He?" Caffar said, amused. "And 'he' also has a name?"

"Indeed. He. Abraham. It took some getting used to, but the girl insists."

"And you obey her orders?" Caffar asked, curious. "You, an apex predator of The Great Domain, now follow the wishes of a child?"

"Unconditionally and with pride."

Dot stepped out from her hiding spot and wandered into the camp, much to the bewilderment of the human soldiers in blue. Her presence shook them even more than the wolf hybrid who pounced from the treetops or the plant hybrid who tore their barbecue shed to scrap metal, for none of them had ever seen a living human child.

"Come, girl," Caffar said to Dot, extending his paw.

"Forgive me if I hesitate," the girl said, "but the last time I saw you..."

"There's no need to be fearful. Not anymore. Caffar and his brothers have stepped into a much larger world. Please, come meet the Apostates."

"Aposta... aposta-whatsit?" Vincent asked.

"Apostates," Dot said, still cautious. "People who've walked away from their religions."

"Dang, I knew Dottie would know. She knows all kinds of stuff!"

Impressed with the girl – perhaps awestruck – one of the human soldiers stood from his place by the fire, a tall man with a freckled face and shaggy brown beard. He walked past the eclectic hybrid creatures and took in the sight of the abnormally normal girl, offering her a warm smile.

"This is James The First," Caffar said to Dot. "He is human, as you are. Is it not comforting to be with your own kind?"

"Not always," Dot said. "My most trusted friends are nothing at all like me."

"I imagine most people are nothing at all like you, kiddo," James The First said in disbelief, his voice clear and confident, a sign of his undisputed authority. "A human child, a little girl who's seemingly in perfect health, who appears educated and who's accompanied by ferocious friends. I'm still not sure if I'm dreaming."

"My mind's spinning, too. We thought you were Purists, but they'd never help a bunch of hybrids."

"Purists?" James said with a long laugh. He turned with his arms outstretched, pointing out his squad's blue military fatigues. "Do we look like Purists?"

"But your equipment..."

"Ah, you noticed that. Yes, that would explain things." James looked about the camp, most of his group's gear confiscated from clashes with Purists troops. "We pick up supplies, weapons, and intel wherever we can, and we've lifted quite a bit of loot from the Greens. But let me start over, kiddo. I'm James The First. For better or worse, I'm the captain of The Honorless Apostates."

"You consider yourselves without honor?" Dot asked.

"No, but that's what everyone calls our motley gang of deserters. Somewhere along the way, the name stuck."

"Deserters? You mean you left the Loyalists?"

"I left the Blues, yes, as did two others. The rest left the Greens."

James The First introduced his squad by order of rank as they remained sitting by the fire, waiting for sunset.

"Hale The Second" was a thin, pale blond woman, a former infantryman with the Loyalists known for her seemingly endless stamina. She smiled at Dot.

"Mort The Third" was a short, stocky man with powerful arms and a permanent scowl, a veteran heavy gunner with decades of Loyalist service behind him. He nodded to Dot and her friends.

Hale and Mort were in the same Loyalist company as James, before the three of them were left behind after a doomed incursion. Inspired by James's cavalier view of a wandering life, they agreed to leave the cause and live off the land as a new unit loyal only to each other.

"Walt The Fourth" was a tall, dark-skinned man with a porkpie hat. He tilted his hat's brim at Dot like the prairie gentleman he fancied himself to be. An old Purist sharpshooter, Walt joined James and company after waking up from a brutal melee that claimed dozens of lives in Wellspring five years prior. Seeing blue uniforms looming above him, he feared imprisonment or execution but was relieved to learn of their defiant kindness and independence, a calling he'd felt his entire life.

"Eve The Fifth" was a petite Asian brunette, a former Purist weapons technician who specialized in automated defense. Like Walt, she long felt the pull of a life untethered and saw James's crew as a path to freedom. She offered Dot a quick grin.

"Grace The Sixth" sat beside Eve. Another weapons tech, the large, dark woman had a shaved head, her hair replaced with a hundred small tattoos: an "X" for every kill. She grunted at the newcomers, her eyes wide and alert. Normally loud and outspoken like the intimidating Mort, she nodded at the girl.

Eve and Grace served in the same Purist company before injuries in battle made them immobile and, therefore, expendable. The two women bled out in a field of fire and watched as their comrades – human and synthetic, equally cold-hearted – packed their gear and drove off in trucks loaded with captured hybrids. The gruesome sight cemented their lingering doubt about their mission. By the time James found them wandering the wild months later, they were open to the idea of joining a rogue faction with no ties, neither blue nor green. The ongoing war never made sense to them, so a life of group survival beckoned.

The six highly trained soldiers banded together to live each day on their own terms, with no orders to kill or capture, no forced hatred for "deviants" or "heathens" or "abominations," people they now saw simply as fellow survivors of a riven world.

"That's quite a crew you've assembled," Dot said.

"And that's quite a statement coming from you," James said, "given your unusual troop."

"It seems the only thing you all have in common is that you deserted your posts."

"My most trusted friends are nothing at all like me," James said, repeating the girl's bold statement from a moment before. "You said we walked away from our religions. That textbook definition isn't far from the truth, kiddo. After a lifetime of taking orders, of never questioning our superiors as we unloaded our rifles on hybrids and artificials and angry humans, we decided their lives were theirs, and our lives were ours. We became the Honorless Apostates, reviled by all for abandoning our stations."

"We don't revile you," Caffar said. "You joined our hunt, saved Juma from a dishonorable death in the Greens' cage. From where Caffar stands, you are predators freely roaming the wild, as we are. For that, you have Caffar's respect."

"You honor us, my large friend, but the only things we prey on are crates of food and belts of ammunition. We avoid fights whenever we can. There are only six of us, after all."

"Six men and women with the spark and gust of an entire company of soldiers."

"Again, you honor me."

Cezar watched the bond between his former Alpha and the Apostates' captain with a tinge of envy. Though Caffar felt relieved to see his younger brother alive and well, he clearly had a stronger connection to the nomadic squad of humans, their views on life seemingly aligned.

Vincent approached the group by the fire.

"I'm Vincent! They also call me Vinny Greenblood, Veggie Vinny, Dim Vin, the Green Fool, Vincent Vines, but Dottie said Vincent is fine because that's what I like to be called and that's okay."

"We used to have a friend named Reggie," Grace said. "He was so afraid of The Worm that he only ate fruits and vegetables, so we called him Veggie Reggie. We liked him a lot."

"In that case, Veggie Vinny is okay, too!"

"Are you sure, Vincent?" Dot asked. "They used that name to taunt you in Colt."

"But these folks aren't from Colt, Dottie."

The overjoyed plant hybrid extended vines in all directions, offering simultaneous "handshakes" to the six humans, for they seemed friendly – even the grouchy ones – their heartfelt greeting a welcome respite after so much animosity and betrayal on the Broken Road. Such cruel behavior never made sense to Vincent in such a desperate world, and he always felt there were good folks to be found if one sought them out.

Startled and amused, the soldiers shook the ends of the vines as Vincent peered into their food supplies.

"Veggie Vinny, you're free to have..." James's voice trailed off as he realized he didn't know what kind of creature Vincent was and therefore didn't know what he ate. "You can have whatever food you like... or need... to eat."

"Thanks, James The One!"

"That's James The First," the captain said with a laugh, "as in 'First in Command.'"

"Got it." Vincent rummaged through their supplies and spied ample game and produce but nothing to complement them. "You guys are in luck. We brought herbs, berries, spices. How long has it been since you seasoned your food?"

"We tend to eat things as they is," Mort said with a grunt. "Meat is meat. A potato is a potato. Don't need nothin' else."

"Aww, you're wrong, and you're in for a treat, because I'm going to make Father's favorite stew! He used to shut his eyes when he ate it, said he savored every bite."

"You cook?" Hale asked in her soft, tinny voice.

"Me cook, yes!"

"Vincent is not a cook," Cezar said. "Vincent is a chef."

"Then I guess we is in for a treat," Mort said, intrigued. "None of us haven't had no real meal in ages. We don't even have no proper pot or pan between us now that I thinks of it."

"Those big empty cans will do the job," Vincent said, spotting several spent ammunition cases.

"The ammo canisters?"

"Yep. Once I clean them, I can cook up a fine stew."

"Then work your magic, Veggie Vinny," Mort said, surprised by the plant-man's enthusiasm.

"I'm starting to like that name. Dinner will be served shortly!"

The pleasantries were cut short by the arrival of Abraham, the giant combat mech emerging from the treeline. Immediately, the Apostates lunged to the ground and grabbed weapons hidden behind the logs near the fire. As they pointed their guns at the giant robot, Cezar quickly held out his hands and stood between his mechanical friend and the soldiers.

"Statement: This unit is not engaged in combat."

"Like hell, you ain't!" Mort said.

"Statement: This unit's weapons remain powered down."

"What's going on?" Vincent asked, confused. "Why all the guns?"

"Stand down!" Cezar said. "Abraham is our ally!"

"Mech ain't no ally to no one!" Mort said as he aimed his heavy rifle at the mech's armored chest.

"Back away, kiddo," James said, his hand resting on a grenade dangling from his utility belt. "Nice and slow."

"My brother speaks truth," Caffar said. "The war machine serves the girl."

"You expect us to believe that?" Grace yelled. "I know that model well. That an A1900! Two of them took out my old company's fort!"

"Ain't no way I'm trusting no machine!" Mort said as he charged his weapon, a monstrous gun made to counter armored vehicles.

"Everyone calm down!" Dot said. She ran to the mech and climbed atop his frame, both to show his passive nature and to deter their attack. "I promise, Abraham won't hurt anyone!"

Gypsy hopped down from Juma's cot and sprinted to the girl's defense, adding further tension to the scene.

"Stand down!" Cezar said again. "The mech has imprinted on the girl! You must believe us!"

"I believe her," Eve said, almost defiantly. "Why would she lie?"

"You trust too easily, Eve," Grace said.

"And you raise your gun too easily, G."

"It's helped keep us alive, or have you forgotten? Don't let the sight of a child blind you."

"Listen to Grace," Mort said as he now looked at Dot's group with disgust. "I sees it now. Healthy little girl. No scars, no smell, no sign of The Worm anywhere on her. Hybrid bodyguards.

Combat mech. They come up on us outta nowhere. Didn't make no sense before, but it does now! You're with them Greens!"

"We're not with the Purists!" Dot said.

"Enough outta you, girl!" Mort said. "Greens always shoot on sight. Don't usually see 'em until there's fire in the sky, but they've reached a new low. Never thought they'd resort to sneaky tricks!"

"Stop!" Juma said, his wheezing voice bellowing across the campsite. It pained the tiger-man to speak, but he strained to be heard. "Juma also doesn't trust war machines, but if Caffar says to stand down, if Cezar says to stand down, then Juma also says stand down!"

The Apostates stared at their large, striped ally in astonishment, his words carrying weight with them.

Juma struggled to stand from his cot. Calah offered help, but the tiger refused, instead clinging to a thick branch that served as a homemade crutch. He hobbled into the center of the standoff, positioning himself between Dot's friends and the alarmed Apostates. In that moment of tense silence, Cezar saw the tiger hybrid was missing his left leg.

"Juma," Cezar said under his breath. "What's happened to you?"

"This body is no longer whole, brother," Juma said in shame. "My hunt is over. Juma has accepted this."

"Who did this to you?"

"Not who, but what. Please understand, the six human soldiers you see here used to be ten before it attacked."

"It?" Vincent asked. "I thought you guys fought a bunch of Greenie clones?"

"Surely, no lowly Automen or measly humans could cripple the mighty Juma," Cezar said, figuring things out. "There must have been another."

"The clones never lifted a gun," Juma said in shame. "They stood and watched from afar as we fought their monster."

"What 'monster' attacked you?" Dot asked.

"They called it 'Azrael.' As tall as the trees, with the arms and legs of a battalion, it wore green armor."

"Identification: They were attacked by an A2500 Azrael-class combat mech." Abraham had detected traces of paint and shorn armor in the dirt, supporting his conclusion.

"Another mech?" Dot said. She remembered the graveyard above Beacon Hill, the Azrael being the largest of the fallen robots, twice the size of her Abraham. If there was another still active somewhere, still serving the Purists...

"Did you destroy it?" Cezar asked, hoping for a victory, though he knew it was unlikely.

"We ran," James said, "launching every smoke grenade we had behind us. We were shocked that we gained any distance from it. No telling where that soulless grim reaper is now."

"Reconnaissance: No humanoid hostiles are detected within a 10-kilometer radius. No humans, artificials, or mechanicals are within my sensory range."

"I suppose I'm relieved," James said.

"That makes one of us," Mort said, keeping his heavy rifle pointed at Abraham.

"I'm sorry for your loss," Dot said to the soldiers, now understanding their cause for alarm. "We've all lost people we care about, but I can promise you that Abraham is a friend."

Juma nodded to his youngest brother, the wolf Calah, and glanced at the others as he limped to Dot. He rested his crutch on one of the mech's massive feet and sat upon the other, showing the group that he trusted the child's faith in her towering war machine.

"Juma believes you, girl," the tiger said. "My brothers believe you."

"Juma speaks truth," Calah said to her, following his older brother's example. "And so you also have Calah's trust."

"Mine, too," James The First said. He held up his open palm, signaling the rest of the Apostates to stand down. They obeyed and lowered their weapons, though they never let the mech out of their sight.

* * *

As promised, Vincent cooked dinner for the camp. He explored the area and found wild mushrooms – morel and chanterelle – close to a patch of fragrant flowers that proved a good substitute for garlic. The soldiers watched as he combined his found treasures with his stock of herbs and some pureed squash within a cleaned ammo canister full of water, simmering his creation over the campfire.

Vincent's intention was to complete the dish with root vegetables, but he stood startled when Calah dropped a cleanly butchered rabbit into the bubbling water, much to the delight of the soldiers.

"Wild boar was never to my brothers' taste," the young wolf hybrid said, "but rabbit makes for a fine stew, don't you all agree?"

The humans and predators grunted and nodded.

"But... it's not part of the recipe for Father's Stew," Vincent said.

"Then let this be Apostates' Stew," Dot said as she took the ladle and stirred the pot. "*Honorable* Apostates' Stew. A new recipe for a new friendship."

"You're smarter than you look, kiddo," James said with a grin, impressed with the girl's maturity and authority.

"Thank you. That means a lot coming from you, Captain."

"I suppose I could say the same." James realized why her friends were so committed to her and soon concluded why she roamed the wild with them. "You're the type of kid who's always full of surprises, aren't you? Well, this old soldier has a surprise or two of his own."

The captain knelt beside the storage trunk near his tent, his back to the group. With the pop of a cork, he rose to his feet and turned to everyone with a newly opened black bottle. He held the cork out to Calah, allowing him to take in its aroma.

"Calah has heard of this," the young wolf-man said, "an ancient drink made from rotted berries."

"We humans call it 'wine,'" James said. "This one is an old Cab. We found it in Whitesbridge years ago. Does your brilliant nose detect any toxins?"

"None."

"Good. It's past its prime, over the hill to be sure. Hell, it's over the hill and through the woods by now, but if it isn't poison at this point, it'll service that rabbit stew quite nicely."

To a bewildered Vincent and a curious Calah, James The First poured half a bottle of 84-year-old Cabernet Sauvignon into the makeshift stewpot and gestured for Dot to stir it in. Instantly, the scent wafting through the air had the inviting, musky aroma of plum, oak, and spiced game.

"I can assure you, Veggie Vincent," James said to their chef, "your father would shut his eyes and savor this stew."

"You're probably right," Vincent said. "Smells pretty good to me. Dottie and I can always pick out the meaty bits."

51

A New Alpha

During the bonding over the community stew, under an overcast sky that darkened and swelled with impending rain, Cezar helped Caffar rebuild the shed at the center of the camp while their older brother Juma rested on his cot within. The two wolves crudely bolted together sheets of corrugated metal to form walls just strong enough to protect supplies from the elements and offer shelter to the recovering tiger.

"This robot you encountered," Cezar said. "How did it compare to my companion?"

"The Azrael mech was a juggernaut, brother," Caffar said. "There's no other word to describe it. Caffar dreams of facing worthy foes but has never imagined an enemy so deadly. It stood taller, larger, fully armed, and showed no signs of heart or soul, not like your machine friend."

"You sense it, also?"

"Your Abraham has a voice," Caffar said, "one of logic and reason, perhaps even compassion. It speaks with you, listens to you, follows some kind of code, just as we wolves do. As strange as it may seem, it appears to be alive and honorable. From what I know about such machines, it's a curiosity, an anomaly."

"Credit the girl," Cezar said. "She has imprinted upon it and insists that it takes no life."

"Then it isn't the great guardian we believe it to be. Caffar knows you, brother. Despite your passive nature, you would kill to keep the child safe, without hesitation, and your plant companion may be a fool, but he would also do anything for her."

"On that, we agree. You are observant and wise as always, Caffar, but know that Vincent and Cezar also avoid death whenever possible. It's another decree from the girl, one that this wolf follows with his heart. Cezar realizes it's hard for you to understand, that such limits would stifle a great hunter..."

"On that, we disagree," the Alpha said to his brother's shock. "Caffar would consider it a challenge, to keep my ward safe while also preserving other life. To succeed in such a difficult mission, Caffar would try but likely fail, but Caffar believes you will emerge triumphant. This hunt, this search for the girl's allies in the east, it was destined for you."

Cezar peered through a gap in the shed's walls, saw Juma nod in agreement, and in their shared praise, the exiled wolf's eyes welled with swirling emotion. Never had he felt the warm embrace of his brethren's acceptance. Inside the walls of the Dominion rainforest, where each night's desperate hunt ended in either feast or famine, Cezar had been branded a coward for sympathizing with and safeguarding prey. Out in the wild world, with deadly enemies of every type scouring the land for his head at all hours, he was the bravest of warriors following a strict code. Such dedicated hunters could only respect that chosen path, for it proved much harder than a predator's life without limits.

"Your words mean a great deal to Cezar," the wolf-man said with a quickened breath. "Your words mean everything."

"You've taken responsibility for a child," Caffar said. "You've had to defy your nature to do so. Caffar realizes now there is no braver act."

"Cezar is glad you approve."

"You no longer need my approval, brother. You lead your own clan now. Caffar can't deny that. What Caffar can do is offer you my blessing."

"Thank you, Caffar. Again, it means everything."

Their repair job done, the wolf-men stood back and took in the sight of the rebuilt shed, its walls buckled and torn but now firmly bolted back in place. It reminded Caffar of its swift destruction earlier, and the strange man who ripped it apart.

"That plant fool of yours," Caffar said. "He's a creature I've never conceived."

"Vincent is special," Cezar said. "Dr. Blum helped create him, said he's one of a kind."

"Caffar is not surprised. It would have taken all of us to reduce this shed to crumpled tin, but he alone ripped apart the walls like paper in mere seconds. I imagine not even he knows the heights of his strength."

"Indeed, Cezar can't fathom his might. He also claims he can't die, and after all we've witnessed, Cezar believes him. If not for his gentle, naive nature, Vincent would be any foe's worst nightmare."

"Be glad he's your ally."

Lynn Harrod

"He's yours as well," Cezar said. "He seems to protect anyone or anything the girl deems a friend."

"You're saying the child views us favorably?" Caffar asked. "After our regrettable confrontation in the rainforest?"

"Cezar spoke with her on your behalf, told her about our ways, our beliefs. She understands."

"Then she truly is intelligent, as Captain James has said."

"Indeed."

"Worthy of your mission," Caffar said.

"On that, we agree," Cezar said. "Where will you go now? You hunted in the wild, saw the threats that hunt you in return. Will you reconsider joining the others in Kellan?"

"Are you still intent on meeting us there?"

"Yes."

"Then that's where we'll go. With Juma now out of the hunt, and the rest of Dominion heading west, we'll heed your advice. We'll bring the Apostates with us, convince them that this city you speak of is real. Does this please you, brother?"

"Nothing in this shattered world could please Cezar more. Cezar will sleep easier knowing you have a destination, a hope for something beyond mere survival."

"Caffar has always taught you that a hunter's life begins and ends with survival, but now..." As difficult as it was for Caffar to abandon his dream of roaming the wild for the rest of his clan's days, their recent defeat, coupled with his brother's inspiring mission, gave him a renewed perspective. "Now you have taught this old wolf that perhaps there is more to life. Surely, there's good hunting to be found in the lands surrounding this Kellan. We'll begin our journey there tomorrow. Caffar swears it."

"You're the Alpha," Cezar said. "No need to swear to Cezar."

"Two Alphas stand here. We both lead our own clans. From now on, we swear to each other."

Cezar relished the words of mutual respect, words he never thought he'd hear from his mentor. "Then Cezar also swears to see you in Kellan."

"Be aware, as an Alpha, your honor binds you to your promise, brother."

"Agreement, as Abraham would say."

From within the shed, Juma smiled upon hearing the two long-feuding brothers reconciling at last, a reunion he'd always wished for, even during times he'd fought against it. He rose from his cot and stepped out of the shed, enjoying the lingering scent of the fragrant rabbit stew.

"Come now, beasts," Caffar said, seeing the tiger on his foot and crutch. "Let's all feast together one last night before we go our separate ways again. There's boar and rabbit and baskets of fish, plenty for all."

As the three hybrid predators headed toward the campfire to join the others, Juma grabbed each of his brothers by a shoulder for a final word.

"This other mech," the tiger-man said. "This Azrael that serves the Purists. Juma's claws meant nothing to its armor. With its many arms, it lifted Juma like a withered flower, tore this body the same way. Juma has never fought such a foe."

"Nor haven't we all," Caffar said, sensing pain in his drifting cadence and tone. "Brother, you don't have to..."

"Please listen." Juma struggled get the words out, a confession that doubled as a warning, one he'd rehearsed in his mind for hours. "For the first time in this tiger's life, Juma felt like the timid, helpless prey we've always pursued. It changed Juma's eyes to the world, as it did Caffar's and Calah's."

Cezar finally understood. He was shocked to hear a quiver in his brother's voice, for the tiger had never feared anyone or anything before. Not only did Juma now know fear, he knew the terror of standing helpless against an unbeatable enemy, a feeling that shook him to his bones. Cezar knew that dread and despair well, particularly whenever Dot was in danger.

"Remember, young Alpha," Juma said, "this metal hell-beast poses a grave threat to you and the girl, even your mighty Abraham, even your unusual friend Vincent."

"Vincent is my blood brother," Cezar said. "His strength, courage, and heart are boundless."

"Of that, we have no doubt," Caffar said.

"He claims he can never die, and Cezar believes him."

"You *want* to believe him," Juma said. "Hunters take the spoils, prey takes the fall, and everything under the sun and moon dies. There is no other end to the hunt. Unless your plant brother is a god, he can die, and Azrael will be the last thing he'll see."

"Cezar will remember. Thank you, brothers."

The tiger and the two wolves joined the others by the fire and enjoyed steaming bowls of rabbit stew, chunks of wild boar, and long filets of trout and bass. They feasted together, drank ancient wine, sang war songs, and regaled each other with stories from the Broken Road as day turned to night, with Abraham's sensors continually sweeping the area.

52

Coffee and Eggs

The following morning, Dot woke up in the one-person tent James The First had provided. With the mesh entry facing the rising sun, she saw the clear silhouette of her dog lying just outside. Gypsy had lain there all night, always her trusty guard. Dot felt the harsh chill of the early morning air and hoped he hadn't endured that cold for hours. She unzipped the mesh and was relieved to see him sleeping on a tarp with a flannel blanket draped over him.

From her tent, she could see the entire camp. The Apostates slept in single-person tents like hers, positioned closer to the now dormant fire. The Dominion predators slept in the shed, rebuilt except for its missing door. Vincent slept on the shed's roof, his unkempt vines dangling down its sides. Abraham stood motionless between the shed and the smoldering fire with only his sensors active.

It took a moment for Dot to locate Cezar, who was perched high in a tree behind the shed, the only other soul awake at such an early hour. She wrapped herself in the long green Purist jacket Eve had given her and stepped outside, careful not to disturb Gypsy. The moment she left her tent, Abraham came to life, turning toward her, his sensors fine-tuned to everyone's movements.

"Abraham," Dot said, her cochlear implant picking up her whispered voice. "Has Cezar been in that tree long?"

"Extrapolation: No one has moved from their current positions since 2300, so one can infer that Cezar has been stationed in the tree for approximately seven hours."

"Can you tell if he slept at all?"

"Conjecture: It is unlikely he slept. His chosen position suggests an observation post."

"Guard duty."

"Correct."

"Cezar can hear you," the wolf said from high atop his Eastern White Pine, 65 feet above the camp. "Cezar's ears are nearly as adept as his nose."

The wolf dropped from his branch, landing on the mossy ground with a soft punch of his long feet. Though he could land from such a great height with ease, Dot still saw fatigue in his eyes.

"You didn't have to watch over the camp," she said. "Abraham's sensors were on, and Gypsy wakes up to the slightest sound."

"Cezar felt it was important for someone to stay awake and alert, no offense to our friends' capabilities."

"You could have taken turns with someone, guard the camp in shifts."

"Cezar proposed that plan, but James The First saw no need. His people installed perimeter alarms and trust them completely."

"If the captain trusts the alarms, then so do I."

"Cezar does not. Any worthy hunter with a keen eye or ear can easily avoid them."

"I'm surprised you consider the Purists worthy hunters," Dot said. "You've never had any respect for the clones before."

"You speak truth, girl. Cezar doesn't believe the Greens and their mindless Automen can see beyond their next footsteps, but there are hunters more clever and devious in the wild. Think of the Gardeners of Beacon Hill. Think of the villagers of Colt you spoke of. They wouldn't simply stomp through here unprepared, without caution."

"Captain James and his soldiers have survived a long time out here. They know what they're doing."

"Tell that to Juma."

KU-KURU-KU-KRUU!

Dot and Gypsy turned toward the startling sound coming from the woods, the loud, raspy crowing of a bird, the first of many to follow.

KU-KURU-KRUK-KRUU!

"Was that... a rooster?" Dot asked, somehow recognizing the call as if she'd heard it every morning in another life.

"Roosters and hens are part of James's perimeter security," Cezar said. "Small camouflaged enclosures every few hundred yards."

KU-KURU-KU-KRUUUUU!

"That's... an interesting system," the girl said.

"Our clan has a battle-hardened German Shepherd and an A1900 combat mech on continuous guard duty. Their clan has chickens. Do you still completely trust the captain's 'alarms'?"

"Well, they are pretty loud," Dot said, unsure, not expecting such a low-tech solution. "I just don't want what happened to Juma to happen to you. If you don't sleep, you won't be much better than a crowing chicken. I can see your droopy eyes and the way your arms hang heavy."

"Cezar promises he will get his rest, girl. Do not worry."

"Okay, good enough for me. Between you, Abraham, and the animals, I suppose we were well covered."

The sheet metal roof of the shed buckled slightly as Vincent stirred awake, coiling in his vines. He sat up and looked around the camp, happy to see three of his friends gathered behind him.

"Good morning!" he said, quickly regretting his loud, animated greeting. He repeated it in a whisper. "Good morning."

"It's alright," James The First said as he emerged from his tent. "The roosters shook us up before you, son." He knelt down and warmed his hands over the glowing embers of the spent fire.

Mort crawled out of his tent with a groan and immediately fed the embers a pile of kindling, fanning it with his loose shirt sleeve. Two minutes and two logs later, the campfire was crackling alive again.

"Dang, you make that look easy!" Vincent said, hopping down from the shed.

"I oughta know how to craft me a fire by now," Mort said, his voice watery and rough. "Been doin' it every sunup for 20-some-odd years."

"And I oughta know how to make a decent breakfast," Hale said as she joined him. "Been flipping hotcakes and eggs after every one of his 20-some-odd years of fires."

Dot, Gypsy, and Cezar returned to the campfire as everyone prepared for the day.

"How's that sound, kiddo?" James asked. "Hotcakes, eggs, chunks of leftover boar chopped up with potatoes and some of your mushrooms?"

"Sounds lovely," Dot said. "But you can have my share of boar."

"You drink coffee?"

"No, sir." Dot realized she knew what coffee was and what it tasted like, even though she had no memory of drinking it. "But I will today, if that's alright."

"Alright? I insist! The day doesn't begin until you get a slug of Hale's burnt sludge in you."

"It gets the job done," Hale said. "It wakes you up, right?"

"That's the one thing it does."

"I used to make coffee for Father," Vincent said as he gazed into the roaring fire. "He liked it sweet with lots of milk."

"No milk or sugar here, son," the captain said. "What we have is strong and black. It'll taste bitter as hell and go down like mud, but it'll get you going, like she said."

"Sometimes we didn't have milk or sugar either. On those days, Father told me to drop an egg in."

"What do you mean?" James asked. "Eggs in your coffee?"

"I likes my eggs up-and-over with buttered toast," Mort said with a snort. "Keep 'em outta my coffee."

"But it's really good!" Vincent said. "I can show you if you like. Father said it made it soft and smooth."

"Lemme guess, the man shut his eyes when he drunk it?" Mort grinned, remembering the plant-man's stories of cooking for his late father.

"He sure did! That's how good I made it!"

"Now this, I gotta see," Hale said. She pulled a small silver bag of ground coffee from the food locker, along with a large steel kettle. "I make the food, you make the brew. You know where we keep the water, Veggie Vinny. Let's see your Father's special egg coffee."

"You actually gonna try this crazy concoction of his?" Mort asked.

"Why not?"

"Vincent is a chef, remember?" Eve said.

Walt The Third, who hadn't spoken more than five words since they all met, simply sat by the fire, amused by the mention of egg coffee. He was surprised that anyone other than himself had even heard of it.

"My mother made something like that when I was little," Walt said. "Cuts down on the acidity. It's an old Swedish tradition going back in her family for generations."

"Swedish?" Mort asked. "What's the hell is that?"

"Don't ask me. I was just a kid."

"Clarification," Abraham said, his clear, synthetic voice startling the soldiers. "Sweden was one of the old nations predating the New World War. It was a country of Nordic origin located in the region formerly known as Eastern Europe."

"Only a damn machine would knows all that," Mort said. "Congratulations, robot, you's officially the brains of our raggedy little outfit."

"Dottie is pretty brainy, too," Vincent said. "She knows a lot about a lot of things! Right, Dottie?"

Dot thought about Sweden and the nation boundaries that existed before billions died of The Worm and the surviving humans formed struggling factions spread out across the continents. Through her scattershot memory, she could almost hear someone teaching her history, world geography, and the ancient traditions of Earth's many peoples.

"Sweden was next to Norway, Finland, and Denmark," the girl said. "Its capital city was Stockholm, with busy ports along the Baltic Sea. At one time, 10 million people lived in Sweden."

The soldiers stared at the girl, not sure what to make of her brief history lesson. They grew up in a world where people fought for their next meal, scrambled to build shelters, and fiercely protected them from outsiders. To them, a population of 500 was considered a rare, large town – a community with a culture – and couldn't imagine millions living together in any semblance of harmony.

"Robot, is the girl makin' up stories?" Mort asked.

"Clarification: Little Miss is correct. Her description is accurate and based in recorded fact."

"Did it just call you 'Little Miss'?" Eve asked.

"The sergeant who imprinted me on Abraham called me that," Dot said. "It was the first thing Abraham heard when he woke up for the first time, and the last thing Sarge said before he died."

"My condolences," Mort said, briefly placing his palm to his heart.

"Sergeant Furst was a good man."

The Apostates looked at each other in grim realization.

They knew that name.

"I've never heard a machine call anyone anything," Grace said, "let alone by a nickname."

"Abraham is my friend," Dot said.

"It certainly looks that way."

"What else can you tell us about Sweden?" Walt said, curious to learn more about his ancestors' heritage. After his family was killed in the crossfire of a battle involving hundreds of troops, and his subsequent upbringing within a Loyalist company, he never thought he'd learn his true origins.

Lynn Harrod

"Let the girl eat, Walt," James said, wanting to avoid depressing discussions of dead relatives and old comrades for now. "We can talk ancient history later. Until then, you can watch Veggie Vinny make your mother's egg coffee."

"You'll never make coffee any other way," Vincent said.

As he filled the kettle with water and placed it over the fire, Caffar, Calah, and Juma had awakened and lumbered out of the shed, Juma already chewing on a slab of raw boar. Vincent cracked an egg into a bowl of ground coffee and stirred it to a black paste. He added the mixture to the water and brought it to a simmer. After ten minutes, the coffee had pulled together, the steeped grounds falling to the bottom of the kettle. Vincent poured it through a clean gas mask filter and served it to the soldiers.

As Walt had described from his childhood memories, the coffee had no bitterness or acidity, pouring a clear, light brown. After decades of harsh black coffee, the Apostates enjoyed the finest cup of their lives.

"Vinny," Mort said. "You made this old man a believer. I thinks I'm gonna add eggs to everything I eats and drinks from now on!"

"It's still strong," Hale said, "but it goes down smooth, real easy."

The predators had no taste for coffee, put off by the intense smell alone. Instead, they drank water mixed with crushed berries as their morning pick-me-up.

Cezar didn't favor the scent either, but he forced himself to swallow a cup, if only to please his friend.

"Cezar doesn't hate it," the wolf said, surprised.

"Thanks, Cezzie," Vincent said.

James The First savored his cup. "Father's Stew last night, Father's Egg Coffee today. The man who raised you had good taste, son."

"Thanks, James The First Soldier Guy," Vincent said.

Hale's breakfast of hotcakes, scrambled eggs, chopped boar, and cubed potatoes proved a hearty meal worthy of the special coffee, and the group enjoyed their time together – swapping war stories and early childhood memories – before packing up camp and returning to the Broken Road to part ways.

53

The Live Oak Trail

The sun sat in the middle of the sky, peering through gathering clouds as Dot and her companions stepped onto the Broken Road once more, now with two of their new friends close behind. James The First and Mort The Third followed on foot. They were hesitant to travel deeper into the East Hills for fear of their infamous and mysterious survivalist clans, but they offered to guide Dot and her companions as they entered that notorious region. They'd emptied several bottles of rum and wine by the time they made that generous offer hours before, beside the late-night fire, but they were men of their word, pie-eyed or not.

Hale The Second and Walt The Fourth stayed behind to pack up camp, folding equipment and cramming supplies into long, narrow motorized all-terrain transports serving as the troop's mechanical pack mules. Eve The Fifth and Grace The Sixth collected the chickens and other "alarms" and traps into a small covered wagon. Its tall, wide wheels provided suitable poultry comfort through the woods for the Apostates rarely used roads.

The central shed – a former office for a loggers' camp that thrived nearly two centuries before – would remain, scarred but sturdy, awaiting other wanderers to discover it. Over the years, it provided shelter for many lost souls and would continue service for as long as its restraightened, reinstalled corrugated steel walls would hold.

Caffar, Calah, and Juma stayed by the campfire, tending its flames. Unlike the humans who covered ground during the day, the predators planned to set out after nightfall. They knew Purist survey equipment was set to detect hybrid life mostly during the day, left behind to recharge during night patrols and raids. Caffar's clan would have better odds of reaching the ridgeline in the dark.

Cezar had shared a final heartfelt goodbye with his brothers, intent on seeing them again one day, hopefully in Kellan, if it actually existed.

As promised, James and Mort escorted Dot's group out of camp, a mile down the road to a break in the trees. A rusty metal sign marked the trailhead of a dirt path, once known as "The Live Oak Trail." After centuries without maintenance, the old hiking trail had become nearly impossible to stumble upon and had to be revealed by an experienced guide. It wound through the woods and around a cluster of boulders, where a well-hidden fork led to a barely discernible choice. The left "tourist trail" was meant for people, recreational day hikers with just a bottle of water and a pair of sandals. The right "service trail" had been reserved for forest rangers, their off-road vehicles, and their pack mules.

"The left trail is steep and technical," Captain James said. "It's a long stone staircase. I suggest you stick to the right trail. It'll take you longer, but the mech will be better able to handle it."

Gypsy ventured down the path to scout for anything that might have escaped Abraham's sensors. After the unexplained ambush by the Regal River, the mech's normally uncanny technology needed to be supported by the good old-fashioned nose of an alert dog.

"This is where we say farewell," James said. "We go any farther, we won't be able to get back fast enough if trouble visits my squad."

"I understand," Dot said.

"You'll be alright, kiddo?"

"I think so."

"Of course she will," Mort said. "She's a sharp one, and with this band of oddball warriors by her side, any roaming squad of Greens or pack of raiders would be fools to engage."

"I don't know if it's because you're little," James said, "or because you're special, but I've come to feel protective of you, just as your friends have. Maybe it's because I just like you, kiddo."

"You're our friend, James," Dot said. "You're one of the few friendly folks we've met out here, and we've met all kinds."

"We ain't good folks," Mort said with a grunt. "We've killed more enemies than made allies, but we knows good from bad, and you ain't half bad, not to me none, anyways." The gruff heavy gunner shrugged off his budding emotion. "But what does an old roughneck like me know?"

"You're both very sweet, even you, Mort, in your own way."

"Don't go tellin' nobody." Mort laughed as he turned away to hide his concern.

The Apostates not only scavenged gear during their travels, but intel as well, and though they didn't share their awareness with her, they knew about the Exceptional Girl who was sought by both the Loyalists and Purists. From an active communications console they took from a Purist squad, they learned all about Dot's misadventures. The six deserters had been secretly following her journey through radio communications, unsure if she was hunted as an enemy of the collective state or as a potential asset. Since meeting Dot, James The First came to care for her like a long-lost niece, but didn't want his crew involved any further for fear of another conflict like the one that claimed the lives of four of his soldiers and Juma's leg. He told himself that the girl's odd entourage would be more than enough to safeguard her from any attack. Still, as he prepared to leave her, he felt some doubt, even as he looked up at the 12-foot combat mech beside her, the powerful wolf hybrid in front of her, and the strong plant thing straggling behind.

"I feel I owe you an apology," James said, much to Mort's dismay. "My squad and I... we know all about you, kiddo. We know the Blues and the Greens are squabbling over you."

"They're doing a lot more than squabbling," Vincent said.

"I figured you knew," Dot said, to James's shock.

"And what made you figure that?" the captain said.

"You're too smart not to know, or at least figure out."

"Your instincts are as sharp as your intellect, kiddo." James looked behind him, at the cracked pavement that led back to his camp, and succumbed to a change of heart. "Maybe... maybe I could spare a couple of... you know... maybe Hale and Grace could join you..."

"Like you said, captain, I have my warriors. I'll be okay."

"If it's any consolation, the patrols never go up this far, never near The Department."

"The Department?"

"That's where this path will take you," James said. "I assume that's where you're heading. We listen in on military com lines to stay a step ahead of our old allegiances, and we've been tracking you. We've kept tabs on you from Wellspring to the North Woods to the South Lands and finally here, in the East Hills. It's where you and your friends all began."

"If you were tracking us, why were you so mistrusting when we met?"

"If you knew about me and my jokers before yesterday, would you have blindly trusted that we meant no harm?"

"What my ramblin' captain means," Mort said, "is that showing kindness to others has ended up burnin' us more times than it didn't. We don't trust nobody right off, not even lost little girls. Besides, how was we to know you somehow tamed a damn war machine?"

"Fair enough, gentlemen," Dot said. "What can you tell us about this 'Department'?"

"Just rumors and legend," James said. "Some say it's where the downfall of humanity began. Others say it's where it'll all end, and where our world will be reborn, if you believe such nonsense."

"How poetical and profounds of you, captain," Mort said. "In other words, girl, we ain't got no clue, but there ain't nothing else up heres."

"How far does the trail go?" Dot asked.

"Six, seven hours."

"Reconnaissance: Much of the trail ahead has been destroyed by the elements."

"Of course it has," Cezar said to the mech. "Every step of our journey has been challenging. Cezar never expected that to change."

"It's actually better that the trail's botched," Mort said. "Makes it harder for the Greens to follows you."

"Recommendation: We must depart soon in order to reach our destination before sunset."

"Not soon, we must leave now," Cezar said. "Captain James, Third Officer Mort, we thank you for your assistance, but if Abraham says we must go..."

"Say no more," James The First said, hesitant to leave the girl. "Maybe we'll see you again. Maybe in... Kellan?"

"That's right," Dot said. "We will. I know we will." Her feigned confidence doubled as encouragement for the soldiers to seek the mythical city, to end their years of wandering the wild while still keeping one eye behind them.

With simple nods to the group, James and Mort headed back down the Broken Road while Dot and her companions started their day-long trek up the obscured, winding trail.

54

D.O.T.

Even though it was the easier of Live Oak's two paths, the decimated, narrow service trail proved barely wide enough to accommodate Abraham. At several points, Cezar and Vincent had to clear brush and boulders to allow their metal friend passage. After almost seven hours, his sensors finally picked up a large compound ahead, a building the size of Dominion sitting in the middle of the property.

"It's just like the rainforest!" Vincent said. He wondered if it was indeed another man-made habitat, a vast, sealed, self-contained ecosystem with a robust hybrid community waiting to be released.

"Dominion was a one-of-a-kind experiment," Cezar said. "This place is likely a post-war fortress." The wolf assumed it was a town fortified by walls, for he'd heard many human cities had followed that extreme strategy in the wake of the New World War, most in vain. "We'll likely find it has become a mass tomb."

"Speculation: The design of the structure comprises GARD architecture."

"Guard?" Dot asked her mech.

"Clarification: GARD is an acronym for the Global Allied Races Delegation, an active department of the world government whose duties originally included the construct of science advancement programs. The angular, Brutalist design suggests this compound is a government facility, a compound of combined biological research and development."

"It may have been commissioned and run by the human overlords in the beginning," Cezar said, "but much can change in two-hundred years."

Dot tried not to form any theories. She only knew – and somehow felt – that the twin Star Girls from The Void were inside, waiting to be rescued. She hoped the dangers the Dark Girl warned her about were behind them, as they had encountered no hostile townships or encampments during their long hike up the trail.

She also hoped to find George along the way. Her dreams hadn't reunited them in The Void for several nights, so she pictured him tracking her during their long journey, just as the Apostates had, pinpointing her whereabouts through overheard communications prior to reaching The Department. As Mort said, there was nothing else of note in the East Hills, nothing aside from rumored pocket communities of savage survivalists, none of which they'd yet seen. She imagined the boy camped out beyond each bend in the trail, his bow and arrows resting beside an inviting fire, just like their night together in the old Wellspring library. She thought of his friendly, handsome smile, his hair dangling in his face, and she imagined running into his open arms.

Such striking affection for the boy took Dot by surprise, and she realized her unique feelings for each of her companions. She regarded her eclectic friends like uncles in a most unusual family.

Vincent was the silly, playful, naive uncle who saw the world anew through his young niece's eyes. Cezar was like the weary, tormented uncle, filled with regret and self-loathing, who didn't want his little one to suffer from his life's missteps. Abraham was the all-business uncle, focused on duty, dedicated by the book to the success of the girl's mission. Even Gypsy played a familial role, as she regarded the German Shepherd like a little brother who felt obliged to protect her.

George felt different in comparison. Perhaps it was because of their time apart, but she viewed him with a heightened affection. She wanted only to be near him, to ensure his safety and happiness, and she hoped he saw her the same way.

The sun's waning amber light passed through the treeline when they finally reached an open area, a pasture bisected by the trail, ending at the large building surrounded by chain-link fencing. The first sight of the gleaming structure and its industrial perimeter brought her plant friend's prediction to mind, a habitat filled with hybrid tribes, but another minute of taking in the sprawling compound brought lost memories to the surface. Dot felt a sudden, alarming urge to flee, and wondered if they made the right choice of abiding the Light Girl's pleas for help rather than heed the persistent warnings of the Dark Girl.

"Abraham," Dot said. "What is this place?"

"Unknown."

"But you said it was probably a research facility."

"Clarification: There is insufficient data to fully support any conclusion to this mission. The facility may have been abandoned and repurposed. As Cezar expressed perfectly, Little Miss, much can change in two-hundred years."

"Can you at least tell us what's inside?"

"Unknown. The building's walls include composite materials similar to the Dominion Research Vivarium."

"That means danger," Vincent said, nervous. "Whatever it is, if Abe doesn't know about this place, it can't be good."

"That's not necessarily true," Cezar said. "The mech's disconnect with his network blinds him to much of the world. Once he reestablishes his connection..."

"There is no network," Dot said, "not anymore."

"How do you know?" Vincent asked. "I mean, we kinda figured, right? But we really don't know for sure..."

"He would have reconnected by now." The girl pieced together her logic as she spoke. "Sergeant Furst said he's the last Abraham mech in the world. When his men found him, he'd never been activated, abandoned in long-term storage. It stands to reason that his support network would be offline."

"Offline? What's that mean?"

"Dead like most of the old world," Cezar said, realizing with dread that Dot was right. "Cezar agrees with the girl. Abraham is partially blind, which means we all are. It's even more reason to withhold fear or hope about this place until we know it with certainty. The hunt continues."

"Abe calls it a mission," Vincent said. "Cezzie calls it a hunt. Which is it?"

"Both," Dot said. "Our mission is to hunt for the truth."

"As always, the girl speaks for us all," Cezar said.

"Dang, I'm not for sure," Vincent said. "Father always said a locked box hides treasures."

"It just as often holds terrors," Cezar said. "Either way, we must push on."

Dot saw her friends looking to her for a decision. It was her quest they followed, and it was her words they hung upon.

"You could all be right," Dot said. "A town, a fort, a lab, or maybe all of those put together. Terrors, treasures, or both. It's risky, but I agree with Cezar. Whatever waits inside, we have to keep going." Dot felt scared and knew she was trying to convince herself as much as her friends that their long journey mustn't be for naught. "We won't know until we know."

"That makes sense," Vincent said. "I usually don't know something until I know it."

"Cezar understands if there is trepidation," the wolf-man said to his friends. "Cezar also believes if we've come this far, it would forever haunt us not to see this trail to its end."

"I'm glad we agree." Dot looked to the sky, at the sun setting behind the intimidating building ahead. "Should we enter the property now or wait until morning? Pick up anything, Abraham?"

"Reconnaissance: No humanoid hostiles are detected within a 10-kilometer radius. No humans, artificials, or mechanicals are within my sensory range."

"But you still can't see inside that building?"

"Correct."

"Cezar says we enter now," the wolf hybrid said, ignoring his growing fear. "Caffar says there's never a better place and time to hunt than here and now."

"I say we go in now, too," Vincent said, enthusiastic yet unsure. He turned to the mech. "What do you say, Abe? Right now or when the sun wakes up?"

"Projection: The chance of danger will not decrease by the coming morning. It can only increase. Hostile forces continue at all hours. Automen need no rest."

Dot wanted her friends to relieve her of the burden of command, but knew they'd follow her lead whichever way she leaned. "We go in now," she said, the words like sharp rocks tumbling from her throat.

The group crossed the pasture and faced an ancient sign hung on the chain-link fence. Its tall, red words startled Dot as she read them.

DEPARTMENT OF TRANSMUTATION.

The girl recognized the typeface. She pulled up her left sleeve and stared at the tattoo atop her hand...

D.O.T.

She thought back to James The First, his parting remark about the trail leading to the place where they all came from.

"Transmutta... transamutata..." Vincent said, confused.

"Transmutation," Dot said.

"Well, whatever that is, this place is the department of it."

"Definition: Transmutation is the action of changing, or the state of being changed, into another form, such as the changing of one element into another by radioactive decay, nuclear bombardment, or other similar physiochemical processes. It is also the conversion or transformation of one species into another..."

"Hybrids," Cezar said with a lump in his throat. "The World Union Government made hybrids here."

"It's where you and your friends all began," Dot said, repeating the Apostate captain's cryptic words.

"But I thought that's what Dominion was for?" Vincent said.

"Dr. Blum said we were all brought to the rainforest as pups, cubs, and calves," Cezar said. "But we began elsewhere in test tubes and petri dishes. This must be that place.

"So, if Dominion was a garden, this Department place made its seeds."

The D.O.T. sign included a lightning bolt symbol, denoting an electrified fence, just like Dominion's. Before Dot could ponder the ominous warning, Cezar leapt high into the air and landed on the other side of the barrier. He entered a security booth and switched off the power, leaving the inactive, locked fence to Abraham.

The combat mech clutched the fence's padlock with two fingers, plucked it off like a flower pedal, and slid the gate aside.

"Good work, guys!" Vincent said. "You made that look easy!"

"Better that the mech opened the fence than the plant," Cezar said. "Vincent would have ripped apart a tangled mess of metal to crawl through."

"So true," Vincent said, nodding. "I've never been very neat."

"There's no turning back," Dot said. "Even though we didn't destroy the gate this time, if someone is still in there, they probably know we're here now."

"Then let us meet them," Cezar said, forcing his courage. "Let us establish who are the hunters and who are the prey."

55

The Impossible Man

Dot's group opened the building's two-story double doors built into a massive five-story front glass wall. It stood as a grand entrance large enough for the mech to navigate through, intimidating enough to make most think twice before venturing forth. As always, Gypsy led the way, scouting the premises for anyone and anything. He picked up a familiar scent, one that eluded even Cezar. Dot couldn't have known, but the scent that her dog detected was her own, and it kept him from offering any warning.

Within the reinforced walls, Abraham's sensors were no longer blocked. "Reconnaissance: There are four humanoids in this facility, all identified as biologically human."

"Four folks in this great big place?" Vincent asked. "That's all, Abe?"

"Correct."

"Dang, that's an awful lot of space for just four humans."

"This building was made to accommodate hundreds," Cezar said. "Perhaps thousands."

"Clarification: This single structure has a maximum capacity of 1,688 people. The compound's outlying support structures increase total capacity by an additional 49."

"That means there used to be..." Vincent said, counting on his hands. "There were... eight plus nine... carry the two... I mean the one... Cezzie, hold up your fingers..."

"1,737 people," Cezar said. "That's how many souls this place was made for."

"Dang, that's almost two thousand! Just like you said!"

"Yet, there are only four left. Curious."

"There could be rooms that block Abraham's sensors," Dot said.

"Negative," Abraham said. "The perimeter walls comprise a sensor-diffusing alloy of iron, lead, and polymer, but all internal walls are made of untreated wood and steel, susceptible to conventional scans."

"That means the walls inside are normal and Abe can see through 'em," Vincent said to Cezar, as if the highly intelligent wolf needed a layperson's explanation. "The big guy knows the place real good now."

"Correct. This unit has composited a complete cognitive map of the premises."

"If there truly are only four souls remaining," the wolf said, "that speaks only death to Cezar."

"Everything's always death to you, Cezzie," Vincent said.

"And your 'Cezzie' is always right."

"Maybe," Dot said. "Maybe not. We're about to find out." Though the girl tried to remain open to any scenario, she couldn't help but agree with the predator yet again. He'd proven to be the wisest of her companions. If his animal instincts gave him a bad feeling, it was worth noting.

Stepping into the structure, the group was greeted by a startling sight. A giant bronze statue of a man stood 50 feet tall with one arm outstretched to the emerging stars as seen through the atrium's five-story glass wall. It presented the open sky to the world like a gift, a gesture Dot knew to be an optimistic view of the future. The golden glow of the sunset reflected off the statue but faded quickly. With no lights on, the massive room would soon be enshrouded in darkness.

"Now this is a big guy," Vincent said in awe. "Shiny, too."

"Does this statue honor a saint or a tyrant?" Cezar asked.

"I'm sure we'll find out soon," Dot said, "but we can't stand and wonder. We're losing light. We need to explore this place fast."

"This time, Dottie, let's stick together," Vincent said.

"Agreed." She held her friend's hand, his long, leafy fingers wrapping around hers. "First, let's figure out how to turn the lights on..."

Upon saying "lights on," the building's automated system recognized her voice, triggering internal lights that flooded the massive space. Banks of ceiling lamps exposed abundant plant life, gleaming marble floors, and long hallways branching in all directions. It all seemed overwhelming until Dot spotted a familiar blue door, barely five feet tall, in the distance behind the statue.

"There." She pointed to the small door. "That's where we start."

"Where you start, or where you end?" a male voice asked. "But does that matter in a circle?"

Dot and her friends turned to a small old man sitting alone on a bench in front of a lush flower bed. The man wore a white lab coat similar to Dr. Blum's, nearly camouflaging him against a row of oversized magnolias, and stared at the girl with a curious smile cracking across his deeply weathered face. He sat cross-legged, almost elegant, as he fed crackers to squirrels, puffed a cigar, and glanced at his wristwatch.

"Professor?" Dot said, not sure why she called him that.

"My girl, I expected you sooner," the old man said through his cloud of cigar smoke. "I'm glad to see you, though I had hoped to be wrong, to never see you again." He held out an open palm to Gypsy. To Dot's surprise, the dog came to him for a warm rub under his collar. "I'm also glad to see this special dog again."

"You know him?" Dot asked, incredulous.

"Man's best friend? How could I not?"

Though the giant statue depicted a proud young man, Dot somehow knew it stood as a tribute to the mysterious elder before them. Forgoing caution and trusting her dog's instincts, she walked up to him and studied his face, every line and blemish, carved and spattered by time. His decrepit features were comforting, as if she'd seen each wrinkle, each cluster of gray hairs and liver spots, many times before. Indeed, she had, as she would soon come to discover.

Unlike the other elderly humans she'd encountered, whose faces belied their true ages due to the straining effects of The Worm, this man seemed genuinely quite old.

"If you don't mind," Dot said, unsure of her own question, "may I ask how old you are?"

"Now, that's an odd way to reintroduce yourself."

"Reintroduce?"

"Reintroduce, reacquaint, restart, reenter one's life."

"Please, your age, I must know," the girl said.

"I find it curious that you ask for my age before my name."

"So do I, now that you point it out."

"Why don't you ask your marvelous mechanical companion?" the old man said. "There's certainly no fooling him."

"Abraham, can you tell me this man's age?"

"Yes, robot, tell us. How old am I? You're an A1900, am I right?"

"Correct," Abraham said.

"Outstanding! Your model was always my favorite. There's nothing like a good old Abraham-class mech. Instead of following a single primary directive, you've been gifted with three: combat, rescue, and recovery. That means you're not just a mindless walking death machine, like most of your kind. You have your massive weapons, to be sure, but you're also equipped with a full sensor array, communications complement, medical diagnostic suite, and scientific survey toolset, all of which is governed by a big, beefy organic-synthetic positronic logic processor... also known as a genuine brain."

"Correct," Abraham said. "Gratitude."

"This Abraham feels gratitude?" the old man said with a smile. "How extraordinary! Even I have never seen a humbled combat mech before, one who recognizes and appreciates a compliment. Your qualitative data processor must have been working overtime!"

"Assessment: You have expert knowledge about this unit's model, construction, purpose, and capabilities."

"Oh, yes, this old goat knows a few things. For example, I imagine the girl has imprinted on you."

"Correct."

"Then proceed, my metal friend, and perform a deep scan on me. Tissue samples, blood make-up, organ health, the whole works."

"Do as he says, Abraham," Cezar said. "Examine this man with every tool, from every angle."

"We must be thorough!" The old man laughed and puffed his cigar.

The mech leaned in close and scanned the mysterious old man with several slow passes of his sensors.

"Analysis: Based on ossification scans of his joints and bone structure, chemical composition and blood viscosity, isotonic saline content, albumin protein, and physiological scans of his heart, lungs, kidneys, liver, and brain, I estimate his age to be approximately 145 years."

"Impressive." The old man smiled through his cigar smoke. "And pretty damn close. The correct answer is 148."

"That's... impossible," Dot said under her breath.

"Surely, you're mistaken, Abraham," Cezar said to the mech. In awe, the wolf-man approached the old professor and scrutinized his face and body, catching his unique scent. It drew like a myriad of many, one that was masked by the magnolias moments before, and could be tied to no other creature he'd ever seen.

"Reanalysis," Abraham said. "Assessment confirmed."

"That would make him the oldest human in history, before or after the pandemic."

"Dang, some hybrids don't even make it that long!" Vincent said, remembering his many fallen peers.

"Maybe he's a hybrid who passes for human," Dot said to her mech. "Like the Widows."

"Clarification: Each of my analyses has been contrasted and cross-indexed for a nearly infallible conclusion. My estimate stands with a three-year margin of error. This man is biologically human, and his proclaimed age of 148 years appears to be correct."

Dot and her friends looked at each other in astonishment. Even if the world hadn't been ravaged by a sinister pathogen that reduced life spans between a few months to a few decades, a sprightly old man could never live to such an advanced age, let alone thrive.

"We love 'impossible' here," the old man said as he stood, amused by their shock. Nothing in his posture, gait, or voice supported the notion that he was a nearly sesquicentennial being. "Impossible is our specialty, my girl. Your unique blood runs through my veins, after all."

"So, the Elders of Beacon Hill were right," Dot said. "If they had drank my blood, it would have counteracted the virus."

"And then some!" Vincent said. "This old guy's more full of life than Father ever was!"

"Such kind words," the old man said. "But no, my girl, ingesting a swallow of your special blood would have done nothing for them. Those desperate fools in their meandering underground tomb would need to be injected with it regularly over many decades for there to be any effect. Even then, there would have been a high probability of rejection. You can rest easy, for you were never the savior they sought."

"Still, what a strange thing," Dot said to her mech. "My blood not only cured him, but prolonged his life."

"Agreement: That is also my conclusion, Little Miss."

"Little Miss?" the old man said, amused, amazed. "My girl, you truly are special, to have a war machine, even an A1900, warmly regard you like a kid sister. I've never seen that before, and believe me, I've seen everything."

"Abraham is my friend," Dot said.

"I can see that." The old man stood and walked up to the tall mech. "You've not only imprinted on him but imparted him with human traits. You've tapped into the organic half of his wondrous mind. It's simply astonishing. I'm not sure how you accomplished it, but if anyone could achieve that small miracle, it would be you."

"Professor, I apologize for what I'm about to ask you," Dot said, "because I feel as though I should know you, that I should know this place, but I must ask... who are you?"

"I'm your creator," the old man said. "I created you all, really. My work at Dominion served as the catalyst for the advanced animal-human hybrid campaign. My research in transmutation also spawned the famously failed plant hybrid program, no offense to your verdant friend."

"None taken," Vincent said. "Thanks for making me... me!"

The old man made a clicking sound with his tongue in cheek, summoning Gypsy again to his side. The normally vigilant dog took to him so easily that Dot could only assume he was also familiar with the man.

"Finally, my concerns and my notes led the Loyalists to search for the last of the old combat mechs. Thus, your metal titan was sought, located, and brought to life. You're welcome."

"On behalf of Abraham," Dot said, "I'll thank you for that."

"It's good to have you back home, Cordelia."

Cordelia?

The old man saw the confusion on the girl's face. "Now, this is most unexpected. The Blessing you received seems to have erased your sense of identity. I wonder what other pieces of your life you've lost."

"I've lost a lot, Professor... Creator... what should I call you?"

"Most call me 'Professor'," the old man said with a puff of his cigar, "for I designed and curated much of the research we've all pursued, training my peers into mastering it. Others call me 'Founder,' for I led the original team behind this sanctuary. Still others call me 'Creator' after I began repopulating the world with my hybrid children, though I've always hated that biblical title. To my colleagues and everyone else, my name is Doctor Domingo Imago. But you, Cordelia, you simply called me 'Father.'"

"Father!" Vincent said. "See, Dottie, you have a father, too!"

"I called you Father?" Dot asked.

"You did indeed," Professor Imago said. "I created you and every non-human you've crossed paths with. I helped give birth to them, though I credit science and the world for their evolution and survival. But you are singularly different, my girl, for unlike the others, I personally raised you within these walls. I tutored you on the history of this world and taught you fundamentals, ideals like right versus wrong, honor contrasted with disgrace, self-preservation balanced with the greater good of all."

Dot thought back to all the moments of uncovered memories, discoveries of forgotten skills, realizations of lost knowledge. Professor Imago – "Father" – was behind them all. His face and voice cast her mind aglow and blew away much of its haze.

"Did the Blessing rob you of your lovely piano concertos?" Imago asked.

"I remember everything you taught me," Dot said, slowly piecing together remnants of her life. "History, culture, art, music, it all stuck. Seeing you here now, I also remember every day of school, and I remember... not being alone."

"You were my best and brightest student, Cordelia. There's no question about that. And you're right, you were never alone in my classroom. I think it's time we walked through that blue door you've no doubt had your heart set on. Gypsy can come with us, though I suggest your three tall friends wait out here while we go in, back to the beginning. Shall we?"

Doctor Domingo Imago held out his palm. To Vincent's curiosity and Cezar's unease, Dot took his hand in hers and together they entered the inner sanctum of the facility, the German Shepherd between them.

"Cezar doesn't like this," the wolf hybrid said under his breath. "Cezar is uncomfortable being apart from the girl."

"Vincent is, too," Vincent said, unknowingly mimicking his friend. "But Dottie respected me when I met my maker again, when I got my memory puzzle-pieced back together, so now I gotta respect hers."

"Agreed," the wolf said. "Out of respect, Cezar will grant her time with her creator, even as my every instinct itches my claws."

Professor Imago guided Dot and Gypsy into a small, round, dim laboratory, its ceiling not much higher than the five-foot door. She could see why he didn't invite her friends. The room's low clearance would have made them uncomfortable, assuming they could even stand upright. Like the atrium before it when they first arrived, the lab was lit only by the golden hue of the sunset beaming in through skylights, just enough light to cast a faint aura atop equipment mounted to the counters and walls.

"Can we turn more lights on?" she asked. As before, the security system recognized the girl's "lights on" and turned up a few of the lab's ceiling lamps at her inadvertent vocal command, slowly revealing a young man slighter taller than Dot. He stood near the equipment and turned upon hearing her voice.

"George?" Dot said in disbelief. "How did you find me?"

"I never lost you."

56

The Source

George Brook winked and grinned at Dot, a gesture he'd been holding on to for over a week, along with his cheesy response to her expected question. The 17-year-old boy still wore his ranger outfit of leather and denim, but hadn't been readily recognized without his many weapons hanging off his belt and shoulder straps. Instead, his bow and arrow, quiver, hunting knife, and pistol rested within their respective outlines on a set of hooks on the wall, as if the space had been tailored for them.

Dot wanted to hug the older boy and spin around in place until they were both dizzy. Instead, she kept her composure and simply walked up to him, placing her hands in his.

"I'm so glad you're okay," Dot said. "No trouble?"

"I got in a few scrapes that almost ended badly."

"Same here. Seriously, how'd you find me? I thought we lost you just before we reached Beacon Hill."

"You did," George said, "but just for a little while. Once I tracked you to the Widows, I returned here to stock up on supplies before coming back for you, but you came to me instead."

"You returned... here?" Dot asked, not sure if it was she or George who was confused.

"Throughout my years in the wild, I've returned here many times. It's become more of a home to me than my old hunting village ever was."

"I don't understand."

"Dot, I have something to confess..."

"Please, just tell me," Dot said. She didn't care if he had a well of secrets. She only hoped that whatever he had to reveal wasn't heartbreaking.

"I returned here because... I mean... what I mean to say is..."

"George works for me," Professor Imago said, letting his colleague off the hook. "He's my assistant, has been for years. He's been my eyes and ears and muscle out in the wild. I suppose that means he works for you as well, my girl."

"Assistant?" Upon hearing that cold title, Dot let her hands slip out of George's. "You work for my father?"

George saw the girl's eyes widen in confusion, heard embarrassment tinged with hurt in her voice. He didn't answer her at first, could barely look at her, but a gentle nod from the old man pushed him forward.

"It was no accident that we met in Wellspring," George said with nervous hesitation. He feared his secret would taint their bond, a relationship he came to treasure as he explored the lonely, desperate world. "I tracked you to the..."

"What... what do you mean?" Dot asked, her trust in the boy teetering on the edge. "Start over, before Wellspring."

"You mean, before we met again?"

"Again?"

George stood flustered, overwhelmed, and afraid. He turned to the old man for help. "I can't. I won't! I mean, I made a promise to you, Professor..."

"It's fine, my boy," Professor Imago said, placing his hand on the ranger's shoulder. "I understand your hesitation, but her mind is becoming clear. I think she's ready. Even if she's not, the time has come." He rubbed his pointy chin and studied their helpless expressions. "Before you met George for the second time? Hmm, if we're going back that far, my girl, perhaps I should explain on his behalf."

As told by the professor, George Brook started out as a devout and dedicated ranger from Colt, an honorable young man of great promise. After his parents succumbed to The Worm, he lived under the mentorship of Senior Wainright back when he, too, was an honorable man. During one particularly harsh winter, Wainright prayed to his serpent lord for guidance, and a vibrant dream led him to believe that the animals around the village – animals infected with the fatal global pathogen – were divinely cleansed and chosen to nourish them. Despite the vision, Wainright had his cooks circumvent the telltale jagged veins, spread out like red-and-blue lightning bolts, but neither careful butchering nor longer roasting times entirely eliminated the virus.

After years of eating tainted game, exposing himself and his followers to gradual, mild doses of The Worm, the village elder's mind slipped into crusading madness. Wainright's increased devotion to his religion – which doubled as a shield against the scary, wild world beyond his village walls – led to a superiority

Lynn Harrod

complex that stoked contempt, blame, and hate. His was an angry, judgmental, discriminant god, and so he would be such a leader.

Wainright leaned into his innate bigotry and started enslaving and trading his hybrid townsfolk with the Purists like livestock. The first to go were the gorilla-man Amos and the dog-man Esau, two respected former woodsman rangers who taught young George how to tap into his animal instincts to track and hunt. When they were ripped from the village, the boy felt like a piece of his heart had been stolen as well. Not once believing the elder's furious sermons about abominations polluting humanity, a disenfranchised George soon lost his faith and left the sheltered community he'd always considered his home.

With great courage and defiance, the young ranger freed several hybrids the night he fled Colt, though none of them met him at their agreed-upon rendezvous upon the coming dawn. Senior Wainright had instructed his hunters to ignore the rebellious teen's attempt at distraction and instead focus their efforts on recapturing and breaking the hybrids for the latest Purist troop on route. Those heartless orders and the chaos that followed allowed George time to distance himself from his suffocating hometown, eluding both the villagers and the interloping Greens.

George wandered the Broken Road, lost and alone, searching for the mythical city he'd heard about in childhood stories, a place many hoped existed but most doubted.

Killian. Kelton. Kaltown. Kellan. Kindman.

Everyone had a different name for it.

The boy spent years searching the North Woods, venturing up the central rocky cliffs and down into the East Hills, surviving day-by-day, often by the skin of his teeth. He had several close conflicts with night raiders and clone soldiers, always outnumbered but never outclassed. He even spent time with both the wise Widows and bitter turncoats of Beacon Hill. George made temporary friends and permanent foes up to the day he discovered the Department of Transmutation, an unexpected, active, hidden facility far above the Victory Garden and the winding Regal River.

Professor Imago welcomed the young man and took him under his wing, tutoring him in the ways of the world. He detailed the social and scientific motivations of his greater purpose, and the woodsman ranger soon came to admire the professor. He quickly made the old man's mission his own, and in doing so, George got to know his three prized daughters.

"Three daughters?" Dot said.

"He's getting there," George said with an awkward laugh. "The old man takes his time."

"A wise old man is only slow to an impatient young boy," Imago said with smiling eyes.

After a year in his care and tutelage, Professor Imago confided in George and revealed his secret lab, the very one Dot stood in that moment. Imago asked for the young ranger's help in safeguarding his special girls from forces seeking to plunder or destroy them. Of the three daughters, George had formed a bond with the eldest of them.

"We've been close for years," George said. "You tried to teach me to read, to speak different languages. You even tried to teach me how to play the trombone and the euphonium."

"So you did know those were musical instruments hung on the wall!" Dot said, thinking back to their night in the old Wellspring library. "You acted like you had no idea what they were, but all along, you were a musician."

"I said you tried to teach me. You were a good teacher, Dot, but I was a poor student. I was just happy we spent every hour of every day together."

"Your bow and blade have always been your instruments," Imago said. "You're a man of action, George. Not everyone is meant to be an artist or scholar."

"Certainly not me."

When the time came for Dot to leave home, Professor Imago tasked George with trailing her from a distance, a secret back-up plan for the well-intentioned Loyalist troop escorting her across the wild. The journey proceeded without incident for over a week, until the fateful day of the skirmish near the bridge to Kellan, one of the rare times George's eyes weren't trained on the military convoy. He'd been away, gathering supplies in nearby Wellspring, and only learned of the troop's tragic end and Dot's memory loss when he found her wandering the old supermarket in town.

"I still don't understand," Dot asked, once again taking him by the hand. "Why pretend we never met? If we were so close, why not tell me?"

"Don't persecute him," Professor Imago said. "He was just following orders, like a good ranger. A good boy."

George felt pangs of guilt. "Please forgive me, Dot. Father made me swear to..."

"Father?" Dot said.

"I sometimes call him Father. Everyone calls him Father."

"Apparently so."

"He told me if you were ever Blessed," George said, uneasy, "that I shouldn't interfere because it might... it might break you."

"What does he mean?" Dot asked the old man. "How would the truth 'break' me?"

"Think of the Blessing as controlled, chemically induced brain damage," Imago said. "If George had blurted out his intimate history with you, it would risk damaging your scattered mind even further. Regaining one's memories is a gradual process. It must be. Otherwise, he might have permanently fractured your identity, impaired your intellect, and we'd have lost you forever."

"It was hard for me to pretend to be just another stranger on the road," George said, "but I always knew we'd find each other again. I thought you might have remembered who I was when you pulled me into your dreams, but even there, I had to be careful."

Dot looked around the dark lab, at the man who she'd just learned was her father and the boy she just realized was her best friend.

"Do you forgive me, Dot?" George asked, afraid of her response. "I wouldn't blame you if you didn't."

"Of course, I forgive you," Dot said without hesitation. "Friend or stranger, you always looked out for me, fought to protect me. How could I curse that? I thought perhaps we had a connection. How little I knew how right I was."

George hugged her, whispering, "I'm sorry" as he held her tight.

"I forgive you both, and I understand. I feel like my mind's been roaming the darkness, and you've only just turned on the lights."

Her analogy served as yet another indirect vocal command. The building's security system once again recognized "lights" in her voice and slowly brought up the lab's overhead lamps' brightness, revealing the rest of the room and the grand secret that long eluded her.

The lab's back wall housed three tall, glass water tanks, two of which held the slender bodies of adolescent girls in flowing gowns.

Their sleeping faces resembled Dot's.

Triplets.

Though she'd just been told she was but one of three, she questioned her sanity not only from seeing herself in those macabre tanks but from the fact that the laboratory now felt like a miniature of The Void, with the five lit humans surrounded by shadows.

"I'm a clone," Dot said in a gasp, the realization landing like a bomb. "I'm just like the Automen."

"No, my girl," Imago said, grabbing her shoulders. "You three are natural, organic, human. The Automen are synthetic, artificial."

"How many of... me... are there?" she asked.

"There's only one of you, Dot," George said. "Always remember that."

"I can more thoroughly answer your question," Imago said. "During the later chapter of my life, what I call my 'Final Act,' I created 23 boys and 23 girls."

"And our mother?" Dot asked.

"That's... that's another story for another day," the old man said. "Just know that of the 46 children I created, only you three stayed home with me. The rest moved on to the next life."

"You mean they died."

The Professor winced at her blunt summary.

"I like to think they briefly lived so that you might flourish. I loved and learned from each of them before they departed, most as infants, toddlers, some approaching adolescence. Their bodies are buried in the gardens around the property. They helped plant those flowers, and oh, how they loved them."

Dot looked to her left, to a six-foot water tank containing the "Dark Girl." Clothed in black, her unconscious body floated within a clear, viscous fluid. The pointed "witch's hat" she wore was actually a cerebral sensor bank and breathing mask attached to a thick cable. The "distant star" behind her was actually a simple 250-watt bulb mounted flush with the glass, doubling as both a light and heat source.

"I know these girls," Dot said as her mind raced, replaying every moment in the dark expanse. More of the fog was lifting. "I know them, just as I know you both. I've seen them in my dreams."

"You didn't just see them, my girl," Imago said. "You were actually with them, and George, it seems, coexisting on a shared metaphysical plane."

"But... how is that possible?"

"It's simple, really, not unlike networking computers. You three children were genetically engineered with chemical transponders that linked your temporal lobes, specifically your hippocampi, merging your abstract thoughts across vast distances during REM sleep while still retaining your individual..." The old man cut himself off when he noticed his daughter's distracted, astonished gaze at the water tanks. "But enough of this technical babble. I imagine your questions aren't about the science but the people."

The Professor was right. Dot had big-picture questions for now, but still felt her memory partially blocked. She itched for the one detail that would bring it all flooding back, as if a single cork kept a great leaking dam from collapse. Everything around her looked familiar while still feeling like heavy discoveries yet to be uncovered.

"Who are they?" Dot asked, looking up at the twin's dormant faces behind glass. "My two fellow survivors."

"This is Goneril," Imago said, turning to the Dark Girl. "Rebellious, always questioning my decisions. Perhaps you remember your horseplay with her, the affectionate taunts and competitive nature of your days together. The discord you shared helped shape your ethics."

"In The Void... our shared dream... she always urged me to flee. She wasn't exactly friendly about it."

"That sounds like Goneril alright," George said.

Dot walked up to the identical tank on her right and faced the "Light Girl." Dressed in white, the apparatus she wore mirrored her counterpart's, as did the way she floated in the life-supporting fluid, eyes closed in a peaceful expression. She, too, wore the hat-like cone that contained her brain sensors and breathing apparatus, backlit by a single bulb.

"This is Regan," the professor said. "Studious, dedicated to aiding my work. I've always thought her gentle nature and maturity rubbed off on you more so than the defiance of your younger sister."

"Sisters?" Dot asked. "So, not clones?"

"No, my girl, certainly not clones. Goneril, Regan, and Cordelia are the genuine triplets of Imago, lab-born of the same single egg to form their own monozygotes."

"But you said I was the oldest."

"Indeed, you are, by a few minutes. You three were the most promising of my lifetime of children."

"We were the only ones who survived," Dot said, remembering more with each passing moment. "We were the only ones who endured through your genetic experiments." She felt it important to correct him whenever he described death in some cold, passive manner.

"That's another way of putting it, yes," Imago said. "You always were the brightest of my daughters, and you never tolerated vague bluster from your old man."

With Dot's palms on the curved glass of her sisters' tanks, memories she assumed had long been erased quickly rewrote themselves, filling her mind with moments from a past life. She used to run around the atrium with Goneril, sprinting down its connecting corridors, each race ending with an aggressive bout of wrestling on the front lawn. She played games of wit and chance with Regan, pitting their intellects against each other, their knowledge of history, science, their familiarity of cultural anthropology. The three girls spoke to each other in multiple languages, performed Beethoven's String Trio No. 2 in G on violin, viola, and cello – though Dot often preferred jazz trombone - and played make-believe in reenacted historical milestones. Dot's favorite roles were Joan of Ark during the Siege of Orléans, George Washington during the U.S. Revolutionary War, and Rand Hawthorne during the New World War in the Founders' Last Stand at Beacon Hill.

In each of her rediscovered early memories, Gypsy ran beside them, for Imago bred him specifically to protect the triplets. From the minute they emerged from their maturation tanks, they had the loyal German Shepherd at their command. Protecting them was his only purpose, and the Loyalist officers helped further forge him into a stalwart guardian who would never waver, never lose sight of his life's mission.

In all of her gathered memories, her creator and identical genetic siblings called her "Cordelia," and in response, she often simply called them "father" and "sisters."

George had always affectionately called her "Dot" from the tattoo on her left hand, for the other girls were never similarly branded, never meant to leave their sheltered compound.

Behind Dot stood a third tank, vacant and empty.

"That was mine, wasn't it?" she asked.

"It was," Imago said. "That's where you were incubated and where you spent most of your life, but that's not where you were matured, my girl. I occasionally took you all out of the safety of your bio-preservation baths and brought you up as my own, as any proud father would. I examined you daily, watched for signs of The Worm, and never saw a trace. After creating dozens of sons and daughters, I finally found my successors. Humanity's successors."

"Why me?" Dot asked her father. "Why did you release me to the Loyalists?"

"You're the Exceptional Girl," George said, repeating the title she'd come to loathe. It now had new meaning.

"Simply put, you were ready," Professor Imago said. "You had the means to make the treacherous journey to Kellan: the brains, the heart, and the courage. Those three traits are all one needs."

"Why keep my sisters here?" the girl asked, her racing mind a blur. "Didn't they also deserve freedom?"

"Sadly, Goneril and Regan needed more time."

"But why wipe my memory?" Dot's many questions formed a long line in her mind. "Why the Blessing?"

"That wasn't the plan, my girl," Imago said with regret. "The soldiers who dedicated their lives to transporting you, protecting you, did what that they had to for your safety. My guess is that when the squad escorting you to the west was ambushed by the Greens, they were forced to hide you, and they decided a Blessing was necessary to keep you safe in the event you were captured. That was the contingency. The idea was, if you didn't know how special you were, if you didn't realize how vital you were to the future of humanity, then they wouldn't, either. It was a foolish assumption, for they targeted anyone remotely different. I should have known. Even with your core memory fragmented, your identity lost, you still came across as a brilliant, resilient, special child. An enhanced human."

"An Exceptional Girl," Dot said. "What is the Blessing exactly? Sergeant Furst told me, but I'm still unclear."

"When you were hidden during the skirmish near Kellan, the brave soldier who spirited you away injected you with a chemical cocktail of my creation. It was a bioengineered compound of benzodiazepines and beta-blockers that blinded you to the history of the world and, most importantly, your central role in its salvation. Had I known it would also affect your sense of identity, I would have never approved of it. I never wanted you to forget who you were, who we were. For that, I'm sorry, my girl. It must have made your difficult, disorienting journey ever more confusing."

"Until now," Dot said. "I remember everything now."

"Interesting," Professor Imago said. "The chemical imbalance we imbued in you started to fall apart upon returning home. For that, I also apologize."

"You wish I were still in the dark?"

"Sadly, yes." Professor Imago checked the time on his watch and took a deep breath. "A compartmentalized mind would have made what's about to happen more... tolerable."

"What does that mean?" Dot asked.

"Yes, Professor," George said, alarmed. "What does that mean?"

"It means... I'm sorry, my girl. As much as I admire your brave companions, please know I had no choice."

"Professor," George said, eyeing his weapons on the wall. "What's about to happen?"

Abraham's synthetic voice cut into the tense exchange, abruptly loud and clear over Dot's cochlear earpiece.

"Warning: The facility is being invaded by 48 Purist soldiers armed with plasma rifles and concussive..."

BOOM!

A sudden explosion of glass and metal in the adjacent room shook the lab's walls and sent shivers through the girl.

BOOM!

"Professor?" George said. "Father?"

BOOM!

To both men's dismay, the third outburst sent Dot running out of the lab, back to her friends in the atrium, where she stood frozen at a terrifying sight.

57

The Final Sunset

The sun and the moon shared the same darkening, overcast sky above the compound, and the atrium's five-story glass wall served as a picture window to the grandiose scene. It was a landscape of peace and beauty that Dot briefly glimpsed from the corner of her eye before smoke and rubble engulfed the room, before she faced her worst fears.

Abraham's frame whined and creaked as he knelt down with plumes of black smoke pouring out of his side, obscuring Dot's view of the rest of the atrium.

"Damage Assessment: Lateral armor plating breached. Forward motor control unit compromised. Suggest..."

BOOM!

Before Dot could answer him, before the mech could orient himself, another shot struck him firm in his upper back, keeping him low to the floor.

"Damage Assessment: Sensor array mounts compromised. Upper articulation points failing. Power module conduits damaged..."

"Abraham!" Dot yelled. "Defend yourself! Where is everyone?"

"Status: Primary power is at 62 percent. Reserve power is at 68 percent. Power rerouted to compensate and aid self-repair..."

BOOM!

"Stop it!" Dot screamed into the blinding black smoke all around her. It stung her eyes as she frantically searched for her other friends. "Stop it! You're killing him!"

George ran out of the lab to join her, his bow at the ready with twin arrows nocked.

"Do something!" Dot said. "He's being attacked..."

BOOM!

Another powerful shot landed square in the mech's lower back, sending him down as flames engulfed his torso. Internal extinguishers spewed chemical flame deterrent foam, barely containing the damage.

His eyes stinging from the belching, polluted fog, George aimed his bow into the foul smoke and let loose five wide volleys of arrows – ten in all – though he couldn't be sure if any had landed on foes. He followed with another barrage, hoping it helped keep the invaders from the girl.

"Run, Dot!" George said.

"Run where?" Dot spun around, turning toward the storm of noise overtaking her senses. "I said stop it! Leave Abraham alone!"

"You heard the little lady!" a male voice said from within the blinding fog. "Cease fire!"

The silence was sudden and stark. As the smoke cleared, Dot saw the hopeless scene in full.

Among the potted plants, across the marble floor, and around the two-story bronze statue honoring the man she'd just rediscovered as her father, four-dozen soldiers in green had stormed in and taken positions, resting their weapons across cover. As Abraham warned moments earlier, Purist forces had entered without warning, once again finding a way to circumvent his sensors. She would soon learn that the militia comprised 47 Automen, one human, and – most frightening of all – the dreaded Azrael combat mech.

As intimidating as Abraham looked, Azrael stood as a living nightmare by comparison, emerging from the black cloud like a demon rising from Hell. The upgraded later-model war machine stood taller and wider than Abraham, so much so that it needed to destroy the already oversized doorway in order to step through it, sending dust and debris high and across the massive room, before bombarding merciless fire on its counterpart. Unlike Abraham's humanoid design of a central torso with two arms and two legs, the Azrael unit had six legs and four arms connected to a horizontal abdomen, resembling a monstrous metal scorpion sans tail.

For the moment, the Azrael mech stood motionless, waiting for its next command, as did the many Automen behind it. As if gathered in the eerie, quiet moment before an apocalyptic storm, everyone in the atrium – the girl, the boy, the professor, the hybrids, the soldiers, and the mechs – simply looked around the room at each other while the smoke from the explosions subsided.

Vincent was scared, confused, not sure why everyone was now just standing around staring.

Cezar waited for the enemy to make the next move and assumed they awaited the same. He had no choice but to hold his position with the Azrael's guns trained on him.

George nocked triple arrows, ready to annihilate anyone or anything that approached.

In the thick of his struggle, Abraham issued futile warnings to surrender. "Command: Surrender or die." With the attack on pause, he privately spoke to the girl over her cochlear earpiece. "Assessment: Present threats outweigh our defensive capabilities. Issuing distress call now. Do not verbally respond, Little Miss."

Dot wasn't sure what Abraham was attempting. With his disconnect to an abandoned global network, she didn't see how a distress call would help. She assumed the futile tactic was simply automated.

"Hang in there, Abe," Vincent said from a corner across the room. Like Cezar, he also stood helpless, with guns pointed at him from all sides.

Dot held her growling dog to her right and kept George in sight to her left. Curiously, she looked past the destruction, past the clone troopers, their firearms, and their doomsday war machine, for it was the lone human soldier who caught her attention. She locked eyes with him as he walked through the gray cloud of smoke toward her, his pistol lowered. In an instant, she recognized him and knew what this turncoat did back in the camp of The Mighty 13th Company of The Loyalists of Man on the edge of the South Lands. The grim realization sickened her.

"Lieutenant Dixon," Dot said with a furrowed brow as the former Loyalist commander approached her. "I'm surprised to see you."

"You know this man?" George asked, lowering his bow.

"Your girlfriend and I go way back, Prince George," Dixon said, "just like you and me. I see you still have that compound bow you stole from my tent."

"It's better in my hands, Dix."

"You're probably right. I'm more of a plasma pistol man, anyway."

"What are you doing here, Lieutenant Dixon?" Dot asked.

"You said you're surprised to find me here. Looks more like 'shocked' to me. And you can forget my rank, Dot, because I told you friends call me 'Dix.'"

"Sergeant Furst thought you were dead... Lieutenant Dixon."

"That's because he was a blind fool," Dixon said, dropping his feigned smile. "Cordelia Imago."

"He thought you died in service to your unit, that you sacrificed yourself to save us."

"Like I said, blind fool."

"Sarge was a great man," Dot said. "He told me to be careful who to trust. It seems I was the blind one, and you're the fool."

"I'm the fool?" Dixon looked around at his superior numbers and at her downed mech, his damaged frame spewing smoke. "Doesn't look that way from where I stand. Did the great man, the honorable, legendary, amazing Sergeant Benjamin Furst, also tell you he lost more men over the years, soldiers both human and synthetic, than any other commanding officer in the Loyalists' movement?"

"Loss is part of war," Dot said, remembering more of Sarge's wisdom. "You must factor that into your strategy."

"Sounds like more of your beloved sergeant's bravado, the man who lost flesh-and-blood soldiers thanks to his poor judgement on the battlefield, and cloned Automen to simple persuasion. He told you that part, too, right? That Automen can choose to switch sides if they feel their mission will fail or their superior officer

Lynn Harrod

turns out to actually be inferior? It completely changes war strategy, doesn't it? Too bad Sarge never quite got that, and apparently, neither did you."

Cezar approached Dixon with dozens of rifles following him.

"An Automan can be forgiven for turning tail," the wolf said. "It's simply following the logic of its programming. But when a soldier of flesh, blood, and bone betrays his brothers in arms, it's called dishonor."

"It's called being a traitor," George said.

"That's rich coming from you two," Dixon said. "The ranger who fled his village in tears, and the wolf who cowardly abandoned his clan. Oh yes, we know all about you."

"You know nothing," the wolf said, seething.

"I know what a traitor is," Dixon said, "because I slaved underneath one for years. A traitor is anyone who puts their legacy and glory above the best interests of humanity. That's what your precious Sarge did. You see, somewhere around the hundredth time we got beat back by the Purists, around the hundredth time we lost good soldiers for no reason other than reckless, ignorant strategy, I realized that both sides of the war want to save the world but only one had any prayer of succeeding."

"I think it's sad that you fought with Sarge a hundred times yet learned nothing from him," Dot said.

"Oh, I learned a little bit." Dixon glanced back at his Azrael mech. "As you know, I used to hate these clunky metal monsters. I figured they were obsolete. But right now, hot damn, I surely love mine. We found it in an abandoned outpost south of Colt. Too bad you missed him when you ran for your lives."

"Why did you attack Abe?" Vincent asked from across the room.

"A silly question from a silly plant-man. Why wouldn't I? You always take down the biggest threat first..."

"That's quite enough!" Imago said, emerging from the lab. "The girl's mech is down and that's all that matters. Let's get this over with, Dixon."

"I know this must be tough on you," Dixon said, "but a deal's a deal, Professor."

Lieutenant Dixon turned to Professor Imago, and Dot's heart sank when she saw no shock or surprise or fear across her father's face. Their familiarity with each other made her nauseous.

Her father's earlier words echoed through her mind.

I'm sorry, my girl.

Her friends were equally dismayed. The mysterious genius they'd been seeking, the brilliant creator who produced the Exceptional Girl, who mentored George and united them in dreams, ended up no better than all the other small-minded, self-serving opportunists they'd encountered on their journey. His lengthy tour of the girl's history was merely a means to stall for time.

"Looks like you were right, Professor," Dixon said, eyeing the German Shepherd by the girl's side. "A loyal dog always returns to its home, and this one brought the girl and her little circus."

"The girl has a name," Imago said.

"And what name is that? Cordelia or Trial Number 43?"

"Her name is Dottie!" Vincent said.

Dixon glared at Vincent. "You will be the first to die, silly plant-man. Even Prince George and the wolf know better than to bark at me like that."

Dot stood in front of her green friend, her eyes never leaving her father's shamed face.

"Professor, what have you done?" Dot asked.

"You used to call me 'Father'," Professor Imago said. "I guess times have changed."

"It seems so."

"My girl, there are many things I've never told you..."

"Then tell me right now! Tell me about 'a deal's a deal'! What are you trading?"

"You," Lieutenant Dixon said, as if it should have been obvious. "He's trading you for peace of mind. Once you and I leave this place hand-in-hand, no battalion or troop or squad will ever disturb his little sanctuary again. This includes the delusional Blues should they ever come knocking, I'll see to it."

"Father, why?" George asked, emotional, confused.

"You'll understand one day, my boy," Imago said. "A man does what he must, and I had to take his deal."

Dot yanked on the Professor's coat collar, forcing him to face her. "You actually believe him? You really think Dixon will honor his word, that he'll help protect you?"

As she looked up at her father's stone face, a blank expression that failed to hide his shame, she realized this wasn't a case of a good man gone bad. She pieced together what surely happened.

Having failed to capture her at the river crossing, the Purists made a beeline for the source – the Department of Transmutation in the East Hills – where Dixon cornered Imago into a cruel agreement. The lieutenant threatened to level the old man's lab, his home, if he refused to cooperate, but promised to allow him two of his three daughters and the freedom to continue his research so long as he surrendered his most successful creation.

Cordelia.

Dot.

Professor Imago knew the consequences of turning down the proposal. The Greens would have taken Goneril and Regan as consolation as they reduced the compound to rubble. Nearly a century of work would have burned in the hills for days, leaving the old man alone with no family and no hope of resuming his lifelong quest for a cure.

"Take her," Imago said to Dixon. "Take her and leave me with my other daughters, as we discussed. Leave the hybrids, the Abraham unit, my son, and my dog, and go about your way."

"You can keep the boy and the dog," Dixon said. "I have no need for them. But our discussion never included the freaks. They didn't strike a deal with me, and we both know they'll seek the girl regardless of what you may tell them. I'm afraid they can't be left behind, not alive, anyway."

Cezar bared his teeth, breathed heavy and deep. "If there's to be a fight, then let it begin!"

"First, we place the girl in the Azrael unit. Then you'll have your fight, wolf. We didn't come all this way just to bring back a dead kid."

The Azrael mech opened its chest and dropped a large, red sphere onto the atrium floor, making room for a passenger. Based on her own mech's design, Dot knew the ominous sphere to be a Lotus bomb, an unforgivingly indiscriminate weapon James The First had described as the "final sunset" for one's enemies.

"I'm not sitting in there!" Dot said as the silent sentinel's open chest awaited like a hungry maw.

"Oh, but you will sit in there," Lieutenant Dixon said, grabbing the girl by the arm. "By now, you should be used to being crammed in tanks and mechs."

"Bastard!" George screamed, helpless, with weapons at his head.

"Some of us here actually want to protect you from what's coming, little girl. If you truly care about saving the world, you'll think on that while you watch us shut down your little circus." He shoved Dot at Azrael's feet and shouted at the professor. "Tell the girl to get in!"

"The girl has a name!" Imago said again.

"Her name is Dottie!" Vincent said, angry, unfurling his vines.

Lieutenant Dixon raised his pistol, pointed it at Vincent's head, and fired a single shot through his brow, sending the plant hybrid cold to the marble floor.

"Vincent!" Dot screamed.

"Pretty sure he won't 'grow back' from a direct headshot from a plasma pistol," Dixon said, "but I kinda hope he survives so I can plug him again."

Gypsy lunged forward and clutched Dixon's leg in his jaws.

Cezar pounced on the lieutenant.

George nocked three arrows.

Abraham rose, unfolded a long-barrel gun from his arm, and turned to Dixon.

The lieutenant struggled to fight off the beasts at his heels before the mech could sharpshoot him, punching and kicking and finally raising his pistol. To Cezar's surprise, Dixon didn't take aim at him or the dog. Instead, he pointed his gun upward and fired a single shot at the ceiling.

The Azrael mech and its supporting clone troops advanced, jolted from their standby positions. The sudden movement of the war machine and four dozen soldiers was startling.

Professor Imago quickly grabbed Dot and hurried her behind a flower bed for cover as her friends engaged the soldiers in an ugly, brutal clash.

58

Contingency

"Protect the girl!" Cezar yelled his command at Gypsy, trying to be heard over the storm of gunfire. The dog didn't heed the order, his jaws still clamped down on Lieutenant Dixon's ankle. "Go! Protect her! Forget the inhuman waste!"

In a lull in the onslaught, Gypsy heard the wolf and immediately ran to join Dot and Professor Imago behind the stone flower bed near the lab entrance. The German Shepherd positioned himself to cover both the girl he was long trained to protect and the man who raised him from the time he was a genetically engineered pup created to be a superior canine.

In the firefight, Professor Imago eyed the laboratory door, waiting for the right moment to rush his beloved Cordelia back to the safety of the reinforced room.

Dot stared at Vincent's lifeless body across the atrium and saw his vines move slightly, unsure if it was a struggle for life or simply the wind blowing in through the destroyed glass wall. She hoped it was his miraculous healing property at work, but braced herself for the cold, likely reality.

As the two mechs clashed, and the wolf hybrid and Colt ranger fought the soldiers, Imago saw their chance to flee. He picked up his daughter and carried her through the blue door, bolting it behind him, locking out the pursuing dog.

"Gypsy!" she said, having seen him barely miss entry to the lab.

"Don't worry about him," Imago said. "Gypsy can take care of himself. Truth is, no matter the outcome, he may very well be the last one left alive."

Through the door's narrow window, Dot watched her friends in what seemed like an impossible battle.

Abraham rushed Azrael, slamming against the giant metal scorpion and entangling with it. He knew his counterpart had superior ranged firepower and wisely narrowed their fight to an up-close melee, minimizing his advantage. Though the odds were still stacked against the damaged Abraham – Azrael's thicker armor and many arms and legs were formidable – a hand-to-hand brawl was his only chance against the much larger, better-armed foe.

George expertly released shot after shot from behind cover, each arrow landing true, a futile effort against an artificial enemy that felt no pain and feared no death.

Cezar took advantage of the dense smoke and foliage of the atrium, stalking the Automen three at a time, slashing through the troop with spread claws and wide open fangs. His powerful strikes would have reduced any human to pulp, but they were synthetic clones whose ability to dismiss injury proved a strength to overcome.

Gypsy used no stealth in his tactics. He charged head-on at the soldiers and mauled anyone unlucky enough to be in his path. Unlike Cezar's wild, wide swings, Gypsy followed his training and clutched the clones' throats, ankles, and abdomens, weak points apt to leak the thick gray blood that allowed them movement, resulting in seized joints and system failure.

Brave as he was, Dot feared her dog would fall at any moment. Watching through the door's small window, that fear vanished when she saw him shot repeatedly, more than she thought he could endure. She wondered how his military vest continued to protect him from the incessant gunfire.

"Gypsy keeps getting shot," Dot said to her father, "but he keeps fighting."

"He's my special dog," Professor Imago said as he raced about the lab, throwing switches and levers as fast as he could.

"You created him." Dot's memory offered another moment from her past, a conversation she once had with Imago when both she and Gypsy were little. "You made him, just like you made me and the others."

"Gypsy has no proper mother or father, if that's what you mean. He didn't come from a litter."

"He came from this lab." Dot watched as her father drained her sisters' tanks. "He doesn't need the vest, does he?"

"The Loyalists gave him his blue vest to identify him as one of theirs, but it doubles as an illusion meant to hide his... unique nature."

Still staring through the window, Dot gasped when she saw Gypsy fall from a shot to the head, only for the dog to rise again

Lynn Harrod

after a moment. The spent bullet tumbled to the marble floor in a puddle of blood.

"Gypsy can't die," the girl said, as she noticed Vincent's body gone. "Just like Vincent."

"Both the dog and the plant-man certainly can die, my girl," Imago said. "This lab doesn't create gods, not that I haven't tried. But Gypsy has the same regenerative gene and healing property that Vincent has, so killing him is quite a challenge. Sadly, it's a challenge that could be met today."

Despite his forced tone of pleasant conversation, the old man hurried to free his sleeping daughters from their draining tanks. He cradled their floating bodies to keep them from collapsing as the tanks' levels lowered, careful not to let them fall. He pulled their breathing masks from their faces and helped them out onto the wet floor.

"Cordelia?" Regan said in a heavy breath as she woke, still orienting herself. "You made it."

"Sorry it took so long," Dot said, her memories of the "Light Girl" flooding back. They painted trees together, read books, played games in different languages.

"You actually came?" Goneril said when she squinted open her eyes and struggled to stand. "You stupid girl. You were supposed to save yourself!"

"Nice to see you, too, Gon." As with her other sister, memories of the "Dark Girl" popped into her mind, times of arguments, pranks, teasing, and rivalry.

The old man enjoyed watching his identical triplets quarrel, once again familiar with each other, but cut off their back-and-forth to return their focus to the situation at hand.

"My girls, we have little time," Professor Imago said. "This lab is heavily reinforced, but with that infernal mech of theirs, they will eventually blast their way in here once they're done with the others. There's no time to lose."

"The others need our help!" Dot said. "We're hiding in here while they're out there fighting for me!"

"They're fighting for us all now, and we must take advantage of the moment. As much as it may hurt, Cordelia, that was the plan."

"I thought the plan was to hand me over to them," Dot said, remembering her father's betrayal.

"That's what Dixon thought. That's what we agreed to, but it was never my plan. When he told me about your friends, I knew I had a chance to save you all. As slim as it is, it was my only chance."

"You used them!"

"I had no choice!" the old man said, snapping back at his daughter with pain in his hoarse voice.

"You always have a choice, Father!"

Professor Imago took a moment to calm himself before returning Dot's incredulous stare, now joined by her identical sisters. "Cordelia's right. I did have a choice. I had to choose between you three girls and the five brave souls fighting for their lives as we speak. And I would choose the same again a thousand times if given the chance. For a father, there's no real decision to make."

"Those five brave souls are also your children," Dot said, pleading. "You said it yourself."

"And I meant it. I love them. I've loved and lost more children over the years than folks you'll ever meet. But I will not lose you."

Still disoriented, barely able to stand, Regan and Goneril nodded, accepting their father's desperate choice.

Dot saw his logic and pain but remained unconvinced. She felt the ensuing battle pulling her away, even as her father offered another way out.

Lynn Harrod

Imago grabbed a large book from a nearby shelf – Shakespeare's *King Lear* – triggering the bookshelf to swing outward, revealing a hidden doorway at the back of the room. A narrow ladder led down to an awaiting tunnel far below. Like the lab, the doorway, the shaft, and the underground passage were barely wide enough for a human, created solely for a thin old man and his adolescent girls.

"This is going to be difficult," he said, trying not to appear nervous as he peered down the dark shaft. "Most difficult, my girls, especially after just barely leaving your sustenance tanks. We'll have to wait a few minutes for your legs to return. But as soon as your feet regain feeling, we must flee while we still can."

The muffled sound of the atrium battle sent sharp pains through Dot's body, as if she felt every wound laid upon her friends.

"I won't abandon them to slaughter," Dot said, making her own tough choice.

"Did you not hear anything Father said?" Goneril asked, shaking her head in disbelief.

"Stop it, Gon," Regan said. "This can't be easy for her."

"But we're finally back together again! She never did listen!"

"I am listening!" Dot said. "But I don't agree!"

"You must let them go, my girl," Professor Imago said, trying to project calm and control on the edge of their doom. He knelt and rubbed their legs and feet with a heated pad. "Your mighty friends, Gypsy, even George. Their lives will go down in service to you, to the greater good, to the only hope this world has. Most aren't so lucky to die with purpose. It's a terrible decision, I know, but it's the only way."

"After everything they've done to bring me here," Dot said, "after all they've sacrificed, there's no real decision to make."

"You might die with them," Regan said.

"Probably," Goneril said.

"Perhaps I will," Dot said. "Perhaps it's best if I die. If I leave with you now, they'll just keep hunting us." She'd always viewed all the violence on her behalf as pointless, and this final confrontation felt like the end of a long, hopeless struggle that only prolonged the inevitable. Soon, her guardians would be gone, but the danger would remain. "After they kill my friends, they'll keep searching for us. Cezar says the hunt is never done."

"Your wolf is wise," her father said. "But he's wrong. The hunt will be done for everyone, including Dixon and his Greens. This slaughter you speak of, it will be theirs as well."

BOOM!

The laboratory shook as a concussion shell exploded against the door.

"They're coming in!" Regan said.

"I still can't feel my legs!" Goneril said. "They're going to get us!"

"They'll surely try, but this laboratory, including that door, is reinforced with seven-inch plate steel augmented by a buffer of inertial dampeners that dissipates nearly all impact. It's impossibly strong. We're standing in what's probably the single most impenetrable room on the planet."

"But they have an Azrael mech," Regan said.

"Which means they have a Lotus bomb," Goneril said. "Even your impossibly strong door won't last long."

"You're right, my girl." Imago said. "But it will last long enough." He continued to rub his daughters' feet and saw their toes wiggle, the first sign that the feeling in their legs was returning. "It's time. We must go." He gestured for them to enter the shaft.

Dot looked down the ladder that descended into darkness. "Father, what did you mean? The slaughter is theirs as well?"

"This entire compound is set to implode. That Lotus bomb they have out there? It's a portable doomsday device, harnessing enough power to level a town."

"So, I was right," Goneril said with a look of despair. "That door won't last against a Lotus bomb."

"Against one, it actually might," Imago said, "but I have nine others embedded in this building's foundation."

"Like the Devil's own pumpkin patch," Goneril said dramatically, her tone and voice identical to her sisters'.

"As soon as we're all in the tunnel, we'll need to get as far from here as we can. 500 meters, to be exact."

"Minimum safe distance," Dot said, "as Abraham puts it."

"That's right. The detonators' sensors are set to our life sign signatures. Once we're all 500 meters away, that minimum safe distance, as you say, the bombs will ignite in a cascade, destroying my life's work and anything still within these walls. You won't have to worry about Lieutenant Dixon or the Azrael mech or any of those Automen ever again. They'll be reduced to ash and dust while we're on our way to the North Woods, to Vincent's former farm. My old colleague Francis Young helped me form this contingency plan long ago."

"Vincent's Father," Dot said.

"His property is well hidden. We'll start anew, away from the eyes of the Greens and Blues and the greedy mitts of raiders. Yes, we'll leave behind fallen comrades, but we'll live on and complete our mission. It's why I created you. It's why I've lived so long. I have to see it through."

"Cowardly," Dot said, "as Cezar would put it."

"Again, your wolf is indeed wise," the professor said. "But sometimes the cowards are the only survivors."

"Listen to Father!" Goneril said.

"Have a heart, Gon," Regan said.

"I'm sorry, Cordelia." Goneril faced her sister with pleading eyes. "I didn't know your friends like you did. I saw them in our dreams, and I know how much they mean to you, but like Father says, this is the only way. Otherwise, you coming back was meaningless."

"If you're so determined to leave them to their deaths," Dot said, "then lead the way, Gon."

After a moment of tense hesitation, a moment to reflect on the grand sacrifice that was about to take place on their behalf, a determined Goneril started down the long ladder, followed by a remorseful Regan.

Professor Imago descended a few rungs and paused. His extended hand and desperate face begged Dot – his beloved Cordelia – to follow him down the shaft. Her hesitation gave him hope. Once he and his children reached the bottom far below, he would seal a hatch from within the tunnel. Their growing distance from the property would soon detonate the compound's bombs, killing friend and foe alike while they fled through the hills.

It felt wrong.

In that moment, both father and daughter knew what must be done.

Though her father's well-laid plan would ensure hope for humanity and keep them together, Dot would lose the new family she'd made on her journey of self-discovery back to her roots, betraying them for her own safety. She questioned whether she made the trek back to save herself or everyone she loved, and she remembered her father's teachings...

Right versus wrong.

Honor contrasted with disgrace.

Self-preservation balanced with the greater good of all.

Dot looked at the ladder, her father, and the blue door behind her as if for the last time.

"If I hadn't come back," she said, "they would have taken everything. My sisters, this place, your work, and your life. So long as you three are safe, my return home wasn't meaningless."

"My girl, no," Professor Imago said in a final attempt to dissuade her. "I can't bear to lose you again."

"Most aren't so lucky to die with purpose."

His eyes welling up, Professor Imago looked at his daughter's determined face and nodded. As he climbed down the ladder, Dot grabbed the bookshelf and swung it shut, concealing the shaft again.

The sounds of gunfire and grenades and metal pounding metal grew deafening as she opened the blue door and returned to the chaos of the atrium. With the sun now well below the hills, she caught sight of the moon rising in the starry sky through the front glass wall, like twinkling lights on a black velvet canvas. It resembled The Void she shared with her sisters and friends and struck her as a beautiful backdrop to what might be the last moments of her life.

She saw no thermal visors on any of the Automen fighting her friends. It offered her one advantage.

"Lights off!"

The ceiling lamps promptly went out, throwing the battle into darkness.

59

Dead or Alive

The full moon shone down through the atrium like a celestial floodlight, casting a faint, cold aura atop the dozens of soldiers. Remembering Sergeant Furst's words, she knew the clones were now blind, lost in the dark without thermal visors. Only the mechs and hybrids could still see, their sharp senses guiding them through the melee.

While Abraham still grappled with the Azrael mech, Cezar took advantage of the dark as he had in the Dominion rainforest. Fighting through his fatigue, fears of failure, and torments of inadequacy, he thought of the girl as he pushed himself to follow his keen nose. Prowling from soldier to soldier, he disarmed them and slashed their lower legs. The wolf hybrid had quickly learned that killing them was not possible, as they rebuilt each other

Lynn Harrod

nearly as fast as he could fell them, but crippling and disarming the soldiers was suddenly an easy task.

Despite his best efforts, the wolf was soon overpowered, held down by a plasma net, a web of electrified cables designed to weaken and restrain even the strongest hybrids. After tracking Dot and her companions across their travels, the Purists had taken an interest in the predator and wanted to subject him to their invasive research.

Vincent's vision actually improved when Dot shut off the lights, his bioluminescent eyes instantly adapting to the dark. From his point of view, the clones glowed like specters, and he evaded them with ease, wrapping his tight vines around them in small groups. With a slight squeeze, he incapacitated them, if only for a brief time. It would have to be enough for now. After recovering from the worst injury he'd ever experienced – the close-range headshot from Lieutenant Dixon – he felt dizzy, weak, and was in no hurry to feel the curious, painful sensation again.

Still reeling from his wound, he, too, was soon outnumbered and captured by the Automen. They held him in a corner with a dense foam specially tailored to clog his porous skin, making it difficult for him to breathe. Though their commander attempted to execute him moments before, they prepared for the possibility that not even a shot point-blank to the forehead could bring him down. Their research teams to the east felt eager to dissect him.

George and Gypsy took cover behind the base of the statue, the dog no longer able to fight. He'd taken enough gunfire to finally weaken him. Like Vincent, the dog's miraculous recovery slowly rebuilt his small frame, but it proved too slow to put him back in the fray.

"Vincent!" Dot yelled. "Cezar, where are you?"

"We're still here, girl!" Cezar screamed from under his painful net, its voltage like a million needles plunged into his skin. "You must run! Leave us with these fools!"

"Run, Dottie!" Vincent yelled, his voice fading as he struggled to breathe.

Dot looked around for her dog, but the darkness and barrage of noise were unforgiving. "Gypsy! Here, boy!"

Despite his weakened state, the German Shepherd obeyed. With George following close behind, the loyal dog limped away from the statue and weaved through the groups of blind soldiers back to Dot at the lab's blue door. What little strength he still had was focused on protecting the girl.

Unable to see him, Dot felt relieved to feel the boy's leather sleeves in the dark while Gypsy fell atop her feet. "George!" She spoke in a lowered voice. "You really are a survivor."

"We're both survivors, Dot," he whispered back, "and we need to stay together now. I think we can make it to that busted window..."

"I'm not leaving, George."

The ongoing clash of the mechs was deafening, and George wondered if he heard her correctly. "Dot, what do you mean..."

"I can't leave." Though she still couldn't see his face, she caught the moonlight reflecting off his eyes, saw their confused expression. "I need you to go with Father."

"What? That Judas?"

"Listen to me! They won't make it without you!"

"I can't... I won't leave you again," the ranger said. "Not here, not with these devils!"

"You have to keep them safe! They're escaping the facility right now."

"How?"

"There's a bookshelf at the back of the lab," the girl said.

"I don't understand..."

"Find the bookshelf. Look for King Lear and a door will open. A ladder leads down to a tunnel. Follow them. They need you."

George realized the plan and knew she was right. If the professor and the girls found a way out, they'd need someone to guide them through the wild, but he couldn't bear to be apart from his beloved Cordelia again. "Come with us, Dot."

"Not yet. I need to stay just a little while longer."

"Why do I feel uneasy with 'a little while longer'?"

"It's the only way, George. You have to trust me..."

"There must be another way!" The boy looked at the shadowy outlines of her desperate, pleading face. He didn't want to lose her, but to refuse her request would be to risk losing everyone. "I was the ranger put in charge of finding you, but you're the one who found me, first at Wellspring, then here at Father's base. Promise you'll find me again when this is all over."

"I promise."

George hugged Dot and held her tight, not wanting to let go. The sound and shudder of the mechs was undercut by nearby footfalls, ripping them from their embrace. The hunting Automen were bound to find them soon.

"Whatever happens, Dot, one way or another, I'll see you in my dreams."

George left Dot and Gypsy, crept through the lab's blue door behind them, back to the bookshelf and the hidden passage.

Lieutenant Dixon surveyed the atrium with a thermal imaging monocular that allowed him limited sight in the dark. He cursed the lack of night vision gear for his men, but felt satisfied that the escalated scene was back under his control.

"Stand down!" Dixon said, calling out to the Azrael mech and the few soldiers still searching the dark. "They're all contained, the ones still with us, anyway, and their machine is barely standing." Dixon lowered his monocular and looked around the vast, dark room at the shiny helmets of his men and the eerie silhouette of his Azrael mech as they lowered their weapons. "Nice trick, child. My guess is your dear old dad and his two other abominations are on the run as we speak, leaving you behind to figure out a way to salvage your situation."

"And my guess is you're stalling to give your troop time to repair," Dot said, holding her dog close. "Nice trick, Lieutenant. I can hear them working on each other. It means you were losing."

Their voices echoed throughout the atrium, making it difficult for the lieutenant to pinpoint her position.

"You're wrong, child," Dixon said. "It just means we took a little longer than planned. We learned from our near-misses on the road. We studied your circus and brought more than guns."

"Too bad you didn't bring thermal visors."

The girl's taunt stung, particularly because most of his soldiers' surveillance gear was destroyed by Abraham when he first awakened and freed her.

"Too bad," he said, mocking her youthful voice. "Too bad your freaks have been taken out of action. The plant and the wolf are mine, and even if they somehow break free, we both know I have the numbers. You have can't win, child, and you can't run off again. They're coming with me. You're all coming with me. The only question is, am I taking you dead or alive?"

"You're the one who's wrong, Lieutenant Dixon."

"Really?" Her defiance amused him. "I have almost 50 soldiers getting ready for Round Two, and a mech that makes yours look like a tin toy. How am I wrong?"

"I'm not trying to 'salvage my situation,' and I don't plan to win or run. I'm here to surrender."

"Is that right?" Dixon said, curious. "Wonderful! Then all that's left is for you is to come to me."

Lieutenant Dixon scanned the room with his thermal monocular again, still unable to locate the small girl behind abundant cover. The many stone flower beds, statuary, metal benches, and dense foliage hid her well.

Dot and Gypsy carefully moved about the dark atrium to avoid her voice giving away her position. It brought the Colt chapel to mind.

"Let them go and I'll show myself," she said.

"A genetically engineered sense of humor," Dixon said. "Imago thought of everything. Why should I believe you?"

"What choice do you have?"

"I can just find you on my own."

"Only my voice can trigger the lights," Dot said, still roaming the immense room with her dog. "We're stuck in the dark until I say so."

"You sure about that?"

"I'm quite sure."

Though Abraham could flood the room with light, Dot knew Azrael could not. She recalled from her fireside conversation with James The First that Azrael had no spotlights like her Abraham. No lights, no reconnaissance sensors, no communications equipment. It had no tools of rescue or recovery or first aid. Every part of the invincible titan's frame was occupied by weaponry. It was built solely to destroy, to kill.

"Take me to Vincent, boy," Dot whispered to Gypsy. She gripped his collar as he limped just ahead of her, until they arrived at the corner where the plant-man laid on the marble floor, covered in restricting foam. She removed her jacket and used it to wipe the dense layer from his body.

"Let's say I do as you ask," Lieutenant Dixon said to the dark, his voice failing to hide his frustration. "What's stopping us from tracking you after we leave this cursed place?"

Dot pointed to the center of the room and made an "O" with her hands. Though she could barely see her plant friend, she knew Vincent could see her and hoped he understood the plan.

Vincent nodded and silently flung a vine to the ceiling rafters, pulling himself up to safety.

"As you said, Lieutenant," Dot said, "we have no chance against you in a fight."

"You really are as smart as they say. Unlike your deluded Sarge, you know when you've been beaten."

She leaned down and whispered "Now Cezar" to her dog. They kept low behind cover and followed the German Shepherd's nose to the wolf, avoiding the many soldiers. With a commanding officer present, the artificial men didn't need to think for themselves. They simply stood blind, awaiting orders.

Dixon climbed atop a flower bed and scanned the room with his thermal monocular. He muttered a curse, realizing the girl was up to something.

"What's your game, child?" he said.

"No game. I'm just waiting for you to make up your mind."

Dot and Gypsy reached Cezar, still trapped under the plasma net. She grabbed the cable and jumped back from the sudden shock. The dog clutched it in his jaws and painfully pulled it off the wolf. Now free, Cezar looked at his ward and saw her form an "O" with her hands, pointing to the center of the room.

Cezar realized her plan and thought it reckless, but followed it without question for he saw no other strategy. He leapt up to the towering statue's extended hand and crouched within its outstretched palm, hiding himself from any moonlit view before dropping to where the girl had instructed.

Dixon finally figured things out and felt foolish for granting her time for her futile efforts.

"Secure the prisoners!" he said, calling out to his soldiers all around.

"We've lost the hybrids," an Automan reported.

"Both of them?" Dixon said. "Dammit, someone get the lights on! Try the lab! There must be a switch in there!"

"Don't bother," Dot said. "There is no button or switch for the lights. It's all controlled by voice, mine and my father's."

As she spoke, more memories came back to her, further familiarity with the property, its operation and purpose. Indeed, there were no light switches to be found, as most of the compound was run by voice command. Simple applications for lighting, food, security, and sanitation were activated by recognizing the voices of Professor Imago and his children. Only the most advanced, specialized equipment could be run manually.

Incubation pods Dot and her sisters slept in as infants...

Maturation chambers they played in as toddlers...

Sustenance tanks they frequently soaked in upon reaching adolescence...

The triplets needed to be contained under controlled conditions, for they were actually advanced hybrid humans. Fusions of plants and animals like Vincent and Cezar were carefully kept in their respective habitats, but unlike her traveling companions – biologically primitive in comparison, each sharing genetic traits with one other creature – Dot and her sisters were master hybrids of multiple species, composites of hundreds of the world's most enduring plant and animal life. That was the elusive key to conquering The Worm and saving the world. The solution lied not in the DNA of any one creature, one hardy plant or resistant animal, but a union of all life on Earth.

Building upon his family's work, Professor Domingo Imago had painstakingly compiled the physiological and biochemical strengths of entire forests, deserts, and jungles across nearly a century of research, distilling them into mutagens for spermatozoa and introducing them to human ova. Along the way, he also used his discoveries to prolong his own life beyond natural means, injecting himself with his children's enhanced blood. Through seemingly endless trial and error, he finally achieved his goal. In the winter of his years, he created a new human paradigm with total immunity to the WN1M pathogen, a virus that burned through the world like a continental cloud of winged parasites.

The strict, controlled environments became necessary when Imago discovered that his children's immunity to The Worm came with a steep cost.

In order to be spared from the inherited vulnerability to the pathogen, the triplets and their sibling predecessors were made immune to every strain of every virus, every bacteria. In creating their perfect immunity systems, they were left unprepared for an imperfect world full of germs and decay, their bodies full of vacancies where a myriad of healthy, symbiotic bacterium should have been. Their robust defenses killed even the ever-present microbes that live on every being's skin, ironically leaving them totally defenseless in the end.

Even the common cold could kill them.

Their early pods and chambers protected them from the world's germs, but the later tanks gradually introduced the girls' bodies to the microbiotic world as they approached adolescence, submerging them in an ongoing, time-released vaccination stream. The transition was meant to boost a learned herd immunity to garden variety illnesses, but the delicate process ended in failure for most of Imago's human children, with only the latest three showing signs of stability. Having spent more time with them than their unfortunate brothers and sisters, Imago bonded with the triplets, naming them after the daughters of King Lear, the main character and namesake of his favorite Shakespearean play.

Cordelia. Regan. Goneril.

As Dot's memories unfolded, she felt a clarity she'd never experienced. The persistent fog of confusion finally dissipated for good. Her brief history suddenly made sense, including the desperate events just before and after the Loyalists selectively wiped her memory, injecting her with the chemical Blessing in order to protect her from interrogation.

The triplets were the first of Imago's children to survive trials past early childhood, their biological recipe of genes striking the perfect balance. Dot was the first of her sisters to complete her term in the sustenance tanks, ready for the world at large. Knowing her value to the world government, including the oppressive forces of GARD, the professor viewed his known facility as too great of a risk and contacted former colleagues for help in safeguarding her.

Dr. Blum offered sanctuary at Dominion, his own work with Vincent having been incorporated in the triplets' DNA. Imago appreciated the offer but didn't consider a lab above a rainforest a proper upbringing for the young girls.

Dr. Artemus offered a home in the subterranean shelter at Beacon Hill. That plan was foiled by the strife of the Widows and their developing civil war.

Dr. Wainright ran the village of Colt, but Professor Imago wisely concluded that the elder had strayed from sanity when he embraced religion over science and declared himself "Senior Wainright," positioning his role as tyrant for a devout cult.

Sergeant Furst of the 13th Company of The Loyalists to Man offered safe transport to the City of Kellan beyond the West Wall, a community that had long been in the planning stage but had yet to be confirmed.

Imago eventually chose Sarge and his troops, the deciding factor being the protection a military escort provided, as well as the option to use The Blessing as a contingency plan. He wanted his first daughter to live a full life in the greater world.

Unfortunately, the professor didn't anticipate a traitor in the Blue ranks.

Lieutenant Albert Dixon had complained about the Loyalist cause, concluding that perhaps the Purists had the numbers, resources, and support needed to secure a future for humanity. To him, the collateral damage of lives lost – human and hybrid – was the price of saving the world.

Professor Imago assumed Sergeant Furst could keep Dixon in line as he had for decades. He didn't know that the disgruntled lieutenant, envious of his sergeant's respect and authority, was quietly persuading their Automen to switch sides, readying them for a late-night mutiny once the Exceptional Girl was secured.

"So, we're left in the dark?" Dixon asked her, looking around at the shadows and silhouettes in the atrium. "Is that what you're saying, child?"

"I'm saying we'll come out of the dark together," Dot said. "Lights on."

To Dixon's surprise, the banks of large dome lamps along the ceiling came to life, flooding the atrium in bright light once again. He turned to see the plasma net empty, the foam-drenched corner vacant, and the Abraham mech still kneeling before his own war machine.

He looked behind him and saw the girl, the wolf, and the plant hybrid sitting atop the volatile red sphere his mech dropped earlier, like an egg laid by a treacherous beast.

Lynn Harrod

"Is this your brilliant plan?" Dixon asked the girl. "Free your friends and hug a Lotus bomb?"

"I already told you. You release them, and I go with you."

"Standby," Dixon said to his soldiers. He laughed upon finally understanding the new situation. "I get it. Our guns are useless so long as your legs are wrapped around that bomb."

"Ten bombs," Dot said. "There are nine others hidden in the foundation of this building. They're set to detonate once my father and sisters are far enough away, like a pumpkin patch of death, as my sister puts it."

"Ten bombs?" Vincent said, hoping it was a grand bluff. "You mean we're all gonna blow up? We're all going to die in the pumpkin patch?"

"Cezar is ready to die," the wolf said, "but Cezar hopes you know what you're doing, girl."

"Sadly, she doesn't have a clue," Dixon said as he walked up to Dot and her friends atop the dreaded Lotus bomb, now clearly seen in the atrium lights. "Terrible plan, child. You expect me to believe the professor would allow his prized creation to die? That he'd sacrifice his beloved first daughter to save the others? I don't think so."

"You could be right," Dot said, "or you could be very wrong."

"From the start, I concluded that he'd never willingly lose you in order to save them. I factored it in, but I also factored being wrong. It's more of that war strategy we were discussing. Either way, I assure you they'll all be mine, whether it's now or later. The girls, the hybrids, the old man's life's work. They've always belonged to the Purists, to save the people of the world. It took me a while to see that. Why can't you?"

"The Greens care nothing for saving the people of the world," Cezar said. "They only care about themselves."

"People?" Dixon asked the wolf. "Is that what you are? You walk and talk but you're not people any more than these mindless artificials and mechs. Real people are natural. They're born, not grown in glass tubes or pieced together in a machine shop." Dixon looked at Dot's determined expression, curious. "Your knowledge is limited, child. I understand that. But you will quickly learn this world is run by and is made for real people who deserve a real future."

"That's also how you see me, isn't it?" Dot asked. "Unnatural? Undeserving? Why should I believe you want me to help you save the world?"

"Let's be clear. You're not the messiah, not the model of a new humanity. You're just a tree with berries ripe for the picking. There's a big difference between finding a cure within you and populating the world with abominations."

"We have different definitions of 'abomination,' Lieutenant. To you, it means anyone who's different. To me, it's anyone who puts themselves, their legacy, and 'their kind' above all others, anyone who sees differences as weaknesses and affronts. To me, you are the abomination."

"I see. More of that genetically-engineered sense of humor."

"Sarge thought highly of you, Lieutenant. But he didn't know that you switched sides, that you're no better than these 'mindless' clones you spoke of, so now I want to be clear. You're not a patriot, not some brave soldier trying to save anything. You're just a scared little man doing anything to survive."

"You're a fair-weather coward," Cezar said, seething.

"Ask yourself, are you absolutely certain about that, child?" Dixon asked. "Talk, talk, talk. All you've done is stalled for time, something you accused me of. I think you should step away from the bomb. The time has come to accept your reality."

Dot heard Abraham in her cochlear earpiece.

"Status: The distress call has been heeded. Reinforcement arrival within one minute."

Dot finally realized the purpose of her mech's distress call.

It wasn't the government global network he'd called out to.

"Now you ask yourself, lieutenant," Dot said, "why exactly have I been stalling?"

Dot's curious question was punctuated by the crashing sound of metal and glass as more soldiers entered the shattered atrium entrance. Dixon turned to the noise and was impressed to see additional Purist soldiers – humans in green fatigues carrying heavy guns.

"It turns out I was waiting for them," Dixon said with a wide grin. "I didn't expect backup so soon, and I guess you didn't either, child."

"Are you 'absolutely certain' about that?" Dot asked.

Dixon looked again and saw more soldiers walking through the drifting smoke. They were dressed in draping red cloaks and hoods, held blades and long spears, many resembling farm tools.

James The First, captain of the Honorless Apostates, leader of the despised deserters, had arrived in unison with the newly united Gardeners of Beacon Hill. They surrounded Dixon's troops, their numbers 52 strong, more than enough to overpower the dozens of Automen still nursing wounds, straining to repair each other.

"Good evening, Dix," James said as he cradled a vicious long-range assault rifle while surveying the room. "It's been a long time since we've been face-to-face."

"Jim," Lieutenant Dixon said, trying to hide his shock. "I see you've brought Big Mort and his big gun, along with the rest of the gang."

"You of all people know I never leave home without 'em."

"Jim... I didn't realize..." The unexpected sight of Region Captain James McAdam and Heavy Gunner Mort Werner, flanked by their infamous cohort, sent chills through Lieutenant Dixon. Deserters, yes, but they were legends among both the Blue and Green, known even by the hooded warriors he'd encountered in the woods. Dix took a slow, deep breath to control his nerves, angry at his own mounting fear. "I thought you died in Bellview. What I mean is... I heard you were ripped to pieces in the Bellview town square by a Hemlock turret."

"I heard I was, too," James said with a grin. "Of all the rumors of my grisly, untimely death, that one has always been my favorite." He looked around at the confused soldiers waiting to see how the scene unfolded. "Damn, Dix, I haven't seen you since we served under Sergeant Furst in the South Lands. I sure miss that old goat. He was a great man, and a damn good soldier."

"The best," Mort The Third said, his heavy gun at the ready.

"The best of us all," Walt The Fourth said, his sniper rifle locked and loaded.

"Abraham told us there was a big party here," Captain James said, "but old Metal Head failed to mention you were the guest of honor, Dix."

"We only want the child!" Lieutenant Dixon said, sweating, struggling to maintain control. "There's no need for our people to decimate each other!"

"Your men aren't people," Cezar said. "You said so yourself. Artificials are mindless and unnatural. Remember?"

"You said that?" James asked in mock disappointment. "You always did have a problem with respect, Dix, demanding it instead of earning it, pounding your fist instead of inspiring leadership."

"Don't tell me how to run my company, Jim!" Dixon turned away from his former colleague in disgust, only to see uncertainty dawning on his clone soldiers' synthetic faces. Facing a fight they'd likely lose, they looked at each other, clearly wavering. "You men serve the Purists of Earth!" Dixon spoke with a slight quiver in his voice that betrayed his fading confidence. "Look at your green uniforms! You men serve me!"

"Your commanding officer doesn't see you as men at all!" James said. "Green, blue, purple, polka-dot, you don't serve him! You serve the likely victor of the battle and the success of the greater cause for humanity! In other words, my synthetic comrades, you now serve me."

One by one, the Purist Automen lowered their weapons and faced Dixon, their sudden and new foe.

The Lieutenant's fear was overtaken by rage as he now found himself alone in the fight. The ability to persuade Automen through logic and coercion, once his secret weapon, had just been turned against him.

"This wasn't the plan!" Dixon yelled. "You're abandoning your mission!"

"Ain't nobody abandoning no mission," Mort the Third said. "We's... what's the word? We's alterin' the mission."

"We're realigning the mission," Hale The Second said.

"Yeah, that's a better word. We's 'realigning' the mission. Consider it a course correction, Dix."

Dot slid off the Lotus bomb and walked up to Dixon. Her lack of fear startled him.

"Your men have changed their unnatural minds," she said, "and you're now outnumbered 100-to-1. I think the time has come for you to accept *your* reality."

Dixon scoffed at the girl's grab for control. He looked up at his last untouchable soldier, the Azrael mech that awaited orders.

"Like I said, I learned one thing from Sarge," Dixon said. "These old mechs don't betray their commanders. This Azrael is imprinted on me. It can level entire towns, so I think it can handle these numbers. Nothing can take it down."

"Actually, there are ten things that can take him down," Dot said, "ten big, red, round pumpkins buried below our feet."

"You do take after your father," Dixon said. "You're both bad at bluffing. You wouldn't let them go off with everyone here. And ten Lotus bombs? There aren't even ten left in the world."

"It's no bluff, Lieutenant. There are ten left, and my father gathered them all here for you, as you'll soon see."

His eyes fixed on the girl's determined face, Dixon held up his palm, signaling the Azrael mech to open its chest, exposing its empty bomb compartment. Before anyone could react, he rushed into his giant mech, and the hatch quickly shut behind him. Once inside the safety of his war machine, he closed his fist in a silent command to engage. Instantly, the robot unfolded its massive guns and attacked the surrounding forces.

"Fire at will!" Captain James yelled.

The combined troops blasted the towering robot, inflicting collective damage that would normally crush the most imposing enemy. They could only look at the metal beast in horror as it continued its onslaught. The captain gestured orders to his troops.

The Gardeners focused on the mech's legs, severing its lubricant lines to slow its lower joints, but its autogenous backups and self-repair system were nearly instantaneous.

The Apostates kept their distance, firing at the war machine's waist from afar to limit its rotation, but one of its many arms shielded it from the attack.

Cezar slashed at the robot's arms, shearing off top layers of ablative armor only to find ample fused alloy underneath.

"We might as well be shootin' rubber bands at it!" Mort said.

"Run, Dottie!" Vincent yelled to the girl.

Gypsy ran with Dot as she sped amidst the chaos, hoping to escape through the blown-open doorway, out to the night beyond.

Vincent whipped all his vines onto one of Azrael's many arms and ripped it from its socket, a sight that shocked everyone. It took all his strength to pull the massive metal tentacle away from the giant mechanized scorpion – a seemingly impossible act – but the remaining appendages attacked his allies uninterrupted.

Abraham slowly rose to his feet, his self-repair efforts not yet caught up with his extensive damage. He struggled to place himself between the girl and the enemy mech and advanced toward his counterpart.

"Status: This unit's reserve power is at 55 percent."

"Abraham, you need to retreat!" Dot said as she made her way to the doorway, ducking behind cover every few feet. "You all do! Tell everyone to run! Command them!"

Abraham grabbed the larger mech and slammed it to the floor, holding it down as he pummeled it with blow after blow, each strike with immeasurable power.

The Azrael mech could not be stopped, but slowed, effectively held in place by the joint effort of the many warriors. It fired mercilessly upon anything and everything around it, with Lieutenant Dixon securely positioned within its central cavity.

"Announcement," Abraham said as it pinned its counterpart to the floor, his booming synthetic voice echoing across the atrium. "All allied parties must vacate the premises immediately. All parties must reach minimum safe distance."

Dot never told Abraham her risky plan, but the mech's calculations concluded the one action that would terminate the Azrael unit – to actually allow the ten Lotus bombs to detonate.

The girl had told the truth when she said she wasn't bluffing.

She gathered her companions and urged them to get everyone out of the structure and away from the compound. As the two mechs grappled, Dot and Gypsy finally emerged from the chaos, out into the cold night air. Cezar convinced the Automen to abandon the fight and flee the premises. Vincent relayed the message to the Apostates and the Gardeners. Together, they all vacated the building, joining the girl and her dog at the perimeter fence.

Knowing that only the two mechs and Lieutenant Dixon remained inside, James The First led everyone else beyond the gate, toward the distant trees. Their collective fear rushed them across the pasture in a blur. Dot realized she and the others covered a lot of ground during their frantic escape and remembered how the bombs' proximity detonators were tied to her position, her sisters', and her father's. She assumed they successfully fled the area a half-hour before and that her presence alone now kept the powerful explosives from destroying the compound.

"Abraham," Dot said. "How far am I from the property?"

"Location," Abraham said over her earpiece as he continued his struggle with Azrael. "You are 425.2 meters from the structure."

To her friends' confusion, Dot stopped and looked back at the facility. She remembered her father's plan. The bombs would go off once he and his children were 500 meters from the property.

"Abraham, forget that other mech," she said. "You need to get out now!"

"Negative."

"Abraham, leave it!"

"Strategy: This unit must remain in the building to restrain the Azrael unit and prevent it from progressing its mission."

"Negative! Forget strategy! Forget its mission!"

"Clarification: The Azrael unit is intent on capturing or terminating you and will not abandon its mission."

"But you must abandon yours!" Dot said, watching the clash of the two sentinels from afar. "We'll form a new strategy later!"

"Clarification: This is the optimum strategy. The Azrael unit must be immobile or inoperable to ensure your safety."

"I won't be safe if you're destroyed!" Dot wiped tears from her cheeks. "I command you to obey me, Abraham!"

"Negative. Your safety is paramount. You must reach the minimum safe distance and allow the Lotus bombs to detonate for this strategy to succeed. I am sorry, Little Miss."

Dot thought about the old Abraham mech that sacrificed itself to save the people of Beacon Hill, a thankless act forgotten in time. It was about to happen again.

"What are you going on about, kiddo?" James asked, doubling back to check on the girl. "Why the heck are we standing here?"

"There are Lotus bombs set to blow once I'm far enough away!"

"More than one? That was true? Then we really do need to move! This compound and anyone nearby will cease to exist!"

"I can't leave him behind!" Dot pleaded. "But he's not listening to me!"

"The Abraham mech?" James asked, incredulous. "Kiddo, I know you got a soft spot for it, but it's a war machine, a giant walking weapon. It's gonna stay back there and fight that thing because war is all it knows."

"You're wrong! He's more than a weapon!"

"He's a dolphin in a big metal suit!" Vincent said, catching up to them. He, too, had doubled back through the fleeing crowd to find the girl. "Abe will figure things out with his smart fish brains!"

James The First looked at his two friends as if they had gone mad. "Look, I don't know what you two are rambling about, but we're lucky to still be alive. Right now, your mech is buying us time to blow up that Azrael. If we want any chance of survival, we gotta do it now before it's too late."

The captain grabbed Dot and carried her further into the trees, away from The Department. She kicked her feet, tried to free herself from his arms.

"Captain, we have to wait! He'll find a way..."

"Kiddo, if that Azrael gets outside and away before your pumpkins go boom, it will stalk us to the ends of the Earth until we are all dead in the ground!"

"Just another minute!"

"Cezar agrees with the captain," the wolf hybrid said, emerging from the troops. "We must take advantage of the situation. We must respect Abraham's strategy."

The soldiers all stood at the treeline, watching the distant battle of titans within the atrium. They wanted to retreat, to find cover or flee far enough away to evade the Azrael's sensors. Had they known that the child's desperate threat about the bombs was genuine – the only thing more frightening than the scorpion mech – they'd have already disappeared into the woods.

Vincent looked at the tense, scared soldiers and the frantic girl who refused to move another foot. He hated seeing her sad and scared, and he knew Abraham could barely handle his counterpart alone.

"I'm gonna go help Big Abe," he said as he ran back to the property. "Dottie, you stay with James The First Guy."

"Vincent! No!"

60

Primary Guardian

Sprinting across the pasture with his vines like an animal with impossibly long legs, Vincent made the long trek back to the atrium within a minute. Inside, he saw its flower beds and trees now engulfed in flames from the massive battle, and he nearly stumbled on chunks of busted concrete as he reached the final fight.

"Dang, this ain't good. Ain't good at all."

Even with his limited intellect, the plant-man could see that Abraham had no chance of defeating Azrael and that perhaps nothing on Earth could. Instead, his metal friend focused on restraining the superior mech long enough for them both to be consumed by the coming firestorm.

Vincent wrapped his vines across Azrael's many arms and pulled them off Abraham.

"You gotta go, Abe!" he yelled. "Dottie needs you! You gotta get her outta here!"

"Disagreement: You must leave and replace this unit as the girl's primary guardian."

"But I can't stick her in my chest! It's gotta be you!"

"Unacceptable."

"Why?"

"Status: Self-repair process is at 52.1 Percent. This unit runs at suboptimal parameters and is insufficient for Little Miss..."

"Abe, I don't know what none of that means but this is what Dottie wants! Sub-optical or not, you'd be better at getting her to Kellan than me! You got the land all mapped out in your head, you can see stuff from far away, and you got those great big guns." Vincent grunted as he kept Azrael off his friend. "You know I ain't wrong."

It took Abraham six seconds to run a multitude of scenarios before concluding that his friend's logic was sound.

"Agreement." Though Vincent missed it, the mech's synthetic voice carried a tone of regret and sorrow. He valued the plant-man, knew how much he meant to the child, and didn't want to leave him alone in a fiery tomb with a heartless devil. "Your strategy offers the best odds of survival for Little Miss, an 81.5 percent increase..."

"Tell me the math later, Abe! You need to go before he makes your power thingy zero percent! Go now! Not sure how long I can hold this guy!"

"Gratitude, Vincent."

Abraham released his grip on the larger mech. He lurched forward, out of the crumbling atrium, as his green friend struggled to keep the mindless war demon behind its walls.

Now alone and entangled with Azrael in the burning building, Vincent found himself stuck in the same predicament as his metal friend. Like Abraham, he couldn't defeat the mech, but could restrain him for the moment. If he tried to flee, Azrael would immediately set course for Dot and the others the moment his vines were loosened.

Vincent looked out through the glass wall and watched Abraham cross the pasture. When he was nearly at the treeline with the others, he felt his vines' grip slipping.

"Dang, you sure are big!" Vincent said. "Even bigger than Abe! I wish there was an even bigger guy helping me!" Upon that odd wish, he looked up and realized they stood in the looming shadow of the 50-foot statue, its arm outstretched to the night sky. "You might be just big enough," he said to the giant bronze man.

Vincent remembered what everyone had been telling him, that he was far stronger than he knew, stronger than Cezar and even Juma. He took a chance and released the fighting mech just long enough to wrap his vines around the statue and pull it down with all his strength. The five-ton statue didn't budge, yet the plant hybrid kept pulling without consideration of its mass. To his surprise, he felt it buckle from its base, and as Azrael turned toward the exit to pursue the girl, the statue slowly toppled.

The bronze giant slammed down on the deadly robot, crushing its torso and pinning it helplessly to the shattered marble floor. With its power module ruptured, processing unit pierced, and primary hydraulics bowed and bent, the previously unstoppable sentinel was now a pile of salvage scrap. After every commanding officer Blue or Green, every soldier of flesh or polymer, had regarded the A2500 Azrael combat mech as "the final sunset" of any battle, an infallible killing machine with no equal, Vincent the plant hybrid destroyed it with his courage, quick thinking, and untapped might. Vincent, the simple, innocent farmer who never wanted to hurt anyone or anything, took down the armored goliath feared by all.

With a final whining of its servos, the mech's many arms and legs stopped flailing, falling to the floor with a thunderous clatter. Its sensors scrambled as all systems shut down completely, throwing the atrium into a sudden silence, like the startling moment when a storm finally subsides.

In the middle of the thick smoke of the atrium and the cloud of dust and debris from the statue's collapse, Vincent also found himself pinned, his left leg trapped underneath the statue's head. Held flat to the floor, Vincent couldn't get a good enough grip to free himself. Even if he could, it would have proved an impossible task. It took every fiber of his being, every ounce of his immense strength, just to pull down Imago's statue. Dead-lifting it off the ground was unthinkable.

"Abe, can you hear me? Big guy? Dottie?"

There was no response. His cochlear earpiece had dislodged and was crushed when the statue fell.

"Father," Vincent said to the night sky. "I think I'm in trouble."

He pulled out his little black book of instructions and flipped pages in search of a solution. Though there were no entries regarding fallen statues or Azrael mechs or Lotus bombs, he found a page late in the book with a macabre header that seemed to fit the situation.

WHAT TO DO WHEN YOU'RE ABOUT TO DIE.

Vincent smiled, for his wise Father had indeed thought of every possible scenario. He read the page twice – a set of four simple steps – and followed its hand-written instructions...

1. Think about all the good in your life and remember how much of it was because of you.

2. Imagine the people you cared about and the people who cared about for you.

3. Leave this book behind for them. They must read it to keep you in their hearts.

4. Remember that you're my son and that I loved you from the moment I brought you into this world.

Vincent thought about all the good days he experienced in his life and reflected on how much of it came from his actions. Those beloved moments naturally led to the people he came to care about.

The kind, brave Exceptional Girl and her stalwart German Shepherd, determined to rescue their family even through a foggy memory and unknown dangers abound. She continued onward while hunted by all, her movements tracked at every hour. Her overwhelming role in curing The Worm and its impossible odds never dampened her spirit.

The imposing wolf hybrid who considered himself an unworthy coward yet proved to be the bravest, most selfless man he'd ever met, who ultimately became one of his closest friends. He was once an outcast in a vast prison habitat, ready to die for his clan, but was driven forward by equal measures of regret and unrequited love.

The old war machine, whose cold primary directives faded as he learned to protect and serve while still preserving and respecting all life, recognizing threats as opportunities for further understanding. His organic-synthetic mind discovered traces of emotion, enough to reveal morals and ethics beyond his base programming.

The enslaved hybrids of Colt who'd lost all hope, accepting their fate of eventually being dissected and discarded by the Purists. They were an ensemble of lost souls who owed their freedom to his newfound bravery and paid it back tenfold by helping the girl and her companions escape the doomed village.

The good Dr. Blum and the forsaken hybrids of Dominion Research Vivarium who'd never imagined life out in the wild world and now traveled across the unknown toward the faint hope of a better future.

The Holy Gardeners of Beacon Hill and the squad of "Honorless" Apostates, wandering warriors who abandoned their first notions of loyalty only to rediscover them to help a lost child and her motley circus of friends.

Behind all the friendly faces in his mind, Vincent thought of "Father" Francis Young, the first person to treat him with unconditional kindness and respect. He taught Vincent about life – as best and as much as he could – before succumbing to decades of pain. After meeting Dot, seeing hope for the world embodied in a fearless little girl, the dying old man knew he'd finally found someone who would continue watching over his unique son, someone who he'd equally care for. That comfort allowed him the peace to finally drift away in his corner chair.

After remembering all those people he'd encountered, some he saved, others who saved him, he placed them all together in his thoughts. He shut his eyes and saw them standing in a group in his own version of The Void, a surreal place where they'd finally be safe together.

CLUNK!

CLANG!

Vincent opened his deep black eyes upon hearing metallic thuds that sounded alarmingly close. They were followed by several more, as if something within the dormant Azrael was trying to awaken. Vincent leaned his head and looked at the fallen mech beside him, hoping it hadn't somehow found the power to free itself.

The noise came not from the machine but the man trapped within. Through the cracked, narrow window in the mech's chest, Lieutenant Dixon pressed his face against the glass. He gave up his futile struggle to escape and saw the tall flames on the walls, the piles of rubble, and the helpless lone plant hybrid trapped a few feet away.

"They're all gone, aren't they?" Dixon said, exhausted, laughing in defeat. "Looks like I ended up serving two lost causes: the outmatched Loyalists and the outwitted Purists. It also looks like it's just you and me in the end."

"Yep, looks that way," Vincent said. "Dottie and the others are far away. You won't be taking her anywhere with you now."

"Then I'll be taking you with me instead... in a sense."

"Dang, you're right," Vincent said. "Unless..." He stretched toward Dixon to free him, but his vines were mostly tangled and trapped within the innards of the fallen war machine. He could only reach one of Azrael's hands. "Sorry, Mr. Lieutenant Guy, but I can't get you out. I guess this is the part where we die. Those big Lotus ball things are gonna explode any moment now... or implode or displode, I forget... kinda like the world's biggest firecrackers."

"Firecrackers?" Dixon laughed again, coughing up blood from his internal injuries. "Boy, I wish I was as dumb as you, that I could see things as simply as you do."

"Thanks, I think. Hey, since it's just us laying here, maybe we're both dumb?"

"You know, that's exactly right. We are both dumb. Too bad we won't be around to see your fireworks."

"Normally, I'd say it was nice meeting you because I like to meet new folks. It's always a new adventure." Vincent wheezed, finding it hard to breathe. "But to be honest, Mr. Lieutenant Sir, it wasn't so nice meeting you. Sorry if that sounds rude."

"The feeling is definitely mutual. I know you're a dullard, but I hope you don't take my actions personally. I was just trying to save the world, like you."

"Nah, not like me," Vincent said, shaking his head. He understood Dixon far better than the lieutenant could know. "Still, it's definitely been an adventure."

Vincent looked at his little black book one more time before placing it in Azrael's palm and closing its massive metal hand around it.

He wouldn't need it anymore.

The plant-man shut his eyes one last time and returned to his personal Void. Facing everyone he cherished once again in the dark expanse, he grinned and waved both hello and farewell.

* * *

Outside at the treeline, Abraham rejoined his companions and the many soldiers accompanying them, signaling James The First to grab the girl once more and rush her further into the woods. Not wanting to leave Vincent behind, Dot screamed in protest and struggled to break free of the captain's hold, but her pleas were ignored as Mort helped James take her away, deeper through the brush.

She looked at the faces all around her, the Gardeners, the Apostates, the liberated Automen, but they all looked away, for they all felt her torment. She shared a concerned glance with Cezar, and they both turned back for one last look at the Department of Transmutation. The compound, surrounded by tall trees and cliffs lit by the full moon, seemed quiet and harmless. The tranquility collapsed as an overpowering dread came over her.

As if she had her mech's sensors embedded in her brain, she somehow knew the precise moment they reached a distance of 500 meters from the property.

"Abraham!" she shouted. "Any sign of Vincent? How far are we from..."

BOOM!

61

When The Smoke Cleared

Vehicle Storage, Maintenance, and Security had their own buildings north and northwest of the central structure. They were spared destruction from the rows of Lotus bombs embedded in the atrium's foundation, its north and south wings, and its inner laboratories. Their mass detonation seemed to turn back time for a moment, with a violent expelling of debris that was quickly sucked back to its source in a powerful implosion, as if a galactic black hole had emerged from the basement.

When the bombs went off, Dot and her companions – both old and new – stared from deep in woods at the immense pillar of fire that rocketed into the moonlit sky with what sounded like the roars of a celestial pride of lions.

"Grab a tree!" Cezar yelled as the thundering, blinding spectacle produced a cloud ring that shot across the land, sending pulverized brick and shattered glass in all directions.

Everyone took cover behind trees to shield themselves from the explosion except for Abraham, who instead grabbed Dot and quickly placed her in his chest. He barely had time to turn his back to the bombs and take the brunt of the blast. Even at half a kilometer away, the mech and the surrounding woods were hit hard by the force of the bombs, with many trees shredded to splinters.

James The First and his squad were familiar with military explosives and knew things could have been far worse. If not for the Lotus bombs' cascading implosion arrangement, a careful design by Professor Imago that contained the blast radius for concentrated damage, the surrounding trees would have been set ablaze and knocked down like dominos across the forest floor, swept away like a hellish, raging river. Few of the people in the woods would have survived if not for the old man's forethought.

Through the narrow window in Abraham's chest, Dot peered through the dense dust cloud, waiting for it to dissipate, hoping to see her leafy green friend emerge unharmed as he always had. After several minutes blind, she reluctantly asked Abraham to scan for Vincent and heard the response she feared.

"Reconnaissance: Vincent is not detected."

"What does that mean?" Dot asked.

"Clarification: There are cellular signs of a plant human-hybrid within the remains of the facility, but none positively identifying as Vincent."

Cezar craned his neck to the full moon and howled in agony, a sustaining dirge of pain and suffering that could surely be heard for miles. The savage outcry would normally strike fear into anyone, but it brought only tears to the girl.

"Please let me out, Abraham," Dot said, shaking. "I think I'm going to throw up."

The mech crouched, opened his chest hatch, and offered his giant hands as stairs to the ground. Dot made it to his first palm before losing her balance and falling to the ripped turf of grass and rocks, feeling weak and empty inside. She stared at the loose soil falling between her clinched fists and at a single torn leaf in her grip. She quietly wept, the flying dust collecting on the trails of her tears. Gypsy curled his body around hers and rested his head atop her feet, feeling the girl's deep despair.

"I'm so sorry, kiddo," James The First said, careful to allow her some space. "I know you two were close."

"He had a good heart," Eve The Fifth said.

"He was a good lad for sure," Mort The Third said. "He told a lot of god-awful jokes, some he said came from the trees by the camp. I laughed at 'em all."

"He said oak trees have a great sense of humor," Dot said, remembering the first time she saw him through the stalks of Father Young's cornfield in the North Woods.

"He said pine trees were also funny," Walt The Fourth said, "but they can be too silly."

"I'll never look at a Christmas Tree the same way again," Grace The Sixth said.

Surrounded by friends sharing her grief, she turned to look at her startling new entourage.

Behind the Apostates stood the Gardeners of Beacon Hill and the newly defected Purist Automen. Seeing them in their long, red hooded cloaks and green fatigues, their weapons sheathed and hatred faded, Dot had to remind herself how suddenly things had changed. Those abandoned and conditioned humans, hybrids, and clones were allies now. Freedom from their oppressors had given them a choice, perhaps for the first time in their lives, and they chose to join her. They stood silent, waiting for instructions from the new human captain.

James felt their stares and tried to think in terms of military strategy, but all he could see in his mind was the plant-man's innocent smile. Before he could ask them for a few minutes of privacy, he turned and saw the dozens of identical Automen gather near.

"Should we reconnoiter the ruins of the compound, Captain?" one Automan asked. "There may be resources."

"The plastic soldier's got a good point," Mort said with a grunt, seeing his duties as a way of coping with his loss. "I mean, we got a helluva lot more mouths to feed and wounds to patch."

James crouched beside the distraught girl. He and Cezar held her hands and together they rose to their feet.

"I apologize," James said, placing his arm around the girl. "I mean, if it feels like we're suddenly back to business so soon after..."

"No, I understand, Captain," Dot said. "We need to take care of each other. Vincent would say the same."

"Very well." James turned to his followers. "I doubt anything of value survived the main building's blast, but the maintenance sheds and vehicle bay might be salvageable."

"Security Office is still standing," Mort said with a glance back at the property. "Worth a look-see."

"Kiddo, you stay here with Cezar. The rest of us are gonna loot the remains."

"You're not afraid of Purist reinforcements?" Dot asked. She eyed the Automan waiting for further orders. "And you're not afraid of the Purists here right now? Lieutenant Dixon said..."

"Dix is dead," James said. "You don't have to worry about anything he said or did. And there ain't no Purists here, not anymore."

"I'm not so sure." Dot lowered her voice and leaned close to the captain. "Some of these Automen killed Sarge. How can you trust them?"

"I get it, kiddo. Sarge was my commanding officer and my good friend, and part of me resents these clones for pulling the trigger. But I also know Dix manipulated them into thinking that Sarge was hurting the cause, that he was the enemy. Dix exploited a logic loop in their programming, forced them to turn on the man and on each other. For most of them, it was a hard call, and they had no control. It must've been painful for them to follow that order. Imagine if someone took control of Abraham and commanded him to betray you."

"That's not supposed to be possible," the girl said. "He imprinted on me."

"Yes, but Dix was there when Abraham came online. If he had also imprinted on him, he could've forced him to harm you, against his will. Believe me when I tell you, if not for Dix's twisting of their minds, these clones would still be following Sarge today."

"Can you promise me we can trust them?"

"Do you trust that Dix and I are different?" James asked.

"Of course."

"Dix lied to them, kiddo. He pressured them to obey, demanded their service. I gave them a little sales pitch, sure, but all I really had to do was point at you, show them I was your protector, not your hunter. That's what flipped the switch back. You want a promise? What I can promise is that I didn't force them into anything. I didn't deceive them or warp their minds. These clones choose to serve me because they're inspired by the stories of the Exceptional Girl, and that's something this old soldier does trust."

"And I trust you, Captain." Dot still felt uneasy around the dozens of Green uniforms, but took comfort in Captain James's confidence. "Thanks for making things a little clearer. It might take some getting used to, but I feel better about it."

"I'm glad." Captain James took Dot to Cezar, away from the Automen clustering around him. "Now, you asked me about Purist reinforcements. Good question. There's plenty still out there. Some of Dix's back-up pals may very well come, but we got ourselves a battalion now, in case you hadn't noticed. And like Mort said, that's a lot of mouths to feed, a lot of shelters to build and hands to arm. So now we gotta pick through the rubble for supplies whether or not anyone's coming. It's the first and last job of any survivalist. Lots of work to be done."

Dot nodded and rested on the roots of an ancient oak alongside Cezar and Gypsy, while Abraham stood nearby, continuing his self-repair efforts.

James joined Mort and Hale, who'd been listening to his talk with the child.

"You really believe what you told the girl?" Mort asked his captain with a snort. "All that business about now trustin' the plastic grunts?"

"You know me, Mort. I wouldn't have said it if I didn't mean it."

"Hell, then I guess I feels a bit better 'bout it, too."

James led the rest of the soldiers back across the now decimated pasture to what used to be the Department of Transmutation, former home to Professor Domingo Imago and the frayed threads of his legacy. The intimidating structure, once a fortress, now stood as a smoldering ruin.

"All those years of work," Mort said as he took in the sight of the total destruction. "Decades of research, all gone forever."

"He was ready to part with it," James said. "The kid and her sisters are alive. They're his life's work, not the notes or files or equipment that were in that place. Those girls have a chance at a future, which means maybe we finally do."

"Crikes, I hopes you's right, Captain."

"I hope I am, too."

James delegated tasks to the vast group without incident. They were all his soldiers now. His original squad of six now swelled to a company over a hundred strong, including a bioengineered military dog, an apex predator hybrid, and an Abraham combat mech. So long as they remained united under his command, no pack of raiders or troop of Greens or any other potential foe would dare cross their path.

As instructed, the Automen patrolled the area, securing the perimeter and repairing any found equipment. The Gardeners rummaged through the surviving outer buildings for supplies and sundries while also harvesting wild herbs and hunting small game.

As James had hoped, the vehicle bay held a fleet of trucks, former troop transports, their solar panels continually charging through the skylights in the ceiling. There was more than enough room in the trucks to accommodate their numbers. The security office had cabinets full of guns and ammunition. The maintenance shed offered tools, clothes, and storage units. After a few hours of scouring the property, the sun had risen, and they had plenty of supplies for everyone moving forward, surely enough to get them back down the Broken Road to the West Wall.

Abraham completed his self-repair to the best of his current ability. Much of his ablative armor was gone, and he needed many internal replacement parts, but he was mostly intact and fully operational. As he absorbed the light of the new dawn, recharging his power module, he spoke to the wolf-man.

"Request: Please accompany this unit to the remains of the atrium. The destroyed Azrael unit may have compatible components for salvage. Your technical prowess and manual dexterity would be of great assistance."

Cezar saw Dot had fallen asleep in tears, exhausted from their traumatic night. He gently lifted her head from the ground and placed it upon the German Shepherd.

"Let us go," the wolf said. "Cezar can take anything you need from that wretched thing."

Upon reaching the site of the conflict, they saw the fallen mech torn to pieces from the cascade implosion, Vincent's dead vines strung out around it. Abraham performed a deep scan of the wreckage, but it was Cezar who noticed something peculiar.

One of Azrael's hands was formed into a tight first, the only part of his frame not splayed out across the cracked marble floor. Within the robot's armored grip, Cezar caught the faint scent of leather and paper, unharmed by the blast. He pried open the massive metal hand with his long claws and found a small black book in its palm.

Vincent's Life Instructions.

"Something to remember him by," Cezar said. "My poor plant must have tucked it in here before he departed this world. He knew his fate and wanted to leave this for us. Brave to the end. Gave his life to save ours. There is no death more honorable, no spirit more pure."

"Agreement."

"Cezar... I... will always remember my blood brother."

"Agreement." The mech turned his head toward the little book. "Request: Allow this unit to scan the booklet's pages."

"Why? Are you actually getting sentimental, Abraham?"

"Analysis: Yes."

"Agreement, as you might say."

The wolf hybrid slowly turned the little book's pages for the mech to archive. The headings caught his attention, covering every conceivable scenario.

"The man was thorough," Cezar said.

Several minutes later, they reached the page entitled "What To Do When You're About to Die," noting the four steps listed. After reflecting on their wisdom and realizing they doubled as steps that everyone should heed throughout their lives, he turned the page and found a fifth and final step reserved for anyone who discovered the book.

"Abraham, scan for any traces of Vincent. Be sure to cover the entire property, including both the interior and..."

"Scan complete," the mech said. "The deceased plant hybrid's remains are positioned in six locations within a 20-meter radius."

"Point them out, please." Cezar braced himself for an unspeakable task.

"Query: What are we do to with the deceased plant hybrid's remains..."

"His name was Vincent!" the wolf bellowed. "And these remains are his body!"

"Correction: What are we to do with Vincent's riven body?"

"We must gather him. It's the right thing to do, and it's also his father's final wish."

"Apology. This unit finds it difficult to speak his name at this time."

The wolf looked up at the mech and felt a lost soul looking back at him within his insectoid camera eyes. "It is Cezar who should apologize. Scanning for any signs that he might be alive, and now for any pieces of his torn body, it clearly pains your large metal heart."

"Agreement."

Abraham shined a narrow beam of light on a severed vine behind them. Cezar picked it up and slung it over his shoulder, barely containing his swelling emotion. The mech saw his tears forming, detected his increased heart rate, change in body chemistry, and unstable stance. Miraculously, the machine felt the beast's pain rather than merely observe it.

"Statement: You have made an intelligent and logical choice in gathering our friend's remains and should feel no anguish in performing this action. With high probability, I surmise Vincent would have wanted us to honor his father's request."

"Even if he hadn't wished it so," the wolf-man said, "Cezar wouldn't leave his brother to rot in tatters in this dreadful place. It's no way to remember a fallen comrade and a good friend."

62

Remembrance

The plan had always been to head west along the high, rocky ridgeline that paralleled much of the Broken Road, past the West Wall, in search of sanctuary. The arduous path would have lessened the chance of detection, for Purist troops rarely ventured in such rough, technical terrain at high altitude, especially at night. A lot changed in the ten days since 15-year-old Cordelia "Dot" Imago emerged from an old oak tree on a steep hillside above the Miracle River Bridge. She awoke alone, without the company of even her own identity. Her entourage now comprised over a hundred trained warriors, all formidably armed and traveling together in four open transport vehicles. For the first time in her life – both before and after her memories were picked, scattered, and erased – she felt completely safe.

Lynn Harrod

The Automen, four-dozen synthetic soldiers formerly of the Purists of Earth, who'd hunted the girl relentlessly for nearly two weeks, now sat beside her as allies and would remain in her service so as long as they felt convinced they were where they belonged. Sergeant Furst had told Dot that Automen switched sides whenever they reassessed their mission and its chances for success, but James The First saw them differently.

From his decades of experience in the field, the veteran captain felt convinced that the identical clone soldiers had a fundamental moral compass and continually assessed not only mission success but also right and wrong, the values of which they took solely from their superior officer. Under Sergeant Furst's command, they believed they served a greater purpose for humanity while still holding a high regard for all life. The disgruntled Lieutenant Dixon, envious of Sarge's station and respect, gradually corrupted them and flipped their loyalty. It didn't matter that a lieutenant technically outranks a sergeant, for he knew the true pecking order and didn't consider Sarge worthy of being above him. That disdain influenced the impressionable clones each day, like children observing their parents' crumbling marriage and taking sides out of innocent ignorance. Dixon exploited their naive viewpoints.

Now, under the leadership of Captain James, their revised mission was to safeguard the girl in the best interests of the world. James assured her he'd maintain their guiding light and would never take their loyalty for granted, something Sarge did toward the end of his life.

The captain's fellow Apostates had accepted their vagabond life of survival, trusting no one outside their small circle, but they felt inspired by Dot's ability to gain trust, even from those who suffered from the mandates of humans. They saw a child gather loyal followers in search of a fabled city beyond the West Wall and realized it was a mission worthy of their devotion, a potential end to their nomadic days.

Mort The Third and Grace The Sixth were still apprehensive about rejoining society but decided that their dream of a permanent home, a city where they no longer needed to look behind them minute-by-minute, was worth the risk. They would still be armed and ready for a fight at all times, but now it would be to protect the greater community.

The Gardeners of Beacon Hill, elite warriors long devoted to their town's three figurehead Widows, anxious Aldermen, and desperate Elders, realized they could now choose the paths of their lives. Adopted by the Widows and conditioned to serve, they were driven by those seen as their saviors. After witnessing the cruel lengths the Elders were willing to go for a slight chance at longer life, and after Cezar officially declared them free from servitude, they left their town in search of a new purpose. That purpose became clear upon receiving the distress call from the Department of Transmutation. They realized who the call came from and why, and dedicated their renewed focus to saving the girl from the harm they knew well.

Dot sat beside Cezar and Abraham in the back of her transport, the first in the convoy of four, as it rumbled west down the road's faded yellow line. Fittingly, each of the long, open-air trucks had "D.O.T." stenciled on their sides in large letters. Both the transports and their passengers were truly hers.

Four of the Apostates – Mort, Walt, Eve, and Grace – drove the transports while James and Hale served as lookouts on the first and last vehicles, respectively.

James lowered his binoculars and smiled at Dot as she stared at the passing trees out the side of the open passenger compartment. The Broken Road felt less desolate and threatening to her, as if it, too, now helped guide her to sanctuary.

"Sorry for the bumpy ride, kiddo," James said. "These old staff transports were always rough, even when they were new."

"After riding inside Abraham for a week," Dot said, "this truck feels like it's gliding on ice."

James laughed, imagining the girl crammed and curled up in the empty central bomb compartment of the mech.

"I've seen a lot of these big troop transports," Dot said. "I can see why the militias used them, but why did my father's lab have so many?"

"Mass transports like these were originally used to evacuate cities and towns during the final stage of the war. Imago's facility later used them to take staff to and from the labs, back before his colleagues died or went their separate ways. The Blues and Greens inherited and repurposed them, but it looks like they missed these four."

"Lucky for us."

"I don't think luck was a factor," James said. "Your father is a brilliant man. He kept these big trucks around just in case he'd need them. Now, I can see why."

Gypsy lay at Dot's feet while Cezar and Abraham sat at the rear of the vehicle, the robot's arms and legs folded in. Cezar carried the large canvas sack that contained Vincent's remains.

"Where should we bury him?" Dot asked.

"Caffar would say to bury him where he last fought," Cezar said. "His grave there would have served as a monument to his sacrifice. But Father Young's final instruction was to bury him where he would have loved to be."

"That's why you brought him with us? To bury him in Kellan?"

"Vincent sought that mythical city just as we did, a new home where hybrids are welcome. Dead or alive, it would honor him to be in such a place, just as it honors Cezar now to carry him there.

We all know he would do the same for any of us. Besides, who are we to deny his father's last request?"

"Maybe we should bury him on his old farm?" Dot said. "It was his home for most of his life."

"Perhaps you're right, but Cezar still believes he would have preferred a grave in the free city, should we find it. He certainly would have preferred to be near you."

Dot held the wolf-man's paw and nodded thanks for the warm regard. "No shady trees. He loved the sun."

"He also loved swimming, didn't he?" Cezar asked.

"He didn't swim so much as soak. He'd just float happily on the water."

Having heard their discussion, Abraham turned to his friends.

"Suggestion: We should locate an area exposed to full sun in proximity to a body of water, conditions that Vincent greatly valued. Examples include the edge of a pond, the bank of a river, or the trails paralleling an irrigation canal."

"Cezar agrees," the wolf said. "Each of those sounds like a beautiful final resting place that would honor anyone."

"I guess we'll know it when we see it," Dot said, touched by her friends' heartfelt ideas.

* * *

The convoy followed the road for hours, its single yellow line hypnotic and peaceful. It passed familiar sights, backtracking much of Dot's journey.

They drove through the town of Beacon Hill and its extensive subterranean shelter, populated by a frightened community of humans who now had to fend for themselves. They crossed a bridge over the Regal River, the same deceptively tranquil river that nearly took their lives, followed by a turnoff to the road that led east to the Dominion Research Vivarium.

"Cezar smells spent ammunition," the wolf said, realizing the facility wasn't far. "Burnt wood, scorched steel, smoldering cinder. After we fled The Great Domain, the Greens must have burned down the rainforest in search of survivors."

"Many of those same Greens travel with us now," Dot said. "How does that make you feel?"

"It's a most peculiar turn of events. Cezar is still unsure about them."

Dot heard the familiar tone of doubt in the wolf's voice, much like her own when speaking with Captain James. "The captain convinced the Automen to join us, just as you convinced the Gardeners. Do you doubt them?"

"No. The red cloaked guards are good soldiers, lost souls who were simply led astray by megalomaniacs. They now serve on their own free will."

"Captain James says the same about the clones."

"Cezar has come to trust the man, just as he's come to trust you," the wolf hybrid said. "Cezar will follow the captain's lead. Together, we will prevail." The scent of the bombed rainforest still hung in the air, a foul odor that only he could pick up. "Sadly, our growing company doesn't change the fact that my old home is now a ruin of decay and lost memories."

"Just like my old home," Dot said. "I'm sorry, Cezar."

"It's for the best, girl. We left in search of a new home. May the old ones harbor the wild now."

* * *

After another few hours, they reentered the South Lands and passed a sign that read "Welcome To Colt – A Neighborhood of Friendship."

"Should we take the north road around the village?" James asked Dot, knowing the girl's history with Senior Wainright's fanatical congregation. "It would take a little more time but..."

"No, we drive straight through it," Dot said, looking around at all the soldiers now loyal to her. "We drive through the heart of that damned village, nice and slow."

"Some of them might see us," Cezar said.

"Let them all see," Dot said. She'd grown tired of always being scared, of always wondering who to trust. Her new armada empowered her to defy those who would harm her and her friends. "I want them to get a good, long look at us."

"As you wish, girl," Cezar said with a slight, proud grin.

Upon seeing the village's eastern outskirts again, she remembered the dog-men and their brethren, their selfless acts as they fled Colt.

"We lost a friend here," Dot said. "A leopard hybrid. She helped us escape this cruel place."

Cezar raised his snout and sniffed the air. "What was her name?"

"Sapphire."

"Cezar smells no leopard nor any other hybrid."

"They might've eaten her," Dot said, clinching her eyes tight in sad disgust.

"If these fools are the zealots you described," James said, "they likely burned her body to cleanse their village of her unholy spilled blood."

"The captain is right," Cezar said. "They saw hybrids as abominations, a curse against nature. In their eyes, to leave her broken body on the ground would be like placing a curse on their town."

"I'm glad they didn't just abandon her there," Dot said. "They did a good thing, burning her, whether or not they knew it."

"May we all remember the leopard Sapphire," the wolf said. "Cezar is humbled by her bravery."

"As am I," James said. "Sounds like she was one tough cat."

* * *

An hour later, heading north, the convoy approached the former campsite where Sergeant Furst gave his life to protect the Exceptional Girl. Dot asked to stop and honor the man, and the four transports parked in the burnt clearing. She expected to see dozens of bodies strewn about the area, but the many Automen engaged in that firefight had either repaired or salvaged each other before moving on with their new commander, Lieutenant Dixon.

Most of them were with her now.

Only Sarge remained on the scorched ground.

Per Dot's request, Cezar picked up Sarge's body, wrapped it in canvas, and placed it in the transport beside Vincent's remains. They would be buried together once they reached their destination.

James The First, Hale The Second, and Mort The Third knew Sarge well. They served with him in their former lives, before his promotion to high command, and grew to admire him. Though the internment in Kellan was yet to come, a ceremony of remembrance at the place of his death felt appropriate. James lit a fire and spoke parting words for his former sergeant as his new battalion gathered around.

"Sarge, you were one of a kind," James said, looking both to the sky and to his assembly. "You believed in a cause with no one cramming it down your throat. You didn't buy into propaganda or idol worship. Like all great leaders, you simply fought for what you believed in, that everyone, human or hybrid or synthetic, had the right to life. You believed being different was a strength, not a weakness or shame, and you believed in this kiddo here with us today. We continue your mission. Wherever you are now, Sarge, know that you didn't die for nothing. I wish I had served under you longer before my departure from the organized religion known as the military. It took this old fool a long time to understand that the only loyalty any good soldier should have is not to his troop nor his clan nor God nor whatever other label you want to use. A good soldier is loyal to the world's citizens. That's what you fought for, and that's what we will keep fighting for in your name."

* * *

After another three hours on the road, rounding out the pilgrimage to nearly ten hours, the convoy finally reached the bridge that spanned the Miracle River, the spot where Dot was unknowingly reintroduced to Gypsy.

An ancient roadside sign partially obscured by weeds read "Kellan Welcomes You – 2 Miles Ahead."

Unlike the former Loyalist camp, the bridge still held the lifeless bodies of Blue and Green soldiers who died for Dot's protection or capture, for most of them were human, including the few who still served the Purists. Mort insisted on also honoring them, giving them a mass burial beside the river. He offered a few words in their honor.

"Some of you was brave souls who fought for the greater good you believed in," Mort said from atop the hood of a transport truck. "Some of you was lost fools who fought for the lies they poisoned you with. Either ways, you deserves to be remembered. That little girl you wanted so badly? She's with us now. Got her right here. It's good that you Greens fumbled 'cause now we're gonna look after her, help raise her right, teach her good from bad and all. That being said, I imagine this old roughneck's got lots to learn from such a sharp runt." He turned to Dot and offered a hand, helping her climb onto the truck hood next to him. "Any words, girl?"

"I'm sorry so many of you died for me," Dot said to the mass grave. Speaking to them was not unlike speaking to the specters of her sisters in The Void. "I'm sorry if you felt like you failed your mission as you died. My hope is that whatever happens next will somehow justify your struggle."

63

Out From The Wild

Sunset approached when they returned to the road a half-hour later. The convoy crossed the bridge and continued another two miles before reaching what they assumed was Kellan, the remnants of a once-prosperous city, one much larger than any other settlement or encampment or town any of them had encountered before. Dot had seen photos of skyscrapers in books and was familiar with the famous ones, but had never gazed up at one in person. Most of the world's major metropolitan areas were heavily bombed during the war, reducing their dazzling sky-high towers to mangled metal amongst piles of rubble. The inner streets and the eight-lane highway that used to serve a population approaching one million were now littered with a sea of derelict cars and trucks left behind during the panic of a mass exodus.

Lynn Harrod

As the convoy drove further into the city, they passed neighborhoods with abandoned homes followed by industrial areas of shuttered factories and commercial districts lined with decimated storefronts. With not another soul in sight, Dot and her companions feared that the stories of the sanctuary city were merely legend turned myth. Perhaps there was once a progressive human-hybrid community here long ago, but as Dot learned, a lot can change over 200 years.

Their despair lifted when they first caught sight of the fabled West Wall, a 50-foot-high concrete barrier that bisected the city, built to withstand assaults from warring factions and raiders.

"You see anyone, Abraham?" Dot asked.

"Reconnaissance: There are three humanoid life signs in a 10-kilometer radius, positioned 308.7 meters ahead. One female hybrid, two male humans."

"Just three?"

"Correct."

"A population of three," James said. "So much for sanctuary."

"We'll become the city's population," Dot said. "As far as I can see, there's still no better place to start over."

"Agreement," Abraham said.

"Disagreement," Cezar said, furrowing his brow. "Cezar will stave off any premature optimism until he meets this mysterious three."

"Don't worry, Cezar," Dot said. "What threat could three people possibly be to us now?"

"Cezar doubts that number. Night is falling, girl, the time for raiders and Greens to run patrols and launch ambushes."

"Trust me, I know."

"You must forgive Cezar if the rising moon makes this old wolf feel... apprehensive."

"If it's any consolation," James said, "this old captain feels the same way. Three people alone with no one else around in this huge city? I don't buy it. Maybe I'm just being paranoid."

"Threat Assessment: The detected three humanoids are heavily armed."

"Paranoia is good," Cezar said, his metal friend having confirmed his suspicions. "Paranoia keeps you alive."

Upon reaching the great barrier that divided the ruins of the city, a woman's voice called out from atop what looked like an immense gateway built into the wall.

"Shut down your vehicles!" the woman said. "Power down your weapons and step out where we can see you! Identify yourselves!"

The four transports parked parallel. Their drivers shut off their humming electric motors. In the silence that followed, the soldiers looked to James The First for orders, and he looked to Dot.

"Well, kiddo, what should we do?" James asked.

"You're asking me?" Dot said, incredulous. "You're the veteran war hero, not me. These soldiers follow your orders."

"True, but I follow yours."

"You honor me, Captain," the girl said, feeling suddenly overwhelmed, "though I can't decide if that comforts or horrifies me."

"Look, I'll do whatever it takes to protect us and our troops. That's on me. I just want to know your thoughts first."

Dot ran the scenario in her mind before stepping out of the transport, exposing herself to the three armed guards atop the wall. If her open gesture was met by a bullet, she wanted to be the first and only to fall, to give the others a chance to fight or flee. After memorializing the dead all day, both friend and foe, she refused to allow another death in her name.

Cezar rose to follow her, but James gestured for him and the others to give her space, granting her time to address the woman above.

"My name is Dot," she called out, holding up her palm to shield her eyes from the setting sun. "My friends and I are..."

"We don't know any Dot!" the woman said. "We see only Purist soldiers!" She'd spied not only Dixon's former clone troops in the open transports as they approached the gate but James's Apostates as well, all dressed in green fatigues.

"They left the Purists!" Dot said.

"Why should that matter to us? A swarm of deserters and lordless clones!"

"They're with me!"

"Turn back now!" the woman said. "We have Hemlocks pointed at you from three directions!"

"Mech, is that true?" James whispered to Abraham in the transport. "Make sure the kid can hear you."

"Reconnaissance," Abraham said to both the captain beside him and to Dot through her cochlear earpiece. "Three unattended caches of armaments are positioned throughout the area. However, if there are remote or automated Hemlock turrets present, this unit cannot identify them until they initiate their power cycles."

"You're saying maybe, but you can't see them until they're about to fire."

"Correct."

James's stomach churned at the possible threat. A Hemlock turret, long rumored to have killed him in battle, was the gun variant of a Lotus bomb, an immeasurably destructive long-range weapon capable of repelling a god, if need be. And there might be three pointed at his people. He looked around at the towering ruins, their blown-out windows staring back like thousands of hollow eyes. If there were indeed hidden turrets about, they could have been anywhere.

Dot's resurgent memory also told her what Hemlock turrets were capable of. After hearing Abraham's report, she trod lightly with the mysterious woman high above.

"My friends call me Dot..."

"You said that."

"...but my real name is Cordelia. I come from..."

Dot silenced herself and watched in shock as the woman jumped from the wall, falling 50 feet until she landed firmly on the pavement with ease.

"Cordelia?" the woman asked. "Cordelia Imago?"

"You know me?"

"If you're telling the truth, yes, I do."

"I have no reason to lie."

"Child, you have every reason to lie, to hide your truth from all those you meet in this unruly world, especially if you really are Cordelia Imago. The question is, are you lying to me now?"

Dot wasn't sure if the stranger's familiarity with her was a good thing or not. Now standing face-to-face, she saw the intimidating, tall woman was clad in plate armor with a long-range rifle strapped to her back, twin pistols at her sides, and a vicious spear in her hand. More arresting than her weapons was her appearance: green-yellow skin, black eyes, and long purple hair like frayed bundles of wild heather. Protruding from the back of her armor were three long vines, raised like snakes around her.

"Identification," Abraham said privately over Dot's earpiece. "The woman is a plant-human hybrid..."

"I can see that, Abraham," Dot said.

"HPG-VCT-006, human-plantae-grandiflora, wildwood calluna vulgarius..."

"I got it, Abraham."

"Threat Assessment: She is armed with a piercing pulse rifle, an acidic plasma spear..."

"Thank you, that's enough, Abraham."

"Are you well, child?" the hybrid woman asked, her hand tightly gripping her long spear. "Who are you talking to?"

Dot considered dismissing her out-of-context comments and offering a vague, comforting response. Instead, she made the risky choice of transparency.

"I was talking to my Abraham-class combat mech.," Dot said, revealing her earpiece.

"You have an A1900?"

"Yes. He's in one of our transports, along with the hundred soldiers you saw."

"That's quite a regiment for one little girl."

"They're my friends."

"Indeed, I saw all your 'friends.' The Purists' soulless clones, Beacon Hill's sadistic Gardeners, human commanding officers, and now, of course, the demonic war machine. We scanned you 20 minutes ago, the moment you entered the city limits. We have a combat mech of our own, nothing like an A1900, but it's locked onto you as we speak."

James and Mort sat up upon hearing the woman's passive threat.

"There's no need for that," Dot said, raising her open hands in front of her. "And you're wrong about them. They're not soulless or sadistic or..."

"Perhaps you are wrong about them!" The plant-woman's voice was deep, hoarse, ominous. She wrapped one of her vines around the girl, feeling for weapons, maybe a bomb.

Captain James watched closely, resting his finger against his rifle's trigger guard.

"Why are you here, child?" The plant-woman asked as she withdrew her vine.

"We're looking for Kellan."

"And who's that? We don't know any Kellan."

"Not who, but where. We seek sanctuary, safety for our hybrids and artificials. We saw the sign..."

"Ferocious friends like these traveling together would be safe wherever they roamed."

"Yes, I suppose that's true," Dot said. "But they wouldn't be free."

"Is that what you seek, child? Freedom? Does it even still exist?"

Dot started to think this stern woman and her two guards with their hidden Hemlock turrets would never willingly let her pass. She considered establishing dominance, issuing an ultimatum, but again chose diplomacy and transparency. The woman's resemblance to her late companion compelled her to earn trust rather than bark threats.

"My close friend was a plant-hybrid like you," the girl said. "His name was Vincent. We wish to bury him here, and our sergeant, if this is Kellan. Please, just let us pass."

"Whether this is or isn't this 'Kellan' you speak of, what will you do if I refuse you?"

"We scanned you as well," Dot said. "You must be formidable if it's just the three of you out here on your own. But it's not just the three of you, is it?"

"You're right," the plant-woman said. "We are formidable. And you're exceptional, right? The Exceptional Girl?"

"I've been called that."

"Are you really Cordelia Imago?"

Dot knew no words would suffice. She pulled up her left sleeve, fully revealing her "DOT" tattoo.

Satisfied, the plant-woman warrior turned and nodded to her comrades on the wall to lower their rifles, just as she lowered her spear.

"Your father is inside," she said, her voice now calm. "He's with your sisters and brother."

"My brother?"

"The young Colt ranger."

"Oh, thank the heavens," Dot said, grateful that her little family was apparently alive. "Thank you... miss.... ummm..."

"I'm Security Chief Magnolia Culluna Wildwood," the plant-woman said, still unsure about the girl. "You can call me 'Maggie' if it's easier."

"If that's what you prefer. Then how do you do, Maggie? You can call me Dot if it's easier."

"If that's what you prefer."

Maggie looked at the open-air transports, at the unnerving sight of Green soldiers staring back at her. She looked up at her two other guards above and shook her head. She had second thoughts.

"You said your friend's name was Vincent?" Maggie asked. "Is he truly dead?" She found the notion of a dead plant hybrid hard to believe, for she knew well that bullets meant nothing to her kind. It was more reason to doubt the child.

"Yes. He was a plant hybrid like you. We thought he was the last of his kind."

"As did I," Security Chief Magnolia said in a curious tone. "It seems we both have siblings we didn't know about. You say you're looking for Kellan, yet you've been traveling through it for the past half-hour."

"You really were tracking us."

"Our Hemlock turrets have long-range sensors. We didn't pick up any plant hybrid. Now, I realize why. I'm sorry for your loss."

"And yours, it seems." Dot looked at the towering gate behind Maggie. "Abraham didn't pick up anyone past the wall. I'm guessing that's where your turrets are."

"The West Wall was built with iron alloy support beams, lead wall span coverings, and polymer composites which…"

"Which interferes with conventional scans." Dot recalled her mech's earlier struggles. "We've encountered this dilemma before, but I think I figured it out."

"Did you?" Maggie asked with an amused laugh. "That would be impressive for a child. Why don't you explain it to me?"

"I'd be glad to." Despite the woman's doubt, Dot finally realized the exploited flaw in Abraham's surveillance. "My friend has first-generation arrays, from way back at the start of the war. Early-model sensors can easily penetrate anything in nature but have a tough time with some man-made materials. Ferrous and dense metals like iron and lead alloys can constrict radiation, countering gamma and x-ray pattern sweeps, and internal fiberglass-vinyl composites hinder radiolocation tools like sonic scans. It's all clear to me now." Looking back at her journey, she realized such materials could augment armor, cover trucks, and perhaps reinforce uniforms.

"That's right," Maggie said, impressed, curious. She didn't expect such keen observation from a young teen. "You must be friends with a mech, as you say, for you certainly talk like one. Tell me, are you really just a little girl?"

"I'm the Exceptional Girl, remember?"

"Indeed." Leveled by Dot's confidence and knowledge, the plant-woman still felt unsure, more confused than before.

"Now you tell me, Maggie, is my family really on the other side of this wall?"

"You have my word, child, Professor Imago and the others are waiting for you. I can offer proof. Can you prove your claims?"

"Just let us pass. Your word is enough. I trust you, and you can trust me."

"I can trust you?" Looking for any reason to suspect the mole of a hidden plot, the warrior leaned in and studied Dot's face. "I would never say those four words to anyone. Where I'm from, trust is earned, not demanded. My mentor's first lesson was to always be wary of those who say, 'you can trust me.' Her wisdom has never failed me."

Dot remembered what Sarge said, that plant hybrids lack intellect. This woman knew her training and nothing else, and it would be hard to gain her full trust.

The plant-woman walked closer to the transports. The presence of so many soldiers who would normally be her foes proved too much to dismiss. How easy it would have been to tattoo an ordinary girl from the squalor of a village, coach her in describing the wall's defense, and use her to sneak hostiles through the gate. The tense scene suddenly felt like a Trojan horse scheme with a simple young girl in place of a wooden statue.

"What if my word wasn't enough?" Security Chief Magnolia asked boldly, defiantly, as if reclaiming control. "What if I'm lying to you now? Perhaps Imago and his kin aren't here. Or perhaps they're my prisoners? What then?"

The vague promises of a stranger no longer held weight, particularly during a challenge, and an exasperated Dot felt angry and toyed with. She'd wanted to avoid threats of violence but saw no choice but to establish dominance, the way Cezar or Dixon would, by making her position ominously clear.

"If you lie to me, Maggie," Dot said, "if you threaten me and keep me from my family, the armada behind us now will likely kill you on the spot."

"Would they?"

"You'd be the first, dead before you hit the ground," Dot said firmly, never taking her eyes off the wavering plant-woman. "It would be out of my hands."

"Our Hemlocks would cut them down."

"They'd do some damage, sure, but not before you'd forever be known as the arrogant guard who died out of ignorance. Is that what you want, Maggie? It breaks my heart that I know for a fact plant hybrids actually can die, as many others have told me. Or do you want to live as the wise woman who delivered the Exceptional Girl? The choice is yours." Dot allowed the plant-woman a long, hard look at her militia in tow, a moment to consider her threat, her logic, and hoped she'd see reason.

In his transport, Captain James silently signaled his Apostates to ready their weapons. Cezar crouched, ready to pounce. Despite the great distance, his claws could easily reach the woman before she knew he was coming.

"The real Exceptional Girl was to arrive with a Loyalist squad," Security Chief Magnolia said, finally revealing her strict orders. "Instead of a small group of Blues, I see a battalion of Greens, artificials, and hoods. You think me a buffoon? Because I'm a plant? You think I intimidate so easily?"

"I think you're a seasoned and intelligent officer," Dot said, pulling back her aggressive tone. "And I think you can tell I'm being genuine. I'm not lying about who I am, and I'm not lying when I say my friends would fire their weapons dry and fight to their last breath, all because you chose to play mind games with a 'little girl.' You wouldn't want all that on your shoulders, would you?"

"No," Security Chief Magnolia said, nervous, now with a burned-in sense of fear. "Of course not."

"I'll be honest, Maggie. I'm tired of people second-guessing me, mistrusting me, especially now that we're so close to the end of our journey after Vincent and Sarge died to get us here. I don't mean to scare you, but a wise wolf once told me that some people only see good intentions after sifting it from a threat. Forget your orders for a moment and search your feelings. Do you really feel like I'm here to trick you?"

The security chief looked at the girl's pleading eyes. "I suppose not."

"Good. Now, open the gate before we question each other further. Please, Maggie, open it now. You really can trust me, and where I'm from, stating that truth means something."

"First, tell your men to power down their weapons."

"Why should they?"

"Because you can also trust me," Security Chief Magnolia said reluctantly, the words burning her throat, making her feel vulnerable. "For all our sakes, I hope your wise wolf is right." She clung to the back of Dot's transport as the girl rejoined her friends. With a wave of her spear, the plant-woman signaled her guards to open the towering gate. It slowly swung apart, revealing a densely populated community. "Welcome to Kellan, child of Imago."

64

A New Home

The scene overwhelmed Dot and her companions as they drove in, their large military vehicles and battered uniforms a stark contrast to the peaceful, thriving community far exceeding anything they'd imagined. Kellan was not merely a village or town or encampment based in the ruins of a collapsed metropolis. It stood as possibly the last living city on Earth.

Humans and hybrids lived and worked together, having rebuilt homes and storefronts. Skyscrapers were repurposed as lush vertical farms, enough to feed thousands of households. Billboards were turned into solar collectors, powering their respective streets. Horses pulled wagons, children played games, and sidewalk vendors sold their wares. Besides the basic supplies of tools, meats, and produce, the street market offered baked treats, art, books, toys, and music. These people weren't just surviving, they were *living*, and they didn't merely coexist, they depended on one another.

It all felt like one of Dot's old picture books, showing the daily routines of the Old World, had suddenly been brought to life. In one sweeping glance, she saw shelters, schools, stores, gardens, playgrounds, all maintained by a diverse, cooperative community of 120,000, hidden from the world by an immense central wall reinforced with all manner of sensor and sound dampeners. Unless Chief Magnolia opened the gate, one would never have suspected such a place existed.

"Thank you again, Maggie," Dot said, done with her intimation tactic. "I apologize for treating you so harshly. I hated speaking to you so."

"I understand, child, and I apologize for my words. As your wolf said, sometimes one has to sift through a threat to find trust, even an empty threat."

"You knew?"

"Not at first, but I searched my feelings, as you said, and felt you wouldn't actually harm us."

"You were right, I never would have. After everything that's happened, I promised myself that no one will die for me ever again."

Chief Magnolia smiled. "Then you really are the child I was waiting for."

Gathered at a tall, active plaza fountain were the liberated hybrids from Colt, adorned in clean clothes. The dog-man Ephraim and his brothers Ezekiel and Elijah wore matching uniforms, serving as members of Kellan's peace officer union, though there seemed to be no urgent need for law enforcement. Near them were the chimp-women, Apphia and Ahlai, along with the leopard-girls in their care, Sherah and Salome. Apphia served as a teacher. She led both hybrid and human children in a group reading lesson, open books all around.

That's day's selection was *The Wonderful Wizard of Oz.*

They spotted Dot as she stepped out of her transport and greeted the old chimp-woman with open arms. Apphia breathed a sigh of relief.

"Tiny Dot," Apphia said. "I knew you'd make it."

Apphia and Ephraim greeted the girl with warm hugs, albeit with an eye on the monstrous wolf-man who never left her side and the Purist soldiers who followed her like a flock of birds. Dot noticed their concern.

"Everyone, this is my friend, Cezar," Dot said, clutching the wolf-man's paw. She felt him tremble and realized he actually felt nervous. "I wouldn't be here if it wasn't for him." She introduced the Colt hybrids by name to her entourage.

"Does the wolf read?" Apphia asked.

Both Dot and Cezar were surprised by the abrupt question.

"He's intelligent and wise," Dot said. "He's proven many times that he..."

"Does the wolf speak?"

"Of course. He's quite eloquent when he..."

"Cezar can read, but not well," the wolf-man said with his ever-present pang of shame in his voice. "Cezar has always learned by listening and doing. My clan did not value literacy."

"Pity," Ephraim said. "Knowledge is the true power of any warrior."

"Cezar agrees. The girl has shown Cezar as much."

"Does the wolf want to read?" Apphia asked, turning toward him.

"Cezar admits... it is a challenge Cezar has long wanted to face."

Lynn Harrod

Apphia held up the classic L. Frank Baum novel her class had been reading.

"I've run across that book before," Dot said, recalling her night in the Wellspring library. "I think you'll like it, Cezar."

"Yes, girl," Cezar said. "What Cezar means is... what I mean... only if there is a book to spare."

"We can share mine," Ahlai said, making room on her bench for the wolf.

"This is James The First," Dot said, grabbing the captain's arm. She looked out at her many other companions, all overwhelmed at the notion of integrating into the community. "And these are the Gardeners of Beacon Hill. Behind them are the Automen who once followed me."

"It seems they still follow you," Ephraim said in awe. "Through the trees and across the rivers, they followed you all the way here to Kellan." The sight of four-dozen Greens would normally fill him with fear, but he clearly saw this troop safeguarded her, just as the wolf, the dog, and the war machine did. "You apparently have a gift for making friends."

"You and I became friends," Dot said to the Alpha dog.

"Indeed, and that's something few have accomplished." Ephraim knelt down to pet Gypsy before rising and offering a handshake to Cezar. "It's an honor to meet a fellow canine hybrid. You kept her safe?"

"We kept each other safe," Cezar said. "It may be difficult to imagine, but... I... owe everything to the girl."

"I know the feeling well, just as I know how odd it feels to join a township for the first time. Consider me and my brothers your guides."

"You honor me."

"Where's Vincent?" Ephraim looked around the group.

"My friend, my blood brother... his hunt has ended." Cezar held the sack of Vincent's remains. "Even now, he honors me as well." He looked down at the sack in sorrow, and the dog-man knew the heavy price of their journey's end.

"He honors us all," Ephraim said, also bowing his head.

"The world shall mourn him," Apphia said. "Every free hybrid will remember his name. My students will hear his stories, sing his songs." She removed a stack of books from a tree stump and turned to the wolf. "This seat was meant for him. You will join us on his behalf?"

Though he was exonerated, Cezar still felt the wound of exile from his clan. The loving and unconditional welcome from the Colt hybrids surprised him, shook him to the core, especially considering their work with human children. In no other place would a disgraced predator like him be allowed with young ones of any species, but here in this wondrous city, as he looked down at the curious, wide eyes upon him, he saw Apphia's invitation as his chance for redemption. No hunt, no death, only acceptance and appreciation. That would be his new sense of honor. His sharp claws would no longer kill, but turn pages. His keen eyes would not seek prey, but knowledge and growth. For the first time in his life, Cezar looked about him and saw a home.

He sat beside Ahlai and together they read the beloved children's tale.

"Little Dot," Apphia said to the girl. "You're free to join us as well, but I assume you're looking for your father. The Professor?"

"Yes, I was told he was here."

"You'll find him in the Founders' Hall down the road."

"Stay, boy," Dot said to Gypsy. She'd noticed the children craning their necks for a peek at her pure dog, likely the first German Shepherd they'd seen.

She left Cezar and Gypsy with the Colt hybrids and continued further into the city, with the Apostates and Automen in tow. Mort took Vincent's remains from the wolf, slinging the heavy sack over his shoulder with a grunt.

They encountered another group of children – again both human and hybrid – playing beside a pond with their human teacher watching over them. Among the youngsters was young Ameri, the fawn-girl from Dominion. Her mother, Ama, sat at a picnic table, preparing lunch. The caribou-woman noticed Dot and her guardians and waved them over.

"I'm glad to see you made it," Ama said.

"I'm glad to see this place is real," Dot said.

"We have plenty of food here, enough for your soldiers."

"Half of them don't eat, but the others would appreciate it, I'm sure."

Dot embraced Ama and gestured for her human companions to take up the generous offer. Ama cut into roast chickens and root vegetables and encouraged everyone to take a plate. The Apostates and Gardeners gladly accepted the meal.

"No Worm here," Ama said. "All the game we eat is raised behind these walls, away from the virus."

"Do you know where I can find the Founders' Hall?" Dot asked.

"The big building with the dome, just a few blocks ahead." Ama looked at the girl's companions. "Is the wolf with you?"

"Cezar? He's reading with another class back in the plaza."

"That's good," Ama said with a smile. "He always looked out for my daughter in the rainforest. I'm happy he made it here with you."

"He'll be happy to know you made it as well."

"Thanks to you," Ama said. "Perhaps I should find him."

"I promise you, he'd love nothing more."

Leaving the Apostates and Gardeners to their lunch, Dot took the sack from Mort and dragged it down the bustling street with Abraham and the Automen behind her. Two streets further, they encountered a service bay, a maintenance facility for agricultural equipment and transport vehicles.

"I know you don't require food," Dot said to her artificial allies, "but surely there are resources here for you all. I'll be okay on my own."

With some initial hesitation, the Automen set down their weapons and explored the workbenches and racks of the bay, outfitted with more than enough tools and supplements to repair and maintain their damaged bodies.

Dot continued down the main thoroughfare, with only Abraham now behind her, something that surprised her. "You sure you don't want to join the clones, Abraham? There's lots of good stuff in that workshop. I know you still need repairs."

"Statement: This unit is sufficiently functional. I shall address my needs once you have addressed yours."

"Gratitude," Dot said.

"Query: Shall I carry Vincent?"

The girl struggled to drag the heavy sack and was tempted to hand it to her towering mech. "No, I prefer to do it, Abraham. I need to do it."

"Acknowledgement."

As they approached the former city hall, its glistening stained-glass dome still intact and beckoning, she felt an unexpected knot in her stomach. "I feel... strange."

"Analysis: Though you have an elevated heart rate and heightened body chemistry, you appear to be in optimum health, Little Miss."

"It think I'm just nervous."

Lynn Harrod

"Query: Why do you feel nervous? You are already familiar with Professor Domingo Imago and your bioengineered siblings."

"It's hard to explain. I've been chasing this moment for so long, literally longer than I can remember, that I'm waiting for it all to fall apart at any moment. Something always seems to go wrong."

"Status: The complement of soldiers at your command, coupled with the city's impenetrable security, suggests that an incursion is next to impossible at any foreseeable time."

"I'm not nervous about any attack," Dot said. "I guess I feel strange because we finally reached our new home together, and... I don't want anything to rip it away."

"Statement: So long as this unit remains functional, no harm will ever come to you again."

"That sounds like a promise," Dot said.

"Clarification: It is this unit's vow of servitude."

"Either way, it's a bold statement coming from a war machine."

"Clarification: The statement comes from a friend."

"I'm glad you're here with me, Abraham."

"Agreement. Gratitude."

"Right now, my heart is pounding like a jackrabbit's feet," Dot said. "I could use the strength of a combat mech."

"Confirmation: You shall always have it."

The giant robot waited outside as Dot carried her large sack into the majestic building.

* * *

The Kellan City Council sat gathered around a long conference table in a grand rotunda, comprising 15 senior members of the city – human and hybrid – elected to represent the citizens from their respective five-block districts. Even after a lifetime of responsibility, of successfully running their neighborhoods as part of a joint effort to minimize the spread of The Worm, they now sat in attention as if they'd returned to Day One. They hung on every word from Professor Imago as he sketched his ideas across a wall-sized map of the city. The council members viewed him in awe, not only because he was a naturally aged man of 148 years, but because he was widely seen as the father of hybrid-human transmutation science and its burgeoning transition program. As far as the council was concerned, he was a living legend who represented both the past and the future of their society.

"I've just returned from surveying the aqueduct with your engineers," Imago said, drawing lines from a central point on the map. "Impressive work, my friends. You are clearly the finest minds of our city. Still, after assessing the treatment plant, the sewage system, and their supporting conduits, we've found many ways to improve the system's efficiency..."

Upon seeing Dot enter the rotunda, the professor's eyes widened, and he stopped short of finishing his proposal.

"My girl," he said with a gasp. He removed his thick glasses and gazed upon her with wide eyes. "Please tell me you're really here." The old man had imagined his daughter's unlikely return so many times that he needed assurance this wasn't yet another daydream.

"I'm here, Father. I'm with you now."

When last he saw his oldest child, she was preparing to sacrifice herself to Lieutenant Dixon and his Purist troops in order to aid him in fleeing the doomed laboratory. After navigating the tunnels deep below the facility and spending long nights traversing the ridgeline eastward, he came to accept her inevitable death as the steep cost of freedom for his other children, both human and hybrid. He knew she was brilliant and brave, but never considered her seemingly fatal decision as having any chance of survival.

"Can we have the room, please," Professor Imago said to the council. No explanation was needed for everyone knew well who this young girl was and what she endured to arrive there. The men and women who led the districts smiled and nodded as they rose from their seats and shuffled out of the room to give the old man space for his reunion.

As Imago approached Dot and took her by the hands, he felt foolish for ever doubting her, never realizing how she'd actually earned her title as the Exceptional Girl.

"You did it," Professor Imago said, astonished, as he placed his hands on her shoulders. "You really are here."

"I had a lot of help. It's the only reason I'm standing in front of you."

"Even with your amazing, faithful friends, I'm ashamed to admit I never expected you to defeat the Greens and make your way to Kellan."

"I didn't defeat them, Father," Dot said. "I brought them with me."

The professor suddenly felt alarmed. "I don't understand. After they hunted you for so long, you would lead them here?"

"Their hunt is over, as Cezar might say, and 'lead' is the appropriate word."

"Is it, now?" Professor Imago struggled to believe her, but he thought about the impressionable nature of Automen coupled with his daughter's uncanny ability to gain the trust of others. The pride on her face was enough. "Amazing! They actually followed you?"

"They're in the service bay right now, repairing each other."

"Are you absolutely sure about them, Cordelia? What about their mission?"

"I'm their mission," Dot said. "I've always been their mission. Captain James realized that was the key. I promise, Father, they don't pose a threat anymore. They'll help protect Kellan from now on. They serve me now, which means they serve you."

"We have Greens working for Kellan?" Imago said with a laugh. "My girl, you truly make the impossible possible." He looked at her proudly, a father whose child had surpassed his greatest ambitions. "All these years, I thought I was working toward a cure for the virus, a way to heal the world. It never occurred to me that the cure went beyond science. You inspired them, and through that, you've healed the world in ways I never could."

"It only works if we work together."

"That was the founding idea of The Department and the backbone of this city."

"It's the new Story of the World," George said from the door. With him were Goneril and Regan, shocked to see their sister alive.

"George!" Dot set down her sack and ran to the boy for a long, warm embrace.

"I dreamed of this moment," Regan said.

"So did I," Goneril said, "but I figured it was just a foolish dream. Looks like Little Miss Know-It-All really does know it all."

Dot reached for her sisters and hugged them together, never taking her hand out of George's.

"I've gotten out of a lot of tight scrapes," the boy ranger said, "but I can't imagine how you got out of that impossible hell."

"I've learned a lot, George. Every moment, every decision, every new friend. I'll tell you all about it."

"You'll teach me, Dot. You've always been a good teacher, but now I promise to be a good student."

"What about Dixon?" Imago asked. "I have a hard time imagining him joining you."

"Lieutenant Dixon remained at your lab," Dot said. "He and his mech... and Vincent... were trapped inside when the building..."

"I see." Professor Imago saw the pride fade from her face, heard the quiver in her voice. "Don't let their deaths haunt you, my girl. You have a big heart, big enough for Sergeant Furst and Vincent but, dare I say, not big enough for Dixon. Even you couldn't sway him."

"They chose their paths, Dot," George said. "We should honor them."

"George is right," the professor said. "Their decisions brought us all here. Sarge and Vincent fought for you. They would be overjoyed to knew you're finally safe and free. As for Dixon, I imagine that implosion was an inevitable end for a man like him. If anyone should feel guilt, it should be this humbled old fool, for I'm the one who failed you. I put you in harm's way, made a devil's deal with the man..."

"You had no choice, Father."

"We always have a choice, my girl. You reminded me of that, and you made the right choice, the brave choice, when I could not."

"I knew you'd figure things out, Cordelia," Regan said. "You always were the smart one."

"And I'm glad you didn't go down in a blaze of glory," Goneril said with a slight smile. "A noble death would've gone to your head."

Dot smirked and looked around at her little family. "I suppose we'll deal with our guilt together. We'll honor Sarge and Vincent for who they were, and even Dixon, for the man he used to be, not who he later became. Captain James is going to bury Sarge in the city cemetery, build a monument to him. I wanted to bury Dixon, too, but there was nothing left of him."

"He didn't deserve your kindness, Dot," George said.

"Maybe not, my boy," Imago said, "but I understand her intentions." He smiled down at his daughter. "Cordelia, out of respect to you, we shall honor Dixon's memory as well. What about poor Vincent?"

"We recovered his remains," Dot said, wiping away a tear. "Well, most of them, anyway." She picked up the heavy sack beside her and handed it to her father.

"There were remains?" the professor asked. "This is Vincent?"

"It was."

"You didn't bury him?"

"Father Young's last request was to bury him in a place he'd love to be. Full sun. Water flowing nearby. We hope to find a spot like that here in Kellan. Seeing how this city has thrived, I think he would have approved..."

"I knew Francis very well," Imago said, raising his hand to interrupt his daughter. "He was a brilliant scientist, my protege, and my friend. I can tell you that Francis Young never made requests. He gave orders, specific instructions."

"That makes sense. It was in Vincent's little instruction book, his way of honoring his only son."

Professor Imago looked inside the sack. "My girl, you still don't understand. That final instruction wasn't meant to honor or remember Vincent. It was meant to grow him back."

65

Rebirth

"Can somebody dig me up? Hello! Anybody?"

Vincent woke up at dusk in a plot of rich, damp soil surrounded by tall oak, lush ferns, wildflowers, a nearby vegetable garden, and a meandering bubbling brook that nourished it all. His head protruded from the earth while his torso and limbs lay underneath, forming spindly new roots that reconnected and rebuilt his body to something resembling his former self. Though his legs still felt thin and tender, his arms were strong enough to dig him out of his resting place.

"Dang, this place sure is pretty."

As he swept aside the soil and pulled himself out of the ground, he turned to see a large group of people a short distance away.

They sat around a campfire, engaged in conversations, their backs to him.

Dot, Cezar, Abraham, Professor Imago, and many others had set up a camp near his "grave" to await his return. It took nearly two weeks, and many had their doubts, but the professor assured them it would eventually happen given enough sunlight, water, and patience.

Cezar sat on a log with Ama and Ameri. The little fawn-girl held a bouquet of lilies that the wolf had picked for her mother.

Professor Imago sat on another log across from them with Goneril and Regan. The girls had just finished knitting a pair of long, colorful striped stockings.

James The First sat on a row of storage lockers with his fellow Apostates. They ate roasted chicken and split a bottle of the captain's ancient wine.

Caffar, Calah, and Juma knelt close to the fire, tending to a large pot beside a wide grill of meat and vegetables. Juma's missing leg was now replaced by a thick wooden prosthetic covered with the names of his friends and doodles by the city's children.

Dot and George sat near a cluster of tents, holding hands while gazing into the fire. They sipped hot chocolate while occasionally watching the fire reflected in each other's eyes. No longer reeking of dirt and sweat, Dot now smelled like lilac and lavender from the homemade soap the city's artisans had given her. Her daily baths were appreciated by all.

Abraham and Gypsy stood at the perimeter of the little camp, always on guard duty. With the mech's upgraded sensors and the dog's keen nose, they were the first to realize their recently deceased friend's unusual return.

"Status: Vincent has regained consciousness."

"He's finally grown back?" Dot asked, anxious, hopeful.

"Correct."

On wobbly legs, Vincent walked up to the camp and plopped down on a log next to Captain James. The group halted their conversations looked at him in silent wonder, regarding him a living miracle, but the welling of emotion escaped the naive plant-man for he'd always been convinced that he couldn't die and that any time away from the girl would only be temporary.

"I sure am hungry," Vincent said. "What's in the pot?"

"Rabbit stew," Cezar said, a smile forming across his long snout.

"Smells good! But I've never eaten a rabbit before."

"My brothers used many vegetables as well."

"Can I have a bowl? You can take my meaty bits, Cezzie."

Everyone sat speechless as Dot stood and sat beside her friend, overjoyed to see him alive, but still unsure if he was truly himself after his resurrection.

"Vincent," she said, "what do you remember?"

Everyone held their breath, awaiting his reply.

"I remember talking with that lieutenant guy. We agreed that we both wanted to save the world, but that we failed because we were both dumb."

"You're many things, Vincent," Dot said in tears, "but never let anyone call you dumb."

"If you say so, Dottie." Vincent took a bowl of stew from Cezar and slurped its broth, his first meal in weeks. "Father used to tell me the same thing. I guess you found his book?"

"We did," Dot said, tears falling down her face. "You were smart to put it in Azrael's hand, protecting it from the fire."

"Me, smart?"

"Brilliant is the word, my boy," Professor Imago said, astonished.

"And you were right, Vincent," Dot said. "Father Young always knew what to do."

"Yep, he sure did. I miss him a lot. I learned that it hurts real bad when someone you love dies."

Dot wrapped her arms around the plant hybrid, burying her face in his chest. He returned the embrace, holding her in his long, leafy vines. He looked around at his gathered friends, distant families ending a day's work in the crops, children playing in the brook, and skyscrapers-turned-vertical gardens surrounding them. Though he'd never been to Kellan, he instantly knew where he was, that they had finally reached their long sought destination.

"Looks like we made it!" Vincent said. "You did it, Dottie! You got us to Kellan! I always knew you would."

Little Ameri gave him her bouquet of lilies. Goneril and Regan gave him their colorful knit stockings.

"Thanks! I love flowers!" Vincent stuck his nose into the lilies and took in their sweet scent before planting them atop his head. "And these long socks will fit me good once my legs get nice and plump again."

"It wasn't me, Vincent," Dot said, wiping away tears. "You did it. You got us here."

"I did? But I thought I got blown up and was growing back in the ground, and I sure don't remember doing anything special. I don't even remember coming here. I'm so confused."

"The girl is right, blood brother," Cezar said. "You're the one who brought us home."

"Home?"

"That's where we are," George said. "That's what you made happen."

"When you're ready, I'm looking forward to some more of your tree jokes," Mort The Third said.

Abraham stepped closer to the camp and looked down at the plant hybrid. "Statement: This unit also values the fact that you continue to be biologically alive and seemingly coherent."

"Aww, what a sweet thing to say, Abe," Vincent said. "And we're all here?"

"Most of us are here," Dot said. "The Widows are in the plaza, and the Gardeners are patrolling the wall. Everyone was eager to see you again."

"Well, that's good to know."

Vincent saw the warm smiles all around and felt the girl holding him tight. He still wasn't sure what happened after his "death" at The Department and wondered if he was now dreaming in some kind of personal Void, his final memory before emerging from the soil moments before. After hearing his friends' kind words and seeing the relief on their faces, he shook his head in confusion until Gypsy trotted up and placed his head in his lap.

"Are you okay, Vincent?" Dot asked. "You still seem out of sorts."

"Sorry if I don't make no sense," Vincent said, rubbing the dog under his collar. "I do that sometimes. But it sure feels good to finally be home."

About the Author

Lynn Harrod is an award-winning writer, artist, filmmaker, and educator with over 30 years of experience crafting short stories, novels, and screenplays. His characters often find their worlds spun sideways by a startling revelation.

Lynn was awarded the PRSA Image Award of Excellence and has placed in the Quarterfinals and Semifinals of the Nicholl Fellowship, the Finals of the Nevada Film Office Competition, the Semifinals of the Writers' Network Competition, and twice in the Semifinals of the FadeIn Awards.

Born in Texas, raised in California's San Joaquin Valley, and educated and trained in Hollywood, Lynn is a writer and partner with Only Human Productions, where several of his works are in development. When he's not spending time with his wife and daughter, or writing all night on his patio, he's usually having a pint with friends.